**Everyone loves
the Ladies of Covington books!**

"There's never a dull moment at the Covington farmhouse of these three older ladies."
                              —*Atlanta Journal-Constitution*

"Medlicott is attuned to the nuances of Southern life
and draws her characters with affectionate understanding and an inspiring message of self-acceptance,
courage, and survival."
                              —*The Dallas Morning News*

"A winner. . . . The three ladies inspire by forming a
community in which they thrive and find new careers
and loves, all with dignity and autonomy."
                              —*Publishers Weekly*

"Medlicott writes convincingly of women's friendship and the burdens and blessings of old age."
                              —*The Herald Sun*

"[A] charming story of small-town life. . . .
Wholesome and appealing."
                              —*Booklist*

"The ladies of Covington sow seeds of courage and community that bloom throughout this small mountain town and deep in the heart of every reader."
— Lynne Hinton, author of *Friendship Cake*

"The issues in *From the Heart of Covington* are as fresh as tomorrow's news. These three women, in their widow's might, inspire us with dignity and confidence, humor and affection."
— Robert Morgan, author of *Gap Creek*

"I began to miss [the characters] as soon as I closed the book. *From the Heart of Covington* is a book that is inspiring and easy to love, one that shows us the true meaning of friendship, family ties, and grace."
— Silas House, author of *Clay's Quilt*

"What a pleasure it is to meet the ladies of Covington once again. Their courage, humor, and wisdom and their sensible, loving regard for the seasons of life and of nature are gifts for us all."
— Nancy Thayer, author of *An Act of Love*

"Proof that a woman's life begins, not ends, at a certain age; that men are nice to have around but women friends are indispensable. A satisfying, warmhearted look at friendship that endures."

—Sandra Dallas, author of *Alice's Tulips*

"Come on the porch for a while with three unforgettable women. Bravo, ladies of Covington, I love you all!"

—Rosemary Rogers, author of *A Reckless Encounter*

"Settle back in a comfortable chair and enjoy your visit to Covington, a town rich with charm and character."

—*New York Times* bestseller Debbie Macomber

ALSO BY JOAN MEDLICOTT

At Home in Covington *
The Three Mrs. Parkers *
The Ladies of Covington Send Their Love
The Gardens of Covington
From the Heart of Covington

* Available from
Pocket Books

JOAN MEDLICOTT

THE SPIRIT of COVINGTON

POCKET STAR BOOKS
New York London Toronto Sydney

The sale of this book without its cover is unauthorized. If you purchased
this book without a cover, you should be aware that it was reported to
the publisher as "unsold and destroyed."   Neither the author nor the
publisher has received payment for the sale of this "stripped book."

This book is a work of fiction. Names, characters, places and incidents
are products of the author's imagination or are used fictitiously. Any
resemblance to actual events or locales or persons, living or dead, is
entirely coincidental.

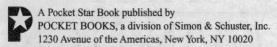 A Pocket Star Book published by
POCKET BOOKS, a division of Simon & Schuster, Inc.
1230 Avenue of the Americas, New York, NY 10020

ISBN 13: 978-0-7434-7037-7
ISBN 10: 0-7434-7037-0

First Pocket Books paperback printing July 2004

10 9 8 7 6 5 4

POCKET STAR BOOKS and colophon are registered
trademarks of Simon & Schuster, Inc.

Cover design by Julienne G. Ha
Illustration by Peter Fiore

Manufactured in the United States of America

For information regarding special discounts for bulk purchases,
please contact Simon & Schuster Special Sales at 1-800-456-6798
or business@simonandschuster.com

To the memory of my beloved grandmother
Rebecca Kushner Paiewonsky
Who taught me that you can rebuild bridges,
that no one is perfect,
and who loved me unconditionally

ACKNOWLEDGMENTS

My gratitude and love to my dear friend, Dianne LaForge, for redrawing the map of Covington to include Bella's Park and Preserve, the new shopping plaza, and other stores on Elk Road.

I would like to express my ongoing appreciation of my agent, Nancy Coffey, whose interest in the ladies of Covington has never faltered and who has worked tirelessly on their and my behalf.

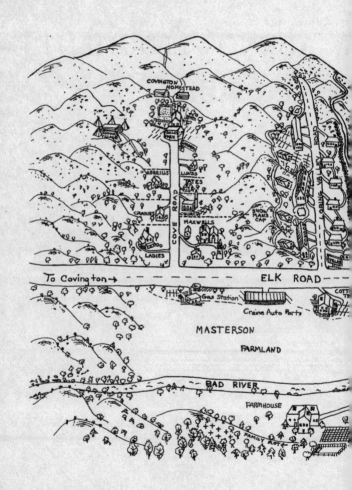

COVINGTON

WATERFALL

MC CORKLE FAMILY

To Mars Hill →

ELK ROAD
MARKET

VINE'S
RENTALS

PAT'S
MEN'S WEAR

LILY'S
BEAUTY

ELK POND
DRUG CO.

...OOM

J.P. Prancer's
Hardware

BAD RIVER

Dairy Factory

MASTERSON LAND

1

WINDS OF CHANGE

At midnight on August 2, the wind slackened, then stirred. Gusts sent leaves scurrying. A tiny spark from a cigarette, casually tossed by eighteen-year-old Brad Herrill returning home from a party, flared to life among dry leaves and snaked toward the woods. In the farmhouses fronting the woods on Cove Road, men, women, and children slept.

By two A.M., a necklace of gold edged the outer fringe of trees, and by three A.M. it had crawled into the woods. Heat from the fire sucked moisture from tree trunks. Bursts of wind stirred the flames, causing widening bands of them to veer across pastures, toward barns and farmhouses. In their stalls, cows and horses snorted and pawed the earth, and still the occupants of the houses slept.

In the farmhouse, Amelia Declose awakened. Through her front window George Maxwell's dairy farm across the road shimmered in an eerie, golden glow in a moonless night. When she raised her window, the caustic smell of smoke filled her nostrils. Smoke drifted into her room and set the battery-powered alarm on her wall jangling.

From Elk Road, the main road through the hamlet of Covington, fire trucks rounded the corner and tore down Cove Road, their sirens wailing. With increasing panic, Amelia watched the line of trucks: four, five, six. Lights came on in Maxwell's farmhouse.

Amelia screamed.

Within seconds her housemates, Grace Singleton and Hannah Parrish, were at her side.

"A fire, where?" Grace asked, suddenly fully awake.

Clutching her neck and shoulder as if feeling the searing pain of burns inflicted by another fire on another night long ago, Amelia stared wild-eyed and pointed toward the window.

"I'm going outside, see where it is," Hannah declared. When Amelia screamed, Hannah had immediately pulled on slacks, shirt, and shoes. Moments later, from the middle of their front lawn, she saw that one of the other farmhouses was ablaze and another spitting flames. Upstairs her housemates were huddled at Amelia's window. "The Herrills' place is on fire, and looks like the Craines' is also," Hannah called.

"What should we do?" Grace shouted to Hannah, though her voice blanched in the roar of a helicopter passing overhead.

"Get dressed," Laura said. Hannah's forty-one-year-old daughter Laura, who had been living with them for a year, stood in the doorway. Her eyes were absent of emotion. Last July, a year ago, she had survived a hurricane in the Caribbean that had destroyed her home, a charter boat, and everything she owned, and killed Marvin, the man she loved. It was déjà vu.

Hannah dashed back upstairs. "Huge blaze. More fire trucks down there than there are people on Cove Road."

"Let's go." Amelia's voice rose shrilly. "Get the car, Grace. Get the car."

Grace put her arm about Amelia's shoulder. Amelia's body quivered like waves stirred by a rising wind. "It's okay, Amelia. They'll have the fire out in no time, I'm sure."

Pulling away from Grace, Amelia fled the house. Halfway down the porch steps, it struck her that she wore only a satin nightgown. The night was delirious with the sounds of shouted orders, revving engines, and low-flying helicopters. A brisk wind wrapped the ends of Amelia's nightgown about her legs, nearly tripping her. Yanking open the door of her car, she stared inside. She had no keys, and Hannah's station wagon blocked her Taurus. Slamming the door, she began to weep. Fifteen feet from the porch, Amelia's legs buckled, and she lay for a time on the grass, grass that was dry and brittle from the summer's drought. Here I am, she thought, barefoot, and barely dressed, sixty-nine years old, and behaving like a hysterical five-year-old.

The Craines' and Herrills' homes and barns were ablaze. Numb and bewildered, the families huddled outside of Cove Road Church with their neighbors the Lunds, the Tates, and Pastor Johnson on the other side of the road. Heat assailed their arms and faces. Acrid smoke stung their eyes as they watched firemen from Madison and Buncombe counties fight a desperate and losing battle to save their homes. On the hills behind the houses arrowheads of flame marked the tree line where helicopters had dumped their vital cargo of fire retardants.

At the ladies' farmhouse everyone was now dressed. Hannah had brought black plastic trash bags upstairs. These she now distributed, one to each of them. "I expect they'll have this fire under control long before it reaches our house, but we can't stay here—the smell of smoke and charred wood will be suffocating. We'll go to Loring Valley and use our children's apartment. Put whatever you think you'll need for a few days, maybe a week, into these bags."

Hiccuping and crying, frantic to flee yet terrified to be alone, Amelia attempted to follow instructions. But when she entered her bedroom, her mind fogged. Everything in the room was the same, yet nothing seemed real. Frenetically she dumped everything on top of her dressing table—brush, comb, cosmetics—into the black plastic bag, and then every pair of shoes she owned.

Hannah and Grace tossed shirts, and slacks, and lingerie, and other bits and pieces of clothing into their bags, and Hannah, ever practical, emptied the file under her desk of papers: the deed to the property, their tax records, wills, birth certificates, and other documents. No one thought of taking Amelia's photographs or antique fan collection, or Grace's treasured clowns or collection of treasured cookbooks, or Hannah's gardening tools and books. Finally, clutching their bags, they stood in the hall. Laura pulled her mother aside.

"Come, look out my window," she whispered.

"Go on down, put your bags in my station wagon—it's last in line. We'll be right down," Hannah said to Grace and Amelia. "Laura's asked me to help her with something." Turning, she followed Laura down the hall.

Laura's window offered a view of the woods and hillsides. Fire raged on the slope behind the Herrills' and marched inexorably across the woods behind the Craines', their closest neighbor. Above the hills a helicopter released its load of fire-retardant liquid.

"Still think they can put it out before it gets to us?" Laura asked.

"With the helicopters helping, yes, certainly. They'll have it under control in no time," Hannah said, feigning optimism while her heart plummeted. Thank God she'd packed their papers, but what else should she, should they, have taken?

Horses neighed fear and protest as men led them across the road, away from their barns. Flames crackled and roared. Roof beams thundered as they toppled. Hoses stretched across Cove Road in order to drench the roofs and walls of the Lunds' and Tates' homes and barns. Standing on a fire truck, the chief yelled orders and demanded that residents evacuate the area. As firefighters turned their hoses on the church, families clambered into vehicles lined up along the road.

The rear of Ted Lund's pickup brimmed with sacks of clothing. A rocking chair leaned against a grandfather clock, and Pastor Johnson, clutching a suitcase, sat on a sack next to the Lund boys, Rick and Alex. Molly, Ted's wife, and her mother, Brenda Tate, squeezed into the front seat. Behind them, water cascaded from the roof of the church.

Suffering from a hangover, and unaware of his role in the destruction, Brad Herrill groaned and held his head as he hunched in the back of his father's big truck. They pulled away and headed for Elk Road. Piled with furniture and clothing, the Craines' two vehicles followed. As the small caravan started up, the chief waved them on. "Get a move on!" he yelled.

In the cul-de-sac, the office and newly constructed living museum sites at the Bella Maxwell Park and Preserve had been thoroughly drenched, although the chief believed that the winds would hold steady, and the park was not in danger. Still, one never knew.

Across from the ladies, at George (Max) Maxwell's dairy farm, a congregation of cows, darkly etched against the

orange glare, were being herded high onto the hills behind the barns. Men with hoses pelted Maxwell's lawn,
windmill, house, and barns with torrents of water. As the
vehicles passed his property, Max broke from among the
firefighters and ran across the road to the ladies, who
stood as if frozen on their porch.

"God, Hannah." He grasped her. "They're evacuating
everyone. Damn. I thought they'd have it under control by
now. Are you all right?"

Terror reigned in Amelia's eyes, numb bewilderment
in Grace's. Unwittingly, Hannah slumped against Max for
a moment. The relief in her eyes was transitory, and
turned to despair. After tossing their bags into Hannah's
wagon, Max shepherded them across the road to his lawn,
then raced back to move the station wagon from their
driveway. And just in time, for shortly after he rejoined
them, they stared in disbelief as fire trucks trammeled
Hannah's rosebushes, as more lengths of hose were unfurled, as great bursts of water struck their home and
showered down windowpanes.

Perhaps it was the proximity, perhaps the sheer irra-
tionality of the moment, but Grace broke from them and
dashed back to their farmhouse. "I'm going after our
things!"

Amelia cringed. Her pupils dilated with fear. "No!"
she screamed. "Grace. No. No."

Before Max could stop her, Hannah raced after Grace.
Max said, "I'll get them. Stay with Amelia, Laura."

Laura drew closer to the older woman, who slumped
against her. The world glowed red.

Dashing past firefighters, Max snatched the women
about their waists and struggled to pull them back. With
amazing strength, Grace broke loose. Max raced after her,
Hannah following across the lawn, up the slippery steps,
and into the farmhouse. The wood floors inside were

slick. The rug in the foyer and the carpeted stairs oozed water. A caustic layer of smoke hunkered about them.

Grace was already upstairs, coughing. They followed. In the hallway, smoke darkened the space.

Max hastened to wet towels. "Cover your mouths and noses. Let's get out of here."

By then, Grace had disappeared into Amelia's room, where the battery-powered fire alarm sounded a faint, intermittent beep. Tearing a pillow from its case, she headed for the dresser, pulled the collection of antique fans from the wall above it, and stuffed them into the pillowcase along with silk and cashmere scarves from a drawer. She couldn't reach the top shelf of the closet, couldn't save Amelia's straw hat, a treasured gift from her husband, Thomas.

Steps thudded on the stairs. A fireman yelled, "You people crazy? Out of here. Out. Now!"

Max yanked Grace's arm. "You heard him. Let's go."

Hannah called to Grace. "Come on. Hurry."

"I want my clown that Bob gave me," Grace called back.

"No time." Max held the towel to his mouth and coughed.

They pulled Grace toward the steps.

"My diabetes medication." Possessed by a rush of strength, Grace tore free of Max and Hannah, brushed away the young fireman, and darted into the smoky, water-drenched kitchen. Looking wildly about, she felt her way, grabbed the bottle of pills from a straw basket on the counter and a cookbook—not a particular cookbook, but the first to touch her fingers. She lurched forward, held her chest, and gasped for air.

Wayne Reynolds, a close friend and volunteer fireman, was beside her. "Outta here, Miss Grace. Back of your house is burning." His strong arms wrested her out onto the lawn and thrust her, stumbling and coughing, toward Hannah, who shuddered when she saw the greenhouse she had sold to Wayne already consumed by flames.

Grace heard a man say, "This house is gone, too." Exhausted, and bent nearly double from choking and coughing, Grace managed to glance at his face. Under the yellow parka, his eyes were red and his tired face damp. A long dark smudge ran down his cheek. He pointed to the ladies' farmhouse just as a paramedic ran up to Grace with an oxygen mask and tank. She held the mask tight and breathed, short gasping breaths and then more deeply.

"Let's get them outta here!" the paramedic shouted to Max above the din as he pressed them away from the house.

Moments later they stood alongside Hannah's station wagon on the road in front of Max's house and watched with horror as flames danced triumphantly on the roof of the farmhouse they had so lovingly renovated and moved into three years ago. Thick gray smoke billowed from its windows and poured from every nook and cranny of the old homestead. Firefighters staggered back.

"Damned fool people running into that house. Risk their lives and ours. Place is dry as tinder," Grace heard someone say. But she'd had to go, didn't they understand? For Amelia, she'd had to go.

A young fireman from Mars Hill, ten miles away, dashed up and demanded, in no uncertain terms, that they leave Cove Road.

"Go to Bob's place!" Maxwell yelled above the din.

Hannah nodded. Four dispirited women, one nearly hysterical, climbed into Hannah's old station wagon and drove, ever so cautiously, toward Elk Road.

2

SHOCK

Hannah's insides quivered. With trembling hands she gripped the wheel and steered her station wagon down Elk Road, then left onto Loring Valley Road. Her own shock, and its concomitant stress, was amplified by Grace and Amelia's weeping, and her daughter's stone-faced silence.

The headlights of the car, as it rounded curve after curve, cast an eerie glow on newly grassed banks which were covered by a blanket of straw to prevent seed erosion. Grace sat beside Hannah in the front, her face mottled with tears and soot. "What are we going to do? What are we going to do?" She twisted her bandanna in and about her fingers, then wound it around her hands.

In a voice hoarse from crying, Amelia said, "We're homeless, out in the street."

"Not out in the street," Hannah said. "Our children's condo is sitting there empty, and we have good friends. That's important at a time like this. Carrying on the way you and Grace are isn't helping anything." Hannah rounded the last curve and headed up the hill to Bob's apartment. "Laura, are you all right?"

"That's a ridiculous question, Mother. Are you all right? Are any of us all right? Our lives are shattered, shattered I tell you, shattered again."

Hannah wished she hadn't asked.

"We've lost everything," Amelia wailed.

"We have each other," Hannah said. In a minute she was going to explode or break into sobs. Fortunately, they had arrived at Bob's condo. Light streamed from the glass panel in the front door, and the exterior floodlight burned bright as if to welcome them. Bob knows, she thought.

Bob knew. At three A.M. the phone had jolted him awake. Annoyance shifted to disbelief and then fear for Grace's safety when Russell barked into the phone, "Dad. There's a major fire over in Cove Road."

"What the hell are you saying?"

"I got up with the baby and couldn't go back to sleep," Russell said, "so I turned on the TV in the den. They interrupted a rerun of *Matlock* with breaking news."

Phone in hand, Bob jumped from bed, strode from his bedroom, crossed the living room, and yanked open the sliding-glass door to the terrace.

His apartment was among those in the highest tier of condominiums in Loring Valley, and the terrace faced towering mountains. Silence dominated the muggy August night. The fire in Cove Road, although separated by acres and acres of steep forested hills and mountains, had dyed the sky brick-red, and the smoke of a thousand woodstoves filled the air. Coughing, Bob hastened inside and slammed the door shut. "My God, the smell's awful. I've heard nothing. Grace, Hannah, the others?" he asked.

"Not sure. I'm coming over," Russell said.

"Wait to hear from me, Russell. I'm going over there soon as I get some clothes on. Hold on, son. Someone's banging on the door." When Bob opened the front door, Grace, smelling for all the world like a smoldering charcoal fire, flung herself into his arms, causing him to stagger back. He held Grace's shaking body. Huddled behind her were Hannah, Laura, and Amelia in various states of rumpled disarray. Reaching beyond Grace, he urged them inside, and as he did so, his hand lost its hold on the phone, which hit the carpet with a soft thud. "Get it for me, will you, Hannah? It's Russell," Bob said.

Hannah bent to retrieve it. "Russell. We're all here. Yes, we're safe. Our home's lost, gone up in flames, the Craines' and Herrills' places, too, and the woods behind the houses." She couldn't go on.

Yet to Bob, Hannah, though drenched and disheveled, seemed oddly calm. Too calm. Putting an arm about Grace's shoulders, he guided her, with the others following, into the kitchen, where he turned a flame under the kettle, opened a box of tea bags, and removed the top of the coffee jar. Bob set mugs on the kitchen table as Hannah dragged chairs from the dining area, and he watched the women huddle about the round table meant for two like puppies in a basket, their shoulders, arms, and legs touching.

Tears trailed down Amelia's cheeks, yet no sound issued from her lips. No one moved to dunk a tea bag or spoon the coffee. Bob placed a teaspoon of strong coffee in one of the mugs, filled it to the brim with water, and eased it toward Hannah. He dunked tea bags, added cream for Grace, sugar and lemon for Amelia. He had no idea what Laura drank, so he made her coffee like her mother's.

They did not touch the drinks, but sat staring vacantly at nothing. Grace and Hannah's hair, though short, hung in wet, ash-streaked clumps. Smudges of soot blotched their arms. Bob realized they were waiting for him to take charge, to determine their next move. So many questions he wanted to ask, but later. "You'll stay here, of course," he said. "You have things in the car?"

"Yes, in the car," Hannah replied. "Black plastic bags in the car. Grace stays here, the rest of us will go to our children's apartment." Like Bob's apartment, that apartment had two bedrooms, each furnished with one king-size bed.

"The three of you won't be comfortable over there," Grace said. "Amelia, you stay here with Bob and me." She stroked Amelia's hand. "You'll have your own room and bath."

It wasn't what Bob wanted. He welcomed the opportunity to live with Grace, just the two of them, and had longed for this ever since Grace turned down his proposal of marriage several years ago. "I adore you," she'd said, "but, please, don't ask me to marry or change the way I live with my friends. We can spend as much time as you'd like together." But Bob knew better. He'd never get enough of Grace. Still, he smiled. "You're welcome here, Amelia. Look, I'll bring all the bags in, and you can tell me which stay, which go."

"I'm so tired," Amelia said. "May I lie down?" She was slight of build, and when she stood, she staggered and nearly fell. Hannah, tall and sturdy, caught her and held her upright. "I must lie down," Amelia whispered.

Slipping their arms about Amelia's waist to steady her, Hannah and Grace led the fragile woman to the guest bedroom. Dark contemporary-style twin beds and a dresser with rounded edges stood out against pale yellow walls. Perhaps, Grace thought, we should have bought something lighter, like maple furniture. But Bob had liked this set, and Tyler, his young grandson who spent many weekends there, loved it, too. Amelia doesn't even know what the room looks like, Grace thought. And that was true, for still in her clothes, shoes and all, Amelia collapsed onto one of the beds, turned on her side, and closed her eyes. Gently Grace removed her shoes, set them neatly on the floor near the end table, and threw a light flannel blanket that had been folded at the bottom of the bed over her. Then she and Hannah tiptoed from the room.

"Amelia's asleep," Grace reported to Bob, who stood in the foyer surrounded by black plastic bags. The smell of smoke hung in the air, and Bob desperately wanted to slide open the terrace door, but Laura and Hannah were kneeling and opening each bag. They set to one side the bags containing their clothing, the financial and other records. Three bags remained: Grace's clothes, Amelia's bag crammed with shoes and cosmetics, and the one that Grace had hastily filled with Amelia's fans and scarves.

"That's it?" Bob asked.

A great weariness sounded in Hannah's voice. "That's all we managed to get out. It happened so fast. We thought the fire would be out long before it reached our house. We expected we'd be gone from home maybe a week, until things settled down. But the fire literally ate the houses, and the trees."

It was clear to Bob that Hannah and Laura needed rest. Picking up their bags, he followed them outside, and piled the two bags back into the station wagon. "Shall I drive you, Hannah?"

She shook her head. "I made it over here. I can get us down the road to a building close to Bob's condo."

"Call me when you get there," Grace said.

Hannah nodded, but she did not call, and it fell to Bob to assure Grace that Hannah was fine and probably didn't remember to phone. "They're fine. They're exhausted, as you must be."

* * *

"I am exhausted." Grace stretched out on the couch, her head in Bob's lap. Bob had covered over the ordinary plaster ceiling with a composite, which simulated a fine, early twentieth-century traditional ceiling in a waffle design, and added a deeper crown molding around the walls. The charm of the room was further enhanced by a stunning Oriental rug with bold, clear reds and blues. Everything about Bob's living room pleased Grace, and as her eyes moved from square to square on the ceiling, she could feel herself beginning to relax.

Bob smoothed the hair about her face. "I'm sorry," he said. "Who would imagine such a thing could happen. How did the fire start, I wonder?"

Grace shuddered. Fiery images hovered a moment, then swooped to consume the pithy center of her mind: scarlet flames devouring their farmhouse; intense heat sucking her into its bowels; the smell of burning wood that nauseated her. She gasped, buried her face in Bob's chest.

Bob held her close, smoothed the damp, sticky hair about her forehead.

When she could talk, Grace murmured, "Bob, love, don't let's talk about it now. My brain's exhausted, more so even than my body."

"Come to bed."

"I wonder if I can sleep?"

"I'll lie right next to you."

Eyes closed, Grace lay awake a long time, seeking something, a word, a vision, a meaning for it all, which would not come to her. Finally she slept, how long she did not know, only that she awakened to Amelia's screams, and the awareness that Bob no longer lay beside her.

3

COMING TO TERMS

When Grace reached Amelia's room, she found her huddled against the headboard, looking worn and faded as beached driftwood against a dark boulder. Bob stood on the far side of the bed looking helpless. "I ran to her when she screamed," he said. "I thought perhaps she had fallen."

In an instant Grace was beside Amelia, holding her.

Amelia's body shook. "Fire, I dreamed of fire." She looked about her. Her lovely blue eyes were glazed. "Where am I?"

"In Bob's guest bedroom. Remember, we decided last night that you'd be more comfortable if you stayed with us. Hannah and Laura are at the apartment our kids bought. It's just a short walk down the hill."

"I vaguely remember," Amelia said softly. She eyed Bob. "I'm sorry for all the fuss."

Bob's eyes sought Grace's. "Shall I put the kettle on?"

"That would be nice, dear." As he started from the room, Grace called, "Bob, wait a second. Look in your room, in that plastic sack of mine, will you? Bring me a bathrobe for Amelia. I think there's one in there."

He pointed to Amelia's bag in the corner. "Her things are here."

"There's no clothing in there, trust me."

"There really was a fire, Grace?" Amelia asked.

"A huge fire. The Herrills' place burned, and the Craines'."

"And our house, Grace?"

"Our house, too, Amelia. I'm sorry."

Amelia gasped, covered her mouth with her hand. "Oh, no! *Mon Dieu.* I can't believe it. I just can't believe it."

"You know how dry it's been all summer. The woods are like tinder, and the fire spread fast, too fast for the firemen to control it."

"Cousin Arthur's farmhouse that he left to me, it's gone?"

Tears formed in the corners of Grace's eyes. "I'm afraid so."

Amelia scanned every corner of the room. "My cameras. Where are my cameras?"

Grace shook her head. "They can be replaced."

Amelia caved against the pillows.

Then Grace remembered the fans. "But your antique fans are safe." Jumping from the bed, she brought the lighter of the two bags to Amelia. One by one, Grace removed the fans and lay them in front of Amelia, who reached forward and touched each lovingly.

"These you couldn't replace, Amelia. You can replace your cameras and equipment, and Mike has the negatives of all your work in his studio in Weaverville." Deeply aware of the losses they had all sustained, Grace's heart tweaked. The fire had changed their world, vanquished their sense of safety, and she saw that in the foreseeable future, one thing was certain. Each of them would reach for something, search for something that had been lost, and regret and grief would visit them again and again.

"I saved my fans," Amelia muttered in a tone of bewil-derment.

Grace did not contradict her.

Months ago, Hannah's older daughter, Miranda, and her husband, Paul, and Grace's son, Roger, and his compan-ion, Charles, partners in a successful party-planning busi-ness in Branston, Pennsylvania, had purchased a vacation apartment in a building down the hill from Bob. Due to time limitations, they had not fully furnished the living room. Now, without washing their hands or faces, without checking to see if the beds were made up, Hannah and Laura collapsed into the two recliners in the living room and waited out what was left of the night. The room was empty save for the recliners, an armoire, which housed the television and other electronic equipment, and several of Amelia's recent color photographs, which brightened the walls.

"At least we have someplace to sit," Laura said. "How long do you think we'll have to live here?"

"Six, eight months, maybe."

"That long?"

"Did you get most of your clothes, Laura?"

"I don't have many clothes, remember?" She didn't tell her mother that she had saved the music box Hannah had given her last Christmas.

"Of course." Hannah was at a loss for words. From the time, a year ago, when Laura, weighted with grief and with her leg in a cast, had reluctantly arrived to stay with them, Hannah worried about her. How would this fire, the loss of their home, affect Laura, who was just recovering from her own devastating losses?

"Maybe this is meant to remind me how impermanent things are, how I can't put my faith in things," Laura said. "I was just starting to feel hopeful about my future. Now I feel defeated, and the whole idea of rebuilding my life seems formidable."

"There are natural disasters, floods, volcanoes. People rebuild their lives."

"Please, Mother, don't tell me about other disasters, or what other people do. Can't you understand how *I* feel? Aren't you incensed at what's happened? Don't you want to rail against fate, to demand to know why?"

"There are no answers to why," Hannah replied. "Events we see as tragic are merely events, arbitrary. It's the picking up of your life and moving on that matters."

"I can't buy that," Laura said. "I can't live in a world that makes no sense."

Hannah was silent. Usually confident and certain of her ability to handle things, Hannah felt humbled, and small, and inadequate, and the enormity of their loss, not just their home, but the loss of their way of life, swept over her. For a moment she covered her face with her hands. Through the sliding-glass doors an indifferent dawn peered in at them.

Back on Cove Road, in the murky light of a new morning, exhausted firefighters doused the last of the smoldering embers, folded their hoses, and with a shifting of gears and a revving of engines roared away. A great hush fell. Feeling as if he were the last man on earth, Max lingered at the edge of his ash-sodden lawn and surveyed the damage across the road. The fire had bequeathed to the ladies a profusion of charred rubble, scorched earth, and ash, and halfway up their hillside it had denuded and blackened once lovely woods. It was the same for the Craines, but at the Herrills the fire had raged higher up their hillside, devouring vegetation to the crest of the hill behind their barn.

To the south, the Bella Maxwell Park and Preserve,

land bought with funds from his deceased wife Bella's trust, had been spared by winds that continued to blow from the south and west. Not a tree or building on that property had been singed, and the intact, vacant homes and the church on his side of Cove Road glistened wet in the morning sunlight. Soon his herd of cows, sent scurrying last night, would swagger down the hillside to the barn for milking. Maxwell heaved a sigh of relief.

Not a religious man, Max said a silent prayer of thanks, and thought of Hannah and the ladies. Grace was probably at Bob's, and the others must be at Hannah and Grace's children's apartment.

Max headed for his truck, then realized that the acrid stench of smoke claimed every crease of his face, every strand of his hair, every fiber of his clothing. Anna, his housekeeper and wife of José, his foreman, met him at the door with a mug of steaming coffee. She followed him to the kitchen, and while he drank, she fingered her rosary beads and repeated Hail Marys in a hushed and anxious voice.

"It's okay, Anna. The fire's out. José and the men will be returning with the cows soon."

"Ah, but Señor Max, nothing be the same. First Missy Bella gone, now the señoras across the road gone. You gonna go, too, yes?"

"Sit down, Anna." He pointed to a chair at the kitchen table. She hesitated a moment, then sat. "The fire's over. Three houses burned. We're here in this house, right?"

"Yes, Señor Max." Her fingers continued to work the beads, though her lips did not move.

"Nothing on our side of the road was touched except by water. The ladies aren't going anywhere." He hoped that was true. "They'll rebuild. So will the others."

"You sure, señor?"

"You're scared, Anna. You remember the fire that

burned your village in Ecuador, when you were a child. This fire last night has picked the lock of your memory, allowed in the old fears." Did she even understand him? Why did he feel he had to explain this to her, talk about picking locks? With her limited grasp of English, she probably wasn't following him at all, so he was surprised when Anna's dark eyes found his. She nodded.

"I get it, Señor Max. I not so much scared for now, but for what happen in my village long ago. I forget. Now I remember. I no like remember."

"That's right," Max replied, thinking that Bella had always said that Anna was very bright, and knew more than she admitted. He appreciated Anna's help, her care of Bella, but he'd never really talked to her. It was José who had told him about the fire of Anna's childhood, how she'd lost her father and three siblings, and how she and her mother had been left destitute. American aid had saved them, José said, for which Anna remained forever grateful.

"I strong," Anna said. "I help the señoras make a new house."

He started to say that builders would do that job, then said, "I know they'll appreciate your help, Anna." He drained the cup and set the mug down.

Anna sprang to her feet and reached for the coffeepot. "More coffee?"

Max waved his hand to indicate no. "I'm going to shower, wash this stink off of me, then I'm going to get some sleep."

"Señora Hannah is fine lady, very strong. Missy Bella, she love her."

Max knew what Anna meant. Bella had urged him not to remain alone. Well, he didn't want any wife but Bella. He heaved himself up. Every muscle ached. He had helped with one of the hoses, which, when distended with water, had been powerful and difficult to manage. A long hot shower would refresh him. "Thanks for the coffee, Anna. Keep an eye out for José. He and the men will be hungry as bears in the spring when they get back."

Anna moved her fingers along the rosary beads. She said, "I pray for señoras rebuild their house."

4

REALITY CHECK

The stunning volatility of the fire, the profundity of the devastation left Hannah, Grace, Amelia, and Laura in a state of disorientation and disbelief. Coming to terms with the ephemeral nature of their safety and way of life would take many months. For now, Amelia buried herself in sleep, while Hannah, unable to sleep, lost herself in crossword puzzles. For long periods of time Grace stared without seeing and seemed barely to understand when Bob spoke to her. Laura, when she was around them, rarely spoke.

Mike, professional photographer and Amelia's former instructor, and now good friend, hastened to be with her, but found himself at a loss when confronted with Amelia's morose silence and withdrawal.

News of the fire made local headlines; it became the lead story on the morning-after news. Brenda Tate, who had fled her smoke-filled house, called from her mother's home in South Carolina.

"We'll be back in a week or so, Grace. As soon as that horrible smell of smoke is gone," Brenda said, after assuring herself that they were all right.

Lurina phoned. "Trouble with bein' so darn old is, Joseph Elisha and me, we're plumb deaf. We never did hear no sirens. Didn't hear nothin' till Joseph Elisha took hisself down to Prancer's Hardware for his mornin' cider and chat with the boys."

Everyone but Lurina called Joseph Elisha Old Man, and Grace smiled hearing Lurina call the old men "boys."

"I near to died till I heard no one was hurt. I figured you'd gone to Bob's place. You okay, Grace, and the others?"

"We're holding up as well as can be expected," Grace said. "We're grateful no one got hurt."

"That's the best way to think on it. People's what counts. Old days, there weren't no fire trucks with sirens to wake folks. One time we had six families who all lost someone. They died in their beds. Buried ten of 'em, women, children, and men folk, all on the same day. Biggest funeral ever 'round these parts."

Lurina loved to tell stories about how folks had died, and the details of their funerals. Grace usually found such stories of the old days and old ways interesting, but not today.

"As I said, we're thankful we're all safe. Thanks for calling, Lurina. Soon as we get out, we'll stop over," Grace said. "Bob's calling me now. I have to go."

"Wait on up a bit," Lurina said. "Want to say, I love you, Grace. You been so good to me, standin' up with me when I married up with Joseph Elisha."

More than a year ago the eighty-one-year-old Lurina had wed Old Man, ten years her senior. That event and all the worrying they had all done about the millennium seemed like so long ago. "I love you, too, Lurina," Grace said.

That same afternoon Wayne, Old Man's grandson, arrived on Bob's doorstep. Grace drew Wayne into Bob's living room, where Hannah, who had come over earlier, sat. Hannah's shoulders sagged. Sadness clouded her eyes.

Wayne shook his head. "I been over to the place. Tried to save your house. Thought we had it there until the wind took to gusting, and those flames went outta control. I was sure scared when Miss Grace ran back into the place. How you ladies doing?"

Hannah looked up at him. "Oh, Wayne. Our greenhouse is gone." Hannah had sold the greenhouse to him, yet she couldn't say "your greenhouse." Wayne didn't seem to mind. She had become, over time, like a mother to him.

"I got it insured just like you told me to," Wayne said. "I can get me another greenhouse, or maybe use the money to get me an education."

Hannah grasped his rough, callused hands. "That would be fine, Wayne. Just fine."

In those first days the phone rang off the hook: teachers from Caster Elementary School, where Grace and Hannah volunteered, and where Brenda Tate was the principal; people whom they knew casually from shopping or doing business. Margaret Olsen, the owner of the Hillside Bed and Breakfast in Mars Hill, where they had stayed when they first came to the area, cried when she called. Mary and Jim Amsterdam, the new owners of Bob and Grace's former Cottage Tearoom, sent over trays of sandwiches with a note that read, *We are so sorry! We're glad no one was hurt.*

The outpouring of concern touched Grace's and Hannah's hearts. Amelia appeared indifferent, and Laura drifted away from them, into a world of her own. Grace phoned to relay the news to her son, Roger, and his companion, Charles.

"You're alive," Roger said. "That's what matters." His

was a practical view. "Now you can build a nice new house with modern conveniences."

Charles cried when he heard the news. "Mother Singleton," he said, using the name he always called her. "Dear God, you could have been hurt or killed. What a terrible shock you've had. Are you sure you're all right? The others, too?"

Grace assured Charles that they were all fine. She refrained from telling them about her own role as rescuer of Amelia's antique fans and scarves. They would think her a fool.

"Now, you eat well, and rest, you hear me?" Charles said.

Hannah phoned her daughter Miranda.

"I'm taking the next plane down," Miranda said.

"Not yet," Hannah said. "We're staying in your condo, Laura and I."

"Mother, are you sure you're telling it to me straight? I know you'll put the best face on it."

"We are fine, Miranda, really. Shaken up but fine."

"How is Laura? My Lord, first a hurricane, now a fire."

"She's going to be fine—we all are. Now, Miranda, I'm getting off the phone. I'll let you know what the insurance people say."

That afternoon Russell, Emily, Tyler, and baby Melissa Grace arrived with a casserole for dinner. The moment they entered, Grace took the baby from Emily. With her blue eyes and long lashes, the five-month-old child strongly favored her mother, but Bob said that with her blue eyes and sturdy little body, the baby resembled Grace, who, of course, was not related by blood. Blood kin or not, Grace could not have loved Tyler or his little sister more. There was something grounding about holding the baby, who looked at Grace with serious eyes as if she knew the way Grace felt.

Questions spilled from eleven-year-old Tyler. "Were you scared? Did the firemen come and wake you up? Did you have to climb out a window on a fireman's ladder? Did the fire burn up all your furniture? What about your clowns, Granny Grace, and Aunt Amelia's pictures?"

Grace stifled tears, and as she answered his questions, Tyler studied her with a look of deep concern. "We'll build you back a nice house, nicer even than the one you had. Every day after school I'll come over and help." Tyler kissed her cheek. "I love you so much, Granny Grace. I'm so glad you're safe here with Grandpa."

Four days after the fire Bob drove Grace, Hannah, and Laura to Cove Road, where reality pounced on them like a fox on a chicken. The eastern side of Cove Road lay charred and abandoned. Three chimneys rose above black and crumbled foundation walls. Burned cars hunkered in driveways, and twisted appliances lay beneath scorched and splintered beams.

With a sinking heart Hannah left the car and walked with hesitant steps toward the site where their home had stood. From the rubble a blistered shoe protruded. Whose shoe was it? Hers? Grace's? Laura's? Even in its distorted form, she could tell that it was too large to be Amelia's. Alongside it lay a slice of mirror reflecting sunlight. Grace's wrought-iron headboard slanted crazily among charred beams.

Like knots on a rope, the loss and grief sustained in her lifetime joined, twisted, and tightened to squeeze Hannah's heart. Her breathing felt labored. Involuntarily Hannah wrapped her hands about her shoulders as if to protect herself from a bludgeoning wind, only no wind raged except in her mind.

Hannah stared for a long time at the soot-covered chimney. Over the last few years the ladies had explored the countryside and occasionally come upon a solitary chimney and foundation long abandoned and smothered with vines. Who had lived there? Why hadn't the owners rebuilt? Now Hannah understood why they had not; sometimes life beat you down so hard that rebuilding seemed too formidable a task.

Hannah's eyes skipped past the soot-stained and blackened stack of their chimney. The apple orchard was gone. Slowly she turned. All of her gardens, so lovingly laid out, were gone. She had invested more of herself here than in all the houses she had ever lived in any- where. Now the despoilment of all she cherished threat- ened to crush her. She hadn't the energy, the gumption to begin again. Closing her eyes, Hannah fought the urge to turn and run, and never look back.

And then Hannah noticed the great oak that had wel- comed them into the shade of its branches their first day in Covington. It was intact, alive, green, its leaves flutter- ing in the summer breeze. "Oh," she cried, hastening to- ward it, and stopped short, stunned to see the opposite side of the trunk leafless, blistered, and blackened.

"Our tree. It survived," Grace said as she came to stand beside her friend.

Hannah lowered her eyes, which fell on their sneakers, stained gray by the ash that powdered the earth. "Only one side of it survived, Grace."

"Will it live?" Grace whispered, looking up at the swaying branches. She clutched Hannah's arm.

"Yes, I think it will. We'll cut away the dead parts. In time it'll fill out." Hannah wasn't sure just what the shape of their oak would be, or how much growth would take place on the charred side, but she hoped for a return of sturdy stems and branches. Suddenly the heavy yoke lightened, and Hannah knew that she would not, could not abandon this place, this land she had come to love and cherish as her home.

"But the hills, Hannah, look at the hills." Grace began to cry.

Bob strode to them and placed a protective arm about Grace's shoulder. "Forests burn all the time. They come back. Look, only half of your hillside's been burned. Lots of trees higher up survived. A few years, you'll never know there was a fire here." He held Grace. "It's going to be all right, you'll see."

Laura stood back, away from the other three, her arms folded tightly across her chest, her jaw set, her eyes angry, yet the look she fastened on Bob at that moment told Hannah that her daughter was certain that nothing would ever be all right. Hannah understood. What she didn't understand was why terrible things happened, loss upon loss: Laura's home and Captain Marvin gone, her broken leg needing to be operated on a second time. Her daughter was just settling down to her new job at Bella's Park, where she researched and re-created the original homestead way of life of the first white settlers, the Covingtons, Harold Tate's ancestors. And now, this fire. It wasn't Laura's house, of course, but it had become her home, for however long she chose to stay with them.

Quietly Laura returned to the car. Moments later the front door of Maxwell's farmhouse flew open, and Max bounded down the steps, raced down his driveway, and across the road. "I know it's devastating," he began as he joined them.

"Hush!" Hannah said. "We know."

"Like you asked, I've arranged for a bulldozer and a truck to get rid of the debris. I'll send over my man with a tiller to turn over the soil."

"Have them take down the chimney," Hannah said. "We start fresh."

"Start what?" Grace asked. Ash in the air mingled with her tears and streaked her face.

"Start rebuilding. We have insurance."

"But the land's destroyed, the woods are gone."

"Look! Not all of our woods and not forever." Hannah took Grace by the shoulders. Her voice choked, and then grew firm. "Listen, my friend. We know about starting over. We've done it. We can do it again."

The sadness and the doubt in Grace's eyes reflected her own, but Hannah could not succumb to either emotion, or she, and Grace, and Amelia would separate. Grace would marry, or, at least, move in with Bob. Amelia would relocate to Asheville, closer to the clubs and theaters she frequented with Mike. Laura? Hannah drew a blank as she considered her own potentially solitary future.

"Can we?" Grace asked feebly, remembering her misery when Roger had insisted that she uproot herself, sell her furniture, rent her home in Dentry, Ohio, and move to Olive Pruitt's boardinghouse for retired ladies in Branston, Pennsylvania. She brightened, then, remembering that she had met Hannah and Amelia at Olive's place, and that it was Amelia who had inherited this property. In time Amelia had changed the deed into all their names, and the three of them built a hope and life together. Grace smiled, and her eyes sought Bob's. It was here in Covington that dear, kind Bob had entered her life and her heart. There was much, still, to be thankful for.

"Of course we can," Hannah was saying as she turned Grace to face Maxwell's property. Hannah needed to remind herself as well as Grace. "Look. Look at Maxwell's hills. In a year or so ours will be green again—not the trees directly next to the pasture, of course, but with ground cover and small shrubs. Nature's wonderful that way. Life springs back. We can spring back. Don't give up, Grace. We *can* rebuild. A house with every nook and cranny just the way we want it." She spoke quickly, painting pictures, seeking to ignite a spark in Grace's soul, in Grace's eyes. "You've always wanted a galley kitchen, and how many times have we talked about bathrooms of our own, your own deep bathtub?"

"Amelia's going to be devastated when she sees this," Grace said.

"Yes, she is. That's why you and I must be united in our resolve."

Hannah waited as Grace, a good foot shorter than Bob, looked up at him. Grace squared her shoulders and took a small step away from Bob. Turning slowly, her eyes scanned Maxwell's hills, low, then rolling higher and taller up to Snowman's Cap, four thousand feet high. Grace's eyes traveled down to the scorched earth beneath her feet, and up to the charred stubble on their once lovely hills. Then she lifted her head, and her eyes, at first questioning, turned hopeful.

"I think maybe we can do it," Grace said. She moved to the living, vibrant side of the oak and touched the bark with her fingertips. "How anyone survives tragedy or manages in this world without supportive family or good friends, I have no idea." She half-circled the tree and tentatively rested the palm of her hand on its black and sooty bark. "Please, come back, tree. We need you." Then she returned to where Bob stood watching her and raised up on her toes to kiss his chin. "You think it's a good idea to rebuild, don't you, Bob?"

Hannah held her breath. This was probably the last thing Bob wanted. Marrying Grace had always been his goal, or at least taking up permanent residence with her.

He chewed his lower lip. Flecks of ash had settled in his thick white hair. Conflict was clearly visible on his face. For a moment he closed his dark deep-set eyes, then he said, "I'll help you do whatever you want."

Grace threw her arms about his neck, and Hannah exhaled, knowing that her ideal life, sharing a home with Amelia and Grace, would continue.

Later that day Amelia listened to their plans without enthusiasm. No spark of interest lit her eyes, and it was two weeks before she allowed them to drive her past their former home, and when they did, she hid her face in her hands and cried.

5

RESILIENCE

"You're a resilient woman," Max said to Hannah. "You have a resilience born of experience. You escaped with your daughters from an abusive husband. You struggled to support yourself and them. You started over, and you succeeded, and there are probably other traumas I don't know about that you've risen above."

"True, but right now I'm feeling wiped out," Hannah replied. "The old punch comes and goes, like a faucet, on–off, on–off. I'm constantly having to bolster myself and the others, too."

"Time," he assured her. "Take a step back from the drama of the fire. Sure, it was a disaster, but no one was killed or maimed, and you don't have to solve everyone's problems, especially not in three weeks."

"Three weeks? It's only three weeks? It seems eons ago. Every day I reach for something that's no longer there, or I remember something else I lost in that fire."

"What do you really want, Hannah?" Max asked. They sat in her office at the Bella Maxwell Park and Preserve, affectionately called Bella's Park. The seven-hundred-acre preserve had been purchased by Max in honor of his wife after her death. The old farmhouse that stood on the land had been renovated into modern offices for the staff who would manage the park development. Historic recreations were planned, and a series of demonstration gardens had already been built, with more to come. *Director of Gardens*, the plaque on the front door of Hannah's office stated.

Max sat on one of the two small couches in the office, and Hannah sat on the other facing him. Max's heart ached for Hannah, for her stunning loss, and there were moments when he had to resist the urge to sit alongside her and hold her hand. If he did, he thought, she might misunderstand the gesture, and he would do nothing to hurt their friendship. "It takes time. Have you heard from the insurance agent?" he asked.

Hannah nodded. "He's been out to see the place. We'll hear from him this week."

"Damned red tape," Max said. "Your place is a total loss—any idiot can see that."

"I'm sure we'll get the insurance money." Hannah was silent for a time, a faraway look in her eyes. "Grace will be fine. It's Amelia I'm worried about. Amelia's been through so much, her nine-year-old daughter dying in her arms from some tropical disease, her husband killed in that fiery crash, her burns. She had a nervous breakdown, you know. It took her years to recover. This fire, losing our home, has really set her back."

"Has she been down to see the place?"

"We drove her by. She hid her face. Mostly she stays in her room, and she hardly leaves Bob's apartment. Keeps saying, 'I can't believe it.' "

"You'd think, having survived all those tragedies, she'd have learned to cope."

"I doubt if resilience is Amelia's strongest suit." Hannah shifted, crossed her legs. "Everyone's different. Amelia's never had much self-confidence, and this has renewed her sense of helplessness, especially after the devastating experience she had last year with that bastard, Lance."

"That was quite something, the way he treated her. Couldn't she see how arrogant and self-centered the man was? I recognized it that first night she met him, when his car struck hers in the fog and I drove by and gave her a ride home."

"What do they say, love is blind?"

Max studied Hannah. She's tall, angular, not beautiful, he thought, not even what he'd term pretty, just, well, a damned good person, clear, honest blue eyes, intelligent, capable, and, well, he had to admit, somehow attractive. He stopped himself. "Cruel as fire is, it sweeps everything clean, and gives you the opportunity to get things right, get what you want," Max said. "What do you want, Hannah?"

"What do I want? Tell you the truth, Max, except for our house, my gardens, and the greenhouse, I pretty much have everything I want. I love my work here at Bella's Park. I'm thrilled to be able to create gardens from scratch, and teach children. I'd like to see Laura settled. Eager for our lives to get back to normal."

He pressed her. "Once you're back in a house with your friends, you'll have all you desire?"

"Yes, essentially." She laughed lightly. "I even have a stack of crossword puzzle books that I work at night when I can't sleep."

His eyes scanned her office: corkboard plastered neatly with drawings of the children's garden, umbrellas in a stand by the door, everything on her desk neat and in place, two of Amelia's lovely photographs on a wall across from her desk. She's self-contained, Max thought. She doesn't need me. Good thing!

Grace wondered at how easily she grew agitated these days. And it scared her that her throat tightened whenever she drank or ate anything, making it hard to swallow. Frightened, she ate only soft foods and sipped drinks though a straw.

Her doctor could find nothing wrong. With the medication she took daily, her blood sugar was under control. He did an EKG and a stress test. Her heart was fine. Her blood pressure and cholesterol were a bit high, but that, he said, was normal considering the fire. "Stress can do that. It'll manifest in all kinds of ways, some physical," her doctor said. "Just eat slowly, small amounts at a time, and go on drinking through a straw. I'm sure it will pass."

Grace hated cold food, and had always been a fast eater. Now she reduced her portions and cut her meat or chicken or fish into fingernail-size bites, which she chewed until they had no taste. Cooking lost its appeal. Still, she struggled against a full-blown hankering for sweet things and dreamed about foot-high Black Forest cake, Vienna cake, and fresh-baked sugar cookies. More and more often she found herself turning to Bob for sex, and for his life-affirming affection. Unwittingly, Grace's weight had begun to come off, and Bob's continual encouragement, and his lovemaking, helped sate her various appetites.

On a Saturday afternoon, several weeks after the fire, Hannah, Grace, and Laura sat in folding chairs under the green side of the great oak. The day was still but for intermittent birdcalls and squirrels rustling leaves above them. The house site had been raked clean of debris, the ash turned under, the chimney and old foundation walls dismantled and removed. During the past two weeks, early-morning sprinkles had nudged irrepressible seeds to life, and tiny green sprouts clustered in spots about their yard. Still, the absence of habitat and the blackened stumps of trees on the hillside spoke of the debacle. A great silent wail of pain hung about the land, and this noiseless wail found its way into their hearts and doubled their pain.

The hush was broken when Grace asked a practical question. "Have we enough money to rebuild?"

Hannah cracked her knuckles, a habit acquired since the fire. "I really don't know. We didn't have replacement-cost insurance," she replied.

"What did you have?" Laura asked.

"Flat amount, a hundred and fifty thousand, and they're prepared to give us that," her mother replied. "We have to have plans drawn, of course, and get building permits, and estimates."

"A hundred and fifty thousand dollars sounds like a lot. Won't that do it?" Grace asked.

"Get us fifteen hundred square feet with building costs at one hundred dollars a square foot," Hannah said.

"Who gave you those figures?" Grace wanted to know.

This was tiresome. Hannah was weary with always having to be in charge, and now to have to answer dumb questions. "Who do you think?" she replied. "Who did the repairs for us when we first came here? Who built yours and Bob's tearoom?"

"Tom Findley," Grace said. "You don't have to be so snappy, Hannah."

"Sorry, I'm out of sorts," Hannah said. "I'm expected to make all the decisions, do all the follow-up, call the insurance agent, buy Amelia clothes, help you find a new car, everything." She held her head with her hands. "Well, I'm human, too, I worry, and fret, and feel at a loss just like you do."

"Take it easy, Mother," Laura said.

Hannah scowled at her daughter. "Don't tell me what to do." Hannah rose and stomped away, and within moments drove away from them toward Bella's Park, leaving them without transportation.

"What Hannah says is true," Grace said. "We do turn to her for everything. Amelia and I have dumped all our stuff on her. I even want her to decide what kind of car to replace mine with. I can hardly think straight, and we all expect her to think for us."

"It's what she gets for wanting people to see her as strong," Laura replied.

"Your mother's tough and resourceful most of the time. She's buoyed us all up, you know that. She's suffered as much as any of us from this fire. Even Hannah's got a breaking point."

Laura sighed. "I may not have owned the house or anything much in it, but the fire's been incredibly traumatic for me, too. I'm having nightmares again."

Leaves fell from the tree. They landed on Laura's arm. Grace brushed them off gently, then said, "I am sorry, Laura. Of course you've suffered. It's your loss, too. This is, was, your home, also."

"Mostly I'm numb. I go about my work at Bella's Park. I stand on the site where the log cabin replications are being built, and I forget why I'm there. My head's a sieve, the way it was after the hurricane took everything away from me. I ache for Marvin as much as I did those first new months."

"It's opened painful wounds."

Laura nodded. "My mother and I were never close, especially during my teen years, but over this last year, I thought we'd come a long way toward mending our relationship." She chewed her lip. "Stress, and living together just the two of us in that apartment. There's no buffer." She fell silent. "But you're right. Everything has fallen on Mother's shoulders, and I haven't been very helpful."

"I know you and your mom have old stuff that gets in the way of your relationship at times. Forgiveness comes into play here, and acceptance. Hannah's not going to change much, Laura, and neither are you, so why not just accept the way she is, and overlook things, especially now, when all our emotions are so raw and exaggerated."

"Why can't she just listen and not always have to fix things?"

"Hannah tries. All her life, she's been the one *expected* to fix things."

"Mother starts giving me advice, and I feel the blood racing to my head, and my gut starts churning. How do I stop that?"

Grace was silent a moment. "Drop your expectations about how she ought to be. Keep in mind that you don't have to take her advice. You and Hannah have a pattern of acting and reacting to each other, and it hurts you both. You can break that pattern."

"How?"

"Try using your mind and not your emotions. Stay in your head. Remind yourself that she wants only good for you. She'd bear your pain if she could. And remember, you're not sixteen. You're a capable adult. Hannah loves you. She means well. It's hard to change, especially for take-charge people."

Laura pulled back. "Don't react, is that what you're saying? Talk to myself? Stop myself from reacting the way I did when I was sixteen?" Laura heaved a deep sigh. "That's a tough order."

"But it works. It starts in the head, and it does take some time to get the right mind-set, but it just might make things easier, at least for now."

"I'll think about that," Laura said. "I'll try." She studied Grace with curiosity. "Where'd you learn all this?"

"Oddly enough, much of it from your mother."

"From my mother?"

"Sometimes it's hard to live the theories we teach, especially when we're deeply emotionally involved."

* * *

At that moment Hannah's station wagon drove up Cove Road and turned into what had been their driveway. With her head bent, Hannah hurried from the car to the place where the greenhouse had stood. She moved in a rectangle, measuring her steps to frame the site. Slowly she walked to where her Chrysler Imperial red rosebushes had graced their driveway. Kneeling, Hannah dug her hands deep into the earth. Soil and ash drizzled from her hands and arms as she lifted a long blackened stem. Then Hannah dropped the stem, lowered her head into her hands, and wept.

Mike, his long brown hair tied back in a ponytail and looking distraught, visited Amelia daily. He brought Amelia a Nikon, a Canon, and a Pentax camera to choose from. She waved them away. "I don't care. You decide," she said.

He brought contact sheets developed from negatives of her work just prior to the fire so that she could choose which shots to send to the New York City gallery that sold her photographs.

"You choose," she said, refusing to look at them. And every now and then, she muttered, "I can't believe our house burned."

Some days Mike kept an appointment with Amelia only to find her sleeping.

"She does sleep a lot," Grace said. "This has hit her harder than the rest of us."

"We can't just let her wallow in self-pity," Mike said.

"Let's give her another few weeks. She'll snap out of it."

"Have you noticed she sighs a lot? I doubt she's aware she's doing it," Mike said. "The zest for life's gone out of her. I'm really worried."

"We have to give her time," Grace replied, but she, too, was worried.

* * *

Several days later Grace and Hannah sat in two comfortable lounge chairs on Bob's porch. Bob was off golfing, Amelia sleeping. Overhead the sky was a platter of blue. Below them, on a patch of hillside, someone had cleared the boulders and rubble deposited by mudslides caused by a storm last year, and had planted a small field of sunflowers, which stood at attention facing the afternoon sun. Across the valley, pines and hardwood trees ran thick against the ridge of mountains, a piercing reminder of their devastated woods.

"I get a sick feeling every time I think of our hillside," Grace said. "Our hills will recover, won't they, Hannah?"

Hannah was sorting newspaper clippings. "Yes, and we'll help the process along. We'll rake in a heavy dose of wildflowers on every bare spot. Think of it. Next summer, along with the first berry bushes and wild grasses, we'll have glorious blooming hillsides. Then the pines will come, and the oaks, and poplars, and maples. After we get a really good rain, and the ash settles, I'm going to walk up there and check it all out. Some of our larger trees haven't been destroyed, and they'll green up next spring. But for a full reforestation, woods like we had, we'll have to wait years."

"Flowering hillsides would make me feel better," Grace said. She sighed. "I guess if we want to walk in the woods like we used to, we'll have to go over to Max's place."

"No," Hannah replied, smiling, "we can wend our way through wildflowers up to where our hills weren't burned, but if we want to walk Max's land, I'm sure that would be fine with him."

"I'm exhausted from all the talk about the fire and what we've lost," Grace said. "My mind's more tired than my body."

"I know that feeling," Hannah said. "But not talking is worse, leads to depression. Look at Amelia."

"What are we going to do about Amelia?"

"I don't know," Hannah said distractedly. She handed Grace a stack of clippings. "Look at these, Grace. Remember that reporter from Charlotte who came up after the fire and asked us all those questions and shot pictures of us and of the remains of our house?"

"He annoyed me, but yes," Grace said.

"Well, he wrote a story about us. 'Golden Age adventurers,' he called us, and 'risk-takers.' "

"Why'd he call us that?"

Hannah lifted her head in a manner that spoke of pride and satisfaction. "Because, he says, we pooled our resources, defied our children and conventional wisdom, and moved from Olive's dreary boardinghouse in Pennsylvania to what he calls 'the boonies' and set up housekeeping. He goes on and on about it being a housing solution for older women on fixed incomes. What were the words he used?" She tapped her temple. " 'Whose finances preclude a Florida retirement-community lifestyle.' Yes, that's it."

"A Florida retirement-community lifestyle. I can't even imagine what that would be like." Grace sipped iced tea through a straw.

"That article he wrote." Hannah waved the clippings. "It went out over the wires and was picked up by newspapers all over the country: Maine, Georgia, Ohio, Wyoming, Arizona, Oregon, to name a few." She handed them to Grace. "Here, you read it, and these, too." Reaching down, Hannah picked up a bulging brown envelope and set it on Grace's lap. "This package just came."

"What is it?" Grace took the heavy envelope. Stamps were plastered across the top. When she shook it, the contents slid from one side to the other.

"Letters. Can you imagine?" Hannah said. "From people sympathizing with us and asking how they can help. Some even sent checks. They wrote us via their newspapers, who forwarded their letters to the reporter in Charlotte. Here's the note from him."

Setting aside the newspaper clippings and the brown package, Grace unfolded the small, square, heavy bond paper with a gray border and read the crisp, perfectly formed hand-printed words.

Dear Ladies of Covington,
As you can see, the poignancy of your situation and your interesting lifestyle has attracted the attention of many people. Best of luck.

In contrast to the meticulously printed words, the reporter's signature devolved into an unintelligible scrawl.

"What do the letters say?" Grace asked. Her curiosity stirred, she tore open the brown envelope. Letters landed in her lap and scattered on the floor. Hannah bent to pick up those nearest her.

"Only read the few he'd opened," Hannah replied. "Mailman left them at the office."

Grace pried one of the envelopes open.

Dear Hannah, Amelia, and Grace,
I was deeply touched by your plight. Fire has always terrified me. Enclosed is a check for $25.00. All I could manage. I hope this helps rebuild your house.
                                                        Jenna Martin

The next letter touched Grace especially.

Dear Ladies,
How brave you are. What courage to move in with one another like you did, and now to lose your home. I am a young, strong sixty-four-year-old woman with no attach-

ments. I offer you my steady hands and strong back to
help you rebuild your home.

> *Sincerely,*
> *Louise Allerton*

"Can you imagine someone offering to come and work?
She must think we're going to build with our own hands."
Grace opened another letter. "This one's to you, Hannah."
"So, read it."

Dear Hannah,
My mother, rest her soul, was named Hannah, and she
was a strong, capable woman, like you must be. I enclose
a check for $15.00. Hope it will help replace a rosebush.

> *Best wishes, a widow,*
> *Mary Louis Franklin*

Another read:

Dear Ladies,
How remarkable that you found a way to share a home
together. I always thought women were too snippy and too
catty for such an enterprise, and yet it intrigues me. As a
woman without children and of limited means, I'd like to
offer you my services in helping rebuild your home in ex-
change for room and board, so that I might see how you
iron out the inevitable problems I imagine come up when
three women try to share a house.

> *Sincerely,*
> *Eileen Collingworth*

The letters astounded Grace. That people would take
the trouble to write. That anyone would be moved to send
money to strangers, and offer help and support, that out
there in the vastness of America women like themselves

yearned for a sense of belonging and community, and felt that she, and Hannah, and Amelia had achieved it. As she read on, for the first time in weeks, Grace's spirits lifted.

> *Dear People,*
> *I read about you in our local paper, and love what you've done. I'm so sorry about the fire. Wish I knew how to find several ladies who'd like to share a home. My husband's dead and the kids are far away. Loneliness is killing me. Enclosed is $50.00 to help wherever needed.*
> *Good luck,*
> *Betty Edmondson*

"I am absolutely dumbfounded by all of this," Hannah said.

They took turns reading the letters aloud and placed the letters with checks in a separate pile. "We'll return them with thanks, and explain that we have insurance money to rebuild," Grace said.

"Let's wait and discuss this with Emily. After all, we have a lawyer in our extended family now," Hannah said.

"Fine. " Then Grace said, "Amelia's got to read these."

The twin beds had been joined, and Amelia sat propped against a headboard staring blankly out the window. She did not turn her head when Grace dashed into her room. "Up and out of here." Grace tugged at the light blanket covering Amelia's legs.

Amelia clutched the blanket. "Leave me alone."

They played tug-of-war with the cover until Grace gave a good yank and nearly fell backward as it came free of Amelia's hands.

"Why can't you just leave me alone?" Amelia yelled.

"Because I love you. I refuse to abandon you to self-centered self-indulgence. Remember who you are. You're

Amelia Declose, profesional photographer, author of a fine coffee-table book of photographs, exhibitor at a New York gallery. You don't achieve all that without guts."

Amelia stared at her blankly.

"Don't look at me that way. Listen, the most amazing thing's happened. Come see. We have letters from women from all over the country." As she spoke, Grace tugged on Amelia's hands.

Slowly Amelia turned, shifted, and swung her paja-maed legs over the edge of the bed. If Amelia's hair were not already white, Grace thought, this fire would have turned it white. Grace could see how thin Amelia had become. Hannah had shopped for Amelia, had bought her pajamas, underwear, T-shirts, and slacks at Rose's in Weaverville. So many things, big and little, had been dumped on Hannah.

A great impatience swept over Grace. It was more than four weeks since the fire. Soon it would be necessary to begin to make major decisions about the land, a new house, and here was Amelia sulking, pitying herself, shutting out life. "That's it," Grace said. "Get dressed. You're not going to sit in here like this getting thin and weak. You trying to kill yourself?"

"It's my life." Amelia waved her arms imperiously. "Get out of here. Leave me alone."

Grace planted herself firmly before Amelia. "No. I will not leave this room without you. There are people all over this country reaching out to us. They're sending money to help us rebuild. They want to know how we work out the differences that arise between us. Let's show them." She held up her fists as if prepared to box. "Shall I tell them this is how we settle things?"

Grace proceeded to hop about the way boxers do on television. "Put up your dukes!"

Amelia's mouth fell open. She stood and edged away from Grace.

"You come with me now, or we fight it out," Grace said. Flushed with a sense of somehow forcing the issue with Amelia, she pranced about the room, turning this way and that, punching the air.

"What the devil's going on?" Hannah asked from the doorway.

"It's a fight to the finish," Grace said.

"Oh, good." Hannah laughed. "I'll referee."

Amelia lifted her chin, lifted her small hands and made fists. With a sudden burst of energy, she struck out wildly in Grace's direction.

Still prancing, Grace moved closer. "Let me have it. Go ahead, hit me, I *dare* you."

"Go away, both of you!" Amelia cried, but her fist caught Grace's shoulder, and she sprang back, startled. "If you could only see your face, Grace. You look like a boxing kangaroo." She began to giggle.

They all laughed, then—laughed until they doubled over and cried, laughed until they collapsed in a heap onto the bed, and the shells encasing their hearts cracked a smidgen. And then Amelia sat up. "I love you both. Thanks for beating up on me."

"Hey!" Grace said. "Who beat up on whom?"

That sent them into further peals of laughter.

6

THE PROBLEM
WITH REBUILDING

The following day Max, Hannah, Grace, and Bob sat at the table in Bob's apartment, where they devoured dishes of *arroz con pollo,* replete with the odor of onions simmering, and the smell of seasoned chicken baked so well it fell apart with the touch of a fork. It had been prepared by Anna and delivered by Max. Amelia hardly spoke and hardly ate, and soon she excused herself and disappeared into her bedroom.

The sliding-glass door to the terrace stood open, admitting a pleasant October breeze, which caught and lifted the ends of the drawing paper Max now spread between them. "Hank prepared a floor plan for you to look at before you go to an architect," Max said. "If you're not clear about what you want, you can waste a lot of time and money."

Hannah glanced at the print, then pushed back from the table. "How can we squeeze four bedrooms and four baths, plus everything else we want, into fifteen hundred square feet?"

Amelia's voice issued from the bedroom. "I want the farmhouse back." Then the television came on in her room.

"She's living in a kind of limbo, except that in her head she still sees us in the farmhouse," Grace explained to Max.

"I think Amelia feels betrayed and angry," Bob said, "as if she's just discovered there's no Santa Claus."

Wind rippled the drawing, and Max rested his large wide hands on it. "Of all people, Amelia should understand the chaos that follows a major life change."

"It's like she's living in the cracks and moving in the shadows, like she did after Thomas died, when she had her nervous breakdown. I'm worried about her," Grace said. "Sometimes at night, I hear her rummaging in the kitchen. At least she's eating. But she may need professional help again, rather than our encouragement." Grace looked from one of them to the other, hoping Max would understand and be more tolerant of Amelia.

They returned to studying the drawing. "In this design all the bedrooms open off of a hall," Max said. "That's more expensive and uses more space than if they opened, say, off of the living room."

The doorbell rang. Max was out of his chair and halfway to the door. "That'll be Hank. I asked him to drop by. He's got something else he wants to show you."

Looking windblown, with their hair helter-skelter about their faces, Laura and Hank strode into the apartment. There was a glow to their skin, as if they had spent the day on a beach, and a brightness in their eyes.

"Greetings, all," Hank said cheerfully as he walked to the table and deposited a small pile of booklets and folders before Hannah and Grace. "These merit looking at. They're modular homes."

"Is that a double-wide mobile home?" Grace asked.

"No. It's not. It's a modular. Mobile homes, what we used to call trailers, are now called manufactured housing. 'Modular' means that the houses are built just like regular houses, the way Max's house and your farmhouse were built. Stick construction, it's called. Modular homes are built like regular houses any contractor would build, using the same stringent building codes. If you'd like to see what they look like, there's a place over west of Asheville where there's a development of them."

Hannah pulled the plans toward her. Bob leaned over to see better, and they looked at several modular styles: two-story Cape Cods, farmhouses with wraparound porches, and ranches. "The only drawback, if you consider it one," Hank said, "is that they're never wider than twenty-eight feet. They come by trailer, like mobile homes do, and fourteen feet is the widest they can transport on highways."

"What's the cost of a modular per square foot?" Bob asked.

"About fifty or sixty dollars. You already have a well and septic, so all you'd need is someone to build a foundation three feet off the ground, but you'd want it that high anyway, what with the occasional flooding of your stream."

Grace and Hannah looked at each other solemnly and nodded. They'd seen that flooding once, and had been relieved that they were up off the ground. They turned back to the designs. "I can't say I like the ranches," Hannah said.

"They'll build to your plans," Hank said. "When the house arrives, a special crew sets it on your foundation, and another crew ties the halves together. After it's finished inside, where the join is, you'd never know it came in two halves. These houses can be as lavish or as simple as you choose. You can order crown molding, marble or tile entryways and bathrooms, carpet, wood or vinyl floors, whatever you want. I've seen simple and fancy interiors."

"I'd like to have a look at them," Bob said.

Grace jiggled her chair. "Can we see them soon?"

"Right now, if you'd like," Hank replied.

Grace turned to Bob. "Oh, let's go now. We can all fit into Bob's Jeep, right?" She looked at him.

"Of course," he replied, standing. "Up and out, then."

"Amelia, what about Amelia?" Laura asked. Amelia had befriended her in those early months, when her leg was still in a cast and she cried for Marvin every single night. Laura worried about Amelia now.

"I'll ask her if she'd like to go." Grace knocked on Amelia's bedroom door. "Amelia, we're all going to see some houses, would you like to come with us?"

"Don't want to see any houses. I want our house back."

Grace's face fell. Bob took her hand. "Come on, honey, you can lead a horse to water and all that."

Within half an hour they had driven into Asheville and were headed west on Patton Avenue, where the traffic grew heavy and drivers scowled their impatience. Another fifteen minutes and Hank directed Bob right. Up, up they climbed until the hillside leveled, and they found themselves on a plateau. HIGHLAND VILLAGE, a sign read. A tall stone arch marked the entrance. Before them were charming homes, many in pastel colors, some two-story, others ranch. As they turned a corner, Grace cried out, "Stop, Bob!" Ahead of them sat a white clapboard house wrapped with a farmhouse porch and with dormer windows above the porch. "Look at that, Hannah, doesn't it remind you of our farmhouse?"

"Indeed it does, on the bottom at least." Squeezed between Hank and Laura, Hannah twisted her head for a better view. A sign on the front lawn read, FOR SALE BY OWNER.

"Can we just knock on their door? Think they'll show us the house?" Grace was so excited she bounced on the front seat.

"Act as if you're a prospective buyer, and they'd probably be glad to show us around," Max said. "Shall we try?"

Grace turned and smiled at him. "Let's do it."

The owners were pleased to give them a tour of their home, which turned out to be a small house, probably no more than fourteeen hundred square feet with a large and impressive porch. But the details included deep crown molding in every room, plus carpeting, arched doorways, a galley kitchen done in mauves, which Grace loved, ample bathrooms with tiled baths and wallpapered walls.

In the car on the way home Hank explained that he could copy the exterior and lengthen the house to give them the space they needed. They could tell him what they absolutely must have, and he'd put something together for them to look at.

Grace and Hannah were delighted. "Now we need Amelia's input on this," Grace said.

Hannah snorted. "Big joke. After our laugh the other day, I thought she'd snap out of the doldrums." She wagged a finger at Grace. "You won't be able to root her out of her room. If she won't participate, we can't hold up everything waiting for her to accept the fact that things have changed. We'll design her a room facing east like she had, lots of windows, a much bigger closet with mirrored doors, and her own bathroom. She'll like it."

Dressed in a blue flannel bathrobe that Hannah had selected for her from Belk's in the Asheville Mall, Amelia joined Grace in the kitchen the next morning. She accepted the tea and English muffin Grace offered, then fidgeted with the ends of the purple and white handwoven place mat. The design on the mat was geometric, and

Amelia traced triangles with her fingernail. "I must have a manicure. They do nails at Lily's Beauty Salon in the new shopping plaza on Elk Road, don't they, Grace?"

Surprised, Grace looked at her. "Vanity, thy name is Amelia" could be said of her friend, but since the fire Amelia had neglected her toilette and coiffure completely. Her hair, usually neatly trimmed and slightly curling about her ears, now hung in uneven strings about her neck. The scarves that Grace had saved, worn to conceal Amelia's burn scars, and usually arranged tastefully and with great refinement, were now tossed inelegantly about her neck. Grace recalled passing Lily's Beauty Salon one day and seeing Alma Craine sitting under the dryer and having her nails done. "Yes, I'm sure they do nails," she assured Amelia.

"Good. When Bob comes home, would you ask him to drive me over there?"

Grace brought her palms flat on the table and leaned toward Amelia. "You know Bob will drive you. Just ask him."

Amelia flushed. *"Mais oui.* He's been incredibly patient having me live here with both of you."

Amelia tossed her head, and Grace realized that Amelia was once again using French expressions she had picked up traveling and living for a time in France. Was the old familiar Amelia reemerging? She certainly hoped so.

"I really should find someplace else to stay," Amelia said.

"Why, Amelia? We're family."

"I've been so unpleasant," Amelia replied, looking away.

"It's been tough on us all, and we've all had our not-so-nice moments. You're staying here with Bob and me, so forget finding another place." Then, grasping the opportunity, Grace plunged into a discussion of rebuilding costs, the possibility of a larger house if they bought a modular. She explained to Amelia what they had learned about modular homes, and she offered to take Amelia to Highland Village.

Slowly disinterest gave way to interest, and Amelia began to make demands. "I must have my bedroom facing east."

"We already figured that. We're all used to the views we had, and we'll locate the bedrooms where they were, only they'll be downstairs instead of upstairs."

"*Pourquoi?*"

"Haven't we fussed about having to climb stairs?" Grace asked.

Amelia frowned, then smiled. "Steps aren't that important. What matters is being with you and Hannah, having our home again."

"Sounds like you're ready to rejoin the world of the living. We miss you, Amelia. We all had great losses; but you know the old adage about the phoenix rising from the ashes. Well, now there are three phoenixes rising. We have our land, and Hannah's going to plant wildflowers on the hillsides that were burned. We can design our own house, just as we'd like it to be. Wouldn't you like a large closet and a darkroom?"

"No. Not a darkroom. I can't abide the smells of chemicals." Her face grew sad. "Oh, Grace, I feel so cheated. If this were the only loss, but there've been so many. Why? Why, Grace?"

Grace nibbled her lower lip. "Don't you think I wonder about that myself? But then I sit back and try to take a long view. I recognize that each sorrow, each loss and disappointment in my life has steered me in a new direction, to new experiences, and new people, often to a happier life. But yes, it raises the old question of meaning for me.

Why are we here on this earth? Ever notice that when we settle in and grow complacent, something happens to shake us loose? I ask myself, are we goaded by a creative discontent, which, if we ignore, leads to situations that make us sit up and take heed: someone dies, we lose a job or a business, there's a fire, flood, or hurricane."

Amelia sat straight. Her eyes lit up. *"Oui,"* she said. "After Caroline died, Thomas retired, and we had a home of our own for the first time in our married life. It was near the beach in New Jersey. I swam all summer that first year. The sea was green, the color of my daughter's eyes. I felt she was right there in the water with me." She smiled. "And living at Olive Pruitt's brought me to you and Hannah."

"Well, then," Grace said, "we can have a more modern house, and our own bathrooms. Come on, Amelia. We can plan it all ourselves, make a new beginning. That's pretty exciting."

7

LIKE PLANTS
UPROOTED

To the residents of Mars Hill, and those in Marshall, the County Seat, and at Hot Springs, on the lower reaches of the French Broad River, and deep within the coves of Madison County, fall, with its golden poplars and bright red sweet gums and maples, held sway for a time. Then protesting gold and crimson leaves rolled onto clenched fists before falling from trees. But to the ladies, absorbed by their losses, autumn's brilliance passed nearly unnoticed.

Having taken up temporary residence with relatives, the members of the Herrill and Craine families were as shell-shocked as Grace, Hannah, and Amelia. Their land had been passed from generation to generation. On this land, their ancestors had conquered the wilderness, survived economic hard times, raised families, and prevailed over illness and death, drought and flood. For the Herrills and the Craines, there was never a question as to whether they would rebuild, merely when. As they waited for word from their insurance agents, one or another of those families could be seen sitting in a car or truck, or standing alone, or with members of their clan in small clusters at the edges of their properties shaking their heads, wiping their eyes, commiserating, or comforting one another, or sometimes, their arms flailing, arguing among themselves.

The Lunds and Brenda Tate returned from South Carolina to soot-stained walls, ash-coated furniture, and carpets soggy and mildewed by water. People from churches around the area gathered to help clean and repaint Cove Road Church. In the lingering light of late summer and early fall, the altar and pews were taken outside, sanded, and stained a rich mahogany. Pastor Johnson, a widower, already gray and stooped, seemed further physically diminished, causing some to wonder if perhaps he might soon be retired and replaced by a younger man with a family.

On a chill October day, Grace and Hannah stood on the site of their former home and considered whether to rebuild closer to Cove Road, or whether to set the house farther back across the stream, and nearer to the hills. Perhaps they should relocate it where their apple orchard had been.

"You know what I feel like, Grace?" Hannah asked. She kicked a small stone. Once airborne the stone seemed to hover as if it, too, found it difficult to return to the land. The stone clunked to earth, stirring up the barely buried ash.

"What do you feel like, Hannah?" Grace asked.

"Well, as if I'd been a well-rooted, thriving plant, and some malevolent hand yanked me from my pot, tore my stem and roots out, and left me dangling, utterly traumatized, in the air." Pausing, Hannah pressed her hand against her chest. "Sometimes it's hard for me to catch my breath."

"That's about how I feel, uprooted, and struggling to survive. I'm sure Amelia would identify with that image, too."

"I can hear that plant screaming, the way I sometimes want to scream," Hannah said.

They headed for the great oak, and Hannah strode around to the rear. Her hand caressed the blackened bark as she carefully examined the scars of the fire. Digging deep into her pants pocket, she retrieved a small penknife, selected a limb, and scraped the dry, brittle bark away. Beneath the charred exterior a pale, green layer was visible. "Look, Grace, look at the cambium. It's green. This is where the new cells grow. This limb's alive."

Grace saw the pale green cambium. "Such a frail, thin layer of life," she said.

"Thin, maybe, but not so frail," Hannah replied, snapping closed the penknife and returning it to her pocket.

Inspired by its ability to survive, and marveling at its resilience, Grace's eyes traveled up to the tallest branches of the oak. "Wonderful, brave tree," she murmured, gently touching its bark. She wanted to put her cheek against the rough charred surface, wanted to communicate to this tree how much it meant to her. "Do you think the tree knows how grateful we are for its survival?" she asked Hannah.

"Yes. I think, like with animals, plants sense our love and our anger. I think a plant cringes when you start cutting its limbs. Before I cut anything, I explain to the plant or flowers why, and apologize, and thank it, too."

Grace closed her eyes and concentrated on telling the oak how much she loved it. When she opened them, Hannah had already begun to walk away, and Grace hastened to catch up with her. Moments later they wandered across the scorched earth to the site of their former porch, the scene of so many pleasant afternoons spent rocking, chatting, and having tea.

"We've all been changed by the fire," Hannah said. "I've softened. You've toughened, and Amelia's in limbo."

"It's temporary. We'll all be fine." Grace sped up her steps to keep pace with Hannah's longer stride.

"Time was, I bounced right back after a trauma," Hannah said.

Grace concurred. "I've been numb longer this time it

seems, and the hopeless, helpless feeling in those first weeks seemed deeper, as if it had settled in my bones."

"And angry," Hannah said. "Lord, I'm still angry at that insipid Herrill boy for tossing his cigarette."

"Are you sure he started the fire?" Grace asked.

"He admitted seeing the glow in the dried leaves, and ignoring it. His father insisted that he tell the authorities. He went to court. They fined him, and ordered him to do thirty hours of community service. After what he cost us all, they should have locked him up."

"That's harsh of you, Hannah, and not like you at all," Grace said.

"Who can feel good about someone who started such a needless fire?" Hannah asked.

"I admire Charlie Herrill for making Brad confess," Grace said.

"I guess I do, too. Velma and Charlie are good people," Hannah said.

"Yes. And they're probably crushed and humiliated knowing that their son is responsible for this whole mess." Grace's eyes traveled across the flat open acres where homes had stood and which now lay vacant. She wondered if the earth had feelings, too, and if it missed its occupants. Silly anthropomorphizing everything like this, Grace thought. Next thing I'll be picking up a handful of soil and chatting with it. "It's going to be better, Hannah," Grace said, "as soon as we have a new home and we're resettled, or repotted, you might say."

"Will we survive the time between uprooting and repotting, though?" Hannah asked.

"Of course we will. We already have."

"You're amazingly optimistic these days," Hannah said.

"Haven't you noticed we take turns being upbeat?" Grace asked. "It's as if sonar passes between us, and we know we can't all be depressed simultaneously. There'll come a time when Amelia will be the most optimistic of the three of us."

Hannah harrumphed. "That'll be the day."

Walking, they ambled past the greenhouse site and meandered down the slope of the pasture to the spot where a small wooden bridge had forged the stream. Neither wide nor deep, but too wide to step across, the stream barred their way. Its clear sandy-bottomed shallows revealed tiny minnows dodging rocks and moseying past squat mounds of sand on their voyage downstream. On the far side, blackened stumps, testaments to the fire, stood where once an orchard had thrived.

"This is hard," Hannah said. "Why is this so much harder than anything else that's ever happened to me?"

"It only seems that way," Grace said. "Each catastrophic event appears, at the time, to be the worst. But think about it. We're lucky. We have pleasant places to live, you've been able to work with your class over at Bella's Park." She placed her hands on Hannah's shoulders. "Most important of all, we have each other."

"I don't like the way things have changed. My lack of optimism scares me. Amelia's lethargy worries me. You're settling in to living with Bob."

Grace's hands were still on Hannah's shoulders and she shook her gently. Her feet had settled a fraction into the freshly tilled, soft dirt-and-ash mix. "You're worrying, again, that our lives will change, that I'll simply move in permanently with Bob, aren't you?"

Hannah nodded.

"We've been over this, Hannah. The way I see it, living with a man is different from living with women, at least with you and Amelia. I haven't much experience, only Ted, really, but he was anything but neat, leaving dirty clothing on the floor or dirty dishes in the sink. I was forever tidying up after him. Also, I like it that we come and go as we please. Ted always wanted to know where I'd been, or where I was going, or when was I coming back. I wonder if Bob and I lived together, would it be the same?"

"Amelia says that Thomas was so neat he almost drove her nuts," Hannah said. "Not all men are sloppy or demanding. You had a bad experience. I get the sense that you'd find Bob neater and more considerate than your Ted was."

After thinking a moment, Grace said, "I adore Bob, you know that. He and I are good together, but for example, Bob pitches his arms and legs about when he sleeps. He doesn't know he's doing it, but some nights, in sheer self-defense, I sleep on the couch in the living room. I miss my own room and bed. Lord, how I miss my bed. I long for my own room, and a bathroom with a deep bathtub and tons of hot water." Grace rubbed her hands together and her eyes darted to the place where their home had been. "I can see it, taste it." She turned toward the hills. The heels of her shoes carved half-circles in the earth. "I can picture wildflowers on our hillside. If those hills had been cleared of trees and planted in grass and flowers when we came, that's what I'd love, so I'm prepared to say goodbye to what was, and anticipate what will be."

In the silence that followed, Hannah studied the site of their home and the hillside. She could see it, too, now, and she smiled. "Thanks, my friend. You've cheered me considerably. Let's rebuild the house exactly where it was."

Without further discussion, they walked toward Cove Road. Then Grace said, "Good thing you remembered to tell Max about our time capsule being buried out back. Where is it, anyway?"

"All cleaned up and safe in my office at Bella's Park. The box didn't burn and everything we put inside is intact. We can dedicate our new house and add new memorabilia to our box before we rebury it."

A car pulled up to the edge of what had been their lawn, and Brenda Tate got out. Brenda had survived a difficult year—first Harold's death to cancer, then months of debilitating inertia. Now, after the shock of the fire, she was proving amazingly resilient, and at the end of August had resumed her duties as principal of Caster Elementary School. Taking long strides, Brenda met Grace and Hannah in the middle of the lawn.

"Greetings, ladies. How are you? Have you had plans drawn for your new house yet?" A gust of wind stirred, tousling Brenda's auburn hair, which seemed to Grace to have lost its luster, and was now splattered white along her hairline.

"We're waiting for Hank to give us a preliminary drawing," Grace said as she hugged Brenda. She was pleased to see Brenda smiling. During Harold's illness and afterward, there had been many nights when Brenda phoned and Grace listened as the recent widow cried and relived her life with Harold. Brenda had also spoken of the fears she felt living alone. Her daughter, Molly, and her grandsons, Rick and Alex, had since intervened, taking turns sleeping over at Brenda's house. But in time they devised a permanent solution. An apartment would be built for Brenda off of her own kitchen. When completed, Molly, Ted, and the boys would move from their smaller house next door to Brenda's large farmhouse. They would be close, but separate.

"How is your apartment coming?" Grace asked.

"We start next week. The builder wants to get the walls up and the roof on before winter sets in. It's a small place, six hundred square feet, but it's all I need. I'll have a tiny kitchen, and a room for mother when she visits."

"Most sensible solution," Hannah said. "We find that

we have to lower our sights, give up things we wanted in a new house because of the cost."

Brenda looked puzzled. "Didn't you have insurance?"

"Fixed amount, not replacement-cost insurance," Grace explained.

"Well, then, take a mortgage for whatever you need to build the kind of house you want," Brenda said.

"A mortgage?" Hannah whacked the side of her head with her palm. "Imagine, we never even considered that possibility."

"Can we get a mortgage at our ages?" Grace asked.

"I think so. Check with your bank," Brenda said, then handed them each a small square envelope. "I stopped to invite you, and anyone you want to bring, to a barbecue we're having this Sunday afternoon after church. Mild weather's predicted. Better enjoy it while we can."

Hannah nodded. "Sounds wonderful. Love to come."

"Molly's already asked Laura, Hank, and Max."

"And Max said yes?" Hannah asked, knowing that Max declined most social invitations.

"He did, and I'm right pleased."

"Well, that's splendid," Hannah replied.

"May I bring the Richardsons?" Grace said.

"Of course. Here's their invite." Brenda handed Grace another envelope. "Pass it on to them, will you, Grace? It'll be nice to see Tyler again. I miss his visits. Before his father married Emily and they moved to Mars Hill, he used to drop into my office regularly just to say hello."

"I still look for him in the halls at school," Grace said. "He misses us and his old friends. They haven't moved but a few miles and yet, for Tyler, it's as if they'd moved him to California."

As if reluctant to part, they ambled toward their cars. "How's Emily doing with the new baby and her law practice?" Brenda asked.

"Melissa's nearly seven months old. Emily worked a bit from home, but she's back at the office now. Russell works at home, you know, and they have a woman named Olga, a friend of Max's housekeeper, Anna, who comes in from ten to four, five days a week, to take care of the baby. I worried that Tyler would resent the baby, but he loves her, and he's very helpful."

Having reached Hannah's wagon, they leaned against its hood. "Where did the summer go?" Hannah asked. "Surely we had a summer before the fire."

"Things do seem to date from August second, don't they?" Brenda said.

"Melissa Grace was born in March. But what happened this past summer? When did we spend the day at Lake Jocassee in South Carolina, Hannah?"

"Last winter, November, or was it December? Miranda, Paul, and the boys were here."

"November," Grace said.

"Yes, November," Brenda said. "After Harold died. I'll be forever grateful to you, Grace, for the wonderful Thanksgiving dinner you sent over for my family."

"It was the least I could do."

Brenda stared across the hood of her car for a moment. "Lake Jocassee. Harold and I used to go down to Lake Jocassee a couple of times a year. We'd rent a boat and fish." Brenda bit her lip and looked away, then heaved away from the car. "I've got to go now, but I'll see you about two on Sunday. Dress informally." And she was in her car and waving as she drove down the road.

"Now that's a woman I really like," Hannah said. "You've been a good friend to her, Grace, but then you're a good friend to all the people you love."

8

A NEW HOUSE

Letters from women around the country kept arriving. This impressed the reporter in Charlotte, who wrote another article about the ladies' plan to rebuild, and he promised his readers a status report later in the year. This, too, went out over the wires, resulting in another rash of mail, some with checks. On the matter of money, Emily suggested a separate bank account for the checks they received, and careful record keeping.

Grace enlisted Bob and Hank, Laura and Mike to help them answer letters. Max offered his kitchen. When the stack of mail grew tall, they gathered for this purpose.

Typical of old farmhouses, Max's kitchen was large and square and painted pale green. A floor-to-ceiling pantry, refrigerator, and freezer stood along one wall, with the stove and sink on the opposite wall. In the center a harvest table accommodated as many as ten dairy hands on those Saturdays when the men worked, and lunch, prepared by Anna, proved an added incentive.

Grace placed the envelopes on the table and with a sweep of her hand spread them out in a fan shape. "I'd like to ask your opinions on how to respond to letters like this," she said as she opened a blue envelope from the top of the heap. She read aloud.

Dear Grace,

I address this to you because the article in my newspaper said that you had lived in a small town most of your life. So did I, before I married a man for whom career advancement meant moving every two years. Two years is barely time to make a friend, find a doctor, help my son adjust to another new school, learn my way around, and we were off again. My son is an agronomist and lives in the Philippines. He has no plans to return to the U. S.

Loneliness is the cloak I wear over my clothing. I looked in the mirror the other day and was horrified to realize that my shoulders slump, my mouth turns down. It's how I feel.

My husband, Arnold, died two years ago, just after we moved to Phoenix. Loneliness, and the inertia of depression, have kept me here. When I read about you ladies in our newspaper, for the first time in months I felt a tinge of hope. Maybe if I could connect with one or several widows, and we could share a home, life would be better for me. Then maybe there'd be someone to talk to late at night when two of us could not sleep, and there'd be someone to share a meal with, or go to a movie.

Your lifestyle has become my dream, but how to achieve it? I appeal to you for guidance. Where do I turn to find other women who feel as I do? What criteria did you use to evaluate one another? What measure of compatibility? What roles do each assume and why? How do you settle disputes? How do you deal when a family member visits or with male visitors? So many questions.

I hope to hear from you.

Sincerely,
Lina Fergusen

* * *

For a few seconds no one responded, and then Amelia broke their silence and distracted them with her comment as she brushed a ladybug off of the table. "Ugh! Anyone else noticed that the ladybugs are here again? Used to be ladybugs would come in spring and then disappear until fall. Now they hang on in cracks and crevices. Why do they always find me?" Then she turned to Grace, who held the letter and was staring at Amelia.

"Criteria?" Amelia said. "Did we have criteria?" She giggled. "Get away from Olive Pruitt and her boarding-house for retired ladies was our criteria."

"We had the advantage of knowing one another," Grace said, "of having lived together. That won't help Lina Fergusen. What will we say to her?"

"Of course, we didn't cook or clean at Olive's except our own rooms," Amelia said, her mind stuck in the past.

Laura dandled an envelope between two fingers. "Just because you ladies knew one another is no guarantee of compatibility anyway. But what would have happened if two of you had disliked the third?" The envelope slid from between her fingers and plunked onto the table.

Hannah shook her head. "Actually I did have criteria, although I've never verbalized it. I knew I could never live with someone who chattered incessantly about noth-ing."

Amelia sobered. "I'd be miserable if someone put me down constantly."

Grace skinned up her nose. "I'd hate living with any-one who left messes for me to clean up the way Ted did: wet towels heaped on the bathroom floor, hair in the sink."

"When that letter came from my cousin Arthur's attor-ney saying that I'd inherited a house and land in a place called Covington, I felt an instant sense of liberation."

Amelia flung her arms wide. "Like a bird let out of a cage. I dreamed that the house would be in perfect condition, warm and welcoming." Her arms dropped heavily, and her eyes misted. "And now it's gone."

"You're forgetting how disappointed you were the first time you saw the house: paint peeling, porch listing, shutters sagging," Hannah reminded her.

Amelia nodded, then frowned. She scratched her cheek. "Truth is, I'd never have come to look at it without you two." She reached to touch their hands. "I'd have been afraid, and probably sold it without ever seeing it." Her voice dropped to a mere whisper. "Like I'm afraid now." Amelia was about to cry

"Isn't it lucky the way it turned out? Listen, Amelia, we're going to have a wonderful new house," Hannah said.

Hank chimed in. "One designed to meet your needs."

Sniffing and wiping her eyes, Amelia nodded. "I feel so, so wimpy. I still need so much bolstering and reminding. I'm sorry."

"Don't be sorry. Everyone deals with things differently. You'll be fine." Grace sat back in her chair and folded her arms across her chest. A twinge of anxiety tickled the edges of her mind, causing her heart to beat faster. There had been no time to talk to Bob about a mortgage, as Brenda had suggested. She worried that at their ages, a bank would never give them a mortgage. Old tapes about men handling the money filled her mind, creating anxiety. Grace forced her thoughts back to the matter at hand. "So, what do we tell these women?"

Hannah shifted in her chair. "That we were accidentally thrown together?"

"Maybe there are no accidents. Maybe there's a reason for everything that happens," Grace said, her voice tentative, almost pleading.

"Fate, accident, whatever," Hannah said. "We snatched the opportunity to change our lives."

Amelia lifted her chin and looked puzzled. "We were so unhappy at Olive's. Maybe we'd have jumped at anything."

"Maybe," Hannah said. "Maybe, if Amelia's cousin Arthur hadn't left her this property, we'd eventually have figured out that we didn't have to stay at Olive's. That we could pool our financial resources and rent a house of our own somewhere."

"Yes," Grace said. "We could have done that, couldn't we?" Her fingertips tapped the edge of the table. "Sometimes one can't see the forest for the trees, as the saying goes. But none of this helps determine what we'll tell Lina Fergusen."

"I'd think it would be important to check someone's police record, get a credit check on them," Max said.

The women hardly heard him.

"We're very different," Grace was saying. "Hannah's independent, raised two girls alone. I was very dependent, scared to take a risk. I'd never been more than twenty miles from Dentry before coming to Branston. I'd never met anyone as sophisticated as Amelia."

Amelia tossed her head. *"Mes chéries,* I'm a small-town girl at heart. I'm well traveled because my husband's work with the Red Cross sent us all over the world."

"Grace is right. You're very different, the three of you," Bob said. "But maybe by the time you met, you had reached a level of tolerance that made it possible to overlook things that might have bothered you about one another at an earlier stage of your lives."

"That's a good point, Bob," Grace replied. "We'd all lost a great deal, which opened us to understanding and accepting one another's foibles."

"Foibles? I have foibles?" Hannah feigned disbelief.

Everyone laughed.

"Why are these letters hazy all of a sudden?" Amelia held up an envelope. "Pass the stamps, please." She placed a stamp equidistant top and side from the edges of an envelope she had addressed.

"Are you having trouble seeing?" Grace asked.

"Since the fire, a trifle." She flicked her wrist. "Too much smoke got into my eyes." She held up a page. "What shall we tell this woman?" She twisted the page to read the signature. "Marlene Baker? She's also asking for ways to find compatible housemates."

Grace set her pen down and studied Amelia.

"I could use more light please, Max," Amelia said.

Max rose and went to the window. He tied back the short canvas curtains and flipped on an under-the-counter light. "That better?"

"Merci!" Amelia said.

"These women who write you, aren't they asking a lot of you ladies?" Hank wanted to know.

"Your situation was unique. You don't have a formula," Laura said. She had arrived with Hank and sat beside him at the table, and Grace wondered if Hannah noticed that their arms touched, and that neither of them made an effort to move apart.

"What can we say to these women?" Grace asked, looking from one to the other. "Trust. We had developed a level of trust. These women probably don't have the advantage of knowing and trusting the people they could conceivably share a home with. Maybe if they could gather a group of interested women in similar circumstances together and meet every week for a few weeks, cook a meal in the same kitchen."

"Maybe travel together. *Pour le meilleur ou pour le pire."* Amelia laughed.

"Like a marriage," Hank said, "for better or worse." The others laughed.

"Potluck. That's what marriage is," Laura said, then looked around the table and blushed.

They worked quietly for a time. A sense of comfort and camaraderie settled over Grace. They accepted one another, overlooked each other's mistakes and quirks, she, and Hannah, and Amelia. It stemmed perhaps from goodwill and the firm resolve to make it work, to push through whatever brambles might beset their path. For a few minutes Grace considered the difficult times they had traversed: the months last year when Amelia abandoned her friends, and her photography, in favor of her new beau, Lance. Setting aside her own needs, she had catered to Lance's inordinate demands for her time and attention. Amelia stopped being there for tea or for hardly anything else. Repeatedly she canceled photo shoots with Mike.

Grace's eyes met Hannah's for a moment. Hannah was stubborn—witness the greenhouse fiasco. As Grace had cautioned Hannah, the work had been too much for her, with the result that a reluctant Hannah sold the greenhouse and her fledgling business in ornamental plants to Wayne Reynolds.

Remembering those early months in Covington caused Grace to blush as she thought about her own immature behavior. A lack of self-confidence and irrational jealousy convinced her that Amelia wanted Bob, and that Amelia could have him. Feeling betrayed and rejected, Grace fled, for a time, to her son's home in Branston. It had taken several months to work through the discomfort and embarrassment of that situation, but they did it. They'd managed to sustain their friendship and persevere through all the crazy tilts that relationships present.

Essentially, Grace thought, it's been our commitment, our intention to preserve our lifestyle, the ability to discuss problems, to apologize and forgive that's worked in our favor. Surely there must be a way to pass all they had learned on to the women who wrote to them.

"We all remember how scary it was and how lonely it was living alone," Grace said. "There are solutions to loneliness. Look at how Brenda and Molly have worked things out. Look at us! We must try at least to help point a way for all the women who have written to us."

"I agree with Grace. Let's sit down and put our heads together," Hannah said. "Maybe we can come up with a list of ways by which women could identify other possible women to share a home with: some way to judge if a person's cooperative or competitive, for instance, or open- or closed-minded, things like that."

"Of course." Amelia brightened. "It doesn't matter if they have the same interests, are early risers or late sleepers, stay-at-homers, or go traveling. It's about accepting someone, and being tolerant of differences." She paused a moment and did a thing with her mouth—teeth covering her lower lip—as she thought. "Kindness and tolerance are important, like you've all been to me, especially now, since the fire."

Reaching across the table, Grace traced the pale blue veins on the back of Amelia's slim hand. "In a way it's committing to being a family, isn't it?"

"And where does that start?" Max interjected, suddenly excited. "In one's head. People tend to build up a case for or against a thing, or a person, in their heads."

Hannah's hands pressed the arms of her chair. She lifted herself a trifle and then settled back into it. "I suggest we write these women that we're working on criteria for housemate selection and will be back in touch."

"You're so smart, Hannah!" Amelia exclaimed.

Grace smiled and picked up her pen. "That way we acknowledge their letters, and it gives us time to consider this whole matter."

* * *

Anna came in then, and her face lit when she saw the ladies. "Ah, señoras! *Buenos días,*" she said. "You like flan? I make today."

"Custard." Grace licked her lips. "My favorite. *Gracias,* Anna."

Anna's broad smile showed how pleased she was to see them, and pleased to offer them flan. "You fix your house, yes?" she asked, looking from Grace to Hannah to Amelia.

Grace nodded.

"They'll fix their house, Anna," Hank said. "And a *casa bonita* it will be. In fact"—he turned to Hannah—"I was going to tell you, I have several sets of floor plans in my car. I was going to follow you home and show them to you, but maybe . . ."

Before he could finish, Grace said, "That's terrific, Hank."

"Let's see them. I can't wait a minute longer," Amelia said.

Anna set the cups of flan on the table and waited expectantly for their reaction, which came as soon as they took their first spoonfuls. "The best custard I ever ate," Grace declared. "You must show me how you get it so smooth, no air bubbles."

"Melts in my mouth," Hannah said, and Amelia, Laura, and the others agreed.

Hank returned with his roll of plans, and they quickly cleared the table of dishes and letters so that he might spread his rolled sheets flat. "You ladies go on that side, and I'll stand over here and point out everything to you," he said.

Hannah stood between and slightly behind Grace and Amelia as they leaned into the table. Bob joined Grace, and Mike slipped in alongside Amelia. Like a convoy of ships, Hank thought as he looked at them lined up across the table. He smoothed the sheet with his hands, then moved his finger along the thin black lines and began to explain. "Remember, these are very preliminary sketches. I've brought two possibilities for you to look at." He tapped the sheet. "Long halls are expensive, so I separated the bedrooms, two at each end of the house with adjoining baths."

They looked at one another blankly.

"You're separating us?" Amelia asked.

"Well, yes, in the sense that there's the living area and kitchen between the two bedroom wings."

"I don't think I like that idea," Grace said. "Do you, Hannah?"

"Let's not react until we see the whole plan," Hannah said. "We got used to proximity at Olive's place and in the farmhouse."

"I have another plan." Hank started to roll the sheet on the table.

"At least look at the concept," Laura said, laying her hand on his arm.

Hannah said, "Not so fast, Hank." She smoothed the plan and placed her palm on one side. Grace followed suit, laying her hands on the other side to stop it from curling.

"The kitchen," Hank explained, "is in the front. Here's a large bay area that extends onto the porch. That's the breakfast room. On the other side of the kitchen, here." He tapped the page. "Here's the dining room/family room all the way to the back of the house. The living room of necessity has to be smaller than yours was."

"Two bedrooms on either end of the house, and each two share a bath?" Grace asked.

"Yes." Hank looked up from the plan. "Four bathrooms are more costly than two."

"We'll never have our farmhouse back," Amelia said. The sadness in her voice indicated that she had found, in the old farmhouse, the home of her dreams.

"It's just one plan," a flustered Hank replied. He was not a house architect, only a landscape architect, but at Max's request, he had agreed to set something on paper. "I've never designed a house," Hank said nervously. He could take acres of bare hillside, or flat, uninteresting yards, and create curves, terraces, arbors, ponds, but a house? He had taken on Max's challenge for two reasons—to help the ladies and to impress Laura. Now he studied the faces of the women: Hannah's speculative, Grace's anxious, Amelia about to weep.

"It's going to take time to reconcile what you want with the amount of money you have," Max was saying. "It might not be so bad to go with this idea of split bedrooms. There's more privacy . . ."

"This floor plan has a name, Split Bedrooms?" Hannah interrupted him.

"Yes. Now, just go along with me for a moment. Close your eyes. See yourselves in your own rooms."

"It's not our farmhouse," Amelia said again.

Silence filled the room then, and Grace thought of Hannah and Laura living together on the other side of the house. She recalled Laura complaining of too much togetherness with her mother, and how such proximity created barriers to their fledgling reconciliation after years of misunderstandings and separation. Grace didn't want to hurt Amelia's feelings, but she felt honor bound to intervene. She swallowed and touched Amelia's hand. "If we were to decide on a plan like this, Laura's much neater than I am about the bathroom, Amelia. How would you feel about being with Laura on the south side of the house? You'd still have the mountain view that you love."

At first Amelia looked at Grace blankly, then she

smiled. She was very fond of Laura. In fact, she, of them all, had most identified with Laura's suffering in those months after Laura came to live with them. She liked to think that their talks, late at night on the porch, and inviting Laura along on photo shoots had helped Laura handle the pain of the loss of her Marvin.

"That would be fine," Amelia said, smiling at Laura. "What worries me, however, is what happens if Laura moves out?"

Hank's eyes found Laura's. Since the fire, he'd wanted to make just such a suggestion. Laura smiled at him, then looked away, neither confirming nor denying his unasked question. Hank's heart skipped a beat. He turned his attention back to the sketch. Before anyone could respond to Amelia's query, he said, "Let me show you another possibility."

With a swish the print rolled back into a tight circle, and Hank fitted a rubber band around it. Then he unrolled a second sketch. "In this one I put the four bedrooms to one side of the house on either side of a hall, like they were in the farmhouse, only downstairs. Bedrooms are smaller, but they're together."

"Ah, like we had before," Amelia said.

"Problem here, if it's a problem at all, is that the two inner bedrooms would have only one wall of windows, to the west in the front bedroom, and east windows in the back."

Amelia turned to Mike. "See, everything's changed. If we had a house like this, whoever took the inside back bedroom would have to look at the burned hillside. I want our farmhouse back."

Mike slipped his arm about her shoulders.

Hank sighed. He'd expected excitement and approval from Amelia, she being the most vivacious and the most impulsive of the three ladies. He could see, now, that he was in way above his head. "Take these sketches home with you and look them over," he suggested. "Use them as a point of reference and draw your own sketch of what you'd like. Remember, hallways and bathrooms add to the cost."

"That's a good idea," Hannah said.

"Thanks for all your work, Hank," Grace said. "We do appreciate it. It's hard to settle for less than we had."

"If only we could have our farmhouse back," Amelia said again. She tugged at Mike's shirtsleeve. "Take me back to the apartment please, Mike."

9

AMELIA DECLOSE

Amelia rolled over in bed, pulled the covers higher, and closed her eyes. Slowly she rocked, back and forth, back and forth. Grace's voice, talking to someone on the living room phone, intruded into the bleak grayness that permeated her days since August 2. Bright-eyed and smiling, Grace would soon knock on her door, insist that she get out of bed, insist that she get dressed, then drag her off somewhere: to the market, to the mall, to Hannah's office, or for a ride in the country. Was Grace really cheerful, or was it all a put-on for Amelia's benefit?

The clock on Amelia's bedside table read nine o'clock. Bob would be gone, off teaching a class at the College for Seniors in Asheville, or golfing, or having breakfast at a restaurant with his son, Russell. Grace would have prepared hers and Amelia's breakfast—waffles, or pancakes, or eggs scrambled and waiting to be stirred into the pan. Why wouldn't the woman just leave her alone?

"I'm not going to let you wallow in your misery," Grace would say, tugging at her arm.

God, but Grace was irritating sometimes. Why should she get up? Why even attempt to shake the sense of nothingness that was her constant companion? Life was meaningless. Recovering meant preparing for the next blow, the next loss. Yesterday she had forced herself to take out the new Pentax camera Mike had brought her. Before the fire she would have been thrilled at the new lens that offered a range from 35mm to 200mm. Amelia had taken the camera out on the terrace, the *balcony* as she called it, of Bob's apartment. It was like looking through a pair of binoculars. The river below sprang into view, so close that Amelia was surprised not to hear its rushing sound. But then overwhelming sadness had intervened, and she nearly dropped the new camera.

Grace's voice stopped. The phone clicked as it hit the cradle. Amelia yanked a pillow over her head. Where would Grace insist that they go today? To another awful meeting with Hank to see houses she didn't want? If she couldn't have the farmhouse back, she wouldn't live anywhere, not anywhere, ever.

The next thing Amelia knew, her blanket, her protective cocoon, was being rudely torn away, then the sheet, and Amelia drew herself into a fetal position, moaned softly, and rocked.

"Up and out," Grace said.

With sure, quick steps Grace reached the window, and Amelia heard the sound of blinds being raised, felt the sunshine on her face. The pale yellow walls of the room sprang to life. Shoes and clothing littered the floor. A blue bath towel hung lopsidedly over a chair.

"Amelia," Grace said. "I think you're willing yourself to die. I'm afraid I'll come in here one morning and find you, well, gone, you know what I mean." She sat beside Amelia on the edge of the bed.

Amelia grunted, and waved her friend away.

Grace said, "I won't go away, not today, not any day. The fire was terrible. We lost much that we loved, but they were material things, and we can replace them. We have one another."

"I can't replace my pictures of Thomas and Caroline, or the straw hat with the cherries that Thomas gave me and I kept all these years."

"I can't replace a lifetime of photographs of my family, either," Grace replied.

"I won't live in any of those houses Hank showed us," Amelia muttered. "Our farmhouse suited us quite well, but it's gone." With her head still under a pillow, Amelia's voice was muffled. "Why can't we rebuild it?"

"We'd all like our farmhouse back, everything back." Grace thought about a mortgage. Hannah had said, "Let's go for it, Grace." And Grace considered all those things Amelia had fussed about in the old farmhouse: the occasional, noisy possum trapped inside the walls, drafts that chilled them, sharing one bathroom. "Nothing stays the same, except perhaps the human spirit, which makes it possible to pick oneself up and go on, rebuild . . ."

Amelia rolled over. Lackluster eyes stared at Grace. "How much am I to endure? Rebuild for what? How many times must I love someone, or something, and lose them? I don't want to go through that again. I'd rather be dead."

"I won't let you die." Her voice was fierce, determined.

"How can you stop me? I refuse to live in those houses we looked at. They're horrible. I want everything like it was. Can you replace the photographs I've taken, the one of the little girl who'd fallen off her bike?"

"Amelia, get real," Grace said. "You know that every negative of every shot you've taken is stored in archival sheets in Mike's photo workshop in Weaverville. Do you hear me moaning about my clown collection? I regret losing my clowns. Bob gave them to me, and I loved the one with the dog balanced on his head. And all my books: ancient Egypt, Greece, the Middle Ages, the Black Plague, first-century B.C., Palestine, books of poetry, my cookbooks. Without an inventory, I can't remember all the names."

Amelia rolled away from Grace.

"Perhaps we can rebuild the farmhouse," Grace said softly.

"We can't. We haven't the money," Amelia said.

"It's nonsense thinking we have to rebuild for the amount received from insurance, and trying to squeeze our lives into tiny rooms in a house none of us really likes," Grace said.

Amelia raised on her elbow and turned to face Grace. "What do you mean?"

"There's such a thing as a mortgage."

"What bank's going to give us a mortgage at our age?"

Grace tapped her temple. "Maybe age doesn't matter. When we're all gone, the bank knows the house will be inherited by someone who'll assume the mortgage, or it will be sold, and they'll be paid off. We must try to get a mortgage. Think of it, Amelia, we wouldn't have to borrow much, maybe fifty thousand dollars in order to get just what we want."

"You really think a bank would give us money?" Amelia asked.

"Why not? This country is all about credit."

"But can we handle a mortgage?" Amelia asked, her voice quavering.

"I think a fifty-thousand-dollar mortgage for thirty years would be about three hundred and fifty dollars a month including taxes and insurance," Grace said. "We can manage it. We'd have to go to a bank of course, and Bob or Max could go with us. Bankers would probably respond more affirmatively to a man than to three ladies who hadn't even had the sense to insure their home for replacement cost. We could ask for a long-term mortgage, thirty years, like Ted and I had on our home in Dentry."

"I don't know much about mortgages," Amelia said. "Thomas and I lived in rentals most of our lives, before we bought the house in Silver Lake in New Jersey."

"What happened to that house after Thomas died?"

"After I used up my savings traveling those first six months, I had to sell it to pay hospital costs. I wasn't sixty-five yet, no Medicare. My insurance carried a limit of ten thousand dollars on psychiatric costs. The hospital was expensive. What I had left, I invested for income. That's what I live on."

"Didn't you have a mortgage on that house?"

"No," Amelia said. "We were older, and Thomas didn't want bills. He didn't want a mortgage. We owned the house."

As they talked, Grace helped Amelia to her feet. She handed her a pair of fresh khaki slacks from the closet and a pale tan blouse. As Amelia exchanged pajamas for slacks and a blouse, Grace straightened the rumpled sheets and pulled the cover over the bed, then steered Amelia to the mirror above the dresser and handed her a brush.

"You didn't have to make up the bed, Grace," Amelia said.

"You, who used to be Mrs. Neatnick, will just crawl back into it all messed up like it is, right?"

Amelia sat heavily in a chair. "I'm so miserable." She covered her chest with both hands. "When will this ache go away?"

"Soon as you get going on some project," Grace replied. "That's why we hardly see Hannah. She's buried herself in work."

"But people have to grieve."

"Hannah grieves. We all grieve, in our own way."

"How are you grieving, Grace?"

Grace finished fluffing the pillows and arranged them neatly on the bed. "I wake up every morning with a heavy heart. I poke Bob awake so I can talk to him. Sometimes I visit our land where the house stood, and I talk to the oak."

Amelia began to cry. "You have Bob. Hannah has Max and Laura. Who do I have?"

"Mike is always there for you," Grace said. "And so are Hannah and I." She moved about the room picking up Amelia's pajamas and slippers, handing her a pair of shoes retrieved from under the bed.

Amelia slipped one foot into a shoe. "I mean someone who is all mine. Mike's wonderful, but he's not interested in sharing his life with a woman, and he's years younger than I am, anyway."

Grace stood still, hands on hips. "I used to think I wasn't a complete person without a man. Remember the old song 'You're Nobody Till Somebody Loves You'? I was raised on stuff like that. So were you, probably. Now I don't think a man is necessary for me to have a happy life, not even Bob, and he's a dear, you know that."

"But you seem so compatible," Amelia said. "Don't you want to live with him?"

"Nope. For example, Bob wants me to watch TV with him in bed at night. I want to read and go to sleep. He'd like me to come to his lectures and go with him for lunch. Many women would adore it that a man wanted their company all the time. I treasure the freedom I have to go and come as I please and not feel guilty about that."

"I've been thinking you'll stay here with Bob, and Hannah will end up marrying Max," Amelia said.

"And you're going to be all alone again?"

Amelia nodded. Tears swamped her sapphire eyes. She bent to put on the other shoe.

"Well, forget it. Hannah and Max? Can you really picture Hannah acquiescing to any man? Placing his needs and wants above hers?" Grace laughed. "Hannah's not about to give up her independence. For years she's been worried that I'd move in with Bob." Grace's face grew serious. "I love Bob, but it's not going to happen, believe me." She studied Amelia. "That's the one thing that hasn't changed." Moving to Amelia, Grace cupped her friend's chin in her hand. "We're still the Three Musketeers, and we'll stay that way."

A trace of a smile rimmed the turned-down corners of Amelia's mouth.

"Come on," said Grace. "Let's go find Hannah and discuss mortgages, and then we can sit down and talk about it with Bob, and Max, and Mike, too, if you'd like."

"You know," Amelia said, "I feel better already."

"But, remember . . ." Grace wagged a finger at Amelia ". . . Brenda's barbecue this weekend."

10

BRENDA TATE'S BARBECUE

A low boxwood hedge, neatly trimmed, enclosed Brenda Tate's backyard within which a half-dozen picnic tables with long benches had been placed. Sheep, raised for wool and much in demand by weavers, grazed in the field beyond or meandered up the slopes of the nearby hillside.

Two grills smoked and sputtered as Brenda's son-in-law, Ted Lund, slapped halves of chicken, slabs of baby back ribs, and ears of corn wrapped in foil over simmering coals. Jugs of cider beckoned from a table near the house and bottles of beer jutted from tubs of ice plunked on the ground near the table. A volleyball net, erected at the far end of the lawn, captured the attention of Paulette, Alma Craine's oldest granddaughter, the Lund boys, Rick and Alex, Tyler, and several other children whom Hannah did not recognize. There was much argument and stamping of feet as Paulette organized the other children into teams. Hannah watched the tableau unfold. One of the unknown children stomped off. Paulette followed, put her arm about his shoulder, talked with him. He laughed. They turned and returned to the net. Had Paulette cajoled, enticed him with some reward, appealed to his sense of fairness?

Relationships with their Cove Road neighbors had undergone a transformation from guarded politeness to genuine warmth. Now the warm smiles and bright eyes of Velma Herrill and Alma Craine welcomed Hannah as their hands reached to clasp hers. Hannah warmed to them, and to the occasion. There had been moments, in those first years, when she was certain that she, Grace, and Amelia would never feel a part of this community. For Hannah, the new overall congeniality of the gathering contained a bittersweet quality. Not so long ago, she had been viewed with suspicion by some of these same neighbors because of her verbal and overt efforts to prevent Jake Anson from selling his land to developers. Someone had cut letters from a newspaper and left a note tacked to their mailbox—YANKEE GO HOME—and Max had warned that she was treading on toes. From some of the locals' point of view, he had said, she was daring to question and to undercut property owners' rights.

The fire that destroyed their homes, and their mutual grief, had changed everything, it seemed. Hannah looked about her. They were all there—Brenda's family, the Herrills, the Craines, Pastor Johnson, Max. Lurina and Joseph Elisha brought Wayne. Lurina's dress smelled of mothballs, an indication that it had been taken from the storage closet set aside for her Sunday best. Old Man roamed from group to group chatting with everyone. Hannah wondered that he had lived contentedly for so many years way back up in the mountains with only his grandson, Wayne, for company.

Lurina strolled up to Hannah and tugged on her arm. "Joseph Elisha," Lurina said, nodding in Old Man's direction. "He tires hisself out chattin' with folks. When we get home, he'll soak his feet in hot water and complain about all the folks wantin' to talk to him, causin' him to be standin' so long." Then she turned serious. "How you ladies doin', Hannah? How's my girl, Grace? I heard Amelia ain't doin' so good."

"Recovery from the shock of the fire takes time," Hannah replied. "Slower for some than others. Grace seems okay. Amelia's coming along. We're trying to decide on a new house."

"I been raised in one house since the day my mama borned me in this world," Lurina said.

"Not many people are so lucky," Hannah replied, thinking how deep folks' roots ran in these parts. She smiled. Folks in these parts? She was starting to think like Lurina talked.

Grace stood with Bob near one of the grills deep in conversation with Charlie Herrill and Frank Craine.

"Maybe you ladies would like to use the same builder Charlie and me is using," Frank Craine said. "It'd be a whole heap cheaper if all the houses get built together."

"That's true," Bob said. "Might as well pour three foundations at the same time."

Grace shuffled from one leg to the other. They had no plans as yet, had not even tried for that mortgage, the idea of which hung at the edges of her mind, tantalizing, yet fraught with anxiety.

"What you ladies gonna build?" Charlie asked.

"We don't know as yet," Grace said.

Frank dipped his fingers in a bowl of water and sprinkled the fire. Drifts of smoke swirled around the grill. Grace coughed, covered her mouth, and moved away from the men and the grill.

"They don't have house plans yet," Grace heard Bob tell the other men. "You guys do?"

"Sure do," Frank said. "Same house we had, only new 'stead of old."

Grace pictured white clapboard farmhouses, barns,

furniture being delivered, and families returning, but when her mind reached their land, she could visualize no house, nothing.

"When do you start building?" Bob asked Charlie.

"Reckon before Thanksgiving," Charlie said.

"Sooner the better," Frank said. "We're cramped at Timmie's place over in Jupiter." The smoke drifted away from them, toward the pasture. "You know how it is, two women in a kitchen."

"How's your auto parts store in the new shopping plaza doing, Frank?" Bob asked. Frank had spoken to them about opening a store well over a year ago, before the shopping center opened.

Frank's frown vanished. His smile softened the lines of his wide, pockmarked face. "Sure doing good. Folks like puttering with their cars. And we're getting business from garages as far as Barnardsville and Marshall."

At the far end of the lawn Molly held a bell above her head. When she lowered her hand, the bell tinkled out across the grass, drawing everyone's attention, urging them to fill their plates and set to eating.

Hannah was famished and filled her plate with ribs and corn. As she ate, she considered the cheerful faces of her neighbors, and wondered which of them had wished her gone? Brad Herrill, the cigarette flipper? One of the Craines? Not Billie, the blond one, recently returned from the Army to work with his dad in the auto parts business. The tall, dark one, over there, what was his name, Tim or Timmie as they called him? He'd married a mousy-looking young woman with an amazingly loud mouth. The youngest son, Junior, was nowhere about.

Although his church had been spared, Pastor Johnson seemed permanently scarred by the fire. Age haunted him, weighted his already hunched shoulders, colored his gray hair snowy white. His eyes, glazed with cataracts, would soon require surgery. Max said that the pastor was pushing seventy-five, yet his manner and demeanor signaled a much older man, older than Hannah, who was seventy-four. She prided herself on her good health. At this stage of life, her clear eyes required no glasses, and her skin, inherited from her mother's side of the family and marked by sunspots, was firm.

A wave of empathy for the pastor swept over her. He was a good man, had been kind to them, even if he never took sides on any issue. Childless, he'd been a widower for more years than anyone could remember. Where would he go, where would he live and with whom if his small congregation retired him and brought in a younger man? Lord in heaven, she was beginning to think like Grace, worrying about Pastor Johnson. Well, was that so bad? Grace tried to see the best in people. She brought out the best in them. Where was Grace, anyway?

Looking about the yard, Hannah was surprised to see their neighbors not sitting, bunched together as families. Grace sat with Brenda and Alma at one table. Bob had joined Frank, Charlie, and Wayne at another. Baby Melissa, alongside her mother, waved her arms wildly from a high chair that Russell had just carried in. Hannah wondered that Grace was not sitting near the baby, then realized that Tyler sat to Grace's right.

Grace waved to Hannah and pointed to the empty space on her left, and Hannah joined them. She found Grace deep in conversation with Brenda.

"It was very fast. He just up and died," Brenda was saying. "Lucy found him. She thought he was sleeping, but when he didn't stir for dinner, she shook him. A terrible shock for the poor child." Brenda shook her head. "He was sure lucky going fast like that, not wearing away like my Harold did."

Grace rested her hand over Brenda's and squeezed gently. "I know," she said. "Wouldn't we all hope to go fast like Lucy's pa did." For a time they ate in silence, but Grace could not get her mind off of Lucy. "Lucy loved her pa very much." There were tears in Grace's eyes. She knew the family, and Pa, as she called him, was stricken with what he called the palsy, probably Parkinson's disease. "When exactly did it happen?" Grace asked.

"Day after the fire. I didn't want to further burden you. The mother has sent off five of the children to relatives down the mountain somewhere near Gastonia. Social Services placed the Down syndrome girl in a residential facility over by Black Mountain. The boy, Randy, is with the mother."

"And Lucy?" Grace asked, deeply concerned.

"The relatives wouldn't take the younger children without Lucy, so she can mind the little ones, I assume." Brenda fixed her gaze intently on Grace, who stopped eating, fork suspended above her plate. "I have a feeling the relatives are the kind of people who won't enroll Lucy in school. Before she left, Lucy came to me. She was nearly hysterical, sobbing, asking for your phone number."

"I never knew, never heard from her," Grace said.

"I didn't give it to her. It was just after the fire. I felt you had all you could handle."

Grace's face clouded with worry. "Poor Lucy. Do you have an address for her?"

"I wish I did. We could try to get it from Myrtle Banks, the mother. The woman is very closemouthed, and Randy sticks to her like paint to a board."

"I must talk to Mrs. Banks."

Brenda bit her lip. Her hand, resting on the table, curled into a fist. "The older I get, the less tolerance I have for ignorance," she said. "Randy would have graduated in June. He's over sixteen, so legally he can leave school."

"He's left school?"

"Afraid so. I checked with the high school."

"I'm heartsick over this. I liked Pa. I love that little girl. I wish I'd known," Grace said. She had fallen in love with Lucy while tutoring her last year.

"I'm sorry I didn't call you," Brenda said. "I wasn't thinking good, I figure."

"I don't blame you. Lord, that fire about put us all out of commission."

Tyler tugged at Grace's arm. "Do you love Lucy as much as you love me?" he asked.

"I love you best of all. You're my grandson, a blessing to me, a grandson I never would have had if you hadn't been your grandpa's grandson. And my heart's so big I love many people. You know that, Tyler."

Tyler sobered, his brows knit as he considered this. "I remember Lucy. She was a grade below me in school. She drew pretty pictures of cows and flowers. I saw them hanging in the hallway. Okay. Let's do something to help Lucy."

Grace hugged him. She loved his generous nature, his open affection, his honesty. He was just eleven. Was Lucy eleven also? "We'll see what we can do," Grace replied.

11

WHAT CAME NEXT

It was late in the afternoon when the ladies said their good-byes, left the barbecue. And walked down to Max's house, where they settled into rocking chairs on his front porch. Grace spoke of a mortgage to rebuild their farmhouse.

"Yes," Bob said. "Why didn't I think of that? Why not apply for a mortgage? You ladies should have the home you prefer, but do you really want stairs again?"

"Actually, I never minded the stairs," Hannah said. "Perhaps they could be laid out differently, half up, then a landing, then up again. That always makes it seem like less of a climb. What do you think?" She turned to Amelia and Grace.

"Stairs are good exercise," Amelia said. Of them all, Amelia seemed to have fussed more about the stairs, yet she appeared to float effortlessly up and down them. Hannah was careful, and always held the railing, while Grace was winded when she reached the top.

"I can't say I love stairs, but I can live with them," Grace replied. "What I'd like to see is a smaller living room, maybe, and an additional bedroom and bath downstairs. Twice now, we've had to convert the dining room to a bedroom, when Hannah had hip surgery and when Laura was laid up after that hurricane beat her up so badly."

"A mortgage is a great idea," Hannah said. "I think we should go for it, and build the kind of house we really want."

"We can have our farmhouse back?" This in a whisper from Amelia.

"That would be quite splendid," Mike said. He squeezed Amelia's arm. "It's what you've dreamed of and hoped for."

"I pray for it every single night." Amelia pushed her hair back from her forehead. "I feel better already."

"Ready for a photography shoot? I've a great area called Sandy Mush that I want to take you to," Mike said.

"Marvelous name, Sandy Mush," Bob said. "Where is it?"

"Turn left off of Leicester Highway toward Haywood County. I can show you. I just don't remember the name of the road you turn west on," Mike said.

"Soon," Amelia said. "We'll go soon."

"So," Max asked. "Who's going to go to the bank about a mortgage?"

"Hannah and I, and perhaps one of you men," Grace replied. "You can pull straws for the honor." She looked at Bob.

"You go with them, Bob," Max said.

Hannah felt foolish. She didn't need a man along, but Grace did, so she let it be, and Bob agreed to accompany them the next day to their bank in Weaverville. But for now, as the light of day faded, they sat on Max's porch enjoying good fellowship even as the smells of cows, manure, and sawdust filled the air.

"Sorry about the smells," Max said. "We tilled and fertilized the back field yesterday and seeded a clover crop." But the odors troubled no one, and seemed totally appropriate for the time and place. A birch tree at the end of the porch glittered golden in the light of the setting sun, and like confetti sent a shower of its leaves to drift past them. At the same time distant voices, soft laughing indicated that Brenda's guests had not all departed. After a time a truck started up and drove by, hands waving from windows. They waved back.

Furnished in cool blues and greens, the lobby of the bank seemed formal to Grace and Hannah. The large upholstered chairs, in which they sat and waited, were firm and comfortable. The minutes ticked by, seeming interminable to Grace, before they were ushered into a wood-paneled office, and an extra chair was brought into the room for Bob by a demure assistant. Introductions over, Bob initiated the conversation.

"The ladies' farmhouse was one of those that burned in the fire over in Covington several weeks ago. Perhaps you heard of the fire?"

"I did. I'm very sorry," replied the loan officer, Ms. Hillary Gray, who looked from one to the other of the women. "I read about it. A terrible fire. Thank God no one was hurt."

Hannah and Grace nodded soberly.

"We lost everything," Grace said.

Hannah explained. "We want to rebuild our farmhouse. The insurance, a hundred and fifty thousand dollars, won't do it, what with construction costs being so high. We'll need another fifty thousand to replace what we had."

Hillary Gray nodded and pulled several sheets of paper from a drawer. "I'll need to ask you some questions, and you'll have to bring in the items listed on this form: the deed to the property, your income taxes for the last three years, a financial statement from each of you two ladies—"

"There are three of us," Grace said, interrupting her.

"You three ladies, then. And your plans for the new building."

"We haven't plans yet," Hannah said. "We hesitated to proceed until we knew whether we could get a mortgage."

Hillary Gray sat back in her leather chair. Behind her, in three silver frames on a high counter, photos of three children smiled across her shoulder. A pot of silk flowers, big, rosy peonies, sat alongside the frames.

"Okay." Hillary Gray smiled at them. "Let me take some information from you, and I can give you some idea where this will come down. First of all, who owns the land?"

"We all do," Grace said.

"That's good." She looked at Bob and back at them. "What are your incomes?"

Bob had handled all the financial matters for the Cottage Tearoom, which he and Grace had opened together, and for an instant Grace giggled nervously. Hannah gave the loan officer the financial information, their ages, and from a slip of paper she extracted from her purse she read off their Social Security numbers. Grace looked at her in admiration. Hannah had thought of everything.

"I'll have credit checks run on each of you," Hillary Gray said.

Grace sighed when they walked from the bank. "They ask for so many things. Do we have all the papers Ms. Gray wants? I marvel that you had the presence of mind, Hannah, to take the files from the house that night."

"I used to wonder what were the most important things to grab and run with if there was a fire," Hannah said. "You can buy new clothing, but personal photo albums would be impossible and business files the most complicated to replace."

"You're right. My biggest loss are my photo albums," Grace said.

"Hillary Gray's questions and requests were routine,"

Bob assured her. "I have a good feeling about this. If none of you ladies has huge credit card debts or other major liabilities, I think you'll get what you want."

"We only have one credit card account, and each of us has a card," Grace said. There was pride in her voice and in her eyes. "We use it for groceries and for our electric bill. We split the cost three ways and pay it in full every month."

"That's good," Bob said. He took their arms and led them across the street to the car.

Within two days Hannah had collected and mailed Hillary Gray all the items on her list, and now they could only wait to hear from her. In November, shortly after the ladies spent a quiet Thanksgiving at Russell and Emily's home, Hillary Gray phoned them. Hannah was at Bob's apartment when the phone rang.

"Mrs. Parrish, how are you? How is Mrs. Singleton? What a nice day we're having."

"Indeed, warm for November," Hannah replied.

Amenities over, Ms. Gray said, "It looks good. I'll need your plans, of course, and the builder's estimate as soon as possible."

Finding an architect, and getting an appointment with him, took another week. Grace changed the calendar page from the rustic November scene of a dark wood porch on which four hound dogs slept to December's picture of pine trees on a hilltop blanketed with snow. December! Where had the year gone? It seemed to Grace, as she slipped the hole at the top of the December page of the calendar over the nail in the wall, that at this time of her life the months passed all too swiftly. At seventy she did not feel old, just the opposite. Even with the shock of the fire, and even though, in those first few weeks, it had been hard to drag herself out of bed each day, Grace felt more energetic, more challenged, more alive than ever.

There were moments, of course, a book she reached for that was no longer there, a favorite dress, a cookbook with a recipe not yet memorized, comfortable old sneakers sorely missed. Gradually she and Hannah had shopped for themselves and for Amelia, and over several weeks replaced clothing, shoes, toothbrushes, combs, cosmetics. The greatest loss was her photo albums: her parents as young people, their wedding picture, her and Ted's wedding pictures, Roger's baby pictures, Sundays at the lake near Dentry, Roger's graduation photograph. Irreplaceable. And for these she grieved, but then, at quiet moments alone, she found that she could close her eyes and see again the gangly twelve-year-old she had been, the blushing bride, the proud mother, her son at six, and twelve, and twenty-two. And the doctor had been right when he had urged her to lose weight. With twelve pounds shed already, she felt light as air.

The ladies asked Hank to sketch out a floor plan for a new and improved farmhouse. To keep it within budget, the bedrooms would be smaller, twelve by fourteen feet instead of the original thirteen by seventeen, but they would have two bathrooms upstairs, and a bedroom and a full bath down. The large, old-fashioned farmhouse kitchen would be replaced by an efficient galley kitchen, with a comfortable five and a half feet between fourteen-foot-long counters. A new breakfast area large enough to accommodate a round table and six chairs would do.

"We must have a pantry, and a mudroom off of a small side porch," Hannah told Hank.

"Shall I fill in the basement or leave it? If we leave it, I could add a couple of high windows down there," Hank said.

Hannah replied, "Let it stay. We never went down there much, not since that night shortly after we'd moved in, when the bathroom flooded and we couldn't find the turn-off valve for the water. But someday it might be useful to one of us."

"I'll put the pump in a closed closet on that back porch, and your water heater can go in a corner of the pantry," Hank said.

"Just make it a big water heater," Grace said. "Amelia and I like long hot baths." They agreed, after much discussion, to forfeit a hobby room.

The architect, a friend of Russell's, agreed to draw the plans quickly so they could have them for the bank in January. "Don't be fooled by Charlie Howard's baby face, and the fact that he hardly looks you in the eye," Russell said to Hannah and Grace as they prepared to leave for their first meeting with the architect. "Charlie's a fine architect but he's a singular introvert, terrible with people. He's happiest hunched over his drawing board. Just take him the floor plan Hank's drawn up for you, and tell him absolutely not to make any changes."

Without looking up at them, architect Charles Howard mumbled a greeting to Hannah and Grace when they entered his small office in Hot Springs. He extended his arm for the rolled floor plan, spread it on a table, and hunched over it. Now and then he nodded. Finally, without looking up, he said, "No changes, right?"

"No changes, Mr. Howard," Hannah said.

"We can't afford to make any changes," Grace said.

"I'll have these for you about mid-January." He dismissed them without saying so. Grace and Hannah looked at each other. They had expected to chat, to discuss the floor plan, to explain their need for a bedroom and bath downstairs, to talk about fixed shutters versus shutters that closed.

In the hall Hannah said to Grace, "Hard to like that

man. I wanted to talk about costs, but I refuse to talk to the top of a head."

That night the ladies gathered in Max's living room. Anna, smiling broadly, served them a dark cake steeped in rum with their beverages.

"This cake is scrumptious," Grace said.

"You want I should give you recipe, *Señora* Grace?"

"I'd love that, Anna, but not tonight, later, when we're back in our own house."

Anna smoothed the small, lace-trimmed apron she wore when company came, and beamed. *"Sí, señora!* You build *una casa grande."* Then she vanished into the kitchen.

"Una casa grande. I like the sound of that," Amelia said.

"If Charlie gets those plans done in January, Tom can probably start in March," Max said. "I'll stay on his back."

"March, why so long?" Amelia asked.

"Processing a mortgage application takes time. Tom has to work you into his schedule, and winter's not the best time to be starting construction."

Tom Findley had renovated the weather-beaten farmhouse for the ladies so that they could move to Covington. Certain, now, that he could bring in the new job below $200,000, Tom came to Max the following day.

"I can put several men to work next week on the foundation. We've got good weather predicted for another week. Might as well get a jump start. Think the ladies have the money?"

"Look, don't bother them now. I'll advance whatever you need. You can reimburse me when you get paid." Max admonished him to secrecy and gave him a check for three thousand dollars.

Three days later stacks of concrete blocks were delivered to the site, followed by a cement mixer and men in work clothes. Using dimensions obtained from the architect, workers erected a three-foot-high foundation wall and were in the process of plastering it smooth when Grace, Max, and Hannah circumnavigated the walls. "Tom's great to go ahead like this. I feel we're half there already," Grace said.

The earth inside the rectangle, where the workmen had stood to work, was packed hard except for the dark, sooty hole that had been their basement. "Actually, I'd like to cover that basement and forget about it," Grace said.

"I'd prefer that we leave it. It's there already," Hannah said. "Tom can put in high windows."

"But why keep it?" Grace asked.

Hannah's shoulders rose and fell. "One or the other of us might need the space sometime."

"With a window air conditioner, vinyl flooring or a bit of carpeting, and good lights it might make a fine hobby room someday," Max said.

"It might flood," Grace said.

"It never has," Hannah replied. She sat on the new foundation, swung her feet over the short wall, and stepped into the space where, in spots, tiny snatches of green poked through dry earth.

"How resilient the land is." Hannah kneeled to smell the earth. "Life's coming back. Most of the ash odor is gone."

"All I smell is fresh plaster," Grace said, "and the fumes from that oil delivery truck." She pointed to a big truck belching exhaust fumes on its way down Cove Road. "I'm going back to Max's place." She started for the road.

As Grace walked away from them, Max offered his hand to Hannah as she climbed back over the wall. They walked back across the dips and ruts impressed into the earth by the tires of fire trucks. Max said, "Once Tom gets started, it will go fast, at least at first. They'll lay the floor. Then the walls will go up, and the roof. When they start finishing the interior, it'll appear to crawl along. You'll think your house will never be finished, but I guarantee you, it will be."

"How long before we're in the house, do you think?" Hannah asked. She trusted Max, and knew that he had quite a bit of experience with having things built.

"Tom's waiting for the plans. If he starts in January or February and spring's not too rainy, they'll get quite a bit done, if not, well . . ."

They joined Grace on the porch. "I'm excited about this. I've never had a home built," Grace said. Her back ached from sleeping on the living room couch. Bob was ignorant of this, however, for she returned to his bed before sunup, and he was a heavy, though restless, sleeper.

Several days later, on a quiet afternoon, Grace and Bob sat alone in the living room. Being a pleasant day, the sliding-glass doors were open and from a distance, on waves of sound, came the steady rumble of a tractor. "Someone over in McCorkle's Creek's turning under corn stalks."

"Isn't it a bit late for that?" Grace asked,

"A bit late. He's probably putting in a crop of clover," Bob said. "By the way, where is Amelia?"

"Off with Mike shooting film."

"And Hannah?"

"Hannah's mulching the children's garden, preparing for winter. You know," she said, then changed the subject, "I'm amazed at how easy it was to get a mortgage."

"I'm not surprised. You have hardly any debt, other than your car payments, and your combined income is over sixty-five thousand. You can certainly cover a small mortgage that's spread out over thirty years."

"Only three hundred and twenty-five dollars a month, split three ways, we'll be fine," Grace said. "We'll have our farmhouse back, only we'll have so many more conveniences. Two to a bathroom instead of four of us."

"Are you sure, honey," Bob asked, "that you won't reconsider and move in permanently with me? You could have your own bathroom." A smile teased his lips. He toyed with a curl of her hair. "I like having you here."

"I love you, Bob." Her eyes softened, and she touched her solar plexus. "I get a thrill in the pit of my stomach when you walk in the door."

"Well, then, we feel the same way. You'll stay?"

She shook her head. "No. This has been special, this time together, but I can't stay."

He appeared hurt, the last thing in the world she wanted.

"I don't understand," Bob said. "We love each other. We're happy living together."

It was quite wonderful, really, to be with someone who loved her and was as considerate as Bob. It was comfortable and felt safe to lie in bed tucked close to him. There were moments, brief moments during the last few weeks, when Grace considered his repeated requests. But hours of agonizing over the matter had only reaffirmed her certainty that living with a man was different than sharing a home with compatible women, and she preferred to leave things as they had been before the fire.

Hannah or Amelia listened patiently, no matter how many times Grace needed to rehash an old anxiety or a new concern in order to clear her mind. Bob would try to fix it, or he would put his arms about her and advise her not to worry about this or that, and in the end she would feel that her concerns were trivial. Perhaps they were, but she needed to come to that conclusion herself.

"What's the problem, then?" Bob asked.

Grace looked at him sideways, raised an eyebrow, and smiled. "Sex is always fresh and highly anticipated. I love when we shower together, and I've lost all my self-consciousness. You've made me love my body." She frowned. "But I wonder, if we lived together, after a time, the thrill I feel in the pit of my stomach when you walk in the door would be gone. The bloom would pass the rose, so to speak. We'd reduce to a mundane relationship, like those couples we see at restaurants who never say a word to each other during their meal."

"Oh, I hardly think so," Bob said.

"Perhaps not. Well, it's not so much a problem as it is a philosophy. I like the independent life I've developed living with Amelia and Hannah." Grace lifted, then dropped her hands in her lap. "It's hard to explain. It's different sharing space with a man than with a woman."

"It's hard for me to understand," he said.

"The last thing in the world I want is to hurt you, Bob. Nothing's changed. I love you with all my heart, only I don't want to be married."

"I'd be content to live with you, Grace," he said.

She didn't want him to beg; she didn't want him to be hurt; she didn't want to lose him. Taking a deep breath, Grace finally explained that he tossed at night and that she slept most nights on the living room sofa. "Why didn't you tell me?" Bob asked, taking her hand. "I'd have slept on the couch."

"I've grown accustomed to a room of my own, where I can be alone, shut out the world, read, or think, or just stare out of the window," Grace said. "If we lived together, I'd have to have a room of my own."

He was silent for a moment before he said, "You could have your own room and bathroom here."

Grace shook her head. "And displace Tyler from a room he considers his? It's hard enough for him now, with Amelia here, and that's temporary. Tyler needs to know he's always got a place with you when he needs to get away from his new baby sister or his stepmother. No matter how much he loves them, he needs time with you, for reassurance if nothing else."

"We could get twin beds and push them together," he said.

They sat in silence for a time. Grace fidgeted in her chair. Bob rubbed his chin. He had not shaved this morning. "I shouldn't have mentioned your tossing," Grace said, placing her hand on his arm. "It's so much more complicated than where I sleep, and yet it's very simple. I want things to be as they were. Can you live with that, now, after this time together?"

"Hard," Bob said, shaking his head. "I don't really understand, although you're right about Tyler and the room. He picked the color and the furniture. He does think of it as his room on loan to Amelia." Lips pursed in a pout, Bob looked at Grace. "We can get a larger bed."

Grace smiled and shook her head.

They were quiet again for a long while, lost in their own thoughts. Bob looked across the valley at the mountains. He didn't like winter, especially living up here on this hillside with its winding roads, impassable in snow and ice conditions. He loved the stillness, the peacefulness of the place, and there were breathtaking moments in winter: a pattern of icicles beneath the eaves of the roof, sunsets that turned the snow to orange sherbet. At those times he longed for Grace to share the moment with him.

Bob looked away from the mountains, and at Grace. Her face was serene. She seemed to be recovering faster and more easily than Amelia certainly, and as for Hannah, Bob thought that Hannah stuffed her feelings, and that, one day, they might explode. "Russell seems to understand your feelings about this, Grace," Bob said. "He keeps telling me not to nag you, to let things be."

"Bless Russell," Grace said.

12

HANNAH'S
BIRTHDAY PARTY

With his flair for the dramatic and his eye for design, Mike was the natural choice for Max to enlist in planning a party to celebrate Hannah's seventy-fifth birthday on December fifteenth.

Mike could have danced with delight. "A fitting end to a difficult year," Mike said. "Something special, something lovely. What kind of budget do I have?"

"Anything you need. I want it to be an evening Hannah will remember," Max replied.

Max turned to Grace for help in developing a guest list. When it was done, the list included the Richardsons, Brenda Tate and her family, Lurina, Old Man, Wayne, Hank, Hannah's foreman at the gardens, Tom Battles, Mary Ann from Bella's Park, and, of course, Pastor Johnson.

Miranda, when Max called her, was delighted, and immediately made plans to come with her family. Although the holiday season in the party-planning business was underway, Hannah's seventy-fifth was too important to miss.

"You absolutely must go," Charles said to Miranda when she told him. "You need a break. You've been beavering away since spring, picking up my pieces mostly."

"But this is our busiest season," Miranda said, brushing aside the fact that Charles looked more and more worn out, and frequently left the shop to rest at home.

"We'll be just fine. It's just for a few days," Roger said.

"But what about you, don't you want to go?" Miranda asked Charles.

"I'm not up to it. This is your mum's big day," Charles said. "Tell her next time we're down, I'll stand her for lunch. You give her a kiss for me."

Miranda acceded. Annoying as it was to have to change planes in Charlotte, the drive down would take too long, so they opted to fly. Since Hannah and Laura occupied the business's apartment in Loring Valley, Miranda accepted Max's invitation for her family to share his large four-bedroom farmhouse.

Grace asked that Ellie Lerner be invited, explaining that Ellie owned the bridal shop where Grace had found the "right" wedding dress for Lurina to wear, and Ellie had graciously delivered the dress herself. Grace and Hannah had talked of having lunch with Ellie, but time passed, and it was not until Ellie's note arrived expressing sadness at the loss of their home, and concern for the three ladies, that Grace realized how remiss they had been regarding Ellie. Max agreed, and Grace was pleased when Ellie's RSVP said that she would be delighted to attend Hannah's party.

When he received the invitation, Roger phoned Grace. "Sorry, we can't come, Mother," he said. "We can't all be away from the business, and besides, Charles isn't feeling up to par."

To Grace this was a red light. "Is something wrong?" she asked, pulling out a chair at the kitchen table and sitting. Grace counted back in her mind, trying to remember when it was that Charles had contracted HIV. Was it seven or eight years? Grace prayed that he would never progress into AIDS, but the threat hovered in the background of their lives like thunderheads over distant peaks.

"He had a flu shot, gets one every year. It knocked him out. Nothing serious," Roger replied.

"Miranda says Charles goes home to rest often. Something you aren't telling me, Roger?"

She could hear the sigh in the silence that followed. Roger said, "Charles's cell count dropped to five hundred this fall. They want to put him on a cocktail of drugs. What we've been trying to avoid for years. He's on a new herbal regime, and acupuncture. His count's up already. Don't worry. He'll be fine."

Grace worried. And then she thought maybe there was more to their not coming for Hannah's birthday. Last January, Amelia and Mike had gone to New York City for the exhibit of Amelia's photographs at a gallery. Roger had planned to rendezvous with Mike in New York after Amelia returned home, only Roger had changed his mind and left Mike sitting, frantic with worry, in a hotel in Manhattan. A devastated Mike had poured out his hurt and anger to Grace. Many weeks later, Roger apologized to Mike, explaining that he had been foolish, had acted precipitously in proposing that they meet, that he had reconsidered and opted for fidelity to Charles. "Blame my mother," Roger had said to Mike. "Blame the values of loyalty and commitment that she instilled in me."

"Roger should have thought about those values before encouraging me," Mike said to Grace when he told her about their conversation. Mike still nursed both anger and hurt. It was better that her son and Charles not come to this event.

"I understand," Grace said to Roger. "Give Charles my

love, and see that he gets plenty of good hot chicken soup."

Grace had assumed correctly, for when she told Mike that Roger and Charles were not coming, anxiety faded from his eyes, and he gave a long sigh of relief.

The invitations contained specific directives. Everyone was sworn to secrecy. Dress was semiformal. Music and cocktails at five in the afternoon. Dinner at six. RSVP requested. Max hired a photographer, whom Mike recommended, to shoot Polaroids throughout the evening.

Mike chose a banquet room at a new resort, the Sky High Country Club and Ski Resort, four thousand feet high in ski country in the mountains of Madison County. The room was intimate and elegant, with a tray ceiling, deep crown molding, as well as decorative molding on the walls. At one end of the room, under a crystal chandelier, a raised platform and small dance floor lent itself to the string quartet Mike suggested that Max hire for the evening.

In an agreement with the management of the resort, light fixtures of no particular interest were replaced with shimmering crystal chandeliers to match the one over the dance floor. Along the walls Mike added delicate, wrought-iron stands topped with clusters of tapered white candles. Lace tableclothes fell gracefully to the floor, and bowls of fall flowers—chrysanthemums, asters amid sprays of baby's breath—graced the tables. China plates with a thick gold band were rented, as were French crystal wineglasses and sterling silver flatwear. Every detail was considered, including individual silver salt and pepper servers.

Mike fumed and fussed right to the last minute. There were not enough candles. The china should be more translucent. The waiters should be wearing tuxedoes, not dark pants and ties and white shirts. But the overall effect was elegant, and Max was more than pleased.

It fell to Grace to deliver Hannah, properly garbed, to the club without revealing why, and to conceal from Hannah that Miranda, Paul, and her grandsons, Sammy and Philip, had arrived in Covington and were staying with Max at his farmhouse.

Days before the fifteenth, Grace convinced a reluctant Hannah that they needed to add something dressy, for the holidays, to their new wardrobes.

In the Asheville mall, Christmas decorations and music, the sense of expectancy on smiling faces, and people carrying wrapped parcels delighted Grace. The festive air, however, produced the opposite effect on Hannah, who grew more and more truculent as they trooped from store to store, and nothing appealed to her.

Grace found a mauve-colored linen skirt with tiny tucks about the waist, a long-sleeved silk shirt, and a linen jacket to match the skirt. Narrow lapels and pearl buttons turned the outfit from good-looking into elegant, a party outfit for an important occasion. Grace twisted and turned before the mirror. "I'm a size smaller, Hannah, isn't that terrific?"

"You look great, and you're terrific, no matter what size you are." Hannah flopped into a chair in the dressing room. "I hate all this," Hannah said, nodding at the holiday shoppers. "Mall's too crowded just before Christmas. Let's get out of here and go home." Hannah tugged at Grace's arm the way Tyler did if Grace took him somewhere and he was tired.

Grace's face fell, and immediately Hannah realized what a lift this shopping spree was for her friend. She sighed. "Okay, one more store."

In the last shop, a small specialty dress shop, Grace

spotted the stunning emerald green pantsuit in a light wool, perfect for Hannah, and when, at Grace's urging, Hannah tried it on, the long jacket settled on her wide shoulders and the arms were a perfect length, as if it had been tailored for her.

"The color's wonderful on you," Grace said. "It brings out the blue of your eyes and makes your skin sparkle."

"Sure," Hannah said, but she studied herself in the full-length mirror. "Right color for Christmas, anyway. Better than red." Gruff as she sounded, Hannah turned this way and that, adjusted the shoulders, shook a pant leg to see where it fell in relation to the sneakers she insisted on shopping in. "I'll have to get a pair of low-heeled pumps for this," she said finally. Glancing into the mirror, Hannah fluffed her thick salt-and-pepper hair. "It's grown out a bit, hasn't it? Should I have it cut?"

"I like your hair longer. It's softer, more feminine."

"Ha," Hannah said. "You're such a romantic." But she remained before the mirror slicking back her hair, then fluffing it out again. "Maybe I'll become a redhead. Then I'll look like a Christmas present."

"A present for whom?" Grace asked, lifting her eyebrows.

"No one, silly woman," Hannah replied, and slipped her arms out of the jacket.

"Bet this outfit sits in my closet for years," Hannah grumbled.

"That green is gorgeous on you," Grace said. "One of these days you'll need something dressy, and you won't have to rush around trying to find it at the last minute."

On the day of her birthday, Grace presented Hannah with a set of stainless-steel garden hand tools with easy-to-grip handles to replace those lost in the fire. The set contained a hand trowel, a transplanter, and a cultivator. Amelia gave Hannah a lightweight, all-purpose weeder. It was a tool Hannah had never had, and it came with a long stainless-steel handle. Bob, at Grace's suggestion, presented Hannah with soft, thick, foam-rubber kneepads and a gardener's apron with pockets for tools.

When she opened the boxes, as she caressed each tool, turning it over in her hand, feeling the easy-grip, elasticized handles, tears welled in Hannah's eyes. "They're wonderful. Much better than my old ones. Thank you, my friends."

"Glad you like them," Grace said.

"Grace, Amelia, and I want to take you someplace special for your birthday," Bob said.

"You don't have to do that," Hannah replied.

"But we want to. We insist," Grace said. "We need to celebrate, and you are our excuse, so let's get out our new outfits, and be ready to leave by four this afternoon."

"So early? Where are we going?" Hannah asked.

"It's a distance, and it's a surprise," Bob said. "All I'll say is that it's an elegant new place."

Amelia, who had committed to helping Mike put the finishing touches to the tables, left Bob's apartment early with her new camera bag, stuffed with her toiletries and cosmetics, slung over her shoulder.

"See you for dinner," she said to Grace and Bob as she went out the door. Her blue chiffon cocktail-length dress and matching shoes and scarf, bought for the occasion, were already secreted in the back of Mike's van.

At four in the afternoon Hannah, Grace, and Bob climbed into Bob's Cherokee and headed for Mars Hill and Highway 19-23. The ride took them past pleasant pastures dotted with rolled mounds of hay for winter fodder. A creek bordered the road. Along both sides of its banks, winter-bare willows leaned toward each other across the gushing water.

"Go slow, Bob," Grace said. "I'm looking for markers so we can find this exact spot to come back to in the summer and have a picnic. Wouldn't that be fun?"

Bob nodded, his eyes intent on the road.

"The light's so soft this time of year," Grace said. "Not harsh like in summer."

"Unless it's snowing," Hannah said. "What has more glare than sun on snow, I ask you?"

"Sun at the beach?" Grace asked, then turned her attention to the hillsides that grew steeper by the moment. Solitary wooden houses tucked into the folds of hills, hidden by trees in summertime, were now visible. Behind some of the homes the earth was contoured, and terraced, and grapevines had been planted.

"I had no idea they grew grapes around here," Hannah said, craning her neck as the car slid past a small, remote vineyard.

"Some families in these parts make quite good wine," Bob said.

"How do you know that?" Hannah asked.

"Old Man and Wayne once took me visiting. I could never find the place again, but it looked somewhat like this, old falling-down house and a vineyard and the best-tasting white wine I've had in a long time. Problem is, they're limited by their land. Not enough of it to produce sufficient grapes to sell their wine."

They nearly missed the sign and arrow pointing to Sky High Country Club and Ski Resort, where Bob turned the car to the right.

The road to the Country Club twisted for several miles up precipitous hillsides and around sharp curves bordered by deep, thick woods. Upon reaching the crest of the mountain, it leveled and widened. A tribute to good planning, condominiums surrounding the ski area had been built into both sides of the mountain, their roofs barely visible from the parking lot.

Hannah stepped down from the backseat of the Cherokee and looked about her. Backlit by afternoon light, the bright stems of red twig dogwoods, planted in clusters here and there along the turnaround, gleamed scarlet. "The winter character of those dogwoods make quite a splash this time of year," Hannah said, walking to one and running her hand along the crimson bark. "And this is quite a view. Must be 360 degrees around. Didn't know about this place. Imagine, a restaurant so far away from everything."

Taking both their arms, Bob escorted Grace and Hannah into the clubhouse. When he opened the door to the banquet room, the glow of candles, the gleam of crystal chandeliers, the blur of faces and bright clothing, and the chorus of "Happy Birthdays!" reached out to envelop Hannah. She took a step back. Miranda, her dark hair pulled back in a large, loose bun, and looking lovely in a blue velvet pantsuit, ran to embrace her mother, and Hannah's grandsons, Sammy and Philip, all grown up now and wearing suits and ties, followed. Hannah hardly knew whether to laugh or cry with pleasure. Her face turned crimson, and her eyes gleamed with delight. Moments later, as if on cue, the sky to the west burst into a flaming sunset, as Mike had hoped it would, which drew them all to a bank of west-facing windows.

"You see," Miranda said, coming to stand beside her mother, "even the sky is celebrating your birthday."

"I'm stunned," Hannah said.

"And surprised, I hope." Max handed Hannah a glass of wine.

In that moment, as she looked at Max, the assembled company dissolved into a blur in the background. With a trembling hand, Hannah accepted the glass he held out to her.

"A toast to you," he said softly.

"You did this, didn't you?" Hannah asked.

"Does it matter?" Max asked. "We all wanted to honor you." Taking her arm, he drew her easily among her friends, all eager to wish her well. Hannah's usual reserve melted, and she laughed, and smiled, then scanned the room, seeking Laura.

Laura stood next to Hank and Paul, Miranda's husband, at the outer edge of the small crowd. Paul was shy, and always hung back. Hannah waved to her daughter. Laura excused herself and made her way to her mother.

"Laura," Hannah whispered as she hugged her. "It's not New Year's yet, but I resolve to listen more and to stop giving you advice."

She would have said more, but Lurina, smelling of a cedar closet, and Old Man, eyes twinkling mischievously, and Wayne, never comfortable in a group, were at her side to hug and be hugged, and Laura drifted away to stand again with Hank.

In the merry-go-round of family and friends, Hannah was aware of musicians tuning their instruments, and then Mozart, softly played, wafted through the room. Looking about, Hannah marveled at the chandeliers, the bright fall flowers on every table, the sparkling tapered candles, and she knew that Mike was responsible for the ambience. Hannah's eyes sought Mike's, found him looking at her, and she smiled, nodded and murmured "thank you."

His brown hair neatly pulled back into a ponytail, and wearing a brown silk Nehru jacket, Mike beamed.

Place cards indicated that Hannah and Max, Miranda and her family, Laura and Hank should sit at one of the round tables, while Grace, Bob, and Tyler joined Brenda, Lurina and Old Man, Ellie Lerner, and Wayne at another table. Mike and Amelia shared the third table with Russell and Emily, Molly and Ted Lund, MaryAnn and Tom Battles, and Pastor Johnson.

Wine was poured all around and toasts were made to Hannah, and then their salads were set before them. Brenda leaned toward Grace. "Lucy Banks is at my house."

"Lucy, here?" Grace asked.

"Poor child. She relates a terrible story. That cousin of hers . . ." Brenda looked furious.

The hair on the back of Grace's neck stood on end. "What happened? Did someone hurt Lucy? I'll, I'll . . ."

"What exactly did Lucy say?" Bob asked.

All at the table fell silent. Still, the buzz from the other tables caused Lurina to turn toward Grace and cup her ear with her hand. "Who's Lucy?" she asked.

"A girl Granny Grace tutored at Caster Elementary," Tyler said in a loud voice. He was hungry, and busy slathering butter on a roll.

"What's happened to Lucy?" Old Man asked, leaning toward his wife and laying his knurled hand protectively over Lurina's bony, age-spotted hand.

All eyes turned to Brenda. "After Lucy's father died, her mother sent most of her children to relatives down near Gastonia. Lucy cooked and cleaned for them and had to mind the younger children, and there were quite a few of them. They never sent Lucy back to school." Brenda's serious eyes found Grace's. Her voice fell. "There was this cousin." She lowered her head.

"A dozen what?" Lurian asked.

"Not dozen," Wayne explained. "Miss Brenda said *cousin*, Lucy's cousin."

"Oh." Lurina looked satisfied.

"So Lucy ran away." Brenda took a deep breath and

continued. "That poor child walked so long she said it felt as if her feet would fall off, and then, when she was 'pure tuckered out,' a trucker gave her a ride as far as Weaverville. She walked the rest of the way."

Grace thought of Hannah, and how, when Hannah had fled with two small daughters from her abusive husband, a trucker had given them a ride all the way from northern Michigan to southern Pennsylvania.

"That's a long walk for a little girl," Bob said.

"She talked?" Lurina said, cupping her ear again. "What did she say?"

"Not talk, Miss Lurina," Wayne said to his step-grand-mother. His voice was gentle and patient. "Lucy walked a long, long way."

"Poor little tyke," Lurina said, "must have been tuck-ered out walkin' all that way and scared to death, wouldn't you say, Joseph Elisha?"

Joseph Elisha nodded gravely, then turned to whisper in Grace's ear, "Lurry's right stubborn, won't get her a hearing piece." He tapped his own hearing aid. "Wayne here talked me into this just before Lurry and I married. Never knew what I wasn't hearin'. Chickens clackin', old pigs of mine snortin', sounds that comfort an old country man like me."

"I gave Lucy dinner before I left and gave her books to read," Brenda continued. "I told her to stay in Molly's old room upstairs, in the back, and not to answer the door if anyone knocked or rang the bell. I'm afraid they'll come looking for her here and—"

Old Man broke in. "We'd be mighty pleased to have Lucy stay with us a bit, right, Lurry?"

Lurry! Where had Grace heard that name? Oh, yes, Lurina had once told her that Lurry had been her father's nickname for her. Lurina was nodding, her head bobbing like a knob on a spring.

"Mighty glad to help in any way. You just let us know," Lurina said.

"How good of you both," Grace said.

"Ain't good, just neighborly."

"Lurina's place might be too close," Bob said.

"Do you think someone will report her missing?" Grace asked.

"Relatives won't, probably, considering they're keeping Lucy out of school," Brenda said. "But you never know. Once her husband died, Lucy's mother fell apart, the social worker told me. Myrtle Banks, that's her name, quit her job at the Sony plant and took to her bed. That's when Randy, the oldest boy, quit school and went to work. Then she shipped off the girls, all but the retarded girl, who the social workers placed in a residential facility. I don't know what Mrs. Banks will do. The relatives may come up here looking for Lucy; they might send back all the children."

No one had touched the salads, except Tyler. Bob picked up his fork. "Let's eat," he said.

Everyone reached for forks. "Maybe Lucy could stay with Russell and Emily for a while," Bob said, "until we figure out how to help her."

Grace looked at Tyler, who had finished his salad and was on his second roll. "Would that be all right with you, Tyler, honey?"

"You bet," Tyler, his mouth full, managed to say.

"I'll talk to Lucy," Bob said.

A sense of irritation rolled over Grace. Bob did not even know Lucy, and yet he was taking charge, saying he would talk to this shy, timid child. Why, it reminded Grace of her own father, an authority on everything, and immediately she felt guilty. Bob wasn't like that. He was only trying to help. Grace reminded herself that since the fire, everything got on her nerves. Cool it, and enjoy Hannah's birthday party, she told herself.

"For now, Lucy is safe, and I suggest," Grace said, "that we focus on Hannah and making this the best party ever."

"Hear. Hear," Tyler said, and hammered the table lightly with the end of his fork.

The beef filet served at dinner melted in their mouths. Pressed through a tube and shaped into rosettes, the mashed potatoes were extraordinary in design and taste. Grace found it easier these days to swallow, although she still drank through a straw. The doctor had been right. The condition was temporary, brought on by stress, and improved by the day. As they finished their meal, everyone at the table focused on keeping the conversation light and pleasant.

"Dance with me," Bob said to Grace as they waited for dessert, coffee, and tea. Grace had never been a good dancer, but with Bob, a masterful dancer, she floated across the floor, feeling graceful and even beautiful. "Have I told you how lovely you look tonight?" he asked

"You're not so bad yourself," she replied. He had used her shampoo, and his thick white hair smelled of watermelon. Freckles trailed across his nose. His smoothly shaved chin was square and self-assured. He had commanded men in the service. They must have followed him gladly, Grace thought.

"Nice of Max to throw this fete for Hannah," Bob said. "What do you think's going on with them?"

"I think they admire each other, and they're good friends," Grace said.

"Nothing more, eh?" Bob asked, whirling her around.

"Nothing more."

Emily and Russell joined them on the dance floor, as did Tom Battles and MaryAnn. "Cute couple," Bob said as Tom and MaryAnn moved past them.

The music ceased. Emily and Russell sauntered over to

Bob and Grace. "You guys look like youngsters on the dance floor," Russell said.

Grace took Emily's arm. They stood for a short time near the windows. "How's my baby Melissa?" Grace asked.

"She's a good child," Emily said. "I thought all babies cried a lot, and you walked the floor all night with them. Not Melissa."

"Are you okay being back at the law firm?" Grace asked.

"I feel like I'm on a merry-go-round. I never stop, it seems. Russell's great, you know that. He food shops, and he's working from home most days, so I don't worry about Melissa, even though she's cared for primarily by Olga, Anna's friend. Tyler's wonderful with the baby, too." Emily's eyes clouded. "You know, Grace, I was raised to think women could have it all—home, kids, career. The baby's only eight months old and I have help, and still, it's incredibly stressful."

"Too many plates in the air," Grace said. "I imagine it would be. The business of lawyering must be stressful." She leaned for a moment against the windowpane, immediately felt the cold against her shoulder, and drew away.

Emily touched the glass with a fingertip. "Cold. Wonder how much colder it is up here at four thousand feet than it is down where we live?"

"Twenty degrees or more, I'd imagine," Grace replied, thinking that she would never live any higher up than the two thousand feet above sea level at Covington. "We better go back to our tables. Dessert's waiting."

Amelia sat between Mike and Emily at the table closest to the window and wondered if no one else felt the chill that penetrated her back and arms. She was freezing. Her own fault for not wearing an undershirt and thicker stockings. She thought about the thick panty hose some women wore in Europe, especially in Germany and Austria. Now, those really kept your legs warm. Recently she'd seen a heavier-weight panty hose in stores in Asheville, but she hadn't bothered to pick up a pair or two. She hadn't bothered with much of anything since the fire. She hadn't gone to the bank with Grace and Hannah, hadn't sat down, except for that one time, with Hank or the architect, hadn't even been over to see the foundation walls. Why look at foundation walls, anyway? Grace would let her know when the walls of the house and the roof were up. Then she'd go to Cove Road to see how the building was coming along, maybe, if she felt, well, more energetic, less downhearted.

Amelia never used the word *depression*. Depression implied doctors and medication, perhaps hospitalization, like after Thomas died. God, she couldn't go through that again. She was much better. Why, she'd even agreed to accompany Mike to a place with the funny name Sandy Mush. That proved she wasn't depressed, just a little sad, and that was normal, one would think, after losing one's home, all the treasured pictures of one's family, and all those boxes filled with her photography book, *Memories and Mist: Mornings on the Blue Ridge*. She had self-published her coffee-table book, and she and Mike had been distributing it, as requested, to local bookstores, to the North Carolina and Virginia welcome centers, as well as to parkway shops. The boxes had been stored in her closet. All gone now. Ashes. The taste of ash, the smell of ash still awakened her at night.

"You're pensive, Amelia," Emily said.

"Am I? I was thinking about this place, Sandy Mush, where Mike's intent on taking me. Ever heard of it?"

Emily shook her head and stirred her coffee. "Great name. You must tell me about it when you get back. When are you going?"

Mike leaned toward Emily. "Soon as I can rout Amelia out, and the weather's decent. They're calling for snow by next weekend, and the forecast is for a cold, snowy winter. Ugh!"

"I could do without that," Emily said to Amelia, then turned to respond to something that Russell said to her.

Hannah preferred a round table. She could see everyone better and hear them better, and she very much wanted to hear every word being said tonight—especially by her daughter and grandsons, whom she had not seen for many months.

Laura had turned to Hannah's grandsons and her nephews, Sammy and Philip, and asked about their plans for college, for careers. Philip replied, "I'm going into theater stage management. I tried acting. Too nerve-racking. Dressing up like a clown for kids like I did when I was in high school was one thing. Standing on stage naked of disguises, so to speak, absolutely terrified me. But I do love the world of greasepaint and make-believe, and I'm good with details, so stage management is the direction I'm heading in."

"And you, Sammy?" Max asked.

Hannah listened carefully. Years ago she worried so about Sammy, after he crashed his car injuring both himself and Philip. Learning that he drank felt like a rerun of a familiar movie: her own father, and her husband, Miranda and Laura's father, had both been alcoholics. Sins of the father visited upon the children, and upon their children? She shuddered to think of it. But Sammy had spent months in rehabilitation, and later at AA. Coca-Cola was now his strongest drink. She was proud of him, and had great hope for him. A psychologist perhaps? Often recovering alcoholics chose a helping profession, but no, that wasn't what Sammy was saying. "You'll never believe this, Grandma." Sammy looked at her across the table. "I'm going to be a Neolithic paleontologist."

"A what?" Hannah asked.

Paul slapped his older son on the back. "My question exactly when he came home and told us."

"I'll be studying artifacts: tools, art, sites that date back maybe twenty-five thousand years. We studied about Neaderthals in anthropology, and I got interested. Imagine, a species much like us, but not like us, roaming the earth, developing tools. We don't believe they used language as we know it. Grunts, sounds, yes, but not language as we think of it."

"I remember reading *The Clan of the Cave Bear* years ago," Miranda said. "They were Neanderthals, right?"

"Yes, in fact, Mom, I found that book in the bathroom one day. That's what got me interested in ancient peoples."

"I am proud of you, Sammy," Hannah said. "That sounds like a most interesting profession. What can you do with it?" She saw him stiffen, realized that it sounded as if she were baiting him, saying one thing but actually disapproving. "I don't mean that in any negative way," Hannah said. "I meant where do Neolithic paleontologists work?"

"I can understand your concern," Sammy said.

He sounded so sure of himself, and mature. Hannah felt ashamed for what seemed her disapproval. She truly hadn't meant it that way.

"We work in museums and at universities," Sammy replied. "I think I'd like fieldwork, excavating." Excitement lit his face. "There's a site right now in the Ukraine where I've applied for an internship next summer. Most sites you can't work in winter, so you dig all summer and collect specimens, bits of bones, a skull if you're lucky, a femur, flints, hand tools." He stopped, embarrassed, but everyone at the table was looking at him appreciatively.

Max clapped. "Good for you, Sammy, my boy," he said. "You've got me wanting to join a dig."

"A most interesting career choice," Laura said.

"It sounds fascinating, Sammy," Hank said.

"I'm amazed and delighted, Sammy," Hannah said. "I'm proud of you, proud of both you boys."

"That makes me feel good, Grandma. Your approval means a lot to me," Sammy said, and Philip nodded. They sat across from one another, and Hannah saw tears in Sammy's eyes, and struggled with the urge to get up and hug him. Instead she gave him two thumbs up.

Then Hannah noticed that Hank and Laura were whispering. "What's the secret, Laura, Hank?" Hannah asked.

Her younger daughter turned crimson, as did Hank, and Hannah realized that theirs was more than a casual working relationship. A romance? Laura and Hank? And she hadn't noticed? Laura and Hank were holding hands on the table. How could she work with them every day and not be aware of shy glances, light touches, hints of intimacy? The fire, of course, had distracted her. She'd found it necessary to focus considerable attention on her work, on plants and designs for gardens, and preparing the gardens for winter, anything to get her through this time, anything to keep her going. There were nights when she did not sleep and her mind wandered so that she couldn't complete a crossword puzzle.

She wasn't one, like Grace, to harangue the universe for meaning. Long ago Hannah had decided that life was arbitrary, that human beings were specks on this vast planet, insignificant considering the numbers of people doubling every year in China, India, South America. But Sammy's talk of ancient peoples caused her to think, and her mind, like a trawl net dragging the sea bottom for fish, spread wide and back in time, capturing a sense of unknown ancients. Had these people queried the stars? Had they wondered about meaning as they struggled to survive? Or had they, like her, gone about their work, their lives, unquestioning until they ceased to be? All this she considered, as the talk went on at the table, laughter, and jokes, and talk of the diary business, and of Miranda's work, of the progress being made in the construction of the early settlers' homesteads over which Hank and Laura had been brought together, he designing, she implementing. Hannah smiled, nodded, and laughed when others did, but her mind wandered to questions that she did not want to ask or to answer.

At Grace's table Ellie had sat quietly all evening. She was, after all, a stranger in their midst. Watching and listening, she ached for the sense of belonging and of family so obvious among these people of different backgrounds and diverse ages. She had no real home, had moved at least twenty times to serve her husband's career. Her heart ached to belong.

"My grandparents immigrated from Europe in the early nineteen hundreds," Ellie told Grace one day, recently, when they finally had lunch in Asheville. "They settled in Chicago. My father was a furniture salesman and a good one, but he was gone a lot. To minimize this, we moved whenever his territory changed. Then we hardly saw my grandparents."

Grace contrasted that with her own life, born and raised, married, and but for her son's insistence that she move, she would probably have lived out her life in Dentry, Ohio. "That must have been hard on you," Grace said.

"It was. I was always the outsider in school. First two grades in Louisville, Kentucky, third and fourth in Dallas,

Texas. Then came Mishawaka, in Indiana, and middle school in Charleston, West Virginia. I went to three high schools, finally ended up my senior year in Maitland, Florida." Ellie had paused, and for a moment stared into space. Her jaw tightened. Tears banked in the corners of her eyes. "That was probably the worst." She let it go at that, and Grace had not pressed her.

"How did you come to live in Asheville?" Grace asked.

"My husband, Seymour, wanted to get away from his family's business in Orlando, and we wanted to live in the mountains. We moved here. Opened the Bridal Shop. He died. Here I am. My sons are in business with their uncle in Orlando."

Grace's heart ached for Ellie. "You must have good friends in Asheville."

"Acquaintances, yes, many of them. Friends? Real friends, someone I could call in the middle of the night . . ." Ellie shook her head. "No. No one like that."

"If I may ask, how old are you, Ellie?"

"Of course you may ask. I've just turned sixty-one, and I'm rootless. I don't feel that I belong in Asheville. I don't belong anywhere." She picked her cuticle. "I come from Jews who lived in shtetls, small, close communities in Europe. In America my grandparents lived in a Jewish section of Chicago. Their children moved away, but they had other people nearby from the Old Country."

Grace had handed her the invitation to Hannah's birthday party then. "You come and be a part of our lives."

So here Ellie was, overwhelmed by the warmth strangers had extended to her, amazed at the closeness of Grace to her surrogate family: Bob, Russell, Emily, the children. Who would have thought that without marriage there could be such bonding? The clapping from the table where Hannah sat drew her attention. They were applauding one of the young men, and Ellie wondered why they clapped, and found that it didn't matter. What mattered was that she wanted to clap with them, to be a part of their lives.

Suddenly Hannah was aware that the table was being cleared, and Sammy and Philip were walking away. Startled, she raised her hand to call them back. Max said, "Hannah, what are you thinking?"

"About work," she lied. And there were Sammy and Philip carrying a large wicker basket, the handles of which were tied with huge blue bows, and bouncing just inside the brim were packages large and small, wrapped in blue, and yellow, and green with bright ribbons. They set the basket on the table before her, and when she looked at it with a stunned expression, Max took her arm and guided her out of her chair. Standing at the table, looking down at the packages Hannah realized they were for her. She stood there unable to speak.

Miranda reached into the basket, picked out a box, and handed it to her. "Open it, Mother," she said.

Inside the box was an alarm clock, just like the one she had lost in the fire, the one she had had beside her bed for so many years, and Miranda remembered. Tears filled Hannah's eyes. It was hard to talk. Someone handed her a glass of water, and she gathered her wits about her while she sipped. Then Hannah hugged Miranda. "Thank you, dear, you remembered. I will treasure this."

They had all tried to replace some item, small or large, including bedroom slippers without backs, just as she liked, and green, her favorite color, and a bedside lamp with tassels, much like the lamp she had toted from house to house, bedroom to bedroom. Max presented her with a box of books, so many different kinds of gardening books that Hannah thought surely he had emptied the shelves of a bookstore. Then her grandsons dashed off and returned with a long, heavy-looking box.

"This is a workbench with shelves above and a place below to store bins of soil, manure, whatever you use," Philip said.

"When you move into the new house," Sammy said, "we'll come back and set it up for you in your yard, and we'll build a shed over it for shade, so you can plant seeds and putter all you want."

Once more the boys disappeared and returned with a crate, one side of which was covered with wire mesh. With the cluck and cackle that issued from it and the feathers that danced to the floor, it didn't take imagination to realize that there were chickens inside, a gift from Lurina and Old Man.

Lurina pushed up from her seat, tugging at Old Man's arm until he stood beside her. "We'll keep 'em back in the henhouse for you until you get home. With the greenhouse gone, you've got plenty room for a nice big henhouse and plenty of fresh eggs. She laughed her wonderful, youthful, infectious laugh. Soon everyone was laughing and clapping.

"Speech. Speech!" Mike called, looking at Hannah. Bob seconded it. Everyone clapped.

Hannah's eyes scanned the room. She was tongue-tied. Couldn't they hear how her heart thudded in her chest? What could she say? Flowery talk was not her style. She would prefer merely to write them all notes of appreciation later. They were looking at her expectantly, eyes wide and happy, and suddenly Hannah found words. "Never in my whole life have I had a party like this. I can't thank you enough. You're all wonderful. Thank you, my dear, dear friends." She sat. The room broke into wild applause. As if that were not enough, Sammy stood and raised his glass of Coke to her.

"Grandma. To me you represent everything noble and strong and fine in a person. If I can be half that person, I'll be content."

Before she could react, Philip rose, with his glass held high. "I admire you, Grandma Hannah, more than I do anyone in the world. You are my inspiration to persevere and succeed."

If she spoke, Hannah knew, she would humiliate herself by bawling like a baby. Emotions long suppressed hurled themselves at the walls of the dungeon where she had assigned them. Hannah opened wide her arms and turning slowly wrapped them all in her love.

13

LUCY BANKS

The day after Hannah's birthday party, Brenda brought Lucy Banks to Bob's apartment. The moment she stepped into the small foyer, Lucy dashed to Grace, wrapped her skinny arms about Grace's waist, and held on tight. "Mrs. Grace, don't let them take me back," Lucy said.

Grace did not try to pry loose from the child's grip. "I won't," she said.

"Promise?"

"I promise." Grace wondered if she could make good on this promise. "I'll do everything I can. We all will."

"No one's come looking for Lucy," Brenda said. "Lucy okay staying here with you?"

"Of course she is," Grace replied. With Lucy still clinging to her, she eased them both to the couch. "Now, you just sit here with me," Grace said to the child. "And we'll have a good talk. Are you hungry? Would you like some milk and cookies?"

Lucy shook her head. Her eyes were swollen from crying. Grace wanted to cry, too. She didn't understand cruelty, didn't understand how anyone could hurt a child.

How could she protect Lucy? Grace did not know, but she would try, they would all try.

"Pa," Lucy was saying. "He laid hisself down and died. Why'd he leave me, Mrs. Grace?" Lucy's bony shoulders shook.

"I'm sure your pa didn't want to leave you, Lucy."

"Why'd God take him, then, Mrs. Grace? I says my prayers every night. Don't God know how much I need Pa?"

Grace had no answers. She held Lucy and rocked her gently, smoothed her hair, and allowed the child her grief. Finally Lucy lifted her head and dried her eyes and cheeks with the red and blue checkered bandanna Grace fished from her pocket.

How gaunt she is, Grace thought. And so afraid. The way her eyes flit around the room, you'd think she expects to see monsters.

At that moment the front door opened. Hannah strode into the living room. "Thought I saw Brenda's car going down the hill. Figured she'd brought Lucy. How are you, girl?" With long strides Hannah marched over to the couch. She lifted one of Lucy's arms. "What have they done to you? Your bones are sticking out, and where'd you get those scratches all over your legs? What's on them, iodine?"

"Yes, ma'am. Mrs. Tate doctored me up best she could." Lucy ran a finger alongside one of the cuts and nodded. "I got cut hiding in a hedge of them wild rose bushes. Figured they weren't gonna look for me in no rosebush. I hid a long while in the dark. When I figured they weren't bothering to hunt me no more, I climbed out. That's when I got cut up. Sure did sting, but I just kept walking." There was pride in the child's voice.

"Well, good for you, girl," Hannah said, knowing first-hand how much courage it took to flee from abusive people whom you were afraid of. "You're a gutsy girl."

Grace noted the admiration in Hannah's face. Good. Hannah would help her. Together they'd find a way to protect Lucy.

Hannah kneeled by the couch. She examined Lucy's legs. "They'll heal up." She turned to Grace. "First thing we have to do, Grace, is talk to Emily. See what the law says about a woman sending her kids to people like those relatives."

"Good idea," Bob said. He came from the kitchen with a tray in his hand. "You drink this milk, Lucy, and have a peanut butter and jelly sandwich."

Shyly, with a quick look at Bob and then away, Lucy accepted the tray. Gingerly she balanced it on her lap. She sipped the milk.

Bob took a chair nearby. He leaned toward Lucy. "When my son, Russell, was about your age, a schoolyard bully beat him up. He was a mess, his eye all swollen, his knees cut and bleeding from falling down. All he'd eat, for days afterward, were peanut butter and jelly sandwiches and milk. Even now, as a grown-up, when Russell's worried about something, he eats peanut butter and jelly sandwiches and has a glass of milk."

Lucy's huge liquid eyes considered Bob. "Did the bully beat up your son a lot?"

"Naw! Just that one time. I took him to the boxing ring and got him lessons. Word got out. That bully stayed clear of Russell from then on. You know, Lucy, people who hurt other people are bullies. When you stand up to them, they generally back down."

Grace remembered what Hannah had said about her alcoholic husband. But if they're bigger and you live with them, they might hit you darn hard, she thought.

"Now, don't you worry anymore," Bob said. "We'll see

no one hurts you. You can stay here awhile, right, Grace? Lucy can sleep on the couch."

Grace nodded. Bob had forgotten that she slept on the couch when he tossed and turned. Well, she'd arrange something with Amelia. There were, after all, two beds in the guest bedroom. "Certainly," she said. This was Bob's apartment, and if he had objected to having Lucy there, what would she have done? Why, she'd have taken Lucy over to the apartment where Hannah and Laura lived, and they'd have bunked up, or Grace would have gone to Brenda's and stayed there with Lucy. They were constructing the addition, but Brenda was still living alone in her big house. None of that was necessary now, however, and she hadn't had to do or say anything. In her heart Grace celebrated the goodness of Bob, and of Hannah, and of Brenda.

Lucy finished the sandwich. A white mustache framed her upper lip. She licked at it with her tongue. "Thank you," she said. "That was right good."

Bob took the tray from Lucy and looked at Grace. "I'm off to meet Martin. We're playing a new golf course down in Hendersonville, can't think of the name this minute."

"I've got the kids from my class coming to the park this afternoon," Hannah said. "I'm off. You rest up now, girl." She waved a finger at Lucy and left.

Grace rose from the couch. "Lie down, Lucy," she said, adjusting a pillow at one end and taking a seat in a nearby chair.

"Mrs. Grace, ain't you gonna ask me about the cousins?"

"I'm not going to ask you anything. When you want to tell me, you know I'm here."

Lucy did not lie down. She straightened her bony shoulders, brushed limp hair from her eyes, and set her feet squarely on the carpet. "Well," she said, "I guess I'm about as ready as I'm gonna be, ma'am."

The air in the room felt heavy with a dark and brooding presence. Grace switched on the lamp on the table alongside her chair. That helped, but there was still this feeling of being closed in, as if she and Lucy were trapped in a cocoon. Grace swallowed hard and leaned forward, waiting for Lucy to continue.

"One day we come home from school, me and Randy, and this here big, old beat-up truck was in our yard. Ma said we girls must each pack us up a bag and take our Sunday dress and shoes. First I figured we was going on a visit, Ma, too, and Randy, but then she ain't packed no suitcase, and Randy was hanging back with his hands shoved in his pockets, looking down, sad like. That's when I knew she was sending us off. She said the man who'd come get us was a cousin of hers. I ain't never seen him in my whole life. I was scared, but the smaller kids were crying, and I figured it was up to me to act brave like. The man brought a boy, older than me, with him, and they threw the bags and all the little kids in the bed of that old truck, and they hoisted up a rail and penned my sisters in like they was cattle.

" 'Set on Jason's lap' is what the man said, and I ain't had no choice. That fellow grabbed a hold of me and yanked me into the truck in the seat next to his pa."

Lucy stopped, and for a moment struggled not to cry. Then she lifted her head and looked square into Grace's eyes. "So I done asked myself, what would Mrs. Grace do? She'd sit still and act dignified. *Dignified*. That's one of those words I looked up in that dictionary you gave me."

Hands clenched in her lap, Grace waited, dreading what she would hear from Lucy.

"Jason, he kept putting his hands on my stomach and sliding them up to . . ." She motioned to tiny points of breasts just beginning to form beneath her shirt. "Ain't no one ever touched me here." Lucy's face, arms, even her skinny legs turned the color of simmering charcoal, and for a moment she covered her face with her hands.

"It's all right, Lucy, dear. It's over. You don't have to tell it all at one time."

Hands fell from Lucy's tear-smeared, distraught face. She leaned forward. Then her voice, nearly frantic, rose. "I got to, Mrs. Grace. I got to tell you everything done happened to me now, 'cause after that I'm gonna dump it out like trash."

Grace nodded. Moments like this, she was at a loss for words. At such times silence and approving eyes were the best responses.

Lucy continued. "They wouldn't let me go to school. Said Ma sent me to take care of the young'uns, and I should be grateful they were helping out Ma. I tried, Mrs. Grace. I watched after my sisters, them that was too young to go to school, and I scrubbed the floors, and did their wash, whatever they told me, I tried to do. There weren't never a chance passed that Jason didn't brush hisself up next to me. He'd corner me up against a wall or a dresser and touch me, here. . . ." Again Lucy pointed to her chest. "And then something really bad happened." Choked with emotion, Lucy could not continue.

Grace wanted to cover her ears. She knew what was coming. These things happened, but not to someone she cared for. "I need a drink of water," she said. "Would you like one, Lucy?"

"Sure, Mrs. Grace."

In the kitchen Grace ran the tap for a long while, letting the water grow cold. She took a drink, filled a second glass, and brought it to Lucy. "It's over now, Lucy. Whatever that boy did to you, it's over now," Grace said. "We'll never let them take you back."

Lucy's eyes were grateful. She drank the water in tiny sips. Grace wished that Lucy would not speak again. She didn't want to hear that that repulsive boy had raped Lucy.

But Lucy seemed determined to say it all. She dried her eyes and continued in a voice so low that Grace bent forward and turned her head to one side to hear the girl.

"We slept in one room, me and my four sisters. We cried ourselves to sleep every night. They had the bed, and I slept in a sleeping bag on the floor. One night I heard the door open, only it creaked so loud, I like to thought everyone would wake up and come a-running.

"Next thing, Jason's tearing at the zipper of my sleeping bag and shoving hisself into the bag with me." Lucy covered her eyes. "He was breathing hard, Mrs. Grace. He was heavy a-top of me." Dropping her hands, she stared at Grace, her eyes wild and huge. "Mrs. Grace, I tried to fight, but he was strong. I screamed and screamed. That's when he tore off and hit me across my face. See." Lucy held her lips back on one side, and Grace saw the empty space where two, maybe three, teeth had been. "Sweet taste in my mouth, blood, nearly choked me, but I kept on a-screaming. That woke up my little sisters, and next I knew somebody was pulling Jason off of me."

Grace wanted to stop her. She reached out her hand to touch Lucy, but Lucy, immersed in the memory, could not stop.

The child went on and on in a flat, dull, heavy voice. "His ma it was, screaming and yanking on him, and then his pa came, and he was screaming what was I good for, I had to pay my way, and things like that.

"They hauled him off me afore he could hurt me. I was so scared, Mrs. Grace, I peed in my pants, but soon as they were outta there, I got dressed and climbed outta that window and took off. I hid in them thornbushes till they stopped calling me and yelling, and then I waited a long while after the lights went out inside."

He hadn't raped her, Grace realized, and released the breath she had been holding. But he would have. He would have raped her that night or another had Lucy stayed.

Grace reached for Lucy's hands. They were cubes of ice. "You did good, Lucy. It's over now, thank God."

Having purged her soul, Lucy kneeled by Grace and buried her face in Grace's lap. "Please, Mrs. Grace, don't send me back," she begged.

"I won't. It's all right now, dear," Grace repeated again and again. And in time, scrunched at Grace's feet, Lucy's breathing slowed, her hiccuping ceased along with the crying. They sat like that for a very long time, Grace murmuring reassurances, smoothing Lucy's lank, damp hair.

Please God, the other girls were safe. She would talk to Mrs. Banks about bringing them home, and soon.

14

A VISIT FROM
BRENDA TATE

Lucy had been with the ladies for one night when Brenda arrived at Bob's apartment with her arms loaded with books. "School goes on Christmas break tomorrow. I've brought the lessons for the last few weeks from Lucy's fifth-grade teacher. Homeschooling can go faster than the classroom. I thought you could inveigle Bob, and Hannah, and Amelia to help bring Lucy up to par with her class, that is, if she's going to come back to school."

"Of course she'll come back to school, and we'll all help," Grace said, thinking of Amelia, uncertain of her and wondering how great an imposition Amelia would consider this request, and the other, more important request that Grace planned to make of her friends.

"I'd love a cup of tea, Grace, and to sit a minute with you," Brenda said, taking off her coat. "I have news about Lucy's family."

A lump formed in Grace's throat, and she led Brenda into the kitchen and waved her toward the round table for two that generally sat three or four of them these days. Hannah had taken Lucy with her to Bella's Park, and

Amelia, where was Amelia? These days, she went and came; they never really knew where she was.

"This tea's good. What kind?" Brenda asked.

"It's a Russian tea. I can't pronounce the name. Want some? I can pick you up a box if you'd like." Grace slipped a half-dozen tea bags into a plastic bag and handed it to Brenda. "Meanwhile, take these home with you," she said.

"You're always so generous, Grace."

"I'm glad you like the tea," Grace replied. "So what's the news? Does it affect Lucy?"

Brenda set her teacup down. She nodded. "Yes, it does. The social worker went out to talk to Lucy's mother and found the other four kids there. With Lucy gone, the relatives brought the girls back to their mother. One of them has a broken arm and bruises on her shoulder and face."

A sharp intake of breath and Grace covered her mouth with her hand.

"Abuse, surely abuse," Brenda said. "But, of course, the relatives told the mother that the child fell down the steps. I wonder how many people use falling down stairs as an excuse when they hurt a child? Damn them!" Anger caused her brows to come together above her eyes and her lips to grow tight. She heaved a deep sigh. "So Mrs. Banks says she wants the social worker to place the four younger girls in foster care. She'll keep Lucy and Randy."

"Oh, no. Foster care, all four of them?" Grace asked. "What kind of woman is she? It sounds as if she's sorting old clothes—throw these out, keep these."

"Yes, that's what it seems like," Brenda agreed. "And there's nothing we can do about it."

"When does she want Lucy home?" Grace asked. She loved Lucy. In her mind Grace had created a fantasy. Lucy would live with them in the new farmhouse—they'd have enough bedrooms. Amelia and Hannah would have to agree to this, of course, but surely in such a circumstance they would. For Amelia it would be like having a daughter back, and she and Hannah could do it right, not make all the mistakes they had made as mothers. They would teach Lucy. She would grow into a secure and competent woman. They'd send her to college. But now, with Mrs. Banks's decision to farm out her younger children and keep Randy and Lucy with her, Grace's dreams for Lucy crumbled. "I cannot bear to think of that child going back into that narrow, limited environment, not when we could give her so much."

"What were you thinking, Grace?" Brenda asked.

"Becoming foster parents," Grace replied. She'd never actually said that to herself, but why not? Maybe they could convince Mrs. Banks to let Lucy live with them.

"Foster parents? You think Social Services will let people your age take on a young child?"

"We don't know that. We can ask, apply," Grace said. She was standing now, her hand gripping the back of the chair.

"You're all flushed, Grace," Brenda said. "Sit down. Have your tea. There's time."

"This apartment is too closed up." Grace moved to the sink, and shoved up the kitchen window. Cold air poured in. Brenda rubbed her arms, but Grace stood at the window, head thrown back, breathing deeply. Then she slammed the window shut and turned to Brenda. "I'm ridiculous, aren't I? What do I think I am, forty years old? You're right. Who would give the upbringing of a child to three old ladies?" Her voice was bitter.

"I never think of you as old ladies. You're vital, active, alive women," Brenda said.

"You know us, but the people in the government agencies don't. They'll stereotype us, have an attitude."

"Perhaps you're right," Brenda said. "But even if they

certified you as foster parents, would Amelia and Hannah go along with this?"

"Hannah, I think she would. Amelia? I certainly hope so." Grace rejoined Brenda at the table, sat, and sipped her tea. When she rested the cup back in its saucer, she said, "Trouble with Amelia is, she's scared."

"What do you mean, scared? Of what, fire?" Brenda asked.

Grace poured them each another cup of tea. "To hear her tell it, it seems that she's been afraid, anxious most of her life. Started in her childhood, I guess. Her parents were always busy with causes and indifferent to her. Good parenting to them meant nannies, clothing, food, shelter, and a pat on the head as they went out the door. Amelia grew up feeling that she didn't matter, and when she married an older man, she worried that she wasn't good enough or smart enough for him. It was 'Yes, Thomas' this, and 'Yes, Thomas' that. You know the old saying, he said, 'Jump' and she said, 'How high?'" Grace stopped to sip her tea. "Hannah and I were a bit put off by Amelia until we heard her story. Amelia's daughter, nine years old, died in her arms on a plane from India, on the way to get medical care. Later a car accident killed her husband and burned her severely. When we met Amelia, she was just out of a hospital and recovering."

Brenda added sugar to her tea. "I didn't know."

"When we came here," Grace continued, "Amelia had a terrible time. She didn't know what she was capable of, or if she were capable of anything. When she took up photography under Mike's tutelage and became successful at it, Amelia had a hard time accepting her success. She was certain she wasn't worthy." Grace placed her hands on the edge of the table and leaned back. "Anyhow, I've watched her change, become more self-confident. And then along came Lance. Her relationship with him started with such excitement. I remember how she looked, so happy, and he turned out to be a liar and a cheat, using Amelia. When it was over, Amelia was devastated and almost back to square one."

"What a shame. But her success in New York, her show?" Brenda asked.

"Mike's not only her instructor and friend, he's been her guardian angel. He arranged that show and went with her."

"Too bad he's gay," Brenda said. "Mike seems to care a great deal about Amelia."

"Amelia was fine until she met Lance. Well, she got over Lance and her work was going well. She's been volunteering with babies at the hospital two days a week, and then this awful fire." Grace leaned forward so fast that she nearly toppled her teacup.

"When someone feels insecure, scared, frightened of life, it can show in behavior that seems selfish, defensive, maybe even downright mean. Essentially Amelia is good and kind, and I've watched her struggle, watched her vacillate between feeling worthy and feeling unworthy." Grace stopped. "I'm sorry, Brenda, I got carried away."

"No," Brenda replied. "I'm glad you've told me. There are times I haven't thought well of Amelia. I've seen her as spoiled and petulant. Goes to show, you can't judge from outward appearances." In the silence that followed they finished their tea. "I admire you, Grace. You're one of the few people I've ever known who can really walk in someone else's shoes."

"You flatter me," Grace said. "I have moments I'm not proud of."

Brenda looked at her watch. "Lord, I must run. Would you like me to arrange a visit with Lucy's mother? Maybe she'll grab at the opportunity you hold out for her daughter."

Grace's face lit up, her body straightened. "You'll arrange a meeting?"

"Certainly, I'm happy to," Brenda replied. "But I still think you ought to discuss this whole thing with the other ladies before you talk to Mrs. Banks."

"I'll do that tonight," Grace said.

15

STANDING ALONE

That evening after dinner Hannah, Amelia, and Grace scrunched around the table in Bob's apartment. "I think best with a warm cup in my hands," Grace said. She had mentioned her plan to Bob earlier that day. His silence indicated his disapproval. Now Grace related Lucy's story, Brenda's visit, the injury to Lucy's little sister, the mother's decision to place her younger children in foster care, and finally the possibility that Lucy might be allowed to live with them in their new farmhouse.

"I'm surprised you're not asking us to take all five of that woman's children," Amelia said. Her eyes blazed a challenge.

Astonished, Grace stared at Amelia. "That's ridiculous. We can't take them all. But we could take Lucy. We could open doors for her. Amelia, please, Lucy's whole life hangs in the balance."

Her jaw set, Amelia looked away.

Grace grew more impassioned. "Do we want Lucy to grow up in poverty with limited aspirations imposed by a limited mother when, with us, she'd be exposed to a whole different world, the possibilities, art, music, books, a meaningful career?"

"You think we can change Lucy?" Amelia asked. "Her formative years are over, the way she speaks, her manners . . . why . . . why . . ."

Hannah's voice stopped Grace from snapping at Amelia. "What exactly is it you're asking us to do, Grace?"

For several minutes Grace sat silent. With one sentence Amelia had challenged and confused her, and Hannah wanted her to clarify her intentions. Before Grace could clear her mind and respond rationally, Hannah said, "Have you given any consideration to the ways in which having an eleven-year-old in the house would change your life, our lives?" Hannah's voice was kind, and for a moment Grace felt encouraged.

"What ways?" She had considered nothing other than protecting Lucy.

Hannah's eyes met Grace's and held them. "I know you care deeply about Lucy. I'm horrified at what's happened to her, but do you really want to take on a project like this? Being responsible for an almost teenager would seriously limit your freedom."

Hannah had twice said "you" or "your," not "us." Grace felt reprimanded, as if *she* were eleven years old. "You mean I'm too old?" Grace asked. Her voice caught on the *old*. She felt young, no different really than when she was forty-five or fifty.

"There's a limit to what we're capable of doing at this age," Amelia said. "Remember how tired you were when you had the tearoom?"

She remembered. But she'd done all the baking, standing on her feet for hours on end, and waiting on people. That was different.

"Spending an afternoon with Tyler's exhausting, isn't it?" Hannah asked.

It was true. And when she baby-sat Melissa, she came home and flopped onto the couch, but that, too, was different. She lifted and carried the baby, who was growing and would soon be walking. Lucy would be living in the house, there would be routines, they would all be involved, or would they?

"There's a time of life for everything. Lucy will be a teenager soon. Who'd deliberately take on raising a teenager?" Amelia's eyebrows shot up.

Hannah nodded.

Grace felt ganged up on. Never before had Hannah sided with Amelia against her. Grace didn't like it, not one bit. "But surely the three of us, together, we could . . ." Grace's voice trailed away.

Amelia crossed her arms over her chest. "Listen, Grace, I lost a child. I'm not getting emotionally involved with another one, not ever again." Her lovely eyes misted. "You love them, lose them, and it breaks your heart. Can't you understand, Grace? I won't risk loving again." For a moment Amelia's face, her whole body seemed to crumble, then she gained control and straightened her shoulders. She swiped the balls of her palms over her eyes. "I'd be glad to help pay for the child's education, or clothes, but live with us? You need to rethink this, Grace."

Grace had felt righteous, noble, virtuous, generous, but such feelings did not, after all, get you through the humdrum, the tedium, and the stress of daily life. For that one needed endless patience, and energy, Grace thought, and it was true, children and especially teenagers could be trying, very trying. She thought of long nights lying awake worrying until Lucy came home from a party, a date. She had forgotten, or chosen to overlook, adolescent mood swings, tears and tantrums, loud music, slamming doors. No, she hadn't thought beyond the moment, hadn't moved beyond her desire to protect Lucy.

"Perhaps," Hannah said, "there's some middle ground. Perhaps we can still help Lucy. Say she works with me when I put in our new gardens at the house . . ."

"Yes, that's it, of course." Amelia brightened. "She could help me with chores, like vacuuming those awful lady bugs off the ceilings, and she could help you in the kitchen, Grace, and baby-sit Melissa, and we could pay her. That way she could be around us weekends during the school year and help her mother financially. Why, she could even sleep over some weekends."

Grace fastened on the last sentence. Lucy could stay over, and Grace would take her to museums and craft fairs. Amelia could take her to the theater. Grace's heart lifted. It wasn't what she'd dreamed, but it was a reasonable compromise, better than having no contact or influence on the child, and better than clashing head-on with her housemates.

16

"NEAR TO BROKE MY HEART"

And so Lucy went home to her mother, and several days before Christmas, Grace, her arms loaded with presents for the children, visited Myrtle Banks in the unpainted house on an unpaved, rutty road in a rural area called Jupiter, which was north and west of Weaverville.

The epitome of hopelessness, Lucy's mother slouched against the frame of the door as Grace walked from her car, careful to step around an overturned trashcan and a squalling skinny cat. Mrs. Banks moved aside to let her in without offering to relieve Grace of her brightly wrapped packages.

Grace introduced herself. Unsmiling, Myrtle Banks nodded.

"These are for the children," Grace said. "For Christmas."

"Ease 'em on down there," the woman said, pointing to a pine branch with three red Christmas ornaments and a string of popcorn that was stuck in a can of sandy earth, and held off the floor by a small square of old and chipped bricks. The poverty of the place overwhelmed Grace. The single gift she had brought for each child seemed totally inadequate. How could this woman work and care for two little girls under five, and two just over five? Grace stood there, facing Lucy's mother. "I want you to know, my friends and I, Hannah and Amelia, that is . . . we'd like to have Lucy visit with us on weekends, when you don't need her at home, of course. There'll be so many things we could use help with when we move into the new house. You know, our house burned down last August."

The woman looked beyond Grace at some far-off place only she could see and remained silent.

Grace's eyes roamed the single room that housed the living and cooking areas. In one corner two mattresses were piled atop each other. Chipped dishes zigzagged in a towering pile in the sink. A pan, smeared with grease, stood end up next to them. The odor of mildew and cheap perfume mingling in the stagnant air caused Grace to feel queasy in her stomach. She wanted to air the place out, fling open the door and the single window, which was covered with plastic.

A well-worn shawl hung across the back and seat of the sagging couch, and from a long gash in a corner of the couch oozed gray stuffing. A curly head and two bright blue eyes peered at Grace from a door to what was probably the only bedroom. Grace smiled at the child, whose eyes quickly found the packages under what must pass for a Christmas tree. The door burst open, and four little girls, stepping stones in size, dashed into the main room and stopped abruptly when they caught their mother's stern eye.

"Mama, we got Christmas," the tallest child said.

A tot of about three, and the prettiest of the children, attached herself to her mother's leg. "Mama. Mama," she said. The woman bent and lifted the child onto her hip. The way the mother looked at this child, Grace saw love and caring, and knew that giving up her children, to anyone, must have been the hardest thing Myrtle Banks had

ever done. In that moment Grace forgot the smells, the
messy room, the dire poverty of the place, and all she
could think was that she must enlist everyone's help to
keep this family intact. There was love here, between the
children, between them and their mother. And Grace suddenly realized that she had never asked Lucy about coming to live with them in the new farmhouse. She had assumed the girl would welcome the change. Lucy had
asked not to be sent back to the cousins, but never had she
suggested that she did not want to live with her family.

A child of about seven approached Grace. Her arm
was in a sling. Her face bore the yellow tinge of fading
bruises.

The mother stepped forward and pulled the child toward her. Tears filled her eyes. "I didn't know they'd beat
up on my girls." The child's head reached the woman's
belly, and she nuzzled against her mother. "Truth be, I
donno what to do. How can I raise up my girls and work
to put food in our mouths? My husband done up and
died. Least he could mind them while I was working."

Poor as they were, it was the death of the father that
had broken the family. He had been the watchdog, the
baby-sitter, the glue that had kept this family together,
even though he was twenty-five years older than the
mother. And Myrtle Banks was not the indifferent slob
Grace had imagined. She was worn out with babies and
work, and alone, now, in a world that demanded more
than she could handle. Surely, Grace thought, we must
help this woman and her children.

"Your girls are beautiful," Grace said. "Must have been
hard for you to send them off with relatives."

"Near to broke my heart," the woman replied, setting
the youngest on the floor of the room.

"It's cold down here, Mama," the little girl whined.

"Hush you up, Audra," her mother said.

Audra slunk to her sisters, wedged herself between them, and the four girls stared at the seven boxes with their huge bright ribbons.

Grace wanted to say, "Go ahead and open them. We'll bring you more." Instead she said, "Well, I have to go now, but Amelia and Hannah, the ladies I share a home with, they also have gifts for the children. May we stop by later today and deliver them?"

Light flickered in those joyless and disconsolate pale blue eyes. "Reckon you're welcome anytime, miss."

"Grace. Please call me Grace."

"Ain't that a right pretty name," Lucy's mother said. Four little girls repeated, "Right purty name, miss." Then the next to oldest child, Martha—Matty, they called her—looked up at Grace. "I done seen you one time you came when Pa was home."

"That's right. I visited when your pa was . . ." She hesitated. "Home," she finished. "You've grown a bit since then, haven't you?"

"Right outta my shoes, see?" Matty extended her foot. The front of the shoe was cut away and her toes hung over the hard brown edge of the sole.

Had she felt comfortable doing so, Grace would have asked for brown paper to trace the child's feet. "We'll be back, then, later today," Grace said, addressing the mother.

Just before the New Year, Brenda Tate and the school counselor paid an unexpected visit to the Banks's small house. They informed Myrtle Banks that an anonymous donor had created a fund from which baby-sitters and other help was available, as well as money for the rent on a larger home for her and her children, on condition that Randy return to finish high school.

17

ENDLESS WINTER

January and February stretched into a chain of cheerless days. In February a fierce storm raged. Before it ended it deposited seven inches of snow on and around Cove Road. Laura did not make it to Loring Valley. She called from her office. "The snow's coming down in buckets," she told Hannah. "I don't want to drive in this weather. I'll stay over at Max's."

When she hung up the phone, Hannah stared out of the window of Bob's apartment. Thick snowflakes blotted out the valley below. Grace turned to Hannah. "Let Bob drive you to your place, get a few things, and stay with us tonight."

"Don't be silly. I'll be fine," Hannah argued.

"But I'll be frantic worrying about you over there alone. We have a gas fireplace. Yours is wood, and there's no wood stored. If the electricity goes out, you'll be freezing."

So Hannah packed a bag. They shoved the twin beds in Amelia's room apart, as they had when Lucy Banks stayed with them, and Hannah moved in with Amelia.

The storm battered the world for a day and two nights. In the cloudy days that followed, Amelia cocooned herself in bed and slept. Hannah couldn't stay still. She paced the living room, listened to the weather report, and tried to be unobtrusive, which proved impossible.

After four days their road cleared sufficiently to be passable, and Max called to announce that Cove Road and Elk Road were free of snow. Hannah collected her things and departed. Once back in her apartment she dressed in layers: a shell without sleeves to keep her chest warm, a T-shirt, a blouse, a sweater. She doubled up on socks, pulled on high-top boots and a hooded coat, and headed to work. Patches of ice forced Hannah to take the turns down the hillside at a crawl. When she finally reached Elk Road her heart was in her mouth. She heaved a sigh of relief.

At eight A.M. Cove Road lay silent beneath its comforter of snow. Bonnets of white capped the roofs of houses and icicles dangled like jagged beards from eaves. On the eastern side of Cove Road, surveyor's markings that separated the ladies' land from that of the Craines, and the Craines land from the Herrills, were obliterated. Stark and forlorn in the still white world, the bare bones of the two half-built houses could, to the unknowing eye, be under construction or in the process of destruction. On the ladies' land, snowdrifts mounded against the recently constructed three-foot concrete foundation and concealed any semblance of a building.

Hannah shivered and thought how much she missed their home. How good it had been to sit in their living room, spiced apple cider in hand, and a cheery fire in the fireplace. She longed to be able to reach out a hand and find exactly what she wanted. But with that thought, reality reentered, and she grew sad knowing that all those things she might reach for would be gone.

Piled high along the curve of the road at Bella's Park, banked snow rose nearly to the top of her station wagon. Hannah eased out and crunched her way across frozen grass to the front door. It was unlocked, yet when she stepped inside, the place was empty. Hannah switched on lights, raised the temperature at the control dial from sixty to seventy-five degrees, and proceeded to her office on the main floor. Once there, she flicked on the switch of the gas fireplace and blessed Max for his foresight, insisting, against her protestations, on having it installed.

Was she alone in the building? she wondered. Rebuttoning the coat she had begun to unbutton, Hannah took the elevator from the lobby to the second floor. A sliver of light slid from beneath Hank's door, indicating that he too had come in early. She knocked. A slight scrambling and then a muffled "Coming" echoed from behind the door.

A key turned in the lock, and the door opened. Beyond a red-faced Hank, Laura stood tucking her blouse into her jeans.

"Excuse me," Hannah said, and, turning, hastened down the hall and down the stairs. Had they spent the night here? She slowed her steps. So what if they had?

Hannah kept a chenille throw close by her desk, for those days when her knees or her shoulders felt chilled; today she pulled it snug about her shoulders. Outside her window a chunk of snow toppled from the roof. It splattered against her window, leaving trails of melting snow on the pane. For a moment she considered wiping the window to clear her view of the meadow and hillside, but to do that she must venture outside, into the snow, which would swallow her boots and zap her toes into cubes of ice. Hannah drew the chenille throw closer, draping an end about her neck.

A half-finished sketch of the Japanese garden she dreamed of lay on her desk, along with pictures of Japanese gardens she had cut from magazines. Japanese gardens possessed clean lines. They calmed the spirit. Once, long ago, on a trip to Florida, Hannah had visited the

Morikami Japanese Gardens in Delray Beach. She had ambled across a wooden bridge, meandered along winding stone pathways, rested on a simple bench to study the golden koi in the moat. Now, planning her own Japanese garden, her mind fastened on stone lanterns, roof tile for the small museum, the sand carefully raked, stones carefully placed, miniature pines. Hannah began to sketch. Later she would send her amateurish drawings up to Hank, and Hank would know exactly what she wanted. He would translate it all into precise plans, and plant materials, and she would begin to order plants, gravel, stone lanterns, material for a bridge over a pond, and to study the habitat necessary for healthy koi.

When the door opened, Hannah lifted her head. Holding hands, Hank and Laura entered her office. A glow framed her daughter's face, and in her eyes a softness replaced the anger and the pain of those days and weeks after the fire.

"Mother." Laura came right to the point. "Hank's asked me to marry him."

Hank chuckled, then appealed to Hannah. "Talk to your daughter, will you, Hannah? I want to make an honest women of her, and she wants us to live—" his fingers made quote marks in the air—"in sin."

"Stop being silly." Laura jostled his shoulder.

Hannah studied them for a moment. She liked Hank. He and Laura would be good for one another. The prospect of a wedding, of Laura settled and living in Covington filled her heart with joy. She wanted to urge Laura to marry Hank, but knew better. "I'd go along with Laura," Hannah said. "Smart gal, knows her mind."

"I'd rather we married," Hank said.

"Why? I told you, if we still want to be married in six months, I'll marry you," Laura said.

Hank looked rueful. "Guess I was raised to believe it

was wrong to live 'in sin.' If you're in love, why not get married?"

"Marvin and I never married. We were together for over seven years," Laura said. "And we were monogamous."

Hannah broke the moment of uncomfortable silence. "So, what's next?" she asked.

"We move in together, I guess," Hank said.

Laura's long slim fingers twined with Hank's long thick fingers. "I lied to you, Mother. I've been staying with Hank these last few days."

Hannah ignored that and counted months. "This is February. August is six months. We ought to be in our new house by then. Want to be married in our garden, like Russell and Emily?"

"Probably not. If we get married we'd prefer a simple wedding, justice-of-the-peace kind of thing," Laura replied.

Hannah squelched her disappointment. "Whatever you want," Hannah said. "Is this public information? Can I tell Grace and Amelia?"

Both Hank and Laura nodded. Hannah rose and embraced her daughter. She felt awkward and stiff. "Congratulations, darling," she said. She squeezed Hank's shoulder. "I'm happy about this."

Moments after Hank and Laura walked from her office, Tom Battle, Hannah's foreman, entered. A transplant from New Jersey, he was in his early thirties, muscular, and of average height with shoulder-length dark hair and hazel eyes. Two small gold earrings, one above the other, glittered from one ear. His T-shirt read *PROTECT WILD PLANTS—THEY CAN HEAL YOU.*

"Snow's melted in the gardens. What a mess."

"I can just imagine," Hannah said.

"Only two of the workmen showed," Tom said. "Guess

roads are still icy down in Marshall." Hands shoved in his jeans, Tom leaned against the door jamb. "I'm gonna put the guys to work cleaning everything."

"And get them to rake the beds well. We want all the leaves and stalks out to discourage disease," Hannah said.

"Yep! We gotta get all that debris and branches outta the gardens. Winds musta been a good thirty miles per hour to blow all that sh . . . ah, crap way over here from the woods."

Then he was gone. Hannah stared out her window. Winter's snowy embrace made her feel sealed off from everything and everyone, and a strange thought came into her mind. What if she stepped outside and her car was gone, and all the houses on Cove Road had vanished, and she was left alone in a vast whiteness? In that instant all of Hannah's losses, past and present, losses she had so scrupulously buried, thrust like crocuses through the snow into the sunlight and pressed for her attention. Hannah rested her head on her arms on her desk and succumbed to tears.

After a time, she wiped away the tears, squared her shoulders, and busied herself with practical matters: how to keep the children in her gardening class at Caster Elementary busy and interested until spring. The saying on Tom's T-shirt sprang to mind. She would give them herbal medicinal recipes to make and try: thyme for a cough, yarrow and plantain for a stuffy head cold, horseradish for a chill. She typed out cards:

Symptom: Coughing

Remedy: Thyme

Brew 2 teaspoons of dried thyme per cup of boiling water, steep 12 minutes and strain. Drink two or three times a day as needed.

Symptom: Stuffy head cold

Remedy: Yarrow and plantain weed

Steep 1 teaspoon each of dried yarrow and dried plantain for every cup of boiling water for 12 minutes. Strain and drink no more than four times a day.

Her mother had used these remedies when Hannah was a child. Hannah had all but forgotten them until last November, when she accidentally unearthed a yellowed herbal in a used-book store. Along with the remedies, she would send a note home with the children assuring their parents that she had been raised on such remedies with no harm done. As she scribbled notes, Hannah remembered a natural remedy for wasp and bee stings. Chew the leaves of the plantain weed and slap it onto the sting. Guaranteed to kill the pain. In the spring she would take her budding gardeners outside, introduce them to plantain, a common weed, and have them chew the leaves. Not tasty, but effective when chewed to a pulp.

18

A PLACE CALLED
SANDY MUSH

Amelia abhorred snow. She experienced none of the tranquility that she knew Grace enjoyed when snowflakes danced to earth. And Hannah, stepping outside, head high, palms open to greet the falling flakes, certainly welcomed snow. Sort of a religious experience for Hannah, Amelia thought.

For Amelia there was no redeeming quality to snow. Snow blocked visibility, isolated you, stranded you, buried you. Beneath its smooth surface it concealed icy roads and sidewalks, and when it melted, it deposited filthy piles of slush. Memories of numbing cold and the chill breath of death still frightened her. Snow brought to mind snow piled to the edge of the porch of her childhood Rhode Island home. She had been five and had wandered outside and stepped off of the porch and fallen down, down into darkness and cold. Unable to call out, she had clawed at wet, cold walls of snow until, exhausted and terrified, she had been rescued by her father.

And another time, as a child at play, she had been pushed hard against a tall, fat snowman, which promptly disintegrated, burying her in its white coldness, obstructing her sight, stifling her breath. For months afterward she awakened from nightmares in which huge balls of snow chased her down streets, around corners, into her bedroom. More recently, only last year, Amelia had nearly lost her life in a snowstorm while out shooting photographs in Barnardsville, a town twenty minutes from Covington. A rogue storm caused her to ditch her car and walk. Near collapse, hardly able to lift a leg in the deepening snow, she had been found by a patrol car and carried home to the farmhouse on Cove Road.

Determined to reawaken Amelia's passion for photography, Mike came to Bob's apartment often. But his presence only annoyed Amelia and stirred questions she dreaded answering: Had the fire that destroyed her home also destroyed her love for her work? Would that love ever return? Without this passion in her life what would she do? Without her work she felt empty, isolated, and that her life was meaningless.

And then, two weeks after the big snowstorm, the day dawned bright and sunny. Mike phoned. "I'm coming to get you, Amelia," he said. "No argument. I've found a special place I want to show you."

"It's too cold," Amelia said.

"It's sixty-four degrees outside and sunny. I'm on my way. Goodbye, now."

Amelia struggled out of bed, dressed, and thirty minutes later, when Mike arrived, she had breakfasted and was ready to sling her camera bag in the backseat of his van.

"Buckle up. I'm taking you to Sandy Mush," Mike said.

Amelia swung the belt across her body, poked around to find the slot, then snapped the buckle into it.

"Up a mountain, down the other side, but it's worth the trip. It's beautiful," Mike said.

"Is it far?" she asked.

"Yes, it is. Have something else to do?"

"No. But why go so far?" Amelia asked. "Lots of places to take photos nearby." The seat belt pressed against her breasts. Amelia tucked her fingers under it and held it away from her chest.

"The name Sandy Mush fascinates me," Mike replied. "You cannot live in this area without making a trip there at least once."

"What kind of name is Sandy Mush?" Amelia asked.

"Seems early explorers camped by a creek and mixed its water with their cornmeal. The porridge was gritty, so they called the creek Sandy Mush Creek, and the valley took the name."

Amelia nodded. She was interested in local history, but not enough to read about it, though she enjoyed tidbits picked up from storytellers and other locals. Now Amelia closed her eyes, and let the hum of the engine and the vibrations of the van lull her. When they turned left, her body slid toward Mike as far as the seat belt allowed, and she opened her eyes. Black squiggles on a yellow sign warned of twists and turns ahead. Fifteen miles an hour, another sign declared. They obeyed, creeping around hairpin curves until they crested the mountain. They began a precipitous descent until the valley opened below them, wide, stretching for miles, a giant basin of rich bottomland, scattered farms, and meandering creeks that seemed to butt into the feet of mountains.

Farmhouses, some old, some of more recent vintage, all with barns and various outbuildings, sat like playthings in the landscape. Rolls of hay, as high as her head, were piled in covered shelters. An old windmill, fallen into disrepair, stood alongside a tilted barn. Sandy Mush was sparsely populated except for cattle. Black-and-white Holsteins and solid Black Angus cattle grazed in fenced pastures. As Mike and Amelia drove past feed lots, the odor of manure permeated the air.

Farther along they drove past a small white church, which caught Amelia's attention. "Go back, will you, Mike? I want to take pictures of that little church."

Mike reversed, turned off the main road onto Sandy Mush Creek Road, crossed a creek, and pulled into the dirt parking area behind the church. "Why this church?" he asked. "The paint's peeling from its foundation to its steeple."

"I don't know," she replied. "It just appeals to me."

Three adolescent boys, wearing denim jackets, stood fishing on the creek that ran between the church property and the main road. They ignored the strangers with their cameras and tripods.

Amelia pressed her forehead hard against a window-pane of the little church and framed her face with her hands. "Look, Mike. It's got yellow walls, nice wooden pews, and an upright piano. Is it in use these days, do you think?"

"Probably. They keep up the cemetery." Mike pointed to a neatly maintained cemetery on the hill overlooking the church.

Amelia moved to another window and stood on tiptoe as she struggled to see inside. "I'd love to go in."

Mike climbed the few rock steps to the front door. "It's padlocked," he said.

Amelia stepped away from the church and circumnavigated it. Then she set up her tripod and camera. Using a long lens, she aimed upward to the steeple. "The bell tower's empty, the bell's gone," she said.

The needle-thin steeple, devoid of paint, reached for the sky. Amelia used half a roll of film taking close-ups of the curling paint, the play of sun and shade on the walls and corners of the building. As she photographed,

Mike sauntered away and stood where he could observe the boys fishing. A yell from one of the boys indicated that he had caught a fish. Voices rose as the boys argued about the weight of the fish.

Amelia hardly heard them. The film she used was black and white. The gallery in New York City, which sold her work, preferred black and white, and they expected a portfolio of new photographs several times a year.

When Amelia was done, they clambered back into Mike's van and drove for miles, seeing neither a store, nor a gas station, nor any semblance of a town. They explored several coves. One was long and narrow, another long and wide with homes scattered here and there and cattle in fields. In one cove, trailers were the residence of choice, some neat with fenced yards and a semblance of gardens, some sorely in need of propping up or of paint. In the windows of several, torn curtains fluttered in open windows. The road ended at a stream. Oversize overalls, sweatpants, checkered shirts, and a cotton print dress hung from a clothesline stretched between trees across the dirt road. On the far side a junkyard of car parts extended along a trickle of a creek.

On the drive back they stopped to photograph a dilapidated relic of an unoccupied, bleached-wood country store sitting in a bed of weeds. Its doors and window were boarded, its roof rusted. Close by, alone and mournful and half hidden in a patch of tall grass, stood an abandoned, miserably faded fire truck. They photographed the truck from a variety of angles: using the grass to frame it, moving beyond the grass for a close-up of the hood, the shattered lights, and dented front bumpers.

The wind captured Amelia's scarf, and it billowed behind her like a wind sock. The wind tousled her fine, silver-white hair, which had grown longer, almost to her shoulders. "I feel good," Amelia said.

"That's what getting out will do for you," Mike said. He hunkered to shoot two collies playing across the road.

The collies raced toward them. Amelia froze, uncertain of their intent, which as it turned out was merely to play. The dogs nuzzled against her legs and lifted their heads to be petted. "The universe is welcoming us to Sandy Mush," Mike said.

"The dogs represent the universe?" Amelia asked. She laughed, and her laughter danced in the air and wafted across winter fields of brown grass.

"All things represent the universe." Mike spread his arms wide. "The day welcomes us, the blue sky welcomes us, the road, the trees, the fields, the dogs, even the cows. You ought to know that. You're the one who's had two out-of-body experiences."

Amelia laughed. It felt good to laugh, to feel light-hearted. "I forget about . . . What do you call them?"

"OBEs," he said.

"Yes. So why haven't they changed my life, like some people claim they do? Why don't I see life as all of a piece, as I did when it was happening? Why am I so wiped out, and angry, instead of philosophical and re-signed about our fire?"

"I don't know, Amelia. Maybe you should take up meditation. It might help you answer those questions."

"I can't. I tried. My mind doesn't want to be quiet. I can't even pray." Amelia turned around slowly, breathing in the mild afternoon air. She stretched her arms above her head. "It is peaceful here. It must be gorgeous in the sum-mertime when the fields are green. Can we come back, Mike?"

He smiled, nodded, and removed his sunglasses to clean them with the end of his shirt. She remained silent while he capped the lenses on both their cameras and loaded the cameras into their respective bags. "Who lives out here?" she asked. "So few houses for all the space. It's like Shangri-La."

"Local folks, and someone told me that thirty years ago the University in Asheville started a pottery program. Some of the students who came to study crafts fell in love with Sandy Mush and settled here. An artsy community developed."

She looked about. "Do they still live here?"

"For the life of me, I can't get a sense of it." Mike shaded his eyes, and he, too, looked left and right across the open fields to houses set back in woods. "Back-to-the-land folks, probably, so they wouldn't have fancy houses, I don't imagine."

"Wouldn't they have signs out, 'pottery sold here' or whatever?" she asked.

Mike shrugged. "In this off-the-track location, with that tortuous road coming in, why bother? They probably sell at craft fairs. Someone told me there's an herb farm somewhere up a mountain, but you need four-wheel drive to get there."

Amelia found a perch on a pile of sand near the fire truck. "Mike," she said, "do you think I'm ever going to be the old Amelia?"

He joined her on the mound. "I certainly do. Why, today you're like your old self."

"But then I slip right back into feeling miserable," she said. "I want to feel upbeat, I want to laugh again. I want to enjoy life. I hate feeling so down." Amelia pulled a long strand of grass from its cluster on the sand pile and ran her fingers along the smooth tubular stem. "There's been too much pain. It seems as if I've just gotten over Lance Lundquist, and now the fire."

"I wish you had never met Lance. First he consumed your time and energy, and then he treated you badly." Mike gave a little shiver. "But you recovered from the trauma of Lance months ago, Amelia." He patted her arm. "Don't worry. When your farmhouse is rebuilt, you'll settle in and be as happy as a bird in its nest."

She was pensive for a time.

"What you thinking?" Mike asked.

"Is a bird happy or does it have to be ever alert to defend against predators?"

"Oh, Amelia, cheer up, think positive," he said.

"Grace wanted the three of us to take Lucy to live with us permanently," Amelia said. "I said no. I'm selfish, aren't I?"

"No, you weren't being selfish, just smart. It would have been too much for all of you. The alternative's much better, all of us chipping in, setting up a trust to help the Banks family."

Amelia was not placated. "It's *how* I said no to Grace, about Lucy living with us. I was sarcastic, mean. She must hate me for acting like that."

"Grace doesn't hold grudges," Mike said. He grasped Amelia's hand and helped her to her feet. "Let's go. The light's just right, shadows are long, and we have a lot of work to do."

They hastened to the van.

"Lucy's family will be all right with the help we're giving them, everyone pledging fifty dollars a month or whatever they can afford," Mike said. "How many of us are in this, anyhow? Bob, Max, Emily and Russell, Brenda and the Lunds, you ladies, and me, of course. Anyone else?"

"I'm really not sure. Grace and Brenda set it up."

"We can all afford something, even if its only fifty dollars a month. It's the right thing to do," Mike said.

"Yes. It is," she replied. "It will keep that family together. It's best for everyone all around."

Mike nodded and shifted the van into gear. They started back through the long valley.

"You really think things will go back to normal when our house gets built?" Amelia asked.

"I do. I certainly do."

"Mike," Amelia said, then fell silent.

"What is it, Amelia?"

"I made an appointment to see a Dr. Pellen in Asheville."

"Dr. Jerry Pellen, the psychiatrist?" he asked, twisting his head to look at her.

"You know him?" she asked.

"Know of him. A friend of mine, John, went to him. John, my friend who died of AIDS. I spent last Christmas taking care of him. Remember? He went to Dr. Pellen when he was first diagnosed." Mike fell silent. They slowed and rounded yet another curve. Then he said, "Pellen helped him deal with dying. John used to say the one thing he wasn't afraid of was death, but when it stared him in the face, he lost all his equanimity and went ballistic." Silence filled the van. They began their descent of the mountain. "That's when you really have to come to terms with what it's all about."

"What do you think happens when we die, Mike?"

He glanced over at her, then fixed his eyes on the road ahead. The precipice to their right seemed steeper and more treacherous than on the drive up. "Well," he said, "in my family they believed in heaven and hell. I don't anymore. I think there's either the loving arms of God held out to receive us, or there's nothing, and when we're dead we're dead." He shrugged.

"It would hurt too much," Amelia said, "if I thought I would never see my Caroline again, so I like to think she'll be waiting for me." They drove for a while in silence before Amelia said, "Calling for an appointment with a psychiatrist wasn't easy for me."

"Then why do it?"

"I had to, Mike. I must get some help, or I'll go crazy."

At the bottom of the mountain, the road grew flat and straight. Tall pines and oaks cast long shadows. Amelia rolled down the window for a moment and shoved her arm outside. The air had grown colder, a portent of the night to come. "Oh, Lord," Amelia said. "When is it going to get warm and stay warm?"

"Not for another month at least," Mike replied.

"I need it to be warm." Amelia rubbed her palms together. "Cold makes getting out of bed harder for me. I lie under the covers and brood about losing our farmhouse. That old building was home to me, in the deepest sense of the word. It brought so many of the good things in my past back to life. Once, when Thomas and I were first married, we lived in an old farmhouse in the south of England. Actually, he was gone so much, I lived there alone most of the time with things that were not mine, not the furniture, nor the curtains, not a pot or a pan, nothing, and yet I loved it. I felt as if I belonged in that quaint little town with its crooked cobblestone streets, and the signs: a mortar and pestle over the pharmacy, a ring over the jewelry store. People called me 'love' when they didn't know my name, and sometimes even when they did. And the creaky fifth step in our farmhouse here reminded me of the creak of those two-hundred-year-old steps."

She paused for a moment. "There was something else. When Grace cooks, the smells take me back to my grandmother's house and Sunday dinners. I'm not even sure what the smells are, seasonings maybe and essences like vanilla, but if I closed my eyes for a moment or two, I'm at my grandmother's, and I'm happy."

Mike drove slowly, listening carefully, thinking of his own memories, of the taste of root beer and ice cream. "Black cows," his Uncle Jerry called the ice-cream floats that he made for his nephews and nieces, and in that moment

Mike hankered for "home." The house he lived in in Fairview, south of Asheville, was a town house with no yard. It did have a small back patio that spilled onto a lawn maintained by the association. What saved the place for him was that the lawn backed on woods, and Mike loved the woods, and the creatures: squirrels, rabbits, a fox, a deer occasionally that darted among the trees.

"I think I get the drift of what you're saying," he said. "It's not the physical space, it's the essence of that space."

"Yes," Amelia said. "The essence of the space."

They were silent, the moment too full to be captured in the confines of language. A car tailing the van caused Mike to drive faster. Their silence was broken when Amelia asked, "Did Dr. Pellen help your friend, John?"

"Yes. He helped John come to terms with dying. John died peacefully."

"Neither of my parents died peacefully," Amelia said. "They fought death to the end. My father had cardiomyopathy. He was angry and bitter. My mother's liver went—too much drinking, I imagine. She was furious at life."

"Sad," Mike said.

"After Thomas died, when I was in the hospital, I was frightened that I'd never recover, never leave the psychiatric unit," Amelia said.

"But you did, and you're going to be fine."

For Amelia, being in a psychiatric unit had been a humiliating ordeal. Never again, she prayed, as she struggled each day since the fire with the unremitting heaviness in her heart. Depression was proving impossible to fight alone, and she had finally called for an appointment with Dr. Pellen. "I'm not sick like I was, Mike," Amelia said, as much to reassure herself as to reassure him. "That other time they literally carried me to the hospital."

"It's good to get help when you need it," Mike said.

"I'll be glad to drive you into Asheville. When is your appointment?"

"March fifteenth at ten in the morning."

"Ah, the Ides of March," he said.

She whirled about. "Why do you say that? Is it bad luck, like Friday the thirteenth?"

"Heavens, no. It goes back to ancient Rome. *Ides* simply meant the day of the full moon, which fell, in the ancient Roman calendar, on the fifteenth of March, May, July, and October, and on the thirteenth day of all the other months."

"Wasn't Julius Caesar killed on the Ides of March, the fifteenth?"

"Amelia, I didn't mean a thing, just old stuff I learned in high school coming to mind."

She rested her hand on his arm for a moment. "Heavens, I'm so sensitive these days. I'm sorry, Mike."

The Ides of March dawned cold and clear and brought with it a brusque wind that whipped about their bodies and tore at Amelia's coat and Mike's jacket. It burned their cheeks and noses. Amelia held her coat collar tight about her neck. "What a horrible day. I keep thinking, how can the men work on our house in weather like this?"

"They've got the walls up and the place closed in. They use heaters. I stopped to see the progress before coming up here to get you," Mike said.

"What if they try putting on the roof and the wind tears it off before they can nail it down?"

"The roof's on, the plywood is, anyway. You need more to worry about?" he asked. "Tom Findley knows what he's doing."

The thirty-minute drive to Asheville passed mostly in silence. Huge trucks roaring by caused Mike's van to weave and sway. Mike slowed and stayed in the right lane.

"Imagine what this road's going to be like when they finish widening it to the Tennessee border. Trucks will own it," Mike said.

Amelia nodded and said nothing. The trucks, the road, none of it mattered, not when she struggled with merely trying to get through the day without crying or sleeping.

The bronze plate on the wall of the lobby indicated that Dr. J. Pellen's office was on the fourth floor, the top floor, of a new medical building off of Sweeten Creek Road in Asheville. The marble walls shone like mirrors. The smell of the hallway reminded Amelia of the interior of a new car. Dr. J. Pellen shared a reception area with five other physicians. The waiting room boasted a high ceiling with skylights, which brightened the room far too much for Amelia, who would have preferred subdued light. She did not remove her sunglasses, not even when the nurse called her name.

Mike patted her hand. "It's going to be just fine, Amelia," he said. Then he rose, took a magazine from a rack, and buried himself in an article about monarch butterflies and their long trip south each winter.

After listening to her history and present situation, Dr. Pellin said, "Mrs. Declose, it seems to me that you're suffering from situational anxiety and depression." His voice sounded upbeat.

"Which means what?" Amelia asked.

"That you've had a trauma that's resulted in depression. We can take care of it, get you back to feeling like your old self."

Relief washed over Amelia.

Dr. Pellen scribbled on his prescription pad.

"What are you giving me?" she asked.

"A mild dose of Celexa. Take three a day. It might be a

week or two before it kicks in, but then you should feel your old self again. Let's get you back in here in four weeks." He closed the folder with her name on it.

Somehow she trusted him. He reminded her of her husband, Thomas: slight of build, good-looking, neatly trimmed mustache, kind brown eyes. She thought of the years since Thomas had been killed in that horrible car crash, the lonely years, and the fruitful years since she came to live in Covington. Thomas might pass her in the street and not know her today with her short white hair. It had been brown. Would he be proud of her photography, or would he diminish her work as he had in those nightmares she had of him when she had first been recognized for her work?

Slowly Amelia walked down the hallway to the reception area where Mike waited. In her hand she clutched the prescription, her lifeline to recovery.

The medication took exactly two weeks to work, and by then it was April. "I feel so very much better, happier, more able to cope," she told Grace. "Now just let our farmhouse get finished."

19

THE MEETING AT FIGHTING DEER CREEK

Three weeks after her visit to Dr. Pellen, Amelia awoke feeling in tune with all creation. She sprang from bed, glad to be alive, eager to share her feelings with Grace and Bob. But when she called to them, she received no answer. The note attached to the refrigerator said they had gone to Asheville.

Amelia looked about her and noticed, for the first time, the waffle ceiling Bob had had installed in the living room. It was beautiful and gave the room a warm, old-fashioned look that pleased her. Amelia moved slowly to the terrace and a moment later stood outside breathing deeply of the fresh, clean air of spring. She flung wide her arms, and after enjoying a cup of tea returned to her room, dressed, gathered up her camera and camefa bag, stuffed with lenses and film, and hastened outside to her car.

She had, with Max and Hannah's encouragement, bought a new Ford Taurus, green this time, to replace the white Taurus the fire had devoured. That's how Amelia thought of all things lost to the fire, not burned or destroyed, but devoured by red, roaring, avaricious jaws that ate across the land, swallowing homes and trees with rapid gulps.

She considered calling Mike, then decided that she preferred being alone today. She would meander through the countryside, travel unexplored roads, and perhaps take photographs.

Amelia turned off Elk Road and headed toward Highway 70-25, which would take her down the mountain to the lower reaches of the French Broad River and the little town of Hot Springs nestled on its bank. But when she reached Hot Springs, she did not stop but continued driving, up and out of town, and followed the road, not knowing where it went, and unconcerned. The day was balmy, the sky morning glory blue and cloudless. The hillsides appeared to be a patchwork: pale green of newly unfurled leaves, tufts of rich, bright greens, and unevenly spaced darker evergreens. Where the tree canopy still remained thin and open to sunshine, dogwoods bloomed like patches of snow in mountain crevices.

North Carolina ended. Tennessee began. The road narrowed. The terrain grew tight, hills close on either side. After a few minutes a weatherworn, lopsided sign nailed to a tree caught Amelia's eye. She slowed her car when she came to the sign FIGHTING DEER CREEK. Amelia braked, hastily sending her camera bag sliding, then toppling to the floor.

A rocky, pitted path sloped and curved to the creek. The short walk demanded concentration. Amelia hugged the camera bag and tripod and placed one foot before the other carefully. Stones along the banks and clusters of stones protruding as peninsulas indicated that this creek, like many tributaries in Madison County and its environs, ran low. The creeks and branches and shallow rivers of North Carolina in no way resembled the wide, deep, navigable rivers of her experience. Still, she loved to watch the flow of water embracing the rocks, leaping over them. Now the splash and slosh met her ears. Expecting to be alone, she was startled to see five towheaded children about eight years old, hunched around a castle constructed from the rough grainy, mustard-colored sand that lined the shore of Fighting Deer Creek. A boy and a girl each looked up at her briefly, said, "Hey," and returned to their work.

"Hi," Amelia replied. She ambled away from them, down the sandy shore of the rapidly rushing creek.

"Whatcha got there, lady?" one of the girls called.

Amelia stopped, turned, and studied the children. Except for the child who had spoken to her, the others remained intent on their work. The girl was pale, her fair hair stringy and uncombed. Bangs obscured her forehead and dangled over her eyes. She brushed them back. Sand drizzled from her arm and elbow.

"It's a camera bag and my tripod," Amelia replied. The ground on which she stood, just above the sandy area, consisted of rough pebbles. To her right uneven rocks and large rounded boulders jutted up and out, blocking further passage along the shore of the creek. In the other direction, behind the children, boulders reared along the shoreline.

"You done mashed the fort!" A boy's voice rose above the rush of the water.

"I ain't done nothing," another replied. For a moment the two boys glared at each other. Then, like two bucks sizing up each other and deciding not to battle, the boys returned to the task of rebuilding the wrecked side of the fort.

The girl who had spoken to Amelia rose and moseyed slowly toward her as Amelia was considering how she would get them to allow her to take their pictures.

"My name's Olivia," the girl said. "I hate my name. The others call me Olive Oyl."

"My name is Amelia, and when I was little, kids teased me and called me Amilamila. I hated that."

"Did you cry?" the child asked. Her jeans were faded and threadbare at the knees, and Amelia wondered how many other children had worn these jeans before they had been passed along to her.

Amelia nodded. "But that only made them tease me more. It's best to act as if you don't care what they call you. Someday, when you're older, you'll see what a pretty name Olivia is."

"Ain't gonna be no someday," the little girl said matter-of-factly.

"Why not?" Amelia set her camera bag and the tripod case on a protruding rock. She squatted, bringing herself eye level with the child. "Why won't you grow older?"

" 'Cause I got me a sickness, and Ma says I ain't long for this world."

"A sickness? What kind of sickness?"

Olivia's frail shoulders rose and fell. "Dunno. Sometimes I turn yellow."

Jaundice? Surely Olivia was wrong. "Would you like me to take your picture?" Amelia asked.

A smile flitted across the pixie face. "I ain't never had my picture took 'cept at school." Olivia glanced furtively at her companions, who were busy fortifying their sand castle with an outer coat of small gray pebbles.

Lofty trees tented the creek. From high above, through wind-blown leaves and branches, dappled light splotched the idyllic terrain and the child's face and shoulders. Olivia looked on curiously while Amelia loaded her camera with 400 ASA film.

"Sit over there." Amelia pointed to a shaded area where the dim light fell more evenly. She raised the camera to her eye and peered through the lens. Behind Olivia, the others had stopped peppering the walls of their sand castle with pebbles and stared at Amelia, their mouths agape. Amelia began to shoot. She was working too fast, without planning. She lowered the camera. "Come on over here," she called to the three boys and the other girl. "I'll let you look through the lens."

They came hesitantly, dragging their feet, their faces a mix of caution and curiosity. They were thin, and their eyes were old beyond their years. Who were they? Where did they live? Were they related?

The tallest and, she assumed, the oldest boy reached her first. "Olive Oyl ain't pretty enough to take no picture of. Take me. I'm the best lookin'."

Arrogant little man, Amelia thought, but she asked, "Is Olivia your sister?"

"Cousin. Stupid cousin." He looked intently at Olivia, whose face was a mask of anger, frustration, and disappointment. "She don't need no picture. She's gonna die soon anyways."

Amelia looked at them. Did the bravado, the rejection, and putting down of Olivia by her cousin stem from his caring and his dread of losing her? "I'll take everyone's picture," Amelia said. "What's your name?" she asked the cousin.

"Luke," he said. His chin tilted up.

"Well, Luke, you come sit right here beside me, and I'll let you look through the lens. Olivia," Amelia said. "Find me a smooth pretty stone with a shiny surface, will you, please?"

Olivia pouted but did as she was asked. As she squatted alongside the creek holding first one and then another stone up to the dappled light, Amelia photographed. Olivia's eyes glowed. She held out to Amelia a shiny dark rock the size of her palm. "This is the best," she said. Amelia nodded and the shutter on the camera clicked and clicked. Amelia lowered the camera and allowed Luke to hold it. "Look through here." She pointed to the lens. "Look at Olivia."

He held the camera as if it were gold and peered into the lens. "She looks funny in this here mirror," Luke declared.

The other children pressed close, wanting to see Olivia through the lens, but with an angry gesture, Olivia turned and flung the rock into the creek. Then she slumped to the ground. "I picked you a right nice, shiny rock." Her voice indicated pain and resentment.

"Try to find it again," Amelia said. "Please do. It was special, I could see that. Shall I help you search for it?" Amelia retrieved the camera from Luke, set it in its place in the bag, and joined Olivia. They kneeled together at water's edge. "We'll hunt for two rocks. I'll have one, and you'll have one, so we remember each other," Amelia said softly. She could feel the girl relax.

"Okay," Olivia said.

Moments later they plunged their hands into the icy water. Immediately Amelia withdrew her hands. Didn't Olivia feel the cold? Didn't her hands ache?

The others joined them, and no one but Amelia appeared to be bothered by the cold water. Everyone dipped in and hunted for a special rock.

Olivia was first to draw out a flat shiny stone. "This here one's for you." She handed it to Amelia, who turned it over in her hand. The stone was icy.

"It's perfect," Amelia said. She reached back into the creek and retrieved a small round stone with glints of green throughout. "This is for you." She handed it to Olivia.

The child reached for it and clutched it in her palm as if it were a golden nugget. She smiled. The resignation in her pale blue eyes vanished for a moment, replaced by glee.

Amelia turned to the other children. "Will you let me take your pictures?"

"Okay," the other girl said.

Luke seemed as shrewd as an old horse trader. "Can we carry the pictures home for our mas to see?" he asked.

"I have to have them developed in a photo shop, and then I'll send them to you if you give me your address."

Their faces went blank.

"I'll bring them to you here in two weeks," Amelia said.

Luke thought about that for a while, then said, "Okay." He nodded to the others. Aggie, the other girl, smoothed her stained T-shirt. Luke slicked back his hair and threw back his shoulders. The others followed suit.

"You, too, Olivia," Amelia said.

Olivia looked at her tentatively, then ran to join the others.

Amelia sat on her haunches and studied the small group on the sand. What was this strange attraction she felt for Olivia? She wanted to snatch up the little girl and take her home. A wave of guilt swept over Amelia. Memories raced through her head: Caroline playing with friends on the banks of the Ganges in India, then toppling headfirst into the river, and Amelia running, struggling to pull her child from the brown, polluted water. A month later she had cradled the small ravaged body of her daughter in her arms on the plane to London. Caroline's trusting blue eyes had found and held hers before closing forever. Amelia had tried and tried to analyze that look. Had it held affection or was it trust? Pain gripped Amelia's heart, pain as deep and wrenching as that day on the plane. Amelia looked about her. Water tumbling over stones in the creek, the dank, dark woods across the creek, the children, and she herself seemed at that instant to be all that remained of the world. A crazy thought ran through her mind. Had she entered a time warp? Was there such a thing as a time warp? Picking up a handful of sand, she rubbed the grains between her palms, felt the grit and chill of it. This was reality—no time warp here, as Luke's rough laugh soon reassured her.

"You look like you seen a ghost, lady," he said.

Embarrassed, Amelia brushed her hands and collected herself. "Why do they call this Fighting Deer Creek?"

Luke dug his toes into the sand. He lifted his chin. "Grandpa says he was huntin' in them woods." Luke pointed into the thick woods across the creek. "Says he met up with a bunch of deer. Two old bucks started to fight. Grandpa backed off and kept moving back and across this here creek, and them two deers just kept fightin' and backin' up until they was in the middle of the creek. Grandpa climbed up on a boulder and watched them. He was gonna kill one, but just as he raised his gun, it was as if them deers knew. They unlocked their horns, and quick as he could blink, Grandpa said, they were up the bank and gone in the woods. People started calling it Fightin' Deer Creek after that."

The other children nodded solemnly. Amelia assumed they had heard the tale over many a winter fire.

"Don't know what name it had afore then," Luke said.

Amelia busied herself preparing to photograph the children. She set up her tripod. The light was so low now that she needed the tripod in order to open the lens wide enough. And she wanted no posed shots. "Are you finished with your castle?" she asked.

"Not the top," Aggie said. "We gotta put the top on."

"Go ahead, then," Amelia said. "I'll take pictures of you building your castle."

They eyed her quizzically, as if she were nuts, and then they began to work and they relaxed. Amelia shot a smiling face, a narrow face deep in concentration, another rubbing sand from his cheek. Then she lined them up, girls in front, boys behind, and took their portrait. As she put away the camera, Amelia said, "Luke, I'll meet you right here in two weeks. I'll bring each of you a framed picture. You can set it on your dresser, or hang it on the wall," she said.

That brought smiles. They walked with her up the steep squiggle of a trail to the road. They touched the shiny new finish of the Taurus, inspected their reflections in the side-view mirrors, and peered with great interest into the trunk of her car, where she stowed her tripod away. "I'll meet you right here two weeks from today at"—she checked her watch—"at three in the afternoon."

They looked doubtful, as if adults made promises they never kept, and they stood in the middle of the road waving goodbye as she drove away from them. Overcome with a sense of loss, Amelia looked back at them. Then she turned a bend, and they were gone, leaving her feeling odd, missing them.

Only after Mike had developed the photos did she speak of Fighting Deer Creek.

Two weeks later Mike accompanied Amelia to the area. The children clustered close to the sign on the road and hung back when they saw Mike. It took several moments before Amelia realized that Olivia was not among them. Her heart sank.

"This is my friend, Mike," Amelia said. Mike lifted the box of framed photos from the trunk of the car and placed it on the grass about ten feet from where they stood.

"Where's Olivia?" Amelia asked.

Luke more leaned than stepped forward. "She's gone."

"Gone where?"

"To God." He shrugged. "That's what the preacher man said."

The ground swayed under Amelia's feet. Mike grasped her about the waist to steady her. Amelia slumped against her car. "To God?"

"We done buried her yesterday," Luke said. His lower lip quivered.

Amelia had been right; the boy had loved his cousin. The pain of her passing was written in the tight draw of his lips, the tears gathering in his eyes.

Luke looked away, then straightened his shoulders and turned again to face Amelia. "Her ma says she'd be right glad to get a picture of Olivia."

"Yes." Slowly Amelia walked to the box, kneeled, and gently moved the frames, until the face of Olivia smiled at her from behind glass. Inside her chest Amelia felt unseen hands tear her heart in two. She wanted to weep, to wail until her cry filled every valley and hollow in the mountains.

Mike understood. Silently he helped her to her feet, and when she seemed steady, he led her back to the car, then brought the box and set it carefully on the hood of the car. Reaching inside, he handed Amelia the photos, which she distributed to the children. As promised, there was also a framed group photograph for each child.

Their shyness vanished as the children exclaimed and marveled at their own likenesses.

For a long while Amelia studied the pixie face, the curious eyes of Olivia, which looked at her from the photograph. Then she handed it to Luke. "For Olivia's mother," she said.

"Gosh, these are okay," Luke said. "Thanks, lady."

"Thanks, lady," the others echoed. The children turned and walked away following a trail through a patch of woods across the road from Fighting Deer Creek.

"Talk to me, Amelia," Mike said. "Don't bottle this up and drift away from us again."

Amelia looked at him. "Have you any idea what that was like? Olivia. You saw her picture. I felt as if I had always known her, and she's gone like Caroline. I keep thinking how that mother must feel."

Mike opened the car door. "I'm sorry, Amelia. Come. Get in. I'll drive you home."

She fastened her seat belt and stared out the window. "You wouldn't know what it is to lose a child," she said.

"I am not without sensitivity," he replied. "Everyone, including me, has lost someone they loved deeply. It's part of life." He held his breath, concerned that he had overstepped his bounds, and then was sure that he had, for they drove for many miles in silence.

20

IN THE SPRING OF
THE YEAR

Amelia did not plunge back into depression as Mike
dreaded. For nights after learning of Olivia's death,
Amelia cried herself to sleep, but even grief must pass,
and as all about her the world offered its gift of spring
and new life, she rallied and began to frequent the construction site, reporting to Grace daily on the progress of
their home.

Amelia sat on a box in the hallway of the house and
watched workmen in overalls smear white gook on lines of
paper that hid the joints of the drywall. When it dried, she
watched them sand it, then paint the first coat, a dull white.
She loved the curve of the staircase railing and ran her
hands along its smooth surface the moment it was installed. From the doorway she watched them spray the popcorn ceiling.

Sometimes, as she sat there, she thought of Olivia,
and, if she were alone, spoke aloud to the girl as she had
to her daughter Caroline after her death. Amelia told
Olivia how the new steps differed and would be easier to
negotiate than the old ones, how there would be a full
bathroom downstairs. It comforted her to think that Caro-

line and Olivia met in heaven and were listening to her and smiling.

Amelia's spirits improved to the point where Grace remarked, "I'm so delighted to see you happier. You probably don't even need that antidepression medication any longer."

Amelia smiled. There were moments, hours, even days when life still seemed meaningless, when her work lacked luster, when her friends seemed not to be enough. "Not yet," Amelia said. "I'm not ready to stop taking it yet; later, when we move back home."

Grace hugged her. "I love you, Amelia. I love spring. It's a special, tender time, sweet as the promise of new love."

The mention of new love sent tiny shivers through Amelia and reminded her of her disappointing romance with Lance Lundquist, and the loss of Caroline and Olivia. Oh, Lord, she prayed silently, let me find joy in nature and my work, in my friends and my home. Let me never again have my heart torn in two.

As the days passed, Amelia was increasingly drawn to the back roads of Madison and Buncombe counties. The countryside, with its stretches of lush pastureland, its views of layered hills and mountains, soothed her, lifted her spirits, and brought tears of gratitude. On hazy days hills pressed shoulder to shoulder against higher hills were both mysterious and heart-stopping lovely. Once, when rain cleansed the atmosphere, Amelia felt as if she could slip a hand between the hills and touch the heart of God. In these moments, Amelia offered prayers of thanksgiving for the world she lived in.

One morning Amelia found Hannah's note saying that she would be staying at Max's. She felt downhearted and somewhat guilty. Needing to bolster her flagging spirits, she decided to wander and photograph. In pastures along her route dew glistened on the tips of grass and in tobacco fields on the pale pink flowers that topped the maturing plants.

Unwittingly Amelia turned off the highway and soon found herself many miles into Barnardsville on a two-lane called Paint Fork. As she followed the twists and turns of the narrow road, a tall pyramid-shaped hill rose before her. Its great height blotted out the morning sun and cast long shadows. At that moment Amelia rounded a corner and was amazed and delighted to see on her left a field of daylilies, neatly cultivated rows of pinks, reds, yellows, oranges, lavenders. A sign to her right, half hidden by shrubs, read CONSIDER THE LILIES. Amelia turned into the gravel driveway and immediately entered another world. A narrow stream shaded by tall trees tumbled over rocks, creating waterfalls. Beyond lay countless beds of daylilies.

Amelia parked her car and stepped out. Under a canopy, behind a well-worn table, sat a woman who waved to her. Without a word Amelia joined her and sat on a bench across from the woman. She was short with graying hair piled atop her head, and serene blue eyes behind wire-rimmed glasses. They were, to Amelia's mind, the eyes of kindness and of peace.

"I'm Marion Mundy," the woman said, a smile lighting her face. "Would you like to see our daylilies? We have over twelve hundred varieties. It's my husband's passion. He plants them: I sell them." Her hands were folded in her lap, but alongside of her sat a basket of green beans waiting to be snapped. Two tabby cats purred and wound soft sleek bodies about her legs. Another curled asleep in a basket on the table. A grandson ran from the house. A bright and curious lad with eyes like his grandmother's.

Amelia and Marion walked among the beds of

daylilies chatting like old friends, and Amelia told the woman about the fire, and about Caroline and Olivia. Marion told Amelia about a terrible accident her son had had and how by the grace of God he had recovered. The daylilies they walked among as they talked were of exciting colors and shapes, some were ruffled, others were spider-shaped, some were huge, while others boasted many more buds than others.

"How does anyone choose?" Amelia said. "My housemate, Hannah, would love these. I'd like to buy that gorgeous bright red one over there, and this deep pink, and that exquisite lemon yellow, it's so tall and elegant. But we've no place to plant them now."

"You can plant them in pots and transfer them later," Marion suggested.

Amelia selected a half dozen.

Later, when Amelia presented the flowers with their roots wrapped in wet newspaper and stored in plastic bags, Hannah beamed as she studied each one, and Grace went wild over the colors.

As May gave way to June, the smile on Amelia's face and the spring in her step came more often and stayed longer, and when she thought about Olivia, it was with a quiet sense that all was well. In that frame of mind Amelia resumed her volunteer work with premature babies in the hospital nursery. The nurses welcomed her warmly.

"They really missed me," Amelia told Mike one afternoon when they were developing negatives at his studio.

"Why wouldn't they miss you? Heavens, I missed you. You're a special person, Amelia, and you have a great deal of love to give."

From that day, whenever Amelia felt blue she had only to remember Mike's words, and the welcoming look on

the nurses' faces in the baby nursery, and she would recover her spirits.

On Cove Road the homes of the Herrills and the Craines
were nearly complete. Soon the ladies' would be, too. Tom
Findley constantly assured them, "You're gonna love this
place when it gets done." Today he waited for them near his
truck and greeted the three women with a broad smile.
"Lemma show you upstairs now that the railing's been installed."

They trailed Tom across the yard, avoiding scattered
pieces of lumber. Amelia looked up at the peak of the
roof. She remembered how upset she had been standing
on this same spot near the road that day when they had
first arrived in Covington, and the sadness and disappointment she had felt on seeing the weatherworn old
building. But they had given it new life, and then it had
died in the fire only to be reborn. Already she loved their
new home.

"We'll have cable TV?" Grace asked. "We used to de-
pend on rabbit ears and only got three stations, one from
Asheville and two from South Carolina."

"They ran cable out here last year. There are TV jacks
in every room," Tom said. "Before we go upstairs, take a
peek at the kitchen. The Formica's been put on the countertops."

It was a wonderful kitchen, and as she stood there,
Grace's heart swelled with pleasure. She had decided on
the design, the color, the appliances, everything, and it
was all she dreamed it would be.

Hannah headed for the mudroom to assure herself that
there was a space where she could sit and take off her
shoes, and a place to stash her gardening tools.

"Where will the washer and dryer be?" Amelia asked
Tom.

"Upstairs, where the bedding and clothing are. Very convenient," Tom replied, and led them up the steps.

Upstairs was much like their old farmhouse, two bedrooms on either side of a hallway, but each set of bedrooms shared a large bathroom with both a shower and bathtub and double sinks. The ladies dallied in each room before moving on to the bedrooms.

"I am going to paint my bedroom green," Amelia said.

Hannah studied the walls of her soon-to-be bedroom. "Some kind of an earthy sand tone for me."

"I'm sticking with apricot," Grace said. She walked to the window that overlooked the stream. It seemed to hum a welcome to her. *Home.* The word pleased Grace, and she said it to herself softly, again and again. Space to roam, hills to meander, and her friends were here. Guilt pinched her heart. Why wasn't Bob enough? Was it the small space they lived in? She didn't really know, only that she was always slightly on edge there, while here, even in this unfinished house, she was content.

Behind her, Hannah was saying, "It won't be much longer and we can get back to normal living."

21

ELLIE LERNER

Life began to return to normal. Grace returned to Caster Elementary to tutor twin sisters. One morning, just as she was finishing a session with the girls, Grace received a message from Brenda asking her to stop by the principal's office.

The familiarity of the hallways, the shuffle of feet, teachers' voices, and children's voices wrapped her in warmth, as did Brenda's outstretched hands. Brenda waved Grace to one of two chairs placed in front of her desk. "How are you doing? Amelia and Hannah okay?"

Grace nodded. "The further along the house is, the happier we all are."

"Thanks for taking on the Talley girls. I know you'll bring them along in their reading skills. You have a way with these children. They fall in love with you, Grace, and want to please you."

"They're nice girls. I think they'll be fine," Grace replied.

Brenda came to the point. "That woman who came to Hannah's birthday party last December, the one you bought Lurina's wedding dress from, what was her name? Can you give me her phone number?"

"Ellie Lerner." Grace rummaged in her purse for a small black address book, flipped through the pages, and read the number to Brenda, who leaned forward and jotted it on a pad on her desk.

"She mentioned she wanted to move to the country. Molly's house is going to be empty, and I'm urging them to rent, not sell it," Brenda explained. "I think property's a good investment. Don't you?" She didn't wait for Grace to respond. "If I come up with a good tenant for them, that'll settle the matter for a while."

"I'm surprised that Ellie would want to live so far from her business," Grace said.

"Oh? I got the impression she couldn't wait to move out of the city."

"That would be something, wouldn't it? Ellie Lerner moving to Covington."

"Why do you say that?" Brenda said.

"She seems so worldly, so citified."

"All she can say is no," Brenda said.

Ellie said yes before seeing the house, and when she did she was ecstatic. "It's so cozy," she said of the living room with its wood-burning fireplace. The bedrooms upstairs reminded her of a dollhouse, and she wandered from room to room, looking out of windows, exclaiming about the mountain, the pasture, without a thought to who would mow the lawn, or what she would do rambling about alone in a two-story, three-bedroom house on a road where most of her neighbors' lights went out by ten and the racket of night critters filled the air.

"Are you sure about this, Ellie?" Grace asked.

Ellie had stopped at Bob's apartment on her way to Cove Road to sign the lease with the Lunds.

"Have you tried staying a night in the house alone?" Bob asked. "It can get pretty dark out here."

"And noisy. Critters, not people, that is," Grace said.

Ellie brushed away their objections. "It's so wonderful. I'll get used to country noises. You did. It's what I've dreamed about, and you'll be just down the road," she replied, all smiles.

"We'll be glad to have you for a neighbor," Grace said.

Ellie shrugged. "What's the worst thing that can happen?" She looked from Bob to Grace. "If I hate living in the country, I'll move back into Asheville when my lease is up."

"Just like that?" Grace asked.

"Sure. If I'm not happy here, I'll move. No big deal. I've moved two dozen times in my life," Ellie replied with a wave of her hand. She looked at Grace. "I loved it out here from that first day when I brought the wedding dresses to Miss Lurina."

"When do you move in?" Grace asked.

"The middle of May, a week after Molly and her family move out."

"We won't be in our house then, not for another few months," Grace said with certainty. She looked at Bob, who sat there rubbing his chest. "What's wrong, Bob?" she asked.

"Bit of indigestion, I guess."

But this bit of so-called "indigestion" would force Grace to make the most difficult decision of her life.

22

OUT OF THE BLUE

Towering trees wrapped the hills behind Lurina's farmhouse, disguising the fact that seventy years ago a virgin forest had succumbed to woodsmen's saws. Timbering once ruled the economy of Covington, of Madison County; Lurina's father had grown rich on timber. Nature's boon and seventy years of growth had produced tall trees under whose thick canopies of leaves and branches lay a world turned green with filtered light and moss.

Hannah and Grace sat with Lurina on her front porch one lazy afternoon. Lurina and Old Man had recently gone for a short walk in the woods behind the house. "Times change, but things don't change a bit," Lurina said. "Time was they cut trees by hand with an ax and a saw, now it's done with big old machines. Nobody 'round these parts would take an ax to a forest like in old times."

"I often give thanks for nature's ability to heal itself," Grace said.

"Wouldn't have to heal itself if men weren't so avaricious," Hannah said.

"I remember when they cut them woods of ours," Lurina said. "When they was near to finished a goosedrownder brung enough mud from those bare hills to nearly fill Bad River over yonder. Mud knocked down the corn and buried most of the chickens, save them that made it up on the back porch railing." Lurina stopped rocking and leaned forward. Her face grew sober as she stared back into time. "Jack, the timber man, wouldn't stop workin', even when Pa said he should. Time he quit, he was standin' in mud high as his thigh, couldn't pull hisself out of that mud. Greedy Jack Bennet stuck right where he was standin'. Couldn't move, couldn't run when that last tree heaved up outta that mud and fell on him."

"A tree fell on him?" Grace gasped.

"Sure nuff! I was small then, and watchin' from Ma and Pa's window upstairs, and wonderin' why Jack kept on hackin' that tree." She slapped her bony knees and threw back her head. "Jack got hisself killed, is what he did. Time they fished him outta that mud, he was caked in it like it was his casket."

Then Lurina settled back in her rocker and folded her hands in her lap, as if she was about to relate another of her dying and burial stories. "This ain't about Jack, though."

Grace raised her hand. "Please, Lurina, not today."

But Lurina would not be stopped. "It's about a huntin' accident. Old Jeb, he lived over in Tennessee, in Laurel Thicket. Jeb knew them woods good as the back of his hand. Nary a soul could figure how he got hisself tangled in a laurel thicket, but he did, and that's how he got hisself shot dead."

Grace remembered that in these mountains folks called rhododendrons laurels, and she knew there were places along forest streams and along gullies where these bushes grew thick and sprawling with tangled branches. How could anyone get into the middle of them?

"Now, Andy Parsons over in Erwin in Tennessee was

out huntin'." She nodded her head. Her eyes were serious. "When he heard the stirrin' and wackin' in them bushes, Andy opened fire. Thought it was a bear. Happened well nigh close to thirty years ago, and those two families ain't talked to one another since."

Before Lurina could tell about Old Jeb's burial, the sharp wail of a siren filled the air. An ambulance tore down Elk Road kicking up gravel as it turned into Loring Valley Road. Less than fifteen minutes later, they watched the ambulance swing back onto Elk Road and dash away toward Asheville.

Hannah hugged herself. "Dread being carried off in an ambulance like that. Wonder who took sick?"

"They ain't never gonna carry me off. I'm gonna die in my bed, just like Pa did," Lurina said. "Maybe when the angel comes for me, I'll see the light just like Pa did afore he passed."

"What if you were in severe pain?" Grace asked Lurina. "Wouldn't you call for help?"

"Nope! They ain't gonna take me to no hospital to die." She looked at them slyly. "There's teas to take for pain," Lurina said. "Ever you wanna know about pain-killin' tea, you just say so. Joseph Elisha and me, we know the old ways."

Hannah dropped Grace off at Bob's apartment. Grace entered, calling, "Bob," and was greeted by the hum of the refrigerator. He's out shopping, she thought, then realized that his car was parked in the driveway. "Bob," she called again. Grace leaned against the wall for support. That ambulance. Impossible. Not Bob. Her mind went blank. Then she noticed the flashing light on the answering machine. With a trembling finger, Grace punched the round gray button on the machine. The deep male voice was unfamiliar.

"Mrs. Singleton," the man said, "I am calling for Bob

Richardson. He's at Mission Memorial Hospital. He'd like you to come immediately." The voice ceased. She heard a click.

"That's it?" Grace demanded of the machine. "No explanation. What happened? How is Bob?" She started to dial Hannah's number, then slammed down the phone, dashed from the apartment, and arrived just as Hannah reversed her wagon out of the driveway and started down the hill. Grace ran, waving her arms and yelling, "Hannah. Hannah!"

The car disappeared around a curve. Grace stood in the middle of the road calling Hannah's name. Tears ran down her cheeks. What would she do? She had not replaced her own car as yet. Stupid! She had never driven Bob's Cherokee. She didn't even know where his keys were.

The sole of Grace's foot hurt. Suddenly she realized that one of her moccasins had vanished. When? And where was it? She searched along the roadside. No moccasin. The pain in her foot increased with every step, and when she arrived at Bob's apartment, to her consternation, the door was locked, and her purse and keys inside. Blood dripped from the cut on her foot. Slumping against the front door of the apartment, Grace sank into a heap on the hard tiles of the entrance stoop, then she wrapped her bandanna around her foot and buried her face in her hands.

As she reversed out of her driveway, Hannah's mind was on Laura and Hank. Earlier that day she noticed that they seemed distant from each other, and that troubled Hannah. Was her daughter feeling guilty for loving someone other than Marvin? Hannah knew what that was like. Several years after Dan Brittan had been killed in a boating accident, she had had an opportunity with a nice country doctor who pursued her. But Hannah could not touch or kiss him without seeing Dan's face. Ultimately she had terminated the relationship and never explained why. If she felt anything, at this stage of her life, it was guilt for not having been honest with the doctor. Being dumped, and never knowing why, could haunt a person for a lifetime. Where was Dr. Frank Ellison now? Was he alive? For a moment she toyed with the idea of trying to find him, to apologize. Did it matter after all this time? Probably not.

Suddenly an awareness of someone running down the hill, her arms waving, came to mind. My God, it was Grace. Gripping the steering wheel, she pulled the station wagon off the road. Wheeling the vehicle about, Hannah took the curves as fast as she dared. Within minutes she reached Bob's apartment, tore from the car, and rushed to Grace, who sat crumpled against the front door.

Grace looked at Hannah with stricken eyes, then relief flooded her face. "It's Bob. A man called from the hospital."

Hannah helped Grace to her feet. "Which hospital?"

"Mission Memorial. When I think that we sat at Lurina's and watched him being carried away. He may be dead! Oh, God, I'm so scared. Hannah, do you think he's dead?"

"Let's listen to the message."

"We can't, Hannah. The door's locked and my keys are inside. I hate myself. I just hate myself."

"Stop it, Grace. Shock can confuse anyone. Get up now, we'll go down to my place and—what's happened to your foot?"

"I cut it."

"Come on. We'll get your foot cleaned up and head for the hospital."

Hannah helped Grace stand. "Where's your other shoe?" she asked.

"I lost it somewhere on the road, but I didn't see it when I came back up here."

They found the moccasin off to the side, about twenty

feet from Bob's apartment, under a shaggy, grayish-colored bush. "You've cut the sole of your foot, and you're bleeding," Hannah said.

Grace grimaced as she slipped her foot into the soft moccasin. "I didn't even feel it at first. Now it hurts like blazes."

Once in her apartment, Hannah cleaned and treated the wound with an antibiotic cream and bandaged it but Grace's moccasin would not accommodate her foot. Hannah dug in her closet and produced a pair of sandals. "May be a bit big for the other foot, but it's better than nothing," she said, handing the sandals to Grace.

The drive into Asheville seemed interminable to Grace. "Can't you go any faster?" she kept asking.

"I'm going sixty-five, ten miles over the speed limit, that's all the police will tolerate. If we get a ticket, it won't get us there faster."

An accident on Highway 240, the bypass north around Asheville, forced them to crawl with traffic. They hardly spoke for fear their frustration would erupt as anger. Twenty minutes later the hospital loomed ahead. "I'll drop you at the front and I'll park," Hannah said.

Grace nodded. Her heart raced. One minute she was hot, the next cold.

Grace entered the hospital, and for a few seconds stood near the entrance confused by the size of the lobby. People entered behind and moved past her. Automatically Grace moved toward the desk in the center of the room, where several volunteers in maroon jackets sat. A gray-haired woman smiled kindly at her.

"Bob Richardson, please," Grace said. "They brought him by ambulance. Someone called me."

The volunteer checked her computer. "You're Mrs. Singleton?"

"Yes, I am."

"There's a note here. Just take that elevator." She pointed to the side and back. "Go to the fifth floor and ask at the desk for Dr. Morris."

"Is Bob, Mr. Richardson, all right?"

"There's only this message, no other information. They'll know more on the floor." She smiled. "You go on up."

Hannah stood beside Grace. "What floor?" she asked.

"Fifth," the woman said. "Ask for Dr. Morris at the desk."

When they left the elevator, the cork floor of the corridor muted their steps. The nurse at the desk asked them to be seated and paged Dr. Morris.

"I'm so scared, Hannah," Grace said.

Another nurse approached them. "Mrs. Singleton?"

Hannah nodded toward Grace.

"I'll take you to Mr. Richardson," she said.

Hannah helped Grace to her feet. In silence, they followed the nurse down the hallway.

The nurse stopped at a door. She turned to them. "Mrs. Singleton only, please."

"I'll wait by the desk, Grace," Hannah said.

The room Grace entered was small, and the bed loomed before her. Behind and alongside it a machine with a computer-like screen blipped and beeped. A tube extended from a bag of fluid on a metal stand down into Bob's arm. Standing at the foot of his bed, Grace felt utterly alone and helpless.

"Bob," she whispered. She crossed her hands over her chest. Her body trembled.

The door opened and a husky, bearded doctor entered. Behind him stood two men in surgical greens with a gurney. The doctor extended his hand to Grace.

"Dr. Morris," he said. "The angiogram showed several severely blocked arteries. We're going to open them up with angioplasties." His voice was deep and reassuring. "This is a pretty routine procedure. He'll be fine. I'm glad you got here. Bob wanted to see you before we got started."

Grace moved to the side of the bed. "Bob."

Bob's eyes fluttered open. "Grace, honey." His speech was slurred, then his eyes closed.

They began to shift Bob from bed to gurney.

Dr. Morris said, "He's sedated. He's going to be fine. Don't you worry."

A moment later they were gone, and Grace walked slowly down the hall to rejoin Hannah.

"They're doing angioplasties on Bob," she told Hannah.

"Better than having bypass surgery," Hannah said.

Grace grated her teeth over her lower lip.

"Seems everyone has had an angiogram or angioplasty these days," said Hannah.

"Who?" Grace asked.

"Tom Findley and Tom Battle, and one of the Herrill boys, I heard," Hannah said.

"Tom Findley? Why don't I know that?

"Because you never want to hear about medical things, people getting sick, so we don't tell you."

"But Bob's never been sick, never had a chest pain. How could this have happened so suddenly?"

"We can't see what's going on inside our bodies," Hannah replied.

"I can't imagine my life without Bob."

"He's going to be fine. From what everyone says, after angioplasty, people feel better than they did before. You had one. Didn't you feel better?"

"My Lord, I forgot. I had only one artery involved. I guess I did feel better, had more energy afterward," Grace said.

An LPN came over and suggested that they might be more comfortable down the hall in the waiting room.

The waiting room was a blessing after the hushed impersonality of the corridors. Grace collapsed into an armchair.

"There's coffee and tea over there," Hannah said. "Want a cup of tea, Grace?"

Grace shook her head. "You get some coffee. It's going to be a long wait."

"We really can't do anything here," Hannah said. "Why not go home?"

"Yes, you're right. Maybe it's best if we go home and wait there." Grace stood. "Give them our number at the desk, Hannah, please."

"They have your number. They already called there, remember?"

"Yes, that's right. They called."

Hannah led Grace to the elevator and out of the hospital, to the small, crowded outdoor lot where she had miraculously found a parking space.

When Grace returned to the hospital the next day, Bob looked well and his eyes were calm. "I'm feeling fine, honey," he said, taking her small hand in his large one. "Just hearing your voice before I went in to have that procedure was a blessing. Glad you got here in time."

"I am, too," Grace said. She hadn't expected Bob to be this upbeat.

"Incredible, what they can do today. My father would have lived many more years if they'd had these advanced techniques," Bob said.

"Your father died of a heart attack?" Grace wondered why they'd never talked about the when and how of their parents' deaths.

"He was forty-nine. Too young to go. My mother re-married several years later. I guess I haven't thought about him much in years."

The nurse said, "Let's keep this visit short. Mr. Richardson needs to rest."

"Of course," Grace said.

Bob squeezed her hand. "I love you, honey."

The nurse's presence inhibited Grace. "Me, too, Bob." She left to join Hannah in the hall.

"How is he?" Hannah asked.

They walked along the corridor, then Grace punched the button for the elevator. "He looks remarkably well, and feels well."

"Imagine that, so soon," Hannah said.

The elevator descended slower than water boils in a watched pot. Grace followed the low humming sounds, the grinding sounds that issued from beyond the walls that encased them. She was never really comfortable in elevators. Now she could not keep away the memories of Ted those last months and her nursing him. Resentment was the emotion she most clearly remembered, mingled with guilt. Their last years together had been years of quiet accepting, and when he became ill, panic followed at the thought of being alone. In the end, in those last months, obligation, not love, carried her through. Would it be that way if she had to take care of Bob?

Never! She loved Bob. But not enough to grant him the one thing he wanted most, to have her move in with him. After all this time, after all his pleas and her re-fusals, would her sense of obligation, and not her choice, grant Bob his wish?

23

TRIALS AND TRIBULATIONS

The elevator settled onto its station on the first floor. The doors eased open to the heat of people waiting to enter. Grace and Hannah pressed their way past them and out into the hallway.

"Why is it that every time I think I've got it all figured out and life's running smoothly, something interferes, makes me have to rethink what I want or need?" Grace asked Hannah as they exited the lobby and stepped into the fading sunshine of a soft evening. To the west among heavy banks of dark gray clouds, a sliver of silver sky, like a slash of lightning, separated the clouds. They were silent as they entered the parking lot, and Hannah concentrated on locating her old station wagon. There it was, sticking out beyond the Volvos, Toyotas, and Tauruses. They settled in and buckled up. Grace noticed Hannah wince as she turned the key in the ignition. "What's the matter?" she asked.

Hannah snapped her hand back and forth as if shaking off a bug. "Hand hurts when I turn the key."

"Does it hurt at any other time?" Grace asked.

"It comes and goes. Initially it felt as if the back of my hand had sustained a blow and the bone was bruised. I had trouble lifting my index finger." Hannah lifted her hand and wiggled her fingers. "That's all I need, now, arthritis in my hand."

"Maybe it's not arthritis. Have you had it checked?"

"Thought I'd start with some over-the-counter medications. See what happens," Hannah said. She opened and closed her hand, stretching out her fingers. "I can do this, and I don't have pain." She pointed to the keys. "It's that closed-fist twisting motion that gets me."

"I think you should go see someone about it," Grace said.

"Who?"

Grace considered a moment. "A hand specialist?"

"Maybe. We'll see."

"Funny, I never feel old. Not until some doctor says, 'Well, you know, Mrs. Singleton, at your age . . .' "

"I know what you mean. I've never had a serious illness, just surgery for my hip and knee. It's a surprise when something hurts, and this hand thing, I don't like it at all. What if I can't use a spade, plant a flower, prune a rosebush? Like a concert pianist having arthritis, being unable to play."

Hannah stepped on the gas, and they shot onto the highway. Grace held her breath until they were safely within the line of traffic. She was never quite sure that some unseen car wouldn't smash into them, especially since Hannah's attitude said, "Driver, look out, I'm coming on in." When Grace had to enter a highway from a feeder lane, she ignored cars beeping behind her and sat there fixed as a boulder until there were absolutely no cars in sight. Only then would she pull onto the road.

Hannah settled into sixty-three miles an hour on Highway 19–23 to Weaverville and Mars Hill. "Can't wait to get into a hot shower," she said.

Immediately Grace imagined soaking in Bob's bathtub.

Bob showered. He tolerated tub soakers. She'd lie in his tub, unable to relax, waiting for the little tap on the door, and then Bob's head would pop in, and he'd ask when she'd be done, and didn't she want to sit on the terrace with him? In the new bathroom she would share with Hannah, the tub would be hers, and Hannah showered in the morning, never at night.

As if reading her mind, Hannah asked. "What are you going to do, Grace? Stay with Bob when we move?"

Grace noted the way Hannah's hands gripped the steering wheel. She weighed her words carefully. "I honestly don't know. Part of me says I owe it to Bob to stay, but it's not what I want to do."

"Bob will never let go of wanting you with him all the time," Hannah said.

Grace's chin lifted. She gave Hannah a defiant look. "Wanting isn't getting."

During the past few weeks Laura had spent more and more nights with Hank. Hannah was alone in the apartment. Having lived alone for much of her life, this should not have fazed Hannah, or so she thought, but it did. To stave off loneliness and depression, Hannah started her day at the office earlier and returned to the apartment later.

And then one afternoon Roger called her at the office. "Any idea when your place will be done?"

"They say by the end of July."

"Darn. Charles and I need a break from the business."

"How soon?"

"Soon as possible. We've been swamped."

"Next week be all right? I'll find another place to stay," Hannah assured him.

That evening, when she and Grace and Amelia were having dinner, she told them about Roger's call.

"I'll call him," Grace said. "Maybe they can go some-where else."

"It's their place; why should they go somewhere else?" Hannah said.

"And Miranda's place," Amelia retorted. "How could Roger do this to you? Surely he knows we have no con-trol over construction."

"Now, wait a minute. Let's not get huffy. Laura's pretty much moved out of the apartment."

"That's as it should be. Laura needs to get on with her life," Amelia said.

Hannah nodded. "True. And I don't think Laura's going to move back into the house with us."

"You think she and Hank . . . ? He's a nice young man," Grace said.

"Max keeps offering me space at his place." Hannah stood abruptly, then stayed behind her chair, her hands on its back, leaning forward. "It'll be all right. Just seems harder to deal with change these days."

"You're right about that," Amelia agreed. "I used to pack and hop a plane at the snap of Thomas's finger. But when I went to New York with Mike for the gallery open-ing of my photographs, I didn't sleep a wink. The bed was hard, the pillows hard." She rolled her eyes. "I missed my down pillows."

"Which you arrange around you in bed like a coffin," Hannah said.

"Do you think that?" Amelia looked surprised. "A cof-fin?" She shook her head. "Not at all. They give me a sense of safely, comfort, and warmth." She smiled. "Sort of like being a child in its crib."

"We do all have our quirks, don't we?" Grace said, changing the subject. "So back to you, Hannah. Where do you want to stay?"

"Miss Lurina and Old Man, maybe. They have a huge old place."

"Ever been in those upstairs bedrooms?" Amelia asked. She pinched her nose with her fingers. "They smell of mothballs or of old age, musty."

"Maybe I'll stay a few days with Ellie Lerner. Heck, that's the last thing I want to do," Hannah said. She turned to Grace, "Why do you think Ellie moved out here anyway? I can't see her living in the country."

"She's lonely, and I think she was captivated by our situation," Grace replied.

"Forget Ellie Lerner. You can share the bedroom here with me," Amelia said. She looked at Grace. "Bob won't mind, will he?"

"Bob's easy."

Hannah looked directly into Grace's eyes. "It may be just you and I, Amelia, when we move back home. Have you decided, Grace?"

"I haven't." Grace wrung her hands and shuffled her feet beneath the table. "I don't know what to do. What if Bob has another heart attack?"

"They cleared his arteries. Isn't that what angioplasty's all about?" Hannah asked.

Amelia's eyes clouded. "Any of us could have an attack of anything, anytime, anywhere. It's the penalty for being alive, isn't it?" Her laugh wore a bitter edge. "Like that verse from the Rubaiyat of Omar Khayyam:

> *"Ah, make the most of what we yet may spend,*
> *Before we too into the Dust descend. . . ."*

"Stop it," Grace said. "We're on edge, all of us. Let's just go about our business and not think about any of this tonight."

* * *

But later, after tossing and turning in the big empty bed, Grace wondered how she would tell Bob that she wanted to move back to the farmhouse. And what would Roger say when he found out? She had gotten closer to Roger this last year, when he confessed his respect for her loyalty and sense of commitment, and explained that when faced with a choice of cheating on Charles, it was her example and her values, instilled in him by her, that dissuaded him. Would he despise her? She couldn't bear that.

Heat spread across Grace's face. For a moment a light breeze caught the blinds at the open bedroom window and rattled them. Still she was roasting. Grace stepped into the living room. The room was warm and welcoming, and its thick carpet filled the spaces between her toes and cushioned her bare feet. Grace crossed the room, flung open the sliding-glass door, and stepped out onto the terrace. A shock of cold tile on the soles of her feet caused her to shudder. Ignoring the discomfort, she stepped to the railing.

There was a complete lack of wind. Bands of mist haunted the valley below, obscuring the villas. For a moment Grace felt weightless and free, as if she were flying high, soaring above the streetlights that in the distance seemed as tiny fireflies casting soft glows, beacons leading one home. Home. Cove Road was home. Grace's fingers found the spaces in the chill ironwork of the railing. Love thrilled, but it could be a tether, and right now she felt hobbled.

24

FEAST OR FAMINE

Grace would remember the days following Bob's home-coming as both wonderful and stressful. Wonderful that Bob looked and felt so well, and stressful in that people arrived at the apartment to visit Bob, and stayed to tell Grace their problems.

Ellie Lerner, who had moved into Molly Lund's house next door to Brenda Tate, appeared first. Once she had inquired about Bob's health, she plunged into a litany of complaints. "You were right about the night sounds, Grace. If I leave my bedroom window open at night, which is one reason I moved out here, the racket is unbearable. Who would have imagined it would be so loud, and so incessant? What's making all that racket?"

"Creatures of the night," Bob said. "Crickets, I imagine, cicadas, frogs, and other critters I might recognize, but whose names I do not know."

"It's much worse than I anticipated," Ellie said.

This is the beginning of her discontent, Grace thought, but she said, "We lived on a heavily trafficked street back in Pennsylvania. At first the cars going by, the horns kept me awake. After a while I didn't hear them. Same when we came here—different sounds, but loud and strange. You'll get used to them."

"Well," Ellie said, "I'll try to get used to them. I don't want to complain about this to the neighbors, don't want them to think I'm a cranky old Yankee."

They laughed, and with that she breezed out of the apartment trailing heady perfume.

"She's really a nice woman," Grace said. "Remember how terrific she was bringing three wedding gowns out for Lurina to try on? I think she's been very lonely since her husband died. She liked us. Maybe she thought she'd become a close part of our lives if she moved out here."

"Probably a mistake her moving to Covington," Bob said.

Grace fixed them each a cup of tea, and when she handed his to Bob, he set it on a table beside his chair, and reached for her hand. "Lord, but it's good to be home, Grace."

"I was so worried, so scared when I got home and you weren't here, and there was that message to come to the hospital," Grace said.

"Don't dwell on that. It turned out fine, didn't it?" He drew her onto his lap.

"Don't," she said, pulling away, starting to rise. "I'm heavy. You might hurt yourself."

"I'm fine. No stitches to pull, no broken bones to mend," he replied, gently easing her back onto his lap. He nuzzled her neck and kissed her eyelids and cheeks. "God, I love you, Grace."

Grace buried her face in his shoulder. Deep within her, passion stirred. That was what was so remarkable. Times like this, she felt seventeen. It was like a shot of adrenaline: She could do and be anything. "I love you, too, Bob. I'm so grateful you're all right." She knew what he wanted, to go to bed, to make love. Love in the afternoon.

She preferred making love at night, a puritanical carry-over from her childhood and the secrecy her mother created about "that sort of thing." And she was frightened for him to exert himself so soon after angioplasty. Surely it was better to wait a week or so.

His hand slid gently across her breast. She wanted to stop him, and she wanted him to continue. The matter was decided when, moments later, the door opened and Amelia entered, lowered her camera bag to the floor, and stood there, her hands at her sides, tears streaming down her face. Grace and Bob pulled apart. Grace braced for a different kind of afternoon.

Amelia seemed unaware that she had interrupted their intimate moment. "Olivia, the little girl from Fighting Deer Creek I told you about a week ago."

Grace remembered. She clambered off Bob's lap and hastened to her friend, circled her shoulders with her arm, and led Amelia to the sofa.

Bob excused himself. "I think I'll go lie down," he said, lifting an eyebrow as he looked at Grace.

Bob wanted her, Grace knew, and she wanted him, but Amelia needed her.

"I've been to see Olivia's mother. Olivia had a serious liver problem. She needed a transplant, but she died before one became available. I cared for that child, Grace. I knew her briefly, yet it seemed as if I knew her forever. I'd taken their pictures, hers and the other children's. Mike went with me to see the child's mother. Her mother was so glad to have Olivia's picture." Amelia's face contorted. Tears trailed along her cheeks and pooled in the corners of her mouth. "It's about Caroline. Will I ever, ever stop grieving for my Caroline? Will every loss, another child, a puppy cause me to come apart like this?"

"Perhaps that's the way grief is. We move past it, or we think we have, and something happens and the old wound opens," Grace said. She'd experienced a nearly forgotten squeezing of her heart when Emily had announced she was pregnant, and Grace worried throughout the nine months, remembering how heartbroken she had been after her own two miscarriages so long ago. That day in the hospital when she held Melissa for the first time, and touched her ten tiny toes and fingers, Grace experienced deep joy, and a sense that her lost daughter, one of the two miscarriages, had been returned to her. She had said a silent prayer of thanksgiving.

"No, I think the pain of loss never really vanishes, just dives out of sight for periods of time, but like a diver, sooner or later, it resurfaces, like now, with Olivia," Grace said.

"I was feeling so much better, happier, and then I came upon those children at that creek. I wish I'd never met them," Amelia muttered.

"No, you don't. This pain you're feeling means you're alive. You care about others, and that's good," Grace said.

"I don't want to care," Amelia replied. She wiped the tears with the back of her hand. Tears gathered again in the corners of her huge blue eyes.

Her eyes are beautiful even when she cries, Grace thought. At seventy she's trim and beautiful, and Grace remembered Lance, and how swept away Amelia had been with him, and how disastrously it had ended. Here they were, three women age seventy and over with busy, full lives, and anticipating moving into a brand-new home. For a moment her own diabetes and Hannah's hand problems came to mind, but she pushed them aside. When the new farmhouse was completed, they would buy new furniture. Hannah would plant gardens. Amelia would hang her photographs. She would cook again. If she moved back home with them. Grace's heart sank.

"I'm going to use Olivia's picture for the cover photo of my new book," Amelia said.

"Won't that make it harder?" Grace asked, glad to think of something else. "Having her on the cover?"

Amelia shrugged. She was silent a moment. "I don't think so." Again her eyes filled with tears. "I'm going to shower now, and then I'll go to Weaverville to Mike's studio. Need anything from the market?"

The next day Bob played nine holes of golf with Martin Hammer.

"Isn't it too soon for golf?" Grace had protested.

"I'll rent a motorized golf cart," Bob promised.

After the marriage of Russell and Emily, Bob and Martin Hammer had become good friends and often followed their golf games with lunch at the club. There was, however, no attempt made to socialize as a foursome that included Grace and Ginger. Loring Valley Clubhouse had been completed, and Ginger, having organized four Scrabble clubs, two in Loring Valley, one at the community center in Mars Hill, and one at the community center in Weaverville, was often referred to around Loring Valley as the high priestess of the game. Ginger had given up trying to involve Hannah, Amelia, or Grace in her activities, and Grace rarely saw her.

It puzzled Grace, however, that Ginger paid so little attention to and spent a minimum of time with her one and only grandchild, Melissa, and she wondered what kind of mother Ginger had been to her daughter, Emily. One day she would ask Emily about her childhood. You could tell a lot about people by what they related of their earliest years, especially their earliest memories.

Her own first memory was a cautionary one. She was about six years old and standing on a steep bank behind her cousins Hank and Sally's home in Dentry. In the gully below, a stream ran shallow in times of drought, exposing the rocky bottom. But after a heavy rain, such as they had had the day before, it raced along, wild and swift, shepherding tree limbs and extraneous debris on its raging bosom.

"I'm going down there and throw rocks in the water," Hank said.

Sally had jumped up and down. "I want to stand in the water and get my feet all wet," she said. Arms flapping wildly, she followed her brother down the slope.

"Don't you kids go down there when that water's high," her uncle had said earlier in his most austere voice and with a scowl. "Or I'll take the hide off of you."

"Come on, Gracie," Hank called up to her.

But Grace had hung back, terrified of disobeying and justifiably so, for her cousins had been yelled at, dragged up the hill, spanked, and grounded after school for three weeks. Caution had paid off, and obedience. Caution became her pattern for years and years, until living with Hannah and Amelia, she had come to realize that she no longer had to react to things and behave as if she were a child. What had been appropriate then was not necessarily appropriate today. She had not flung all caution to the wind, and she was definitely not a physical risk taker. She wouldn't ride the rapids of some river, which everyone was so crazy about doing around here, or drive fast, or cross the street on a yellow light. But she wasn't an old stick-in-the-mud, as Tyler called some of his pals.

Bob's friends continued to phone. It was, Grace thought, as if his angioplasty was a wake-up call: Mike, who was starting to put on a paunch, joined a gym, Russell started walking every day, Martin talked about becoming a vegetarian. Russell or Emily phoned daily, and a new ritual was initiated as Grace and Bob began to have lunch at their home in Mars Hill every Sunday. That delighted Tyler, who never stopped complaining that he hated his new school, and that he did not see enough of his Granny Grace since they had moved.

Mars Hill was home to Mars Hill College and the popular Southern Appalachian Repertory Theater. Green rolling hills sprawled upward from the town. Russell and Emily had purchased an older two-story brick home on three gently rolling acres with a breathtaking view down a long valley and out to layers of mountains. In the afternoon, as haze shifted and settled between the ranges, the effect was that of a Chinese painting. It quite took Grace's breath away, and after lunch, when Tyler and the Richardson men played checkers, and Emily insisted on cleaning up the kitchen alone, Grace retired to the covered porch with Melissa on her lap, until the child grew restless and pushed away to run the length of the porch on chubby legs. Then Grace would turn to her, hold wide her arms, and ask, "Who is Granny's darling?" From the end of the porch a grin spread across Melissa's bright little face. Fastening her eyes on Grace, she would run pell-mell down the length of the porch to fling herself into Grace's outstretched arms.

One afternoon, on their way back to Covington from Mars Hill, Grace said to Bob, "There can be no doubt in that little girl's mind that I love her."

"Nor in Tyler's. That's one of your greatest gifts, my dear." Bob turned slightly to smile at her. "Your ability to love."

And Grace thought, If I am so loving, why do I agonize so about moving in permanently with you?

25

TIME GOES BY

By summer, with its white siding and yellow shutters, its freshly painted front porch, the ladies' farmhouse appeared ready for occupancy. The interior was another matter. They had just taken another tour of the place with Tom assuring them it was going along very well. But they had come to expect delays: Inspectors were late, as were the bathroom countertops. The wrong moldings arrived and were sent back. The drywall finishers for the bedrooms upstairs were delayed. The construction process was exasperatingly slow and emotionally draining.

"Lord," Amelia said, "it wears me out waiting to move in."

"Well, it can't be much longer," Hannah said.

"You're beginning to sound like Tom Findley," Grace said.

"Have you seen those inspectors?" Amelia asked. "They don't give a hoot if we ever move in. They poke at everything, climb into the attic, then they have long chats with Tom, and he stands there nodding, and when they're gone, Tom looks furious."

"It can't be much longer," Hannah repeated.

Grass sprouted all about the house, bringing with it delightful wild white daisies and tiny brilliant yellow flowers. On the damaged side of the great oak, new tender branches reached for light. Grace placed four folding chairs in the shade of the oak. They came, sometimes the three of them, sometimes with Laura or Bob, several afternoons a week after four P.M., after the workmen picked up their tools and departed. It was good to sit beside their home and dream about returning.

Today there were only the three of them, and that was especially pleasant to Grace.

"It's going to be wonderful moving back home," Amelia said. "I don't mind the bedrooms being smaller, do you, Grace? I'd so much rather have the other bathroom."

Grace agreed.

"I think I would have settled for a ranch-style house if you hadn't made such a fuss, Amelia." Hannah poked her arm lightly.

A speculative look crossed Amelia's face. She studied Grace, who leaned back in her chair, folded her arms behind her head, and closed her eyes. "Suppose you had never moved to Branston? What if you were living alone in your house in Dentry? Would you have stayed there?"

"Stayed there?" Grace said softly. She unfolded her arms and raised herself in the chair. "I don't know. Taxes and insurance were going up. Repairs. When I look back, it was a blessing Roger insisting that I move. I didn't think so at the time, of course."

"Ever consider renting a room to some nice woman?" Hannah said. "That would have helped financially."

"Heavens, no, not some stranger in my house," Grace said. Then, quickly, she covered her mouth with her hand.

Hannah leaned forward so fast she nearly toppled the chair. "What are you saying, Grace? If you feel that way, how can we make helpful suggestions to the women writing us about choosing housemates?"

"I never expected that answer from you," Amelia said.

"I'm so sorry. I don't know where that came from," a flustered and blushing Grace replied.

"I do," Hannah said.

"Where?" Grace asked.

"From Mrs. Ted Singleton and Grace whatever-your-maiden-name-was."

"Please, Hannah, Amelia, don't look at me like that. I wouldn't have had the courage to invite anyone in back then. I'd be thinking, How do I know this person won't rob me blind? But it's different now. I'm a different person."

"Of course you are," Hannah said. "We all are. In the last three and a half years we've all changed, and for the better, I'd say."

"But that's a legitimate concern," Amelia said. "How do you know a person is trustworthy, honest, reliable? We were lucky. We knew one another beforehand."

"Which is why it's so hard to know what to write to all those women asking us how to find housemates," Hannah said.

"We're going to have to decide on something," Grace said.

"Come on, let's go wander about our bedrooms again," said Amelia. "You can tell me where you think the bed should go." Amelia rose then, as did Grace, but Hannah sat there. They stared down at her as she worked her fingers, open and closed. "I'm going to have to see a doctor," Hannah said.

Grace bent over and took one of Hannah's hands in hers.

"I'd have them checked sooner rather than later," Amelia said. "Need a hand up?"

"I am perfectly capable of pushing myself up from this chair," Hannah said.

* * *

After waiting for two hours in the waiting room of Dr. Emile Alexander's office, the door to the office opened, and Hannah heard her name called. She'd been resisting walking out by focusing on the fish tank on the far wall. Such tiny goldfish. She was certain they were as unhappy as she. Hannah followed the nurse into the office and into Room 4, where she waited another ten minutes. By the time Dr. Alexander entered, Hannah was annoyed and resentful.

"Sorry to keep you waiting," he said.

Sorry? Like hell you're sorry, Hannah thought. Then, at his direction, she placed her right hand palm up on the table and explained about the sore feeling, the ache when she lifted her middle finger, the pain in her little finger when she squeezed or twisted anything.

"Are you right-handed?" he asked.

"Yes, I am."

Now he was poking at the pockets of flesh on her palm just below her fingers. "Does this hurt?"

"Ouch," Hannah said.

"Thought so," he commented. He sat back.

"Let's get X rays." He opened the door and beckoned a tall, solemn-faced nurse.

Doesn't anyone in here smile? Hannah wondered as she followed the woman down the hall and around a corner.

"How long does it take to develop X rays?" Hannah asked when they were finished.

"Couple of minutes," the woman said, and pointed the way back to Room 4, where Hannah waited another twenty minutes.

When Dr. Alexander reentered the room, he carried an envelope containing the X rays, and slapped them onto the brightly lit board alongside the desk. Hannah saw her bones, long, slender, no knobby joints as she expected.

"Fingers look good. No enlarged joints. No sign of arthritis."

"So, what have I got?" Hannah asked.

"You've got stenosing tenosynovitis, commonly known as trigger finger,"

"Isn't that where your finger locks up on you?" she asked. "I don't have that."

He took her hand, palm up again, and pressed on the pads beneath her fingers. "Feel here," he said.

Hannah placed her finger on the spot.

"Now close and open your fingers," he directed.

She complied. Something moved beneath her fingertips.

"Feel the movement?" he asked.

"I think so. I'm not sure."

"Well, it's there," the doctor said with utmost assurance. "There are pulleys and tendons in your hand that bend your fingers. The pulleys form a tunnel under which the tendons must glide. Trigger finger happens when the tendon develops a swelling or a nodule, like you've got. When the tendon swells, it must squeeze through the opening of the tunnel, and that's what causes pain, inflammation, and more swelling."

"If you say so," Hannah muttered. "So what will help it?"

"A shot of cortisone."

"Cortisone?" She shook her head.

"You could try anti-inflammatory pills, like ibuprofen, but if you want immediate relief, cortisone's the best way," Dr. Alexander replied.

Hannah hesitated. She felt suddenly cold. A bead of perspiration formed above her lip. She must decide now, this minute, to either have the shot or walk out of the office. But if she had to come back, another two-hour wait?

Hannah squared her shoulders. "Okay, let's do it." She extended her palm.

The doctor rose, left the room, and returned moments later with two syringes and two needles, one short and fine, the other nearly as long as her finger. He dabbed the fleshy puff under her fingers with an iodine substance, then inserted the tiny needle.

"This will numb the area," he said.

"Before the big assault," Hannah muttered. She fixed her eyes on a place on the wall behind his head. The cortisone shot hurt, and hurt some more. It hurt, and when it was over, all the fingers of her hand grew numb.

"Go on taking anti-inflammatories, morning and evening, with food. Come see me in a month," he said.

All that night her fingers remained numb, and all the next day her fingertips tingled, but the pain was gone.

26

ALTERNATIVES

The next day was Friday, and all morning, people were coming and going to and from Hannah's office at Bella's Park. MaryAnn dashed in, dabbing at her eyes with a handkerchief. "My brother just called. Mom's been taken to the hospital. She fell, broke her hip. I have to go home. Please, Mrs. Parrish, will you tell Mr. Maxwell for me? I need to hit the road before rush hour." MaryAnn ran her hands through her golden hair. "Will you tell him, please?"

Hannah waved her out the door. "I hope your mother will be all right. I'll tell Mr. Maxwell. Drive carefully, now."

Moments later Hannah's foreman arrived. "The new path into the woods turns out to be over fifty feet. I curved it twice. The plan called for one curve." He spread the smudged and wrinkled landscape plan on her desk.

She smoothed its edges and leaned over it. "It will look wonderful with two curves."

He rolled the print, tucked it under his arm, and departed.

Hank and Laura sauntered in all smiles and holding hands. Hank's hair was, as usual, rumpled and out of place, as was his shirt. Appearances. What did they really matter? Hank was, without a doubt, a kind and thoughtful man. A good man. Hannah was pleased with her daughter's choice.

"We've found a charming little bungalow on the road to Mars Hill," Laura said. "I'll have all my things out of the apartment by this evening."

"If it goes as we hope," Hank said, "we'll be married by the end of summer."

She'd miss Laura. Things had been tense between them since the fire, and then living so close, just the two of them, in the apartment. But it seemed to Hannah that their relationship had softened and lightened since Laura fell in love with Hank.

When her daughters were babies, Hannah envisioned being close to them as they grew older, close in ways impossible with her own distant and "stiff upper lip" mother. She anticipated being an intimate part of her daughters' lives. She even believed the old adage: *"A son is a son till he gets him a wife; a daughter's a daughter for all of her life."* But it hadn't worked that way. Never enough time. Being sole parent and breadwinner had left her exhausted at the end of a day, and easily provoked to anger and sharp words.

Miranda came to mind. They were closer now that they no longer lived near each other. Were they closer because of the distance? No, Hannah said to herself. It's because we talk to each other now, say things unsaid for all those years, like "I respect you," or "admire you," or a simple "I love you." Although never quite comfortable with touchy-feely stuff, Hannah was better these days at showing affection. Reaching out, she hugged Laura and Hank. "I'm so happy for you both." For a moment her hand stroked her daughter's cheek. "Be kind to each other."

Laura's hand covered her mother's. Lifting it to her lips, she kissed it. "Thank you, Mother, for all your patience. I've been a pill, and I'm sorry."

When they walked from her office, Hannah sank into her chair and turned it toward the window. Laura had looked at her with love and tenderness. For a moment Hannah forgot how tired she was: tired of living out of a suitcase, of not having a rocker or even a recliner that suited her long legs, tired of sleeping in a bed she had not chosen, tired of a view of mountains that seemed to block her in. Her mind trailed from Laura to Roger and Charles. She could move in and share the bedroom with Amelia, but she hated the perfume smells and scented soaps. It seemed the alternatives all carried a caveat.

Outside her window, gently rolling hillsides spilled from higher mountains; the woods seemed to beckon her. A tiny creature, dark brown with a darker stripe down its back, scurried across the flagstone paving, drawing her attention. The door behind her swung open. Hannah heard Max's breathing, heavy from a brisk walk. She smelled the morning dew on his clothes and arms and the musk of his aftershave. He sat in a chair across from her desk, and she imagined him stretching out his long legs. She turned her chair to face him.

His first words, repeated daily since she had told him about Roger's call, came almost as a plea: "Stay at my place, Hannah. Two big, empty bedrooms."

Repeating a gesture, grown familiar to them both, she waved away the idea and shook her head. "Zachary might come home. Didn't he write you that he'd arrive and surprise you? I don't want to be his surprise."

"I don't build my life around Zachary," Max said. "He went off after his mother died, and God knows what part of the world he's in now."

"Kind of wonderful, though, to be so adventurous and young enough to plunge ahead, not knowing where the next wind will take you," Hannah said. "When he comes home, he'll probably be ready to settle down. What do you hear from him?"

"Last month his letter was postmarked Delhi. Now, that's the end of the world."

"Well, one day when you least expect him, he'll walk in the door," she replied, "and you'll be glad to be alone together, to get to know your son again." Hannah pushed her chair back from her desk and crossed her legs. "But seriously, Max, I wouldn't feel comfortable staying at your house, with or without your son."

"What are you afraid of, Hannah?" He pulled a chair close to her desk. "I'm not going to attack you."

She studied him, smiled, uncrossed her legs, and leaned forward. They'd been sublimating feelings for each other for a long time. "Maybe"—she swallowed hard—"maybe I'd attack you." And then Hannah blushed and looked away, ashamed at her forwardness, but not before she noted the momentary flicker of his eyes, the way he drew back slightly in his chair. Her heart sank. She had made a fool of herself. Seeing his apprehension, however tentative, Hannah felt hurt. She crossed her arms about her chest.

"I've talked to Ellie Lerner. I'm moving in with her until our place is ready."

Max rose. He towered over Hannah's desk. She felt his loneliness and for a moment wondered how long it would be until he found a companion, if not a wife. Hannah stifled the urge to get up and go to him.

"As you like," he said. His voice lost its softness and became professional. "I'll see you later. Maybe we can walk up the hill and see how the Covington Homestead's coming along. That daughter of yours is doing one hell of a fine job."

"Sure," Hannah replied.

Burying herself in work, she forgot about their walk to the homestead until late afternoon when he stood in her doorway. "Ready?" he asked. He held the door wide, avoiding contact with her as she hastened past him. Their footsteps echoed in the empty reception room. Briskly they moved to the rear exit door, and out onto the flag-stone patio. Across green fields they lengthened their strides as the land rose gently to a place from where they could see the worn gray shingles of an 1880s homestead gleaming silver in the afternoon sun.

"All the wood used in the reconstruction came from hundred-year-old barns and tumbledown cottages your daughter found. How she located them, I'll never know, but find them she did."

His praise of Laura gratified her.

On the porch of the smaller of the two log cabins, they sat on a bench fashioned from the trunk of a tree. It had been sanded smooth and the grain of the wood created a dark V surrounded by lighter wood. Close by, men split wood for a rail fence.

"Sheep pen," Max said. "They're getting ready to build a sheep pen." He extended his hand. "Come see the inside of the cabin."

The walls of the single room were chinked with red clay. It housed the kitchen, work, and sleeping areas. A large iron pot, black as the belly of a cave, hung over a blackened hearth. To one side, four cane-bottom chairs surrounded a plank table, and from the walls hung ladles, pots, a broom made from rushes. A butter churn and a small three-legged stool sat solidly near a wall. Hannah had the sense of a woman bending to her task, making butter. A rough-carved wooden bowl filled with eggs sat in the center of the table.

"Guinea hen eggs," Max said, picking one up and heft-ing it in his palm as if weighing it. "Guineas are prolific egg layers. We bought two dozen hens. I tell the men to help themselves to the eggs. No sense wasting good eggs."

The bed, at the other end of the room, with its oak foot-
and headboards streaked from a lifetime of scrubbing,
looked oddly out of place. An oft-washed quilt covered
the husk mattress and jammed against the foot of the bed
folded quilts topped a gouged and scarred wooden chest,
which served as storage for clothing. From pegs on the
wall hung a pair of stiff blue overalls, a blacksmith's
leather apron, a woman's Sunday bonnet with bits of lace
to tie beneath her chin, and a pair of high-top boots held
together by their laces. Max walked over to the boots.
"Laces made from goat hide. Laura's had luck finding
old-timers who remember how to do these things."

A miniature bed, replete with cornhusk doll, sat alongside the larger bed, indicating that long ago a little girl
lived here. "Laura suggested we hire historical inter-
preters for a couple of hours on Saturday afternoons all
summer. She's interviewing staff now."

As a child, Laura had been organized and excellent at
tracking down information when she needed it. Children,
Hannah thought, were born with innate skills and abili-
ties, which they would use for a lifetime.

Max had walked on ahead, and Hannah hurried to
catch up with him as he headed toward a small one-room
structure. "Laura didn't miss a thing." He pointed out the
corncrib, the smokehouse. "Hogs were a major source of
food, you know. Folks used all parts of a hog. Smoked the
meat over hickory wood so it lasted all winter."

"How do you know all this?" Hannah asked

"Laura. Harold Tate left an oral record, which Molly
shared with her, and she's gotten hold of the Foxfire
books. They do a great job of preserving the past."

From somewhere a sheep bleated. Max said, "Did you
know the settlers only ate male baby sheep?" He winked
at her. "Practical. Only needed a couple of rams to service the herd."

Hannah turned her attention to the loom house. Pegs on the walls housed spindles of carded wool waiting to be threaded onto the loom to be woven into jackets, skirts, and pants. She pictured the spinner bent over the spinning wheel, or throwing the shuttle across the threaded loom, which stood silent nearby.

Max motioned and they walked on past neatly tilled patches of vegetable and flower gardens, past the sheep-sheering pen, to the second log cabin, which was larger than the first, for it had two stories and long, narrow windows upstairs and an exterior staircase leading to the sleeping rooms. The floors of both log houses were made of planked wood and raised above the ground on stone pilings. Hannah noticed that nothing was wasted. The exterior porch walls were lined with hooks holding shearing tools, shoemakers' tools, blacksmith tools. Tags underneath identified each tool and its use.

"It's splendid what's been done here," Max said. "This homestead's about finished, your gardens are ready to open to the public. We have to talk about an opening date, Hannah."

"How about the end of June?"

"Or just after the Fourth of July, or if we wanted to do fireworks, the Fourth itself." Max slapped the side of his thigh. "God, Bella would be thrilled with all this."

"I'm sure she would," Hannah replied. "It's what she would have liked to see happen to this land. She'd be so proud that you did this for her."

"Not only for her, Hannah," Max said. He looked pointedly into Hannah's blue eyes. She looked away. Then, lost in their own thoughts, and without another word spoken, they retraced their steps across the grass to the office.

The lowering sun cast long, cool shadows across heat-doused fields. Hannah thought of Amelia and how she talked about photographing the soft shadows of afternoon, and she wondered where Amelia was today. Mike had mentioned that since Olivia's death, Amelia photographed with wild abandon, in direct contrast to her usual gentle approach to photography, one that kept her glued to one spot for an undetermined amount of time waiting for the right light, the right shadows.

Mike had also said that recently he found it difficult to keep up with Amelia, and she was fifteen years his senior. "She never stops moving, and her work's changing. It's darker, more dramatic, it asks questions where before her photographs were more sentimental, the kind of scene that stirred a sense of peace, or brought tears to your eyes."

"Grace and I haven't seen any of her new work," Hannah had replied.

"I think she's embarrassed by the change," Mike said. "It's something I don't believe she's integrated. I develop a photo, and she stares at it as if it were someone else's work." He tossed his head and smiled. His teeth shone as if he'd had them whitened. He scratched the side of his jaw. "You know, transitions are exciting, especially in art," Mike said. "They're going to show her new work in New York."

Hannah had been pondering that word, *transition,* ever since. Now she said to Max. "Do you ever think about the ways in which people handle change?"

"Not easily, it seems to me," he said.

"You wouldn't think, at our ages, after all we've seen and been through, that a fire in which no one was injured would create such a sense of confusion, and that the effects of it would linger in so many ways. Is it harder? I wonder," Hannah asked, "which is worse, do you think, a major change imposed on you, or a change initiated by you?"

"I think you feel more in control when you've started things in motion," Max said.

But Hannah wasn't sure this was true. She had planned to and finally fled from her abusive husband with two small girls, and the trauma of it, the fears, and the adjustments required had been formidable. The event, so long ago, seemed to have left permanent scars on herself and her daughters. She trusted men when she married Bill Parrish. His abuse left her disillusioned with men until she'd met Dan Brittan. She trusted Dan, but that was probably silly, for had he lived, he would probably never have left his wife. She didn't want to get into her past with Max, so she said, "It's the process of coming to terms with change that interests me. It is a process, and it takes time."

"I understand that," he replied, stopping to move a fallen branch from their path.

"It causes people to reevaluate their lives: what they really want, who they really are. Each of us handles the process differently."

"Amelia least well, I imagine," he said, extending his hand to help her across a small gully that heavy rains had forged where a tractor left ruts in the pasture. "Got to get this filled in," he muttered.

Hannah looked at him. He tolerated Amelia, she knew that. She accepted his hand, stepped wide across the depression in the earth, and released his hand. "No," she replied, "oddly enough Amelia coped by withdrawing. This was not necessarily bad. It scared us, but she needed that time to heal and gain a perspective on her old fears. She needed a plateau, a place to rest a while."

"Who, then?" he asked.

"Grace, oddly. I watch her. She's continually struggling with what's right and wrong, the honorable thing, and you know, Bob never eases up the pressure on her to move in permanently with him. She sleeps most nights on the couch because he tosses around so much. I'd have to say this transition time is hardest for her. She may not move back into the house with us, not after Bob's angioplasty." Exasperation was obvious on Hannah's face. She knew it. Did not know how to control it. "Doesn't she realize that any one of us could be stricken with anything at a time when we are alone somewhere?"

"I guess she feels a commitment to Bob," he replied.

Hannah wanted to say, What about her commitment to us, to the lifestyle we have developed? Instead she said, "But it's not what Grace wants to do. What matters most? What she wants or what Bob wants?"

Max stared at her pointedly. "Sometimes we do what we feel we have to whether we want to or not. Life keeps handing us challenges."

"Problems, I'd say, one after the other, small and large, it's always something."

"I can't look at them as problems. It's easier if I consider them challenges. I guess if you expect life to run smoothly, it's harder."

"Expectations. Yes. We do get trapped in our expectations about how things ought to be."

"Guess I wised up years ago, when I realized that Bella wasn't going to fit in in Covington, no matter what I suggested she do with or say to the neighbors." He stopped. Hannah stepped to the side to avoid bumping into him.

"Sorry," Max said, picking up his pace. "I had this idea we'd integrate into the community, join the church, be social with everyone. Bella would have none of it. It was going to be her way or no way. She left once, went home to her family in Atlanta. That's when I knew I'd rather have Bella as she was than be a part of the local community."

"It's hard when people want different things, like Bob and Grace."

"Or like you not using the extra rooms in my house," he said, looking at her out of the corner of his eye and grinning.

"Well, maybe if I can't find a place to roost," she said.

27

FOUR'S A CROWD

Back in the office Max asked, "Want to go into Asheville and have a leisurely dinner at some nice restaurant? Maybe take in a movie?"

Hannah thought of the empty apartment she would go home to. Still she shook her head. His invitation sounded too much like a date, and much as she would have enjoyed such an evening, it was important, she felt, to maintain a professional relationship. "Don't feel like a trip to Asheville. I have some things to finish up here."

"All work and no play . . ." he said.

Hannah waved him away. "I know." She rounded her desk. "I'll be here maybe a half hour. I'll lock up."

When he was gone, Hannah pulled a sheet of writing paper from her desk. She had never been one for writing. She could weave the words in her mind, words of affection, words of description, but when she tried to put her thoughts on paper, they whirled away tangled in a great swirl of wind.

Her letterhead read *The Gardens of Covington* and beneath in dark, raised letters, HANNAH PARRISH, DIRECTOR. Hannah smoothed the sheet of paper.

Sometimes it all seemed a dream that at seventy-five she would be in charge of a major creative endeavor. A last hoorah. Her swan song.

"Why do people keep saying 'swan song'?" she'd asked Grace once last year, when Amelia was off with Lance, and they were alone having tea.

"It's a romantic concept, I guess," Grace replied, "I looked it up once in a dictionary of the origin of words and phrases. 'Kept alive by Shakespeare, Coleridge, and Spenser,' it said."

Hannah turned her attention to the letter. Why write? She would call Roger. Her hand settled on the phone, then pulled back, and she picked up the pen. She wasn't in the mood for chatting, and if Charles answered, he'd want to chat. The note was brief, devoid of prating, or of indebtedness, though she was deeply grateful.

Dear Roger and Charles, Thank you very much for the use of your apartment. It was a blessing. I shall be moving out tomorrow.

She paused, pen poised, and turned her chair to look out of the window.

It was growing darker; exterior lights switched on automatically. Light pooled on flagstones on the patio. Her stomach rumbled. It was eight o'clock. She had been here longer than a half hour.

Looking forward to seeing you and Charles. Fondly, Hannah.

Hannah signed the letter, sealed and stamped it, then studied the one she had begun to her grandson, Sammy, the formerly irascible teenager who, at twenty-one, graduated with honors from college, turned into a pillar of respectability, and was now dating the mayor of Branston's daughter.

A knock on the front door of the building startled Hannah. Switching on lights, Hannah moved across the reception area. Peering though the peephole, she was surprised to see Ellie Lerner. When she had told Max that she was moving in with Ellie, she had not been telling the truth. She had never mentioned it to the woman, nor did she really want to live with Ellie.

"I ran into Max. He told me you might be here." Ellie Lerner looked as if she'd stepped out of an L.L.Bean catalog with her crisp tailored shirt, chino slacks, and her hair slicked back and twisted into a knot. Hannah thought of Ellie's elegant bridal shop in Asheville and wondered what had motivated the woman to rent Molly Lund's house and move to the country, a good thirty-five or forty minutes' commute from the city.

"Got a minute?" Ellie asked.

"Sure." Hannah waved her inside and locked the door behind them.

"It's late. Have you eaten?" Ellie asked. "I haven't. Can I take you to dinner?"

Grace and Bob were baby-sitting at Russell and Emily's, and Amelia was in Asheville with Mike at a concert at the Diana Wortham Theater. Hannah thought of the empty apartment. "Dutch treat, okay?" Hannah asked.

"I invited you," Ellie protested. "Athens Restaurant in Weaverville, okay? I don't feel like driving back into Asheville."

"Yes, that's fine, I won't have to stop and change my clothes, and it's Dutch treat." She would mail the letter to Roger at the new post office in Weaverville, which was just down the road from the Athens Restaurant.

Ellie said, "I'll be glad to drive."

Hannah was happy to have her drive. Ellie's BMW was more reliable than her own old station wagon, which had been coughing and sputtering of late.

As they proceeded down Cove Road, Velma Herrill's

new Subaru turned into her brand-new driveway, and they waved.

"They've moved back in," Hannah said. "Wish I could say the same for us." She missed their farmhouse. The old house had character, and challenges: broken water pipes, ancient fuse boxes, ubiquitous drafts, standing in the hall waiting to use their one bathroom, creaking floorboards, possums living inside the walls. The old house had given herself, Grace, and Amelia a new sense of identity, as if they were, like their ancestors had once been, pioneers. You couldn't be a pioneer in a modern new house, now, could you? "With all the construction on Cove Road, it's beginning to feel like a new development," Hannah said.

"I don't think so," Ellie replied. "The houses look the same to me."

Hannah did not share her thoughts, but she worried that their new farmhouse, so modern, so well insulated that there would be no room for possums inside the walls, would be sterile, not as cozy and welcoming as the old one had been. Expectations. Give them up. Stop thinking like this, she warned herself. It's gone. Stop looking back.

Brenda, her arm about her younger grandson, sat rocking on the swing on the porch of her home. The porch light cast a halo around them. They waved as Ellie's BMW rolled past. Lights inside the church illuminated the single stained-glass window over the front door. Stained-glass windows always reminded Hannah of the Catholic Church where she had gone to admonish and rail against God after Dan Brittan's death. She had left that church, and stood outside wanting to throw rocks, to smash those windows.

A slick black van, which Hannah did not recognize, sat in Max's driveway, and the front door of the house stood ajar. Could Zachary have returned? And who was that woman in an Indian sari stepping out of the house onto the porch?

They turned the corner onto Elk Road. "I was crazy about my husband," Ellie said suddenly. "When he died of a heart attack, I was inconsolable. I hated the way people didn't know what to say to me, or what to do. They couldn't look me in the eye. It was awful, their embarrassment, their clumsy, well-intended condolences. God, that was a terrible time."

"How long ago did he pass away?" Hannah asked.

"Four years, now."

"It's true what you say. Many people don't know what to do or say when a friend or relative has a great loss." Hannah's eyes checked the cars lined up for gas at the gas station, which hadn't changed one iota since they had come to Covington. It stood there, barely off the road, with its old gas pump slightly tipped to one side, its dilapidated screen door, its unpainted roof.

"Someday," Ellie said, "someone's going to build a new station and put this eyesore out of business."

Regret swept through Hannah. The weatherworn station and mini food store had a certain charm; it made a statement about the quality of things rather than appearances. Over the years they had run to this odd little store for a jar of peanut butter, a gallon of milk, butter, or a video movie for a rainy night, and Buddy Herrill would be there, smiling, opening the door, welcoming them, chatting, and offering tidbits of news about this one's grandmother in Atlanta, or someone's child winning a track meet. It was also the gathering spot for the older men in the community. What was odd and incongruous was Ellie Lerner, from New York City, choosing to live in rural Covington. Suddenly Hannah regretted saying yes to dinner. "Why did you move way out here, Ellie?" she asked.

"A dream, I guess. I wanted it to be like it is with you ladies."

"You won't get that living alone," Hannah replied. There was something pathetic about Ellie, a successful businesswoman, and so restless, it seemed to Hannah, and so lonely. Hadn't she made friends in Asheville over the years she had lived there?

"I thought once I had the house, other women would want to move in for the companionship," Ellie said. "I even took an ad in the newspaper. I've had a few calls, but no one sounded right."

"What would 'right' be?"

They entered the highway, and Ellie set cruise control at sixty-five. The Forks of Ivy, Barnardsville, then the Flat Creek exits flew by. They got off onto Monticello Road, where Hannah came to buy perennials at Reems Creek Valley Nursery, and mulch and pavers at the Feed and Seed next door. This set Hannah thinking about her new garden she would create at their new home, about the beds of annuals, zinnias, marigolds, salvias, and cosmos planted along with hardy perennials. Wayne would help prepare the new beds. He was at the technical college now, studying horticulture, but their lives had come together, braided, unbraided, and remained connected at the roots, like family.

"What would be 'right'?" Ellie said, interrupting Hannah's mental landscaping. "Well, I guess I'd like someone who enjoyed the things I do, theater, eating out, shopping. A nonsmoker, heavens, not a smoker."

"Let's see, Amelia loves theater, enjoys eating out once a week or so, and hates to shop. Grace hates shopping, doesn't care one way or the other about theater, and prefers to eat at home, and I definitely prefer to eat and be at home."

"But the life you have together seems so warm and caring and—"

"It didn't happen overnight. We found ourselves in that boardinghouse in Pennsylvania feeling as if we'd come to the end of the road. I never stop being grateful to Amelia's cousin for leaving her the old farmhouse."

"They must have been very close."

"Actually, Amelia never knew him. He found her through genealogy. She turned out to be his only living relative. But we'd had a year living in the same house, getting to know one another. We knew it wouldn't be perfect, but we were willing to take a chance on one another."

"Did you have problems?" Ellie asked.

"Certainly. It wasn't always easy. For one thing, initially, Amelia's helplessness irritated me."

"I never think of her as being helpless."

"She's undergone a miraculous transformation in the last few years," Hannah said, remembering Amelia's difficulty learning the mechanics of photography, and her obsessive guilt at her own success when she began to sell her work.

"But you got along with her, right?"

Hannah sighed. "It's funny, when you move from friend to FRIEND, it's because your feelings change. You know the person's good and bad points, and you've come to accept them. That's what makes a person a FRIEND. Acceptance! You cross a line in your mind, and affirm rather than critique them. They just are who they are and you take them that way."

"Sounds so complicated. It must take so much time," Ellie said. "I guess I'll never find the perfect housemate."

They reached the post office. "Depends on how much you're willing to put into it," Hannah replied, handing Ellie her letter to slide into the slot of the drive-up mailbox.

* * *

The Athens Restaurant was decidedly a family-oriented place with its blue-and-white check tablecloths. The waitress, Polly, whom Hannah had come to know and like, seated them in a booth in the back, Hannah's preferred seating. Ellie ordered a vegetable pizza, and Hannah chose chicken gyro and a Greek salad. Hannah recognized several women at another table, women who worked at the plant nursery, and greeted them.

"You know so many people," Ellie said.

"Don't you run into people you know in Asheville?" Hannah asked.

"Not often. Asheville's a changing city, people move in and out, or they have their own little clique and pretty much stay with them."

For whatever reason, Ellie Lerner did not feel integrated into her community, and Hannah wasn't about to pursue the matter. Ellie Lerner exhausted her, for she chatted on and on about how much older women were when they married these days, and how hard it was to find and keep good help at the bridal shop. What Hannah wanted was to finish their meal and return to the apartment to pack.

When they had eaten and the waitress brought their check, Ellie blurted out, "What if I moved in with you, and Grace, and Amelia? You have another bedroom, and your daughter won't be with you."

The idea stunned Hannah, set her mind spinning around the "no" she wanted to shout. "Well, I'm not sure. That's certainly not something I can decide alone."

Ellie's hand shot across the table and grabbed the check. "You will talk to the others?"

Firmly but gently Hannah removed the check from Ellie's hand, took a ten-dollar bill from her purse, and handed it, and the check, back to her. "Now you can take care of this."

"You'll ask them about my living with all of you?" Ellie pleaded. Her fingers squeezed the money and check.

"I'll ask Amelia and Grace," Hannah said. She knew that she would never move in, even temporarily, with Ellie. It would be preferable to move into Bob's apartment and share a room with Amelia.

Back at the apartment Hannah began to pack and considered how quickly one's worldly goods could be reduced to three small boxes. She showered, changed into pajamas and a bathrobe, slipped her feet into her slippers, and strode out onto the terrace. Evening brought cool, sometimes chilly temperatures, and Hannah pulled her fleece robe tighter about her and settled into a chair.

So much to consider: Max's repeated invitation. Bob pressuring Grace to stay with him. Why didn't the two men move in together? They could live at Max's. Anna could cook for them and take care of them. Hannah smiled, thinking of all those letters women had written asking the ladies how they worked out living arrangements, assigned tasks, handled differences. The big question was, of course, How could they find compatible housemates?

Grace and Amelia acknowledged the letters with cards, but they had all been too frayed and stressed to sit down and determine what, or if, they would make specific recommendations to the women. Soon they would have to discuss this, but there was so much to do, to consider. Hannah clasped her head in her hands. And now, of all the annoying things, Ellie wanted to move in with them.

It was not that Hannah disliked Ellie. She just didn't particularly enjoy her company. Ellie was too needy, too much on edge. On the other hand, Hannah reminded herself, she'd been totally turned off by Amelia when she'd first seen her standing in Olive Pruitt's foyer in that white linen ensemble with a hat, and that silk scarf settled with studied casualness about her neck. Pretentious! Hannah retreated to her room. But then, gradually, as they lived together, Hannah had grown accustomed to Amelia. Yet it had not been until that day under the great oak tree, when they first visited Covington, and Amelia told them about her daughter and husband's deaths and her breakdown and hospitalization, that Amelia became a real person to Hannah.

Hannah sighed. She'd have to pass along Ellie's request to Amelia and Grace. No way to avoid that. Ellie would ask Grace, and they'd have to present a united front. Hannah realized her toes were cold. She should go in, but, well, it was such a star-studded night. Often it was too hazy to see the stars. Tonight they glittered as clear and crisp as she remembered them from her childhood before the veil of pollution shut out the night sky. One of her happiest childhood memories centered on a summer camp experience and a star-spangled sky that left little space for darkness. Tyler, Hannah thought, and the baby, Melissa Grace, would never know the night sky as she had known it, not if they lived near a city on the East Coast of America. Sad. Ah, well.

Hannah pushed herself up from the chair. Tomorrow she would clean the apartment thoroughly, stifle her consternation at having to vacate the place, and move in with Amelia. How, with her long legs and arms, she would ever sleep in a twin-size bed, she did not know. How she would tolerate Grace running around trying to satisfy every unspoken need of Bob's, she did not know.

28

CHANGING ROOMS

Amelia's presence pervaded her bedroom. The warm, dark wood of the dresser top vanished under a plethora of lipsticks, powders, other cosmetics, bottles of toilet water and cologne, combs and brushes, wadded clumps of netting that Amelia slipped over her head at night to assure that every stand of hair remained in place. Slacks and a long-sleeved blouse dangled over the back of a chair. Amelia's shoes were more or less lined up alongside her bed, the side facing the bed Hannah would use.

"They're over there so I don't stumble over them," Amelia explained.

Hannah said not a word. So, what about me stumbling? she thought. But it was, after all, Amelia's room. In the bathroom Hannah stared at the dizzying array of scented soaps, lavender body scrub, loofahs, hair and body sprays, shampoos, and conditioners. She remembered, now, why she never visited Amelia in her room in the old farmhouse.

"You're going to have to leave off the perfume," Hannah told Amelia when she agreed to move in with her. "Just for this little while. It makes me sick."

An exasperated Amelia huffed, "This is all just too much for me." Scowling, she lifted each bottle of eau de cologne, as if it were a precious jewel, from the dresser top and placed it in a drawer.

Now, as Hannah stood in the doorway of the room, anger rose in her, anger at the fire that relegated her to such a vulnerable position, anger at Roger for wanting the apartment at this time, anger at Amelia, well, for just being Amelia. "You could move in with Ellie Lerner. She's powdered and scented, just like you are," Hannah said, and was about to stalk from the room when Grace appeared in the doorway.

"You two arguing?" Grace asked. She kept her voice light, with a touch of humor. "It won't be much longer, and we'll all be back in our own rooms in our own home." She remembered reading of an experiment where scientists increased the rat population in a cage with the result that formerly docile rats turned against one another and newcomers.

Hannah stalked from the room, ignoring Grace.

"Everyone thinks I'm prissy. Well, what about her?" Amelia asked. Her hands were firmly planted on her hips, and she challenged Grace with her eyes.

"We're all stressed out, and it's affecting our tempers. We've all overreacted at one time or another these last few months," Grace said. "Is there any way I can help you?"

"Sure, you can ask Bob to go stay at his son's, and Hannah can share his room with you." With a toss of her head Amelia flounced into the bathroom and slammed the door behind her.

The weight of the world settled on Grace's shoulders. Her nerves were frayed. She wanted to scream. Everyone's temper, it seemed, escalated daily, and would soon register a seven on the Richter scale, and she was expected to function as peacemaker. She was tired of that role, bone-weary tired. Without another word Grace left the apartment and got into her new Camry. Within minutes Grace reached the valley. Once on Elk Road she debated continuing into Weaverville, or maybe Asheville— it might distract her to roam the mall. Instead, without thinking, she turned onto the dirt road leading to Lurina's farmhouse. A cup of tea, rocking on the porch would be soothing, and it didn't matter if Lurina talked nonstop about old times or burials; that at least was familiar and asked nothing of her but to sit quietly and nod occasionally.

"I'm tickled pink to see you," Lurina welcomed her. "Come and set a while. Porch would be nice. Ain't no clouds about."

A short while later, with a cup of tea in their hands, they settled into two squeaky rockers on the porch, and for a time only the grind of the rockers and the dull echo of cars on Elk Road intruded into the silence. And then all hell broke loose.

Old Man appeared in the doorway, suitcase in hand. "I'm a-leavin' then, Lurrie," he said.

Lurina rocked harder. She avoided his eyes. "Suit yourself," she replied.

When he saw Grace, Old Man nodded and set down the suitcase. "Maybe, Grace, you can talk some sense into this here hardheaded woman." He leaned against the railing, pulled a pipe and pouch of tobacco from his shirt pocket, and began to stuff the pipe.

Oh, my Lord, Grace thought, not trouble here, too. She braced herself and took a deep breath. "What is going on?"

"He ain't gonna tear up this house belonged to Ma and Pa. 'Twas good enough for them until they passed, and it's good enough for me."

Grace lifted both hands in the air. "Who wants to tear up what?"

"It's too many steps, Grace," Old Man replied. "My old legs can't take steps no more."

"Steps are good for a body, keeps the blood movin'," Lurina said, averting her eyes from Old Man.

"We gotta convert one of the rooms downstairs into a bedroom," Old Man said. He struck a match and tipped the bowl of his pipe to receive the flame. Smoke drifted up. He sucked at the stem of the pipe. Grace turned her head to avoid the smoke, which circled Old Man's head before journeying on.

"All in his thick skull," Lurina muttered. "Ain't one of us sick a day. Steps is good for you."

Old Man stood his ground. "Not for me. I never had no knee-joint pains until now."

Grace looked from one to the other. They were both hardheaded, and she didn't want to be in the middle of all this.

"Well, I'll be off, then." Old Man shifted from one bandy leg to the other, reached down for his leather suitcase, scarred with time and use, and started down the front steps. "I'm outta here."

"Wait." Grace couldn't stop herself. "Surely you aren't going to separate, break up your marriage over whether you make a bedroom downstairs or not?"

"Yessiree, sure as rain." Old Man stopped, set down the suitcase again, and bent to rub his left knee. "All my years I ain't never had no arthritis, and I got it now, and it's them stairs. I keep it up, I'll be a-lying in that bed up there and never get me down." His eyes fell on Lurina, hopefully, but she refused to look at him. "Well, Lurrie, I'll send Wayne for the pigs." And with that, he lifted the suitcase and, bent even more than he was by time and nature, started down the driveway.

"How are you getting up the mountain?" Grace called after him.

"I'll head me over to the gas station. Buddy will see I get me a ride home," he called over his shoulder.

Grace couldn't let him walk across the pasture, and then down Elk Road to the gas station. "I'm going to drive him over there," she said to Lurina, and instead of the argument she expected, Lurina nodded and went on rocking.

"I'll come back," Grace said. "Soon as I drop Old Man off."

"Suit yourself," Lurina muttered.

Once in the car Grace asked, "I thought you sold your mobile home."

"Changed my mind."

"Wayne said he tore down the pigpen."

"They's got wood to make another."

"Why not stay a few days in Covington, until Wayne gets a new one built."

Grace considered everyone she knew. Ellie Lerner had an extra room, and Max did. Max. She'd ask Max to put Old Man up. She would talk to Lurina. Before the wedding, when the choice of a burial site for the two of them threatened to cancel the event, she had been able to convince Lurina that the Reynolds Cemetery was better maintained than the Masterson family cemetery, and would be a fine place for her and Old Man to be buried. It took hours of gentle persuasion, inspecting both sites, and Amelia's pictures of the cemeteries laid side by side to convince Lurina.

At the gas station several old men with furrowed, sun-burned faces sat tilted back on creaking chairs on the covered porch. Crooked wood poles, some with chunks hacked out, held up the tin roof. Old Man set his suitcase alongside a chair and sat. Someone handed him a bottle of soda. Old Man rubbed the cool bottle against his face before screwing off the top and drinking.

Grace found Buddy inside. She explained briefly. "Keep him here for an hour or so, will you? I'm going to find him a place to stay for a few days until this tiff with Lurina blows over."

"You'd think, old as they are, they'd be too worn out to hassle," Buddy said.

"Those two aren't what you'd call worn out," Grace said. "They can still spit fire."

Buddy chuckled. "I can just see them two old codgers sitting on their porch spitting out fire, like some baby Mount Saint Helens."

"Just don't get him a ride up to his old place. No one's there."

"Sure thing, Miss Grace. I'll see he don't go nowhere."

The front door of Max's farmhouse opened to reveal a tall, dark-haired young man with a beard and mustache. Grace gasped and stepped back. Had she made a mistake? Wasn't this Max's house? Yes, it surely was, the rockers were lined up on the porch, the table and chairs were as they always were, close by the kitchen. The daffodils they had planted with Bella that spring before she died were close to the end of blooming. Grace heard Anna's voice from the interior.

"*Señora* Grace. You come in, come in. You no recognize Zachary?" She leaned over, hands on her thighs, and laughed. "See," she said to the young man, "I tell you, better shave. You look like *bandito.*"

"More like a pirate home from the sea." Grace opened her arms. "Welcome home, Zachary. How pleased your father must be."

A slim young woman in a sari of sunset shades approached them. Her skin was olive, her ebony hair hung to her waist, and a red dot marked the center of her forehead.

"Señor Zachary's *esposa*."

"My wife, Sarina." Zachary reached for the young woman's hand, but she clasped her hands together, and bowed her head slightly. Grace followed suit, bowing slightly.

"It is a great pleasure to meet the friends of my husband," Sarina said in perfect soft, lilting British English.

"And for me to meet you," Grace said. "Is this your first visit to America? How do you like our country?"

"I have been several times with my parents to New York, on holiday," the young woman replied.

Zachary drew both women inside to the parlor. Anna bustled about opening the blinds and offering tea or coffee. "No, thank you, Anna, I can't stay long. I came to speak to Mr. Maxwell," Grace said.

"He in barn with José. I get him," Anna replied.

The newlyweds sat together on the couch. Zachery held Sarina's hand protectively. She's shy, Grace thought, and probably confused by all the new people, and the surroundings.

"How long have you been home?" Grace asked.

"Yesterday. We arrived yesterday. I wrote Dad that I'd surprise him." Zachary laughed. "He wasn't prepared for just how much of a surprise." Zachary looked tenderly at his wife.

The young woman looked so solemn. Grace wished she would smile. "Does Hannah know you're here?"

"Dad's probably told her. He's been down to the office, but then José called him back. Some problem with a cow having trouble calving."

Anna appeared in the doorway looking anxious, wringing her hands. "*Señor* Max, he say no can come. Very bad with cow."

"It's all right," Grace said. "I'll call him, later." She stood. The couple stood. Sarina clasped her hands again and bowed her head. Grace reciprocated, then walked briskly to the door. "Good to have you back, Zachary, and congratulations." She looked at Sarina. "Welcome to our part of the world, my dear. I hope you enjoy your stay."

Putting Old Man up at Maxwell's place was out of the question, Grace thought as she walked down the porch steps to her car. Would Ellie, with all her concerns about living in the country and her distractedness, take him in? Without thinking about the day or time, or that Ellie would be at the bridal shop in Asheville, Grace turned into the driveway of the Lund house. It was only after standing at the door for several minutes ringing the bell that she realized Ellie was not there. "I'll call her," she said, and hastened back to the car and on to Hannah's office at the end of Cove Road.

Hannah sat at her desk poring over two landscape plans that Hank had presented to her: an annual flower (cutting) garden and a Japanese garden. Her first night's sleep in the twin bed in Amelia's room had been a nightmare. Her feet drooped off the end of the bed, and the width afforded no space for bending her legs. Amelia snored. Short little grunty snores that rose and fell like gusts of wind. If she could afford one of those extended-stay motels, she would move there, but over the weeks it would add up to thousands of dollars.

Just then the door burst open, and Max almost fell into her office.

"What are you running from?" she asked.

Max righted himself against her file cabinet. "You're never going to believe this, but Zachary's come home."

"How wonderful. Told you he'd come."

"And not alone. Zachary married an Indian girl from

some town in northern India. Her father's a big-deal merchant, trades in silk and fine carpets. Mother's carried about the grounds of their estate in a litter. Can you believe that? A litter? Who lives like that today?"

"Obviously the very rich in India," Hannah had replied. "Sit down. Want a Coke or a beer?" She kept both for him in the small refrigerator next to the file cabinet.

"I need four beers."

"There's only one, followed by as many Coke chasers as you'd like."

He sat and opened the beer she handed him.

"When I got home last night, they were there, waiting for me. Don't ask if I was shocked, and frankly disappointed that he never wrote he was getting married. But then I figured, what the hell, he's here." Max drank deeply, then balanced the can on his knee. "You ought to see how he looks. If you passed him on the street, you'd tighten your hold on your purse."

"That raunchy?"

"Beard, mustache, hair long," Max said. "Well, after we'd done some catching up, Zachary tells me he's going to live permanently in India, enter her family's business. Her name's Sarina and something unpronounceable. He doesn't want my house, my business. Never wants to see Covington again. Buncombe County, Madison County are too provincial. He's seen the world. Been wooed by the exotic. Says he prefers the genteel manners of the East, the tight family structure, even the nepotism."

He paused then and emptied the can of beer. "They came because his wife insisted that she wanted to meet his father. She's very respectful, shy, pleasant. Speaks well. She was educated in England. She's a lawyer. There is no son in the family."

"So your Zachary is to be their son?"

"Looks that way. Sure there isn't another beer in that

fridge of yours?" He opened the under-counter refrigerator and poked about. "Nope. Just Coke."

"I'd hoped that Zachary would get his fill of travel and come home to stay," Hannah said.

"Kick in the ass." Max snorted. "Remember our talking about expectations? Here's a perfect example of how they don't pay off."

"Still, it's good they came, that you met his wife."

"I guess I have to do something, eh? Have friends over? Take them out for a fancy dinner?"

At this point the call came from José. "Got to go," Max said. "Cow's having trouble birthing a calf." And he was gone.

Hours later Grace, her mind consumed with thoughts of Zachary and his wife, opened the door to Hannah's office. "I knocked. Didn't you hear me?"

"I'm a bit distracted," Hannah said. "Come on in."

Grace was out of breath. "I met Max's son and new daughter-in-law."

"What do you think?"

"She's a refined young woman. He looks like a bandit or a pirate. Let his hair grow, beard, mustache," Grace said.

"I wonder, does he walk around like that in India?"

"Who knows? But that's not what I came to tell you." Grace perched on the arm of one of the loveseats.

"What could supersede such news?" Hannah asked.

"Old Man and Lurina have had a fight. He's walked out."

"Walked out?" Hannah said. "Walked where?"

"He's at the gas station. Buddy's keeping his eye on him. I have to find him somewhere to stay until I can talk to Lurina."

"What's the argument about?" Hannah asked. She

rolled the blueprint and slipped a rubber band around it, then squeezed it into a high round basket alongside her desk, a basket that burgeoned with rolls of prints.

"Old Man says the stairs hurt his knees. He wants to convert one of the downstairs rooms to a bedroom. Lurina says the house must remain as her parents built it, no changes."

"That old woman can be so darn intractable," Hannah said.

"If one of them were to get sick, imagine one being confined upstairs, and the other one up and down, up and down," Grace said.

"And you hope to convince Lurina, right?"

"Maybe I can. I did about the cemetery."

Hannah folded her arms across her chest. "So, what's the plan?"

"Keep Old Man in Covington a few days. He wants to go back up the mountain."

"Wayne is out in Haywood County. Old Man would be alone."

"I went by Max's. I thought Max wouldn't mind having him for a few days,"

"He probably wouldn't," Hannah said.

"But now he's got Zachary and his wife," Grace said.

"He has four bedrooms," Hannah said.

"I was thinking Ellie."

Hannah laughed. "Ellie? You think she'll take him in? Why, she wants to move in with us—" She clasped her hand across her mouth.

Grace's face went red. "Ellie wants to move in with us? She asked you? You didn't tell us? And you said what to her?" Grace had been thinking how she would tell Bob that she was committed financially to Amelia and Grace, especially now that they had taken on a mortgage. If Ellie moved in, Grace would be superfluous. Tears filled her eyes, and to hide them she moved swiftly past Hannah's desk to the window.

"The last thing in the world I want to do is live with Ellie Lerner," Hannah said. "This just came up, and I hadn't a chance to tell you and Amelia, to ask you to back me in saying no to her."

Grace blew her nose. Turning from the window, she raised her hands. "What's wrong with me, Hannah? I think I can solve everyone else's problem, and I can't solve my own."

"Well, since you don't have to decide about Bob today, we can deal first with finding Old Man some place to stay for a few days."

Grace slumped against the wall. "Why isn't our house ready? I hate all this waiting. Roger and Charles will be here any day now."

"I think we should ask Max first; Ellie, for me, is a last resort."

"You'll ask him with me?" Grace said. Tiredness, as much mental as physical, washed over Grace. She could hardly move. Weary with being the caretaker, she longed to be taken care of.

Hannah put her arm about Grace's shoulder. "Come on, my friend, let's see what we can do."

Grace wiped her cheeks with her bandanna, and they walked arm in arm from the office into the reception area and out to Hannah's car. "I'll drive," Hannah said.

Anna opened the door. *"Dios mío."* She rolled her eyes and slapped the side of her head lightly with her palm. "Good you come. They make big argue, *Señor* Max and *Señor* Zachary." She urged them inside.

The men stood at separate windows. Max's fists were clenched. Zachary turned, his eyes defiant, daring Grace and Hannah to interfere.

"I can see this isn't a good time," Hannah said.

"For you, it's always a good time. Come in." Max waved them in.

Sarina appeared in the doorway, her pretty face puffy, her eyes red.

What a shame, Hannah thought. Hard for a young bride to be so far from her people. She smiled at Sarina, who bowed her head slightly, then fastened her eyes on her husband. Zachary, angry and defiant, stared at her for a moment, then he smiled and moved to take her hand. Backing from the room, Sarina drew him with her.

Max slumped into a chair and buried his face in his hands. His voice was muffled. "Damn it. I let my temper get the best of me, fool that I am."

The women said nothing, and in a moment he collected himself and lifted his head. "Tried to talk him into settling here, going back to college. He's a grown man, experienced, seen and done more than his mother and I put together, and I'm insisting he tie himself to Covington and a dairy farm. I'm a goddamned fool. Driving him away permanently is what I'm doing."

"I'm sorry," Grace said.

Hannah sat there, her mind whirling. A philosophy that preached accepting what life handed you was one thing; the living of it was another. Her heart hurt for Max. If anyone knew the pain of alienation from one's children, she did. She wanted to go to him, put her arms about him. Instead Hannah squeezed her fingers together until her knuckles hurt.

"Well, ladies," Max said. "You've seen me at my worst."

"You're only human," Hannah said. "Lately none of us has been at our best."

"What's my excuse? You had the fire."

"You fought to save our home and your farm from that fire. You've been a rock for all of us," Grace said.

"You're kind, both of you, but there's no excuse for what I've said to Zachary. Money on it, right this minute those kids are packing to leave, and I don't blame them. Sarina looked terrified—all the yelling."

"Sarina strikes me as a young woman who can handle a family disagreement," Hannah said. "She's probably up there calming him down. Well, we must go." Hannah started to get up, but Max waved her back. "Don't go, please." He ran his hands through his hair, buttoned a button that had opened midway down his shirt. "Did you come for anything special?"

"It's not important," Grace said.

"Tell me anyway," Max said.

From the kitchen came the sound of china clinking, a cup on a saucer, perhaps. Anna was making coffee.

"It's Old Man and Lurina. He wants a bedroom downstairs. She refuses. He walked out." Grace looked hesitantly at Hannah. "We're trying to find a place for Old Man to bunk for a few days, until we can talk with Lurina and see what we can do. If we had our own place . . ."

"Be glad to have the old codger. Characters, those two. Old habits die hard. Wondered if it would work, marrying at such an age."

"Is it about age?' Hannah asked. "Or a matter of cooperation, understanding, commitment?"

Max studied Hannah. He raised an eyebrow. "All of those things, I imagine, but more difficult to practice the older one gets, wouldn't you say?"

Grace intervened. "You say you'll have Old Man? With what's happened?"

"I've got four bedrooms. Only two are occupied as of this moment, and maybe only one, if Zachary leaves."

"I don't think they're leaving," Grace said, tilting her head toward the stairs.

A sheepish-looking Zachary and his wife came down

the stairs and walked toward them. Zachary ignored the
women and extended his hand to his father. "I dishonored
you, I am sorry."

"No. I was rude, demanding, hardheaded. I'm sorry."

"Then we shall have no further argument. It is settled,"
Sarina said in her soft, lilting accent. "We shall enjoy the
remainder of our visit. Your country"—she turned to
Grace and Hannah—"is very beautiful. My home is as
lush as it is here."

"I've seen pictures," Grace said. "Magnificent country."

Sarina nodded. "A vast and many-faceted land, India."

Zachary's arm circled Sarina's waist. "We're going to
take a ride, Dad. Maybe relax in one of those hot tubs
down in Hot Springs."

After appropriate farewells to Grace and Hannah, the
young couple ambled to the door. From the kitchen came
Anna's whispered, *"Madre de Dios, gracias."*

Grace and Hannah took Old Man to Bob's apartment for
dinner, or supper, as he called it, and then they delivered
him with his old suitcase to Max's farmhouse. When
Anna opened the door, Max welcomed Old Man and led
him up a flight of stairs. It was plain to see that Old Man
had trouble with steps, the way he clutched the banister,
the laborious climb, one carefully placed foot at a time.

"I'm sorry about the steps," Max said.

"I'll make it," Old Man said, and he stopped to catch his
breath. "Ain't for long. Wayne'll have me a place fixed up in
no time. Grace," he said, turning his head, "somebody's got
to feed those pigs of mine."

"I'll take care of that for you," Grace said.

Old Man's face relaxed.

The room faced the pasture. Mooing cows were being
shepherded to the barn to be milked. Old Man looked out of

the window and smiled. "Sure feels like home," he said. "You're mighty kind, Mr. Maxwell. I'll just pull me a chair to this here window and watch the cows comin' home. Don't it look like my place up the mountain, Hannah?"

It didn't. Old Man had lived in a valley with a stream cutting through the center and surrounded by hills, but Hannah nodded. "Smells like it, too," she said.

"Sure does." He poked his head out of the unscreened window and drew a deep breath. "Nature's perfume," he said, and chuckled.

29

HANNAH MOVES
TO MAX'S

Hannah turned over, again, in the twin bed. She had gone to bed at nine P.M., hoping to be asleep before Amelia returned from the theater, where she had gone with Mike, Ellie, and Brenda. Hannah tucked her legs in, then she straightened them. There was no way to be comfortable in a twin bed, so why was she doing this when every day Max urged her to stay at his place?

"God, Hannah," he said. "There are three other bedrooms besides mine. Why do this to yourself?"

The glowing hands of the clock at her bedside read ten P.M. It seemed as if she had been tossing for hours. Hannah decided to phone Max. If he picked up by the second ring, fine, if not, well, she sighed, she'd be stuck right where she was.

Max answered the phone on the first ring. "Hello?"

"I'm eating crow," she said. "May I stay a night or two at your place?"

"You know you're always welcome," he replied. "Come on over. I'll be waiting."

It took Hannah no time to transfer three boxes to her car. Bob and Grace's door was closed. No light came from beneath it. She left a note for Amelia on her pillow, and one for Grace under a magnet on the refrigerator, then Hannah pulled the front door quietly behind her. Within a minute her wagon was halfway down the mountain.

Max waited for her on the front porch. "Need help with your suitcase?"

"Not now. I need to sit and collect myself. Being impulsive isn't my thing, as you know, but I couldn't bear another sleepless night." She sat heavily in a rocker, and he took the adjoining rocker.

"It's been hard for all of you, I know. It won't be much longer. Tom tells me he's in the home stretch," Max said.

The night was scented with a flowering vine whose leafy stems twisted about the fretwork. "What is that wonderful smell?" Hannah asked.

"Night-blooming jasmine. Bella planted it. We'd sit out here nights when the jasmine was in bloom, and she'd listen to me go on and on about a cow not giving as much milk, or the potential for the new crop of calves. Patient woman."

Suddenly Hannah stopped rocking. "She was a wonderful woman." They were silent for a time, then Hannah asked, "Is that a light I see in our house?" She pointed across the street.

"Tom leaves a light burning."

"Why?"

"I don't know. I like it. Friendly seeing the light. Makes me think you're right there across the street."

"I wish we were."

Again silence. The Herrill and Craine households, farther down Cove Road, were dark. Night sounds rose like birds from cover. "I'd forgotten how loud the night is," Hannah said. "Bob likes it quiet, dark, and cool, so the air-conditioning is on, and we don't open windows. I wonder how Grace is going to like that if she goes on living with him? She loved to sit at her open window at night and listen to the sound of our stream competing with the crickets."

"Hard to give up one's habits," he said.

She nodded. "What are your habits, Max?"

"Well, I'm a pretty regular guy. After dinner I watch the news, read the paper. I like a good mystery on TV, a bit of sports sometimes. I read mostly Westerns. I know I've been dozing in my chair when the book hits the floor. Then I do a walk-through of the house, make sure the doors and windows on the ground floor are locked. By eleven I'm in bed."

"Every night?"

"Every night. Bella painted at night. She said nighttime had a certain feel that inspired her. She went to bed sometimes one or two o'clock. We had separate rooms, adjoining rooms, for years. She used to say that she could set her clock by me. After she died, I found it easier to keep up the routine. It felt comfortable. My life changed, but at least the everyday small things stayed the same."

"True. You're left at odds and ends at a time like that. Old habits offer something to hold on to."

"What are your habits?" he asked.

"I'm an early riser. I don't like waiting for people. I try never to be late for an appointment. I do not procrastinate."

He leaned toward her and their arms touched. Hannah moved back, resting her hands in her lap, but there had been something comforting in that brief touch. "Sometimes I wake up at night feeling lonely so I slip downstairs, close the kitchen door, and whip up a milk shake. Coffee. I like coffee milkshakes. Then I go to my room, sit, and drink it slowly. It soothes me. I've always thought that overweight people eat to fill an emptiness inside."

"You're not overweight," Max said.

"Lucky for me, I rarely feel empty or lonely in the dead of night." Hannah reached out her foot and stopped the rocker. "It must be late. Help me with my boxes?"

"Boxes?" he asked.

"Live out of three boxes these days. Amazing how little one really needs to get by."

With a box under each arm, Max led the way upstairs. Hannah carried the third. The hall was wide and lined with Bella's paintings. At the end of the hall, he stopped before a tall door and opened it. Had all the doors they passed been as high as this one?

"This was Bella's room," Max said, and she remembered him saying that he and Bella had adjoining rooms. Was there a lock? Max set down the boxes and flipped a switch. The Tiffany lamp by the bed came on. The bed was high, a fine old mahogany four-poster. The covers were turned down. "Did you run up here and turn down the covers when I called?"

"No," he said. "Anna does that every night. In the morning she freshens up the room, opens the windows. Had she known you were coming, you can be sure there would have been flowers."

"I feel odd sleeping in your wife's bed."

"If there's anyone Bella would have been happy to have sleep in her bed, it's you, Hannah. You do know how much she cared for you?"

"And I for her." Hannah stepped to the open window. It faced their house across the road. If his room was next door, then he, too, could see their house and into her bedroom, which, like Amelia's, faced west. The lace curtains stirred. In the distance a dog barked. A car drove slowly down Cove Road. Sometimes she recognized whose vehicle it was by the hum of its engine. There was a constant cough to Pastor Johnson's old Chevy. Brad Herrill revved his truck's motor, as if determined to announce his presence. But this car had no distinguishing sound, perhaps Ellie and Brenda returning from the theater. "I appreciate your letting me come. I'll sleep well tonight." She was dismissing him. She hoped he understood her need to bring their unanticipated evening to an end.

He yawned. "I'm bushed. See you in the morning." He closed the door softly behind him.

Hannah scrutinized the large, lovely room. A lace canopy framed the four-poster bed. She slipped off her shoes. The Oriental rug felt like velvet beneath her feet. At the foot of the bed stood a Queen Anne sofa, a coffee table, and two armchairs with delicately curved legs. Had Bella entertained in her bedroom? Hannah noticed two doors on opposite walls. Which was the bathroom, and did she share it with Max? Which door led to Max's bedroom? Hannah approached a wall and pressed her ear against it. Nothing. She did the same on the other side of the room. Was that a shoe dropping? Carefully she tried the knob on the first door. It turned, revealing a bathroom that took her breath away with its marble floors and counters, claw-foot tub, glass-enclosed marble tiled shower, and gold-plated fixtures. And it was all hers, for there was no door at the other end. The sound that issued from her lips was somewhere between a sigh and a gasp of pleasure.

Hannah showered. Her arms went slack. Her shoulders relaxed as hot spikes of water prickled her back and slithered down the curve of her waist and hips. She wallowed in warmth, felt every muscle go limp. Afterward she wrapped herself in the thick, oversize bath towel, dried her hair and brushed it back from her face. She smiled at her naked self in the full-length mirror. How firm her breasts had been, how strong her thighs. She ran a hand over her right thigh. It was still tight and firm from all the garden work she had done over the years, and without the cellulite that worried Amelia. She twisted and turned. No denying that her breasts sagged, and she was rounder around the middle. Oh, well. Hannah pulled on her plaid cotton pajamas, climbed into the comfortable queen-size bed, sighed with contentment, and fell immediately asleep.

30

UPSTAIRS, DOWNSTAIRS

Hannah's note on the refrigerator disturbed but did not surprise Grace. Disturbed because it highlighted the growing tension between Hannah and Amelia, which threatened the harmony of their household. How could anyone share a room with Amelia considering the smells of perfumes, powders, and hair sprays employed in her daily toilette? It was logical Hannah should stay at Max's. Grace wished she could be there, too.

Grace heard the door of the bathroom close. Bob showered immediately on rising and by eight-thirty A.M. he was gone to the golf course for most of the day. Because he never showered at night, he brought the odor of a day's sweat to bed with him. Funny about habits: Hannah's need for time alone, Amelia's need to "put on her face" and dress first thing in the morning, as if she were going to town, even when she was not leaving the house. Amelia and Hannah tolerated Grace's off-key humming and singing.

Grace missed the quiet time at night before she went to bed, and pined to sit by her window and listen for the sound of wind in the trees and the flow of the stream. She had become adept now at reading weather signs: a clear sky and rushing water signaled heavy rain in the higher mountains, while the turning of leaves, their undersides visible, announced rain. This sense of being in tune with wind and water enhanced her feeling of belonging to the land, of being at home on Cove Road. If only she felt at home in this apartment, this box perched on a mountainside with no flat area to walk on, and no yard. To stay with Bob, here, would diminish her life. Not Bob per se but the environment. It was a decision Grace preferred to defer.

Because Grace had risen earlier than usual, she made a pot of coffee for Bob and set the coffeemaker on WARM. She set the table: plates and mugs, butter and jam. She removed a package of bread (he liked wheat berry) from the refrigerator and set it alongside the toaster, placed a juice glass by his plate on the table, and made certain that the container of orange juice was in front of the milk in the refrigerator.

Lurina, she knew, rose early. She would go there now, have a cup of tea, and try to reason with her about a room downstairs.

Outside, a late-season frost filmed the windshield of her car. Where was her scraper? Grace searched her car, under the seats, in the glove compartment, the trunk. No scraper. She hit the side of her head gently. Of course not. That, too, burned in the fire, and she had not thought to replace it, especially since Bob scraped both their cars' windshields during the winter. Back at the farmhouse Grace generally deferred leaving the house in winter until the sun defrosted her windshield, but Hannah had given her the scraper. Now it was gone, and seemed, suddenly, an enormous loss.

So many things to replace. So many things to remember. Grace rubbed the frosty windshield with the butt of her hand. Cold. Stupid. Returning to the apartment, she took the spatula from the kitchen drawer. Within moments of haphazard scrapping, the frost released its hold and slid in tiny crystals down the windshield. The moment she cleared a space large enough to see through, Grace was in her car and away.

Lights blazed in Lurina's farmhouse. The old lady opened the front door. She smiled at Grace, but her eyes were puffy and red. "Knew you'd be comin' back," she said. "What'd you do with Joseph Elisha? Stubborn old man. Makin' such a fuss about a couple of steps."

Grace's eyes went to the steep staircase. "Couple of steps, eh? I'd find them hard to go up and down."

"Whatcha sayin'? You got steps in your place," Lurina said.

"These seem steeper somehow; maybe it's because there are more of them, shorter steps, and closer together, so you have to be more careful, I don't know."

"You get used to them," Lurina said.

"So what is it, exactly, that Old Man proposed?"

Lurina pulled Grace toward the dining room. "In here. If he had his way we wouldn't have us no dinin' room."

"He wants to make a bedroom here?" Grace looked about. The room was large, maybe twelve feet by eighteen feet and crammed with oversize oak sideboards, a large, solid round table and chairs, and boxes of all shapes and sizes everywhere. Grace noted a large storage pantry that could be converted to a bathroom, and there was room for two closets, one on either side of the window. It made sense to Grace, but she said nothing.

Lurina marched around the room, touched the walls, the furniture. "Ma and Pa, they'd have folks by for dinner after church on Sunday. Ma loved to cook, like you, Grace. I never did see a real good cook who wasn't plump, like you and Ma, Grace. Times I see you comin' you remind me of Ma."

Grace had lost nearly twenty pounds and did not feel plump anymore. Lurina's comparison made her feel like Ma. "You and Old Man entertain a lot? People come after church?"

Lurina shook her head. "Don't got no people but Wayne and you ladies visitin'."

"All you'd need to do is ask, and folks would be glad to come for dinner after church," Grace said. She had learned, when speaking to someone local, to refer to lunch as dinner. Now she must tread carefully, not rile up the old lady.

"If that's a joke, Grace, I ain't laughin'. I'm long past the days when I want to stand in a hot kitchen waitin' for food to cook."

"Maybe Old Man could cook."

Lurina laughed. Her face lit up. Spiderweb lines shivered when she laughed. Grace could not help but laugh with her.

"I can just see Old Man with an apron standing over a pot," Grace said.

"Not Joseph Elisha, he's shy of kitchens. Be in my grave afore that happens." Lurina wiped her face with the back of her arm.

"Let's go upstairs. I want to experience those stairs myself," Grace said.

Lurina led the way. The odor of mothballs increased with every step they took. Did Old Man complain about that? Grace noticed that Lurina stopped every few steps and her breath came in short gasps when they reached the top. Grace did not comment.

"See," Lurina said between breaths. " 'Tain't nothin'."

Grace rested her hand over her own heart. "Shows you how out of shape I am. My heart's thudding. Feel it." Taking Lurina's hand, Grace placed it over her heart.

"Lordy me, that's a racin'. Sit you down, Grace. You live here, I'd have to make you a room downstairs."

"Well, now," Grace said, "that would be kind of you."

Lurina looked away. "Ready to make it back down?"

Grace nodded. "I think so."

Lurina descended gingerly, clutching the railing with both hands as they returned to the first floor. "It feels, in here, Grace," Lurina said, tapping her chest, "like I'm goin' against Ma and Pa not to keep the dinin' room like they had it."

"It must have been hard for you tending your pa, up and down the stairs, when he was sick," Grace said. "I remember how my legs and my back hurt at the end of every day when my husband was sick. I used to wish we had a bedroom on the ground floor, but I understand how you feel, not wanting to do anything against your parents."

Lurina led the way into the kitchen, a dim room, painted green, at the rear of the old farmhouse, and filled a kettle with water from the tap. Her hands quivered slightly as she carried the shiny blue kettle, a wedding present from Amelia, to the stove. "Ma wouldn't let Pa take the piped water the government offered. Time was, when our well ran dry, we hauled water from Bad River." She plopped into a chair across from Grace at the table. "You think I'm a stubborn old woman and old-time thinkin' like Ma, don't you, Grace?"

"I respect your wishes. You'd as soon live alone than do anything against your Ma and Pa."

Lurina began to cry, short, dry sobs and sniffles. Grace pulled the bandanna from her belt and handed it to Lurina. "He didn't ask," Lurina said. "Just telled me what to do. I ain't used to nobody tellin' me what to do."

"You mean you wouldn't mind having a bedroom downstairs?"

"Lord a mercy, no, Grace. Times are, I think I ain't gonna make it up them old steps." She tilted her chin. "But I got my pride."

"I don't like anyone telling me what to do, either, Lurina."

"We're alike Grace, you and me, that's why I love you like you was my own child."

A shrill whistle reminded them of tea, and Grace rose, dunked two tea bags into the pot, and set the pot on the yellow tablecloth.

"There's rolls and jam in the fridge," Lurina said.

A comfortable silence filled the room, a silence between good friends.

Grace dabbled blueberry jam on her roll and used Sweet'n Low in her tea. It wasn't sugar, but she was gradually adjusting to the taste. When she had washed the few dishes, Grace asked, "What do you want to do, Lurina?"

The old lady's lips tightened and her eyes, already slits, slid deeper into their sockets. "Let him worry a day or two. Gonna be mighty lonely up that mountain. He ain't even got his pigs."

Grace gasped. "Lord, he asked me to feed his pigs until Wayne can come to get them."

Lurina put her hands on her hips. "Think I'd leave poor dumb animals to starve? I fed them yesterday and this mornin'." She laughed, leaned forward, and put a hand on Grace's arm. "Now, don't you tell him. Let him stew a bit."

Grace nodded. "So what now? Want me to ask Tom Findley to come talk to you about whether he can even convert your dining room?"

" 'Course he can. It's a right fine room, big, got a window, make a bathroom outta that there storage closet. But you don't tell Joseph Elisha, now, promise me, girl."

"I promise." Grace had no intention of keeping Old

Man upset, but she refrained from telling Lurina that her estranged husband was probably enjoying a big breakfast with a group of people in Maxwell's kitchen, and Anna was probably fussing over him. Grace wished that she were a member of that household. No strings attached over there, or were there, for Hannah?

"Come," Grace said to Lurina, "I have a surprise for you."

31

MORNING AT MAX'S

Hannah awakened, lay in the big bed, and savored the white, butter-soft sheets, softer than any sheets she had ever slept under. Bella's room was a vision in white—walls, canopy, curtains—idyllic and serene. Max had said they would have a late freeze, just a crusting, last night. Hannah drew the covers close under her chin, covering her shoulders. She had awakened once during the night because the sheet and blanket had fallen away, exposing her shoulder and arm to the chill night air. Now she stretched her legs. No cramps. Warm feet. No tingling toes from hanging off the bed. Wonderful.

Had Max visited Bella in this room, in this bed? Had his head lain on one of the pillows on which her head now rested? Or on one of the other pillows beside her? A shock of pleasure caused a tingle along her spine. This room was so definitely a woman's lair. She could not imagine Max, with his long legs, being comfortable on that delicate sofa or chairs, but she could conceive of him heaving himself up onto this high canopied bed.

Her eyes scanned the room, fastened on Bella's pastels on the far wall. One painting showed a red fence over which cascades of white roses hung, the red peeping through like polka dots here and there. The other painting was of a weatherworn dock that stretched into the ocean. A pagoda sat at the end of the dock. Behind, where sand met shore, children built sand castles. It fetched memories of Long Beach, on Lake Erie in Canada, where she and Bill vacationed when her daughters were young, before the darkness of Bill's drinking exploded into violence. In those early days of her marriage, she *had* walked with a jaunty step, and laughed, and hummed tunes while cooking. Hannah closed her eyes, and for a moment revisited that tall young woman, head thrown back, hair streaming behind her as she ran with her little daughters on the grainy sand of Lake Erie.

Through the open window floated the warm, earthy odor of fresh-mown hay. In the hallway a board creaked beneath heavy feet. Old Man? Max? Zachary? Steps moved down the hall. Hannah glanced at the gilded clock on the night table. It was nine A.M., way past the time she usually rose.

Anna had set breakfast at the dining room table. Grace was there, and Lurina, too, and Old Man, and Zachary and his bride, and Max at the head of the table looking the satisfied patriarch. He rose to pull out a chair to the right of his own for Hannah. Anna hastened toward her with a pot of coffee. Platters of scrambled eggs and bacon, pancakes, syrup, and small muffins were passed. There was about all of this something of a dream, as if they belonged in this house together, except of course Bob was missing, and Amelia.

"You look well rested, Hannah," Grace said. She dipped a slice of pancake in a pool of syrup on her plate, ate it, and closed her eyes.

"That good, eh?" Hannah asked.

"That good. The best I ever had, Anna," Grace said.

Anna beamed. "Recipe I get from Missy Bella."

Bella's name brought a flush to Hannah's cheeks.

"Was the room too cold last night? Temperature took a dip," Max said.

"I was just fine," Hannah said.

Zachary laid his napkin neatly folded on the table. "Sarina and I will be leaving tomorrow."

"Leaving so soon?" Hannah asked.

"We have shopping to do in New York before we fly back."

Max's face remained passive, almost indifferent.

"You must get my father to visit us in India," Zachary said to Hannah.

She waved her hand. "I don't have that kind of influence with your father."

Dark eyebrows raised above calm dark eyes. "Really? Don't you?" Zachary asked.

"Well, I see Tom Findley arriving across the road." Grace had been unable to hide Old Man's whereabouts from Lurina. "Lurina, Old Man, and I are going to ask him to come over to Lurina's place to check out that dining room as a potential bedroom."

Lurina's eyes peered at Max from squinty eyes. "Mighty good of you to have us for breakfast. Best I had in more years than I can think on."

Old Man rose and walked slowly to Max. "You been mighty good to me, and I thank you. I'm gonna roast you the best hog you ever tasted afore this summer's out. And this young lady"—he pinched Anna's cheek—"she can cook us up a pot of rice and red beans to go along with it."

Anna blushed and nodded.

A look passed between Hannah and Grace as Grace stood, pushed in her chair, and prepared to follow the two old people out of the room, a look that said, Isn't this great? We belong. We have a family, albeit adopted.

32

WHERE SHALL I SLEEP TONIGHT?

Hannah stood beside Max on the steps of his farmhouse and waved goodbye as Zachary's rented van eased from their driveway onto Cove Road and moments later disappeared from sight on Elk Road.

"So short a visit," Hannah said. "Did you have a chance to talk, to catch up?"

"He wanted his mother's jewelry—engagement ring, pearls, diamond earrings—for Sarena."

They moved from the rail and sat side by side in two rockers.

"And?"

Max passed a hand across his forehead. He looked suddenly drained, and old, as if his son had captured his father's vitality and taken it with him. "I gave him the whole damned box, wedding ring, gold bracelets, everything."

"Oh," Hannah said. It was not her nature to probe, to intrude.

"You disapprove? Think I was a damned fool?"

"Certainly not," she replied. "Bella would have given them to him herself if she were here."

He nodded. "Yes. She would have." He struck one palm

with the fist of his other hand. "What I resent is the brevity of his visit," Max replied. "I resent not being notified or invited to their wedding."

"Yes. I understand." After a time Hannah said, "She seems a fine young woman, educated, considerate."

"I don't object to her. It's the way my son has conducted this whole thing."

Hannah wiped the sweat from her upper lip. Heat curled the hair about her forehead. "Is it hotter this year, do you think?"

"If I didn't believe in natural weather cycles, I'd swear we were experiencing the damned greenhouse effect scientists are always screaming about," he replied. Then he shifted gears. "Well, Hannah, what do you think about August eighteenth for the grand opening of Bella's Park?"

"It's a good date," she said as she brushed away a fly that buzzed about her face. "More flies this year, too."

He looked into her eyes. "Now that they're all gone, you'll be moving back to the apartment, I presume? Will you have dinner with me before you go?"

It took courage. Aside from the sheer comfort of Bella's room, she enjoyed Max's company. Hannah said, "Tell you the truth, Max, I'd like to stay."

The darkness and sense of loss and loneliness she saw in his face and eyes vanished, replaced by surprise and pleasure. He seemed to gather into himself, as if remembering that she would move into her own home in the not-too-distant future, and his eyes shadowed. "Stay as long as you'd like, until you're ready to move home," Max said. He pointed, then, to the trucks arriving across the road. "Looks like Tom's added men to his finishing crew. Won't be long." He looked down at his watch. "Seven-thirty. Zachary and his wife. They couldn't wait to have breakfast with us." His broad shoulders rose and fell with his sigh. "What say we have a good, solid breakfast before we head to work?"

* * *

It seemed as if the universe understood Max's need to stay busy. First, the tractor broke; Max dashed off to get the part to repair it. In the afternoon one of the men working on the Indian Settlement fell from a ladder, tore a tendon in his leg, and had to be transported to the hospital in Asheville. Max drove him.

Hannah's day passed more smoothly. She and her foreman, Tom Battle, began to lay out the paths and the location of the pond in what would be the Japanese Garden. It was one o'clock before she slumped into her chair in her office, caught her breath, and grabbed crackers and cheese she kept for just such a moment. Eating slowly, Hannah let her mind wander to the prospect of another and yet another night in Max's house.

Should she switch to a different room, one without a connecting door? She enjoyed Bella's bedroom. The bed cradled her, comforted her. Not since the fire had she slept as well. Could they, for the remaining weeks of her exile from home, live together like siblings? Certainly. They were mature adults. They understood the parameters of friendship, for that was all it was, friendship.

Hannah doodled on the side of the appointment calendar, which covered the center of her desk. Dated squares reminded her that she had agreed to shop with Grace for kitchen appliances on Wednesday, followed by a meeting with a plumber about the waterline for the pond in the Japanese garden. Lunch with Laura on Thursday. Would they talk about Laura and Hank's wedding? On Friday she and Tom Battle were scheduled to visit an aquatic nursery about koi for the pond: how many koi to how many gallons or area of water?

Hannah looked down. She had doodled rings, intertwined rings. Zachary and Sarina's visit, or had Laura and Hank prompted the imagery? Digging in her top drawer,

Hannah found a thick, square eraser and, pressing hard, rubbed out the doodles.

Hannah followed Grace through the appliance section of the store, from stoves to dishwashers and refrigerators, where Grace questioned the salesman about energy efficiency. Finally they stood before washing machines and dryers.

"What exactly does extra-large capacity mean?" Grace asked as she opened the top of the washing machine. "Will it handle lightweight summer blankets?"

"Yes," the salesman replied.

"How many blankets at a time?" Grace asked.

"Two, surely, maybe three if they're twin size." He consulted a chart he had picked up from the counter. "It depends on the size of the blanket. Now, a king-size is different. You'll want to wash it by itself."

Grace turned to the dryer. "How can I tell if the dryer's insulated and installed properly so I never have a fire caused by lint?"

The salesman stared at her.

"I heard on TV about fires started by lint in dryers," Grace said.

"We've never had such an incident with our product," the salesman said.

"Would you tell us if you had?" Hannah asked.

"I would suggest that you clean the filter after every use," the man replied.

"I do that," Grace said. She tapped a machine. "We'll take this one, in almond, everything in almond, please."

"Yes," the man replied.

As they left the store, Grace said to Hannah. "See why I need you? I'd never have asked him that question."

"I don't see that we got much of a response from him," Hannah said.

"But you let him know we're not dumb shoppers," Grace said. "How about stopping for a glass of iced coffee at one of the bookstores?"

"No bookstore," Hannah said. "We get in a bookstore, we'll never leave. I know you, and I have to meet with a plumber this afternoon."

Later, at one of the chain restaurants on Tunnel Road, they ordered iced teas. After a long sip Hannah said, "Grace. I'm comfortable at Max's. Going to stay there until we move."

"You've been miserable sharing a room with Amelia."

"Surely have. It's not really Amelia, it's her cologne and hair spray."

"Bob fusses privately about that, also. The place is small. Odors carry," Grace said.

Hannah's elbow missed the table as she leaned forward. It struck the edge. "Ouch." She rubbed her elbow. After a while she asked, "You make a decision about staying on with Bob?"

"I worry a lot about what's the right thing to do." Grace ran her hands across the lower part of her face. "I want to come home with you and Amelia. I want to sit by my window and listen to our stream. I . . . I long for time to myself."

"I'd miss you terribly if you didn't come home," Hannah said.

"What if you and Max . . . ?"

Hannah pulled back. "Don't be ridiculous."

"Sorry."

The room filled with young people. Someone changed the music, and the beat of drums resounded in Grace's head. She covered her ears. "I've got to get out of here."

"Need to get going, too," Hannah said.

Ten minutes later they had turned left from 240 onto 19–23 and were headed to Covington.

33

THE GIFT

There were days when Amelia awoke bursting with energy and enthusiasm. Those days she shot prodigious amounts of film. But some days, like today, the day after stumbling upon Consider the Daylilies, putting one leg in front of the other required effort.

"Dr. Johnson assures me that in time I'll be my old self again." Amelia rolled her eyes. "But Lord, when?" she said to Grace that morning. "To quote him, 'Your lassitude is the direct result of the stress of the fire.' Seems to me there's no end to the results of the fire, wouldn't you say?"

She sprawled on the living room couch, shoes off, feet propped on one arm of the couch, a romance novel in her hands. Bob had departed early for a day of golf with Martin, and Grace sat at the kitchen table writing a note of acknowledgment to yet another inquiry from a woman who wanted to find housemates. "Where do I start?" the writer had asked.

"I agree, Amelia. It's turned all our lives topsy-turvy," Grace replied.

The doorbell rang. Amelia shifted her feet, wiggled her toes, and ignored it. After the second ring Grace set aside her pen and went to open the door. Randy Banks, six feet tall now, stood behind his mother. He carried Audra, his youngest sister, who squeezed a small silver box against her chest. In the doorway Mrs. Banks clasped and unclasped her hands, hugged her elbows, allowed her arms to fall limply to her sides, then hugged her elbows again. Three little girls and Lucy stood in a row before their mother, their shiny clean faces lifted expectantly to Grace.

Grace smiled. "Come in. Come in," she said, making way for them.

Tentatively, clustering like sheep in a pen, the small troop entered the apartment. The girls' bright eyes flitted from one wall to the other, then up, fastening on the chandelier that hung from the ceiling. Lucy looked down at one of her sisters, who tugged at her hand and pointed up. "That's a special kind of light fixture, Matty," Lucy explained. "See, it's got many lights, not just one bulb."

Grace moved to the wall and flipped the switch. The fixture blazed with light. Matty gasped, another covered her mouth, another giggled. The mother's hands passed from shoulder to shoulder in an attempt to hold her younger children in place next to one another.

"How nice to see you all," Grace said. "How are you doing, Randy? Been able to catch up in school?"

"Yes, ma'am, Mrs. Grace," Randy said. "I'm gonna graduate with my class."

"Good. I'm very glad to hear that." His returning to school had been a condition of the trust she had been instrumental in setting up to help the family.

Grace brought chairs from the kitchen into the living room. Amelia sat up and set aside her book.

"We come to thank you, Mrs. Grace," Myrtle Banks said. "Gimme the box, Randy."

The box Randy handed to her was about six inches long and maybe three inches high. "We brung you a present," the mother said, handing it to Grace. "It's something the boy"—she nodded toward Randy—"made for you, but we all come to thank you."

"You didn't have to do that," Grace said as she accepted the gift. It was wrapped in aluminum foil with an emerald green bow affixed in the center.

"Open it, Mrs. Grace," Lucy urged.

Grace sat in one of the chairs and unwrapped the package. One of the girls, perhaps the four-year-old—Grace was never sure which child was which or what their ages were—sidled up to her and leaned against her knee. Matty gathered up and held to her chest a tan chenille-covered throw pillow that Amelia had tossed to one end of the couch. She snuggled it, then brought it to her cheek. The look of sheer delight in that little face made Grace want to catch her up and hold her close.

Their mother sat stiffly on the edge of a kitchen chair. Randy stood protectively behind her as Grace folded the foil carefully into a neat rectangle, as if it had been the finest wrapping paper. "Will you hold this for me, please?" Grace asked little Audra, who leaned against her knee.

Smiling, Audra clasped the square of foil with both hands.

Lying in the box on cotton batting, the kind women use for quilt backing, lay a small wooden rose, beautifully carved, its petals precise and delicate. "It's beautiful! Look, Amelia, see how beautifully it's crafted." Grace held the rose in the palm of her hand so that Amelia could see it. "You did this, Randy?" she asked

"Yes, ma'am," he replied.

Myrtle Banks beamed. "We come to thank you," she said again. " 'Cause of you, our family can stay together."

Still cuddling the pillow, the oldest girl after Lucy moseyed over to Grace. Reaching with one hand, she touched

Grace's cheek. "Randy done it for you. I sawed him. It had a bump in the middle, so he made a flower."

"It's very beautiful." Grace leaned forward and hugged the child, whose skin was sticky and warm. Tiny ringlets of damp hair framed her forehead. The pillow in her arms squashed between them. Suddenly all the children surrounded Grace. They touched her hands and leaned against her knees in a manner so easy, so comfortable that it filled Grace's heart with warmth. Ted, her deceased husband, would be proud of what she had done for this family.

"I'll give to our church; I'll work in the food kitchen," Ted used to say, "but I am not giving my hard-earned money to some organization for their administrative costs."

This tied in with her own father's oft-repeated dictum. "Charity starts right here, at home."

Grace couldn't remember her father being particularly generous to anyone, certainly not to his children, but the words sounded firm and certain. Now, as she looked at these children, she felt a deep satisfaction knowing that she had helped keep this family together. She wanted to gather all the children onto her lap.

"Mrs. Grace gotta breathe, Aggie," Lucy said. She took the arm of one of her sisters and pulled her back.

"I'm fine. It's okay, Lucy," Grace said. Then she gave her full attention to Lucy. "Could you go with me to town next week to help me pick out napkins and tablecloths for our new house? We'll have lunch in town."

"I been baby-sittin' down the street, Mrs. Grace," Lucy said, "but so's I let Mrs. Parker know I'm not comin', I can go with you, right, Mama?" Lucy turned to her mother. "You always say how Mrs. Grace comes first, if she needs me."

Her mother nodded. "Mrs. Grace first."

Grace flushed, embarrassed by unaccustomed preferential treatment. Whatever she had done for this family came from her heart, and from a sense of righteous indignation at the world for poverty in the midst of plenty. She held up the carving. "I thank you very much for this lovely gift." She looked at Randy. "I will treasure it always."

They were silent and stood looking at her.

"How about some ice cream?" she asked.

That broke the spell. "Hooray, ice cream, you got chocolate?" Aggie asked.

"I've got chocolate, vanilla, Rocky Road, and mint chocolate chip."

Mrs. Banks rose to help Grace in the kitchen, and Grace let her, knowing the woman needed something to do with her hands.

Later that night, as Bob lay snoring softly beside her, Grace recalled every moment of the visit with the Banks family. It was so easy to lose oneself in the mundane affairs of one's own life, and so satisfying to be able to help someone else. But then Grace looked over at Bob, his face reposed in sleep, his lips parted to vent a snore. He had told her how terrified he had been the day of his heart attack. Knowing that, if she left him alone, would she be utterly selfish? Would she lie awake at night in the farmhouse berating herself for her self-centeredness?

"Selfishness is a sin," her mother said so often it had become her mantra. "It's a blessing to put the needs of others first."

Why did that dictum, which Grace had lived by without question for so many years in Dentry, still arise to confound her present-day decision-making? Hadn't she changed her viewpoint about what was selfish and what was not? She had come to believe that to live by someone else's values—Ted's, her parents'—was to live *their* lives, not her own. Help me choose wisely, she prayed silently.

34

HANNAH'S PROMISE

On Thursday Hannah and Laura drove into Asheville for lunch. Hannah would have preferred someplace closer to Covington, but Laura said, "I've got this craving for Chinese food."

The morning had begun with fog that settled along the edges of Cove Road and did not lift until well after ten A.M. Now a heavy dullness permeated the air.

"I hate the way haze hides the mountains this time of year," Laura said.

"Seems worse every year, or maybe I don't remember," Hannah said as she glanced at her daughter. Laura's eyes were bright, her cheeks flushed a paler shade of the terra-cotta Lands' End shirt she wore.

Max had called a meeting of the staff for eight that morning to announce the date of the grand opening of the park, August 18.

"That's only a month away," Hank said.

"You know what they say," Max replied. "Work expands to fit the time allotted for it. If the date were January of next year, we'd be busy until then. The Indian Settlement's ready, the Covington Homestead's an ongoing project, as are the gardens, but enough is finished, and we want to open before winter." He looked from one to the other. "You've all worked hard, and I'm grateful. August eighteenth, then. Time for others to appreciate what you've accomplished. Let's plan the event."

They had worked all morning sketching out entertainment, food, advertising, and it was after twelve when they finished. Now, as she and her daughter drove to Asheville, Hannah said, "August eighteenth. Well, it's one thing doing your job day to day, another having a major event staring you in the face."

"Isn't this whole garden thing a bit much for you, Mother? I mean at your age and all?" Laura asked.

"I have good help, and frankly, I've never felt so good. I can't wait to get to the office in the morning."

"I envy your passion for gardening," Laura said.

"This work you're doing at the park, it hasn't captured your passion, has it? You do it so well."

"I'm a good organizer, that's all." Laura stared out of the window. "I loved the sea, loved the boat, and Marvin."

Hannah could see how her daughter struggled not to cry. "I know you did," she said. They drove in silence past the New Stock exit before Laura said, "Mother, I'm scared."

"Why, Laura? What are you scared of?"

Silence again. Hannah waited, remembering fear: standing with clammy hands on stage at Penfield High School, down to the final two contestants, she and Jim Bakerson. *"Acclaim"*—a simple word called by the spelling-bee coordinator. Scared. The word, *acclaim*, stuck in her throat. And her wedding day, and Bill throwing a fit and cursing, about what she could not recall. Walking down the aisle on her father's arm. Scared. Anticipating the birth of Laura after a twenty-eight-hour labor with

Miranda. Terrified. Somewhere she had read a book about facing fear. You could run from it, but if you did, it would haunt you, or you could plunge ahead, do that which you feared and overcome it.

They pulled into the parking lot of the restaurant. Hannah's hand rested on the door handle, but Laura did not turn off the motor of the car. Instead she hunched over the steering wheel. "I'm pregnant." The words came out strangled, knotted, pulled as tight as the last stitch in a line of sewing.

"Pregnant?" Hannah asked. "But how wonderful."

"I didn't think I could have children, all those years Marvin and I tried . . ."

"When is the baby due?" Hannah asked.

"March."

It was a stupid question, perhaps, but Hannah asked it, anyway. "Does Hank know?"

Laura lifted a defiant chin. "No, he doesn't know, and I don't want him to know. I'm thinking about an abortion."

A gray cloud settled over Hannah's mind. A lump rose in her throat. She struggled for clarity, for the right words. "An abortion?" *Careful, Hannah, careful. Laura will clam up on you.* "Well, yes, you could do that," Hannah said. "Tell me why you'd want to."

"I'm over forty for one thing, and it doesn't seem fair."

"Not fair to whom?" Hannah asked.

"Marvin. He wanted a child so badly." Laura placed her hand on her flat stomach and lifted it quickly, as if she had touched a hot stove. "It's early. It's hardly a baby yet."

Hannah had always been pro-choice. "No one should bring an unwanted child into the world," she'd said on more than one occasion. But now, faced with the possible termination of Laura's pregnancy, of the end of her possible grandchild, her whole being revolted against the idea.

Laura was confused, functioning out of guilt and the pain of loss compounded by the fire. Logic, reason, arguing with Laura would serve no purpose. Grace had this way of answering a question with a question. How would Grace handle this? Hannah took a deep breath.

"Marvin loved you dearly, didn't he?"

Laura nodded.

"What do you think he would want for you?"

"He'd want me to be happy," Laura said. She sniffled.

"Would a baby make you unhappy?"

"I don't know."

"Tell me, Laura, do you love Hank?"

"I do love him. It's different from Marvin. It's more in the middle, a calm sea." For a moment her eyes lit up. "With Marvin, it was majestic waves cresting." Her eyes clouded. Tears pooled. "High, like the waves that washed over our boat and killed him." Laura burst into tears.

Cry my child. Cry. In time, your tears will wash away the worst of your pain. Hannah knew. She was silent and allowed her daughter to fully vent her anguish. When Laura dried her eyes, Hannah asked, "Want to pick up something at Taco Bell or Burger King?"

"Yes," Laura said. "I don't want to go into a restaurant looking like this, and I do need to eat something."

They ate in the car and sat for a long time in the parking lot of a nearby mall. Laura spoke of other fears. "I'd probably be a lousy mother. Forgive me for saying this, Mother, but I don't want my relationship with my child to be like yours and mine has been."

Hannah cringed. Would she forever carry the blame? Had she asked for a drunken, often violent husband? Had she wanted to be a single mother and the sole support of a family? It had been so hard, so very hard. Would her daughter never offer a comforting, "I understand, Mother"?

"It doesn't have to be that way," Hannah said. "Your

circumstances are different. For one thing, Hank doesn't drink."

"I know, but how can you know what's going to happen? Hank might die, he might be killed in a car crash, or have a heart attack."

"Or he might live to be ninety years old."

"How can I take that chance and have a baby I might have to raise alone?"

Hannah wanted to yell at Laura, "You're not alone, as I was!" But her mind urged, Don't argue, whatever you do, don't argue with Laura. Hannah waited a moment. "You don't have to marry him. You don't have to have this baby."

"But I want to marry Hank. He's good and steady. He's what I need in my life. I'm frightened."

"You have time. Why not wait a few days before making any decision?" Hannah said.

Laura lifted a tear-smeared face. "Yes, I do have time, don't I? A week or two at least. I can think about it." She sat taller. "I'll think about it. Please, Mother, don't tell Grace or Amelia."

"I won't."

"Promise?"

"I promise."

The heat of summer yielded to cool nights. Heavily burdened by her promise to Laura, Hannah lay awake under a light blanket in Bella's big bed and tried to ignore the mating call of a tomcat somewhere on Cove Road. It drifted through her open window sounding for all the world like a cry of pain. Down the hallway a door closed. Hannah stiffened. The seventh step on the stair creaked. Max? It must be Max going downstairs for a glass of milk.

"If you hear someone walking about at night, it's only

me. I go down for milk. It helps me sleep," he had told Hannah.

She pictured him sitting at the kitchen table, probably in the worn blue terrycloth bathrobe she'd seen him wear over his pajamas. She had come upon him watching TV one night, and he had jumped up and offered to dress.

"Nonsense," she'd replied. "Be comfortable." Hannah had considered joining him downstairs in the study for the eleven o' clock news in her pajamas and gray terrycloth robe. But, since that was a bit too cozy, she watched the news upstairs, propped up against the high mahogany headboard.

Again, the cat wailed, long, drawn out, pitiful. Hannah raised herself on her elbows and stretched her neck to see out of the window. If the cat were black, would she even see him? She settled back onto the pillows. She had promised Laura not to tell Grace or Amelia, but, Hannah rationalized, Laura made no mention of Max. Hannah needed to share her concern with someone.

With resolve, Hannah shoved back the covers, donned her bathrobe, tied it snug about her waist, and slipped her feet into her slippers. She turned the lock on the door and eased her way along the hallway. If she counted right, she could step over the seventh step. At the top of the stairs Hannah stopped. What was she doing? If she was descending the stairs to talk to Max, why this cat's-paw approach? Let him hear the creaking step, prepare for her arrival.

Max sat at the kitchen table, a mug of milk and a plate of Grace's sugar cookies, that Anna had baked, in front of him. He looked up and smiled when Hannah entered. "Well, this is a surprise. Want a cookie, milk, coffee?" He half rose, and she waved him down. "Anna left a pot of decaf on the stove. You couldn't sleep, either, eh? Air feels heavy, like it's gonna rain."

"I'm upset," she said. "This afternoon my daughter shared a serious problem with me, and I can't stop thinking about it."

"Wanna talk about it?" he asked.

Hannah poured a mug of coffee and put it into the microwave. When it dinged, she carried the mug to the table and pulled out a chair across from Max.

"What did Laura say? She and Hank want to elope?" he asked.

"I don't know what she wants to do about a wedding. What she did tell me was that she's pregnant." The instant the words left her lips, Hannah felt that she had betrayed Laura's trust.

"Well, they're getting married, aren't they? Saw them in the hall yesterday—lovebirds if I ever saw any," Max said. He ran his hands through tousled hair. A fine stubble shadowed his chin and cheeks.

"My daughter isn't sure she wants to have the baby."

Max leaned on the table. "Isn't sure she wants to have the baby, eh? Well, now I've heard it all. You'd think at her age, she'd be thrilled to be pregnant."

"Laura's afraid she'll be a lousy mother, like her mother was."

Max sat back. "So, you were a lousy mother, were you? That's what she thinks, eh?"

Hannah's shoulders slumped. "I was, Max. I worked two jobs just to keep us all in food, rent, clothes, and all the other things growing children need, want, you want for them, ballet lessons, piano lessons. You know."

He nodded. "I know. It's always something. With Zachary it was soccer camp, swimming lessons, drum lessons, tennis. You do your best for them." He cocked his head. "And she thinks you're a lousy mother, eh? I'd say Laura's damned ungrateful."

"It's complicated. Our circumstances were so reduced when I left their father. They resented the change, resented me. I've tried to explain. Miranda gets it, maybe because she's a mother, but Laura has a most tenacious memory."

"You've done so much for her this last year. She arrived by ambulance all beat up from that hurricane." He shook his head again. "You turned your household upside down for her."

"Maybe men are immune to the kind of guilt women are heir to."

His hand came down hard on the table. The spoon in Hannah's mug rattled. "Not guilty? What do you think keeps me awake at night?" His large palms wrapped about his head. "If I'd paid more attention to Zachary when he was growing up, gotten closer to him, not felt jealous when I saw that he preferred his mother's company, not withdrawn . . . If we'd been closer, would he have run off after his mother died and married without telling anyone?"

"*What-ifs* don't help. Parents never know," Hannah said. "Seems to me our children are born with a will, a personality of their own, and a direction, you might say. It's as if we parents present ourselves like an array of foodstuff at the grocery, and they pick what they want. 'I'll take responsibility,' one says. 'I'll be a daredevil,' says another. Another child takes to your religion, or refuses to go to church, or to wear *that* kind of shoes, whatever." Max looked haggard. Dark circles ringed his eyes. This is a low ebb in the tide of his life, Hannah thought.

"So," he said, "I'm to believe that Zachary chose his

mother over me because he identified with more of her ways?"

"Something like that," Hannah said.

"Isn't that a cop-out for me?" Max asked.

"Maybe. The longer I live, the more sense it makes to me. I think as parents it's incumbent on us to accept who our children are, accept whatever wife, or husband, or career they choose," Hannah said.

"That's a tall order. I've worked to build this business for my son."

"Have you really, Max? Haven't you built this business because it's what you love to do?"

Max pushed back from the table. There was a smile on his lips when he looked at Hannah. "You won't let me get away with anything, will you, woman?"

"Not about this. I know how you love your land, how you enjoy tromping your woods. Why, you even appreciate the smell of cows and manure."

Max laughed. "True enough."

Hannah pushed back her chair from the table. "Coffee?" she asked.

He lifted his mug. "More milk, if you don't mind."

She rose to refill her cup and poured him another mug of milk.

"Back to Laura," Max said. "What did you tell her?"

"I didn't tell her anything, just suggested that she give it a few days' thought, and I asked her what she thought Marvin would want for her. Laura feels guilty to be pregnant. She and Marvin tried for years to have a baby, and now, with Hank, she's pregnant."

"Well, personally, I think she ought to be celebrating," Max said.

Here they were interacting like an old married couple. "I don't want her to abort the baby," she said, "and frankly, I don't know how to stop her."

"You tell her that?"

"No. I try not to suggest anything to Laura. She'll often do the exact opposite of what I want."

"What does Hank say?"

"He doesn't even know she's pregnant," Hannah said. *Was it the coffee this late at night that was making her head throb?*

"And she made you promise not to tell him, right, and not to tell Grace and Amelia? That why you're telling me?"

"Max. I need your support."

He rose then, rounded the table, and lay his hands gently on her shoulders. "You've got my support. Whatever you want. You just tell me how I can help." He bent then and kissed her neck as lightly as the brush of a dove's wing.

With one hand she reached back and grasped one of his hands. "Thank you."

"Come on up to bed, now. Daylight, things look clearer, and you can't settle anything about Laura tonight," Max said.

Whose bed? The question dispatched scurries of anxiety through Hannah.

She did not resist, but welcomed his arm about her waist as they mounted the stairs. Blood throbbed in her temples. Her heart drummed. At her bedroom door, they turned to face each other. He held her hands. Would he kiss her?

Max said. "Go on to bed now, get some sleep. Things will look better tomorrow."

Hannah slipped into Bella's bedroom, and for a long while leaned against the door, hoping for his knock, dreading his knock, which never came.

At every turn she took during the next few days, Hannah missed her daughter. Laura was never in her office, and once, when Hannah heard Laura's step in the lobby, and rushed to open her office door, the front door was just closing. By the time Hannah reached the entrance to the building, Laura's car was halfway down Cove Road. As she watched the car disappear onto Elk Road, Hannah's frustration increased, and by the third night, as she and Max watched the six-thirty news in his living room, Hannah found herself agitated.

"Laura's avoiding me. I'm sure of it," Hannah said.

"She's busy, in and out these last few days," Max said. "A lot to do with the opening a month away."

"Avoiding her mother, most likely."

Max ignored that and looked at Hannah. "I've been thinking. I have a proposal for you."

"Shoot," Hannah said, certain that it applied to work at the park.

"Zachary, as you well know, doesn't want this land, this business. He will get a trust his mother set up for him when he's thirty."

"Why thirty?"

"Bella had the idea a person wasn't mature enough to handle a large sum of money until they were thirty."

Max rose, offered his hand. "Come on. Let's sit outside."

"It's late."

"So what? Nice outside this time of year."

The air was cool and sweet. A stout wind caused a hanging pot of petunias to seesaw and bang against a post. Max removed the pot from its hook and set it on the floor. At the end of the porch, the doors on the old china cabinet rattled, while in the front yard, tall pink and white cleome flowers arced and swayed, and overhead, clouds played peekaboo with the half-moon.

"It's too darn windy to rain," Max said.

"Those cleome need to be staked and tied back," Hannah said. "Shall I do that for you tomorrow?"

"Thanks," Max replied.

Across the road, in the ladies' yard, a tarp had ripped loose, exposing a stack of wood and a palette of floor tile waiting to be removed. In the front yard a sea of tall grasses and weeds genuflected to the dazzling white farmhouse with its red sheet-metal roof.

"We're going to have to plow up the entire lawn and reseed," Hannah said. She studied the house with its yellow shutters. "So soft, the yellow. I like it," Hannah said. "I love the dowels on the front porch railing. I like the roundness of them."

"You'll be moving in soon. Have you money to refurnish?"

"Some savings. Tom said he thought there'd be a few thousand from our insurance account for furnishings."

"The insurance company just hand you that cash?"

"That's right."

They settled into rockers. The creaking sound on the uneven porch floor felt homey to Hannah. She leaned back and closed her eyes.

"Hannah, would you consider marrying me?"

35

MAX'S PROPOSAL

"What?" Dumbstruck, Hannah gripped the arms of the rocker. What was Max asking? Surely she had misunderstood him.

"Will you marry me?" Max said. "I've been to see my lawyer."

His lawyer? Marriage? Ridiculous.

Max continued. "I'm changing my will and leaving this property, the house, the land, the livestock to you. My lawyer pointed out that you'd pay a large inheritance tax, lose as much as half of it in taxes, but if you were my wife, it would simply go to you, no taxes, nothing."

"You're asking me to marry you so that you can leave me your estate, and I won't have to pay taxes on it? Why would you want to leave anything to me?" Hannah began to laugh. This was incredible. A ludicrous proposal.

"Because Zachary has made it clear he doesn't want my land or the business. I have no other family." His eyes bored deep into hers. "I trust you."

"But I'm your age. You might outlive me."

"I'll make changes, then, if that happens, but if not, I know that whatever you do, whomever you might pass this estate on to, would be right, and well thought out, like my decision is." Silence yawned between them. Perfectly at ease, he smiled at her. "Would you marry me if I asked you to be my wife in every sense of the word, live here with me, change your whole life?"

She shook her head. "At this stage of my life, Max, I'd have to say no. Much as I care for you, and I do, I have no desire for a husband, especially not 'in every sense of the word.' "

"That's what I thought," Max said. "So this is what I propose. We marry. Nothing changes. I live here. You continue to share your home across the road with Grace and Amelia. All that's different is that when I die, you own the whole estate."

"Stop talking about dying. You'll be around for a long time," Hannah said. She began to rock again and suppressed the urge to laugh. Yet his proposal intrigued her. A twist on marriage, her kind of twist. Clever Max. Was this a ruse to woo her, to bind her to him? She understood that he cared for her: his thoughtfulness, the times she'd caught him looking at her tenderly, heard the softening of his voice when he spoke to her, the way his eyes lit when he saw her. And she cared a great deal for him. But the caveat? First it would be fine living across the street. Then he would phone and invite her for dinner. "Stay the night," he'd urge. They would be married. Would she stay? Would they cuddle in his bed, in the room next door to Bella's, a room which, as yet, she had never entered? That would be enough for her. But would it be for him? Long ago she had extinguished her sex drive and had been relieved to let it go. There were stirrings she felt with him, at moments. Would she be tempted?

"I don't want sex. I'm done with that," she said.

"Bella didn't much care, and we let that part of our lives fade out long ago," Max replied.

"You're joking. Why, you look so, so . . ."

"Virile?" he asked. He smiled. "Bella used to kid about what a sexy couple we looked like. 'If folks only knew,' she'd say, and we'd laugh and hold hands. That's all that seemed necessary. Being together, holding hands."

A large tabby cat raced across the lawn. So you're the one making all the noise at night, Hannah thought. Having subsided, the breeze merely tweaked the tips of leaves. Max rose and rehung the pot of petunias. "I don't know what to say to you," Hannah said.

"Don't say anything. There's time. It's all going to be yours one way or the other."

For a moment the prospect of all that money intrigued her. "If I say yes, will you think it's out of greed?"

"You're not a greedy woman," he said. There was trust and softness in his voice. "I feel right about this, Hannah. Take your time. Talk to Grace and Amelia if you care to. Miranda, Laura, anyone you choose. I'm not going anywhere."

"Let's not discuss this any more right now," Hannah said.

They rocked in silence. Hannah felt, at that moment, both separate from and merged with Max.

36

AMELIA AND
GRACE'S REACTION

It had become a habit in the afternoons, after the work-men's trucks pulled out of the driveway of their farm-house, for Hannah to cross Cove Road and visit the new farmhouse. She missed the lived-in feel of the old place and the sense of history interred with the fire, but she preferred the new stairs, much easier to climb, and the additional bathrooms up- and downstairs. No more shiv-ering in the shower when the water in the old heater went cold. Their new water heater was huge and gas operated.

"Plenty of hot water for all of you to shower or bathe at the same time," Tom Findley said when he urged them to go with the larger gas appliance.

As she toured the house, Hannah's mind whirled. Laura had dashed in and out of her mother's office earlier today. "I'm reconsidering my decision," she said. "Talk to you later." Although relieved by this news, Hannah wanted to discuss it with Grace and Amelia, but she must honor her promise to Laura.

Meanwhile, August 18 loomed. One small section of the Children's Garden, a bed of squash, was unfinished, and it fell to Hannah to locate and contract with jugglers, clowns, and artists who would paint children's faces on the back patio. She had assumed responsibility for training her fifth- and sixth-graders from Caster Elementary to lead the smaller children through their special garden. And then there was Max's astonishing announcement about his will. She had not responded further to his blunt proposal of marriage, and he had not pressed her.

Unless Grace or Amelia stopped by her office, Hannah rarely saw them. Considering how close they'd been, both emotionally and physically, Hannah missed them. She missed their daily tête-à-têtes, missed slipping into Grace's room at night for a last catch-up, or to continue a conversation started earlier in the day and interrupted.

Now, as she signed requisition forms that Tom Battle placed on her desk for pathway stone, concrete decorative lanterns, and special rocks for the Japanese Garden, Hannah's mind resisted focusing. She handed the forms to Tom. "So much to do. My head's swimming."

"It's all under control," Tom said. "Max said not to bother you, just go ahead and hire a couple more guys. Done that." He waved the papers he held. "Japanese Garden doesn't have to be completed by the eighteenth. Everything else will be in top shape, Hannah. The English Garden, Herb Garden, Canal Garden, and the Children's Garden will all do you proud. Not to worry."

Her foreman headed out of the door, and Hannah swung her chair to face the window. Its high back cradled her head, but her mind and spirit would not be contained within these four walls. All her life nature had welcomed her in ways most people had not. If she believed in God, it was a God of nature, a God who lived in all living things. On a nearby hillside Max and two men strode along, then disappeared over the crest of the hill on their way to inspect the Indian Settlement.

Max's proposal had flattered and confounded her, and left her feeling ambivalent. Didn't he care enough to want her to live with him? But had he suggested that, she would have rejected him instantly. And if she said yes to his proposal, could she modify her life with Grace and Amelia in order to integrate Max into it? Integrate him how? So far, she had refrained from sharing his proposal with anyone. Like a kid with a new ball, she determined to bounce it alone for a while. Now suddenly Hannah ached to discuss it with Grace and Amelia.

Picking up the phone, she dialed Bob's apartment. The phone rang and rang before the answering machine kicked in and Bob's voice said, "We are not at home. Please leave a message for Bob, or Grace, or Amelia."

"Grace, Amelia." Hannah spoke rapidly. "Meet me this afternoon at three-thirty on our new porch. Bring folding chairs, one for me, too, please. It's important." Hannah set the phone on its cradle. This afternoon she would tell them about Max's proposal.

"He asked you to do what?" Amelia asked.

"Marry him," Hannah said softly.

They sat in folding chairs on their front porch. In the yard, under a hot afternoon sun, two workmen loaded shovels full of building debris into wheelbarrows, carted them to a truck waiting at the edge of the road, pushed them up a ramp, and dumped them into the belly of the vehicle.

Tom Findley stepped from the house onto the porch. He leaned against the doorframe, his hands in his pants pockets, a big grin on his face. "Well, ladies, not much left to do now: crown molding in the last bedroom, closet doors to install, air and heat vents to set, couple of odds and ends to tie up, cleanup, and a last inspection. I'd say you can start moving in by the third week of August." He started down the steps, calling to a workman. "Hey, Jerry, bring the barrow inside when you're done—use the ramp off the kitchen porch. We got cleanup in the kitchen and pantry." Moments later he climbed into his big blue pickup, reversed from the driveway, and drove out onto Cove Road.

"Let me see if I understand this," Grace said. "Max wants to marry you because he's leaving you everything he owns, and he doesn't want you to pay inheritance taxes, and you can continue to live here, with us, even though you're married to him. Is that right?"

"You've got it. Funny, don't you think?"

"Wish someone would leave me an inheritance," Amelia said.

Hannah and Grace stared at Amelia.

"Amelia. What's wrong with you? Someone did," Hannah said. "Your Cousin Arthur, bless his soul, left you the farmhouse, and land, and the cash to fix it up."

Amelia gasped. "Lord, how could I forget that?" She tapped her temple with a finger. "I must be losing it."

"We all have too many things on our minds these days," Grace said. "Now, let me think." But Grace's mind was garbled. Their commitment to sharing a home seemed to be falling apart. Here she was desperately trying to find a way *not* to stay with Bob and not hurt his feelings. If Hannah became Mrs. George Maxwell, would Max, as Bob had done for years, pressure Hannah for more and more of her time and attention? What husband wouldn't want that? First it would be a night, then a weekend, and before you knew it, Hannah would be moving permanently across the road. Smile, Grace. You can't stand in the way of Hannah's happiness. "You must do what you think is best, Hannah," Grace said.

"That's crap," Hannah said. "Mealymouthed words that disavow your real feelings about this, Grace. Tell me what you really think, feel."

Like a jack-in-the-box, Grace raised her arms, dropped them, raised them again, then down, then up, and finally she plopped her hands into her lap. "What do you want me to say—that I'd be devastated if you moved out, the same as you've indicated you'd be if I stay with Bob? I can't pressure you, I can't." She began to cry, and made no effort to hide the tears.

"Grace, my Lord, see what you've done to her," Amelia said. She tugged at the bandanna tucked into Grace's belt until it came loose and handed it to Grace. "Well, I have something to say. I do." Amelia stamped her feet on the new wood deck. "You both have men in your lives. Both of you could move out, and I'd be left alone in this big house. We came here together intending to stay together. I feel as if I'm going to be abandoned by both of you." Her eyes blazed from beneath raised eyebrows. Her nostrils flared. She leaned her chair back at a perilous angle.

Hannah reached out her hand to steady Amelia's chair. "Whoa! Slow down, Amelia. Have I said I'm going to marry Max? I don't want to marry anyone."

Amelia's chair banged forward. The flush and anger in her face modulated to embarrassment. "Marrying him would make you a very rich woman."

"Isn't that why we took out home health and nursing care insurance? So we wouldn't have to worry about our money running out on us?" Hannah asked. "I've got all the money I need. I don't want Max's."

"He must really love you," Grace said in a low voice. "Whoever said that love is easy?"

"Love?" Hannah crossed her arms over her chest. "I'm not talking about love. I'm talking about a financial arrangement."

Grace dried her cheeks, pressed the bandanna against her eyes, and held it there. "An arrangement, of course. It was such a shock, your news. We overreacted, Amelia and I."

"I meant every word I said," Amelia muttered.

"If Max really means for you to live apart, for it to be a marriage for legal reasons only, how do *you* feel about it, Hannah?" Grace sniffled and blew her nose.

Hannah looked deep into the eyes of her friends: Grace's anxious, Amelia's calculating, scared. Hannah loved these women. She loved Max, too, since that day more than a year ago in their front yard when he had informed her that he had bought Jake Anson's land and asked her to create gardens, to be director of gardens for the proposed park. All this time, from across the road, she had loved Max. Not with fierce passion, but steadily, quietly. They worked together five days a week, all day long. Before the fire destroyed their home, Max had eaten with them once or twice a week, as had Bob. Her mind spun fantasies. Anna, she had discovered, would love to cook for them all, and she'd be happy to help Grace, who was struggling to prepare new diabetic recipes she didn't really like. Some evenings they could all eat at Max's place, like a family. She raised her head. There was no need to ever move out of their home, no need to upset the pattern of their days. It was a matter of organizing her time, coming home earlier in summer so she could join Amelia and Grace for tea. This need be only as complicated as Hannah let it become.

"I feel so many things," Hannah said. "Confused, flattered, amazed, sad for Max's disappointment with Zachary. I don't want to change our living arrangements. As I look at you two, I think of the years that we've been together in Covington. I remember all the difficult, but mostly the wonderful times: Christmases in our living room, the time capsule we buried, Russell and Emily's wedding in our garden, the way you took Laura in and helped her. We've built a life together." Suddenly it was easy for Hannah to lean forward to hug them, and to speak words of affection. "I love you both. Impossible to walk out on you, my sisters, my friends."

Grace grew very still. She could feel her prickling skin settling, her jangled nerves quieting. Then her heart tumbled. How was she going to cope with Bob? How was she going to walk out on him, abandon him when he needed her, especially now with Hannah dedicated to their lives together?

37

HEARING VOICES

There was something about Sundays; *enervating, languorous, logy* all sounded more acceptable to Grace than plain old *lazy*. On Sundays Grace preferred not to make the bed, or cook, or get dressed until late afternoon, when it was time to go to Russell and Emily's for dinner. On Sundays the answering machine took calls, and she allowed the newspaper to spill off the couch onto the floor.

Bob golfed on Sundays, as he did every other day. As long as it wasn't freezing cold, or snowing, or pouring rain, he was up and out before Grace opened her eyes. Bob spent more time golfing, now, than he spent teaching classes, or doing anything else. His dedication to the game amazed her. She could not imagine following a small white ball for miles on end.

"It's not about the ball," Bob had explained one Sunday as he was about to leave. "It's being out in the fresh air. Walking is great exercise. It's companionship, the chance to talk about things."

"What things?" she had asked as she lay under the sheets and stretched her arms high above her head.

Bob slipped his hands into his poplin jacket pockets.

The jacket was green with a white golf ball and crossed golf clubs on the collar. "Life," he said. "Martin and I talk about our lives, travels, work, things like that." He bent to kiss her forehead.

Today he left the house before she awakened, and she relished being alone in the big empty bed. Lying there, Grace's mind turned again to the issue of moving into the house with Amelia and Hannah. Indecision was driving her crazy. Bob did not appear to be a man in need of anything. He had recovered rapidly from his angioplasty, joked about having a better ticker than before the procedure, and his energy and sex drive had certainly been given a boost. Yet when they were alone together, he would take her hand and tell her how much he loved her, needed her, relished her company, loved waking up with her beside him, how all day long, no matter what else he was involved in, he anticipated coming home to her. Flattering, but she was beginning to feel like a favorite stuffed animal set aside all day and reached for at night for security, perhaps, and comfort in the long dark hours.

"I think," Grace told Hannah, "that Bob is afraid of being alone at night. After my one angioplasty, I was frightened to be alone, especially at night, for a long time."

"I assume you got over that?" Hannah asked.

"In time, I did. You have to or you go nuts. Haven't given it a thought in years until Bob had his heart attack."

"And Bob will get over it. Men are babies when it comes to being sick," Hannah replied. "You have to remember, Bob wanted you to marry him, or, at the very least, live with him since day one. His heart is an excuse, one he's sure you can't walk away from."

"That's true," Grace had agreed. "Only, how do I tell him?"

"You say, 'Bob, I'm moving to the farmhouse when it's finished.'"

So why was it so hard to say that? Because, Grace told herself, it sounded abrupt, cold, and unfeeling, and it was selfish, almost cruel. Bob's fears were real to him, if not to her, and she had to respect them and help him in any way she could. She loved him. She owed him that. Around and around would go the arguments in her mind, even as she set up a shopping trip to buy furniture for her bedroom in the new house. Grace felt as if she lived in two worlds and walked a tightrope between them.

The doorbell rang. Darn. She would have liked to loll in bed longer. Grace rose, slipped on her bathrobe, and hastened to the door, which was now being knocked on by determined knuckles. Hannah. It had to be Hannah. It was Hannah.

"Know what time it is? Almost noon. We need to drive into Asheville, have brunch, and do our shopping. Remember, Grace, we're going to shop for furniture?"

"I haven't forgotten. Is Amelia coming?" Grace raked her hair, which hung in uncombed straggles about her face.

"No. She's off with Mike somewhere."

"Shouldn't we wait for her?" Grace asked.

"Amelia said she knew exactly what she wanted for her room and planned to order from a catalog."

"Really?" Grace poured herself a glass of orange juice. "Tide me over until we get to the Uptown Café in Asheville for brunch."

"Glad you remembered," Hannah said. She poured herself a cup of coffee Bob had made. One sip, and she stuck the mug into the microwave. "Hate cold coffee. Hurry up, now, get dressed, and don't stop to shower, just slip on whatever, and let's get going."

"You are merciless, Hannah."

"We have a lot to do this afternoon."

Hannah followed Grace into the bedroom, lifted Bob's bathrobe from a chair, handed it to Grace, and sat.

"What kind of a bedroom set are you thinking of?" Grace asked from the bathroom. The door stood ajar.

"Shaker," Hannah said. "Light wood, simple bed frame, tall narrow dresser with lots of drawers. And I'm going to put up a rack with knobs to hang clothes on. I like being able to take off a shirt and hang it on a knob instead of a hanger in the closet."

Grace stepped from the bathroom, her hair wet and slicked back, wearing a blue shirtwaist dress of some crinkle material that required no ironing and hung almost to her ankles. "I'm ready." She had lost eighteen pounds and few of the clothes bought after the fire fit; still Grace had not replaced them. "I'm waiting until I take off another five pounds," she said. "No sense shopping twice."

They headed for the door. Once in the car Grace said, "About my bedroom furniture, I want a pretty padded headboard, no more wrought iron. I need to be comfortable when I prop up and read in bed. I want big night tables with drawers for my pajamas and underwear, and since I'll have a wood floor in my bedroom, I want a beautiful Oriental rug, lots of colors swirling . . ."

"All right, I get it," Hannah said.

"A bookcase, of course, and an upholstered rocking chair with a hassock for my feet. You know, Hannah, at night my toes tingle and sting. I don't know why. I keep changing shoes to see if that's the problem, but it hardly makes any difference."

They were zipping along and had nearly reached the highway into Asheville. "You ought to tell your doctor. Diabetes can cause something called neuropathy in your toes," Hannah said.

"What's neuropathy?" Grace asked.

"Something about nerve cells dying, and having tingling or burning sensations in one's extremities."

"That sounds just horrible. I can't have anything like that." Grace skinned up her nose and frowned.

"Your feet have probably gotten flatter, wider, and it's the shoes," Hannah said.

"It better be the shoes," Grace said. She turned to look out of the window. "The hills are so clear today." Her mind returned to furnishing her bedroom. "I was thinking about a lace bedspread, but then lace is rough on the skin."

"Stick to a comforter. Practical. Looks good all year," Hannah said.

They exited in Asheville, drove past the Catholic cathedral, past the Civic Center, past Malaprop's Book Store and Café on Haywood Street, then turned right on Battery Park, where they found a parking place in front of the restaurant. The restaurant was small but cozy. People spoke in low voices. The music was unobtrusive. Brunch began with orange juice in frosted glasses. Muffins bulged with nuts and fruit. They ordered eggs Benedict.

While they waited, Grace said, "So, tell me what's going on with Max."

"This morning, early, I went to the English Garden to sit quietly and think, and there came Max, apologizing for interrupting me, but doing so nevertheless."

"What did he say?" Grace asked.

"That he knows, legally, whereof he speaks. That he's leaving me his property regardless, so why should I pay taxes. I told him I didn't want the property, and that I have all I need. He's like a man obsessed, as if some soothsayer had predicted his demise."

"Is he sick?" Grace asked.

Hannah shook her head. "Not that I know of."

Grace fastened her eyes on Hannah's. "I know you like Max, and you're good friends. I can tell you're comfortable staying at his house. But how do you really feel about Max in here?" She pointed a finger at her heart.

Hannah waved her hands and hit the water glass. Water splattered. Within moments the waitress whisked away the wet place mat and replaced it with a dry one.

"I am so sorry," Hannah said.

"It's nothing," the waitress said. "See, it's all fixed. Enjoy your meal."

Noting Hannah's red face, and that she cast embarrassed glances about the room, Grace buttered a muffin and waited a few minutes. "Now, you collect yourself and answer my question," Grace said.

Hannah was given a reprieve when the waitress returned with the eggs Benedict and mounds of hash browns. "Looks delicious." Grace picked up her fork and knife.

They ate for a time in silence. People left the room, others arrived and were seated. There was no sense of hurry. Grace finished first, then sat back, folded her napkin, and set it judiciously alongside her plate. The waitress removed her plate and brought hot tea. Grace squeezed a lemon into it and added Sweet'n Low.

"Okay," Grace said. "You haven't answered my question. What do you really want?"

Hannah bit her lower lip. "I wish I knew. I'm not sure, Grace, what kind of obligations marrying him brings. He says none, but how can I be sure?"

"You could take him at his word, not sleep over there, not be over there every day. You know the old saying, 'Actions speak louder than words.' "

"What do your actions say? Bob thinks you're going to stay with him, and you go shopping for bedroom furniture." Suddenly Hannah laughed. "Tell me, Grace, for two ladies in our seventies, what's going on?" She clasped her hands and rested them on the table. "Femme fatales, that's what we are. Who would have thought?" Hannah laughed lightly. "Look around. Imagine, if the folks in here knew we had suitors. Quite funny, Grace, don't you think? Would you say it's a reversal of natural law?"

"To heck with natural law." Grace laughed. "Maybe natural law's on our side."

Hannah grew serious. "And I still haven't a clue what to do."

"Have you discussed this with Laura, or Miranda?"

"Heck, no. They'd be biased. What with suddenly having a potential inheritance from me."

"Right." Grace turned a spoon over and over in her hand.

"And there's something else I want to tell you, Grace." Hannah sat forward and lowered her voice. "Laura swore me to silence, but what the heck. Laura's pregnant."

"Another baby in our family. Wonderful."

"Wait up. Hear the rest of it. Initially Laura wanted to abort it."

"My God, no."

"She's changed her mind." In Grace's face and eyes Hannah saw her own emotions reflected. Grace's face first glowed with pleasure, then lost its luster. Her eyes grew sad. Her cheeks and mouth drooped, but then, at the final news, Grace smiled, her face suffused with joy.

"I am so glad she's decided to keep the baby," Grace said.

"When Laura first told me, she seemed adamant about not having the baby, and I kept thinking, what would Grace say? I knew I couldn't tell her what to do, and she raved on and on about Marvin wanting a child and being cheated. I suggested she wait a few days before making the decision, and that she consider what Marvin would want for her. Well, Saturday she told me that she had done just that. She hiked into the woods and sat on a boulder to think. You know Laura's not given to believing in prophetic dreams or anything out of the ordinary, but she told me, and Grace, you should have seen her face. My Laura absolutely oozed happiness. Anyway, she said she heard Marvin's voice."

Grace bent halfway across the table. "Heard his voice? Really? What did he say?"

"That Marvin is thrilled for her, that the baby will be a boy, and he would like his name to be Andrew, his father's name."

"You believe she heard him?" Grace asked.

Hannah sat silent, and for a moment, pensive. Then she smiled, the widest, brightest smile Grace had ever seen on Hannah's face. In a voice filled with wonder, Hannah said, "Does it matter if Laura had a vision, or she imagined the entire thing? Marvin's voice could have been squirrels gathering nuts or the wind in the branches for all I care. What matters is that I'm going to have a grandbaby to love and spoil." Hannah grasped Grace's hand. "A chance to do grandmothering right." She sighed, then relaxed against the tufted back of the seat. Hannah's face changed. Her eyes had that practical, determined look Grace recognized. "Grace, this baby coming makes marrying Max worth considering."

"It gives you a practical reason for saying yes to Max?" Grace asked.

"Exactly. I can deal with the rest of it."

With a clear vision of what kind of furniture they wanted, it took hardly any time at the very first store to make their selections. When the saleswoman stepped away, Grace asked, "Are we going too fast?"

"I hate shopping, and you do, too. They have what we want, let's get it."

The store agreed to hold the furniture for several weeks without a storage fee.

"What do you think Amelia's going to get for her bedroom?" Grace asked as they waited for the sales slips to be prepared.

"Amelia stopped by to take pictures of the gardens last Friday, and while she was there, she hauled me out to her car and unrolled a panel she bought, rice paper painted with a Japanese design, tall willowy stems and flowers that look like peonies. Pretty. She's planning to hang the panel behind the bed in place of a headboard. Mike's having it mounted on a sturdy frame for her."

"Hardly practical," Grace said, then laughed. "But who cares?"

They stepped out of the cool store and immediately recoiled as heat from the macadam parking lot rose in waves and walloped their faces. Grace brought her hands to her cheeks. "Mercy, it's hot."

"We finished so early. Let's go on over to the Folk Art Center on the Parkway. It'll be cool inside, and it's always pleasant," Hannah said. "I'm all churned up about the baby and thinking what to say to Max."

"Sounds good to me." Grace slipped her arm in Hannah's. "Let's do that."

As they settled into Hannah's station wagon, Grace was still thinking about Amelia's hanging screen. "Don't you remember, Hannah, Amelia never reads in bed. She sits in her lounge chair, and when the book falls to the floor, she startles awake and staggers to bed." Grace leaned forward and formed her arms into a loose barrel-like pose, neck stretched forward, bobbing.

Hannah laughed. "You've got her down pat, Grace. Lord, but I do miss our home."

"I miss the unfettered companionship. Odd how the presence of a man changes things. We speak less freely to one another in Bob's or Max's or even Mike's presence. Why is that so, do you think?" Grace asked.

Hannah turned off the Parkway into the drive and up into the parking area of the Folk Art Center. They sat a minute in the cool car. "Men and women see and hear things differently. Whether it's genes or learned behavior, I wouldn't presume to know, but there's a difference, that I am sure of."

"Bob cannot fathom why I would prefer living with you two than with him."

"There's an isolation, I think, living with a man that you don't get living with women," Hannah said.

"Not always," Grace said. "I felt pretty isolated with my mother. I doubt that we ever said a deeply personal thing to each other."

"True. For years I've certainly felt isolated from my daughters," Hannah said. "Maybe that's a mother–daughter thing as well and a man–women thing. I don't know. Our children and their fathers both presume that they come first."

"Well, I was certainly raised to think my husband came first because he worked for a living, while being a homemaker had little value, or appreciation." Grace swung open her door. Hannah did the same, and they walked up wide steps to the large wood-and-stone building. Not that they had settled the issue of men and women, but just talking about it, acknowledging their concerns, was comforting.

The crape myrtle shrubs that lined the path had been trimmed to form trees with multiple slender trunks. They could see through the trunks to a lawn and benches, see a small black-and-white dog on a leash and four children who all appeared to be under six years of age and in the charge of an older gray-haired man. The children began a game of tag, and the dog's leash trailed behind it on the grass as it raced after the children. "Looks like fun," Grace said.

"Too darn hot to run around in the sun," Hannah said, and they continued to the steps that led to the front door.

Inside, people milled about. Some were lined up at a kiosk run by the Park Service, buying compasses, maps, calendars, postcards, books. Beyond this counter the room expanded into a large gift store. A wide ramp led to the second floor. They walked up slowly to where quilts comprised the feature exhibit. Quilts covered every wall and draped across chairs and old headboards set up for that purpose.

Grace was immediately drawn to a quilt whose riot of colorful five-inch squares were made from scraps, the label said. She studied it carefully for a time, trying to count the squares and considering the manner in which the quilter had joined the colors to create a harmonious whole. Then her attention shifted to a red, white, and blue quilt labeled *Fourth of July,* which hung center stage on the largest wall, then on to a quilt with a mix of stitching and appliquéd flowers, which touted itself as being an original design. Traditional quilts, among them wedding ring and log cabin, were duly represented, as were quilts with an African motif, a Western motif, one covered with appliquéd, irregularly shaped birdcages. "Gorgeous color combinations," Grace said. She tugged at Hannah's sleeve. "Look at these prices, six hundred dollars, a thousand dollars."

Finally Hannah said, "Let's go to the gift shop and buy something wonderful for our new house."

On the first floor they wandered through the gift shop and stopped to admire pottery bowls and vases, goblets, and dinnerware. They expressed appreciation for the intricately woven baskets for bread, newspapers, magazines, and storage of all kinds, and they admired handmade jewelry, some pieces bold and colorful, others delicate, boasting a single gemstone, or none at all. They came upon shelves of wooden bowls.

"Let's buy a bowl," Grace said. "Something decorative, something we would never put food in."

Almost at the same instant their eyes fell upon a large deep bowl, finely wrought and nearly paper thin, whose pale wood dark indigenous swirls added to the bowl's exotic character. It was priced at one hundred twenty dollars.

Without another word they bought it.

"So, when are you going to tell Bob?" Hannah asked as the saleswoman wrapped the bowl.

"I will, when the time is right."

38

CHARLES AND
ROGER

Troubled by the pressure of the sheet on her tingling toes,
Grace wandered out to the terrace. The full moon revealed details of the landscape: hills ebony against the
sky, a glint of silvery water as the river below wound past
the villas, brilliant white flowers blooming on a moon
vine planted in a large pot.

After their trip to Asheville, Hannah looked up *neuropathy* on her computer, and what Grace read there thoroughly
frightened her. Nerve cells were dying in her toes. She
could, in time, lose all sensation. Why, she might not be
able to feel a cut on her toes, or a crack in the skin between
them, or a toenail poking into the flesh of its neighbor. Infections might not be curable. She could lose a toe, several
toes, her foot. The long-term prospects were horrendous.
She gleaned from reading that her tingling, burning toes
represented the initial stages of neuropathy, and that sometimes a topical ointment, like capsaicin, a cream containing
pepper, helped. Last night she had rubbed that cream into
her toes and inadvertently touched her hand to her lips.
They burned for an hour. She would phone for an appointment with her doctor in the morning. Maybe there was

something else she could use. But more important, since she could not, according to present literature on the subject, reverse the damage to the nerves, she could at least try to stop the progression? Maybe, she thought, as she turned to walk back into the bedroom, her doctor would have the answer she was seeking.

To further compound her worries, Roger had called earlier in the evening and told her that Charles had moved from uninfected HIV to infected HIV or AIDS. "I wanted to warn you. Charles looks wan, and he tires easily."

"Are you sure he's got AIDS?" Grace asked.

"Yes. There are tests that measure the amount of the virus in the blood," Charles said.

"What kinds of tests?"

"White blood cells help our bodies fight disease. This disease targets these cells and cripples them. In healthy people, you for instance, your T cell count would be between 800 and 1200. Charles has had his blood checked regularly. For years his T cell count was acceptable, then it plunged to 200, and he started medication."

Grace gasped. "You didn't tell me."

"Why worry you? With medication, the count went back up." Over the phone she could hear him crack his knuckles. "When there are too few white cells left in the blood to fight infection, you get the serious infections of AIDS. So far he hasn't contracted any of the really horrible things you can get with AIDS."

"Will Charles be all right?" Grace asked.

Roger laughed a hoarse, bitter laugh. "All right? In what sense? The first drugs they had on the market blocked an enzyme the virus needs to grow, the newer drugs work by stopping the final growth stage of the virus. They all have side effects."

"Charles tried so hard to avoid having to take medications."

"Vitamins and minerals, massage, yoga, meditation, acupuncture. We even flew out to California and set up a regimen for treatment with herbs from a Chinese medicine clinic," Roger said. Tears trembled in his voice. "Acupuncture seemed to help for a while, but in Charles's case the doctors think the herbal treatments may have activated rather than suppressed the virus. There's so damn much they still don't know. So now we're on the medical track with a combination of drugs that seem to have arrested the spread of the virus, and given Charles a breathing spell. At least the night sweats and the nausea and the shortness of breath have stopped."

Grace spent a restless day waiting and worrying. She phoned her doctor for an appointment, and visited over breakfast with Amelia before Amelia went off with Mike.

"I lost so much time with my work those months after the fire," Amelia said. "I've got to make it up. The gallery in New York pesters me for more prints, new prints."

"What about the second book you were planning?" Grace asked.

"I've set that on the back burner. By the way, what did you decide? Are you coming home with us?" Amelia asked.

By way of reply Grace said, "I bought my bedroom furniture yesterday. I had some money saved."

"Bet Bob was upset when you told him," Amelia said. She headed for the door, her camera bag slung over one shoulder, her tripod balanced on the other.

"Actually, I haven't had a chance to tell him," Grace replied. But Amelia was gone, and Grace's words faded in the air.

The opportunity to tell Bob receded in the face of Roger and Charles's arrival a few days later. The day after they came, Roger assured Grace that Charles was eagerly anticipating her visit. Grace walked down the hill to their apartment. What would he look like? What would she say to him?

Charles sat in one of the two recliners in the living room. Pale scrawny legs protruded from his plaid shorts. How drawn his face was, how shadowed his eyes. Her heart plummeted.

"Charles, dear Charles." Grace came to stand beside his chair.

He turned his face to hers, and his eyes brightened. "How good to see you," he said as she bent to kiss his dry wan cheek. "I've had a bad spell, but I feel much better. I've started gaining back some of the weight I lost. See." He flexed his arm to show firm biceps, which were not there.

Grace said, "Yes. Soon your strength will come back." It broke her heart to see how his hair had thinned, how pale his face and arms and legs were, how wrinkled his neck. A wasting disease, she thought, like cancer.

"People have bouts of illness with this, and they recover," Charles said. A smile tugged at the corners of his lips. "I've had a good run, Mother Singleton. Many symptom-free years, good years with Roger. He's been kinder, more devoted than I ever dreamed possible."

"I'm glad to hear that," Grace said. All she had read about AIDS spelled disaster, illness, death.

He reached for Grace's hand, and she pulled a chair close and held both of his. "You've always accepted me, never treated me as a pariah," Charles said. "I want you to know how much I've treasured our friendship."

"I love you as a son," Grace said simply.

"And I love you, deeply. When I go—" He held up his hand to protest her speaking. "When I go, please be there for Roger."

"I pray it will be a long time before you go anywhere," she said.

"But when it happens. Promise me you'll be there. He doesn't cope well with loss."

"I'll do everything I can," she replied.

Charles sighed deeply and relaxed. He seemed to grow smaller, to lose himself in the large chair. "Good. I know he likes Mike. Make that happen, will you? I want Roger to be happy. Mike is a good man."

Grace struggled with tears. "Don't worry yourself with that now. You look tired."

"I tucker out easily," Charles said.

"I'd better leave you to rest. Shall I turn on the TV?"

"No. But would you help me outside? I'd like to look at the mountains. I can lie on the lounge out there as easily as sit here."

Suddenly Roger was there. "I'll do that, Mother," he said. "Charles is heavier than he looks."

Mainly supported by Roger, but with Grace assisting, they helped Charles from the living room and settled him on the terrace. Grace tucked a light blanket about his legs, and Roger wrapped a shawl about Charles's shoulders. "I'll be right back," Roger said. "I'll get you a cup of good strong tea." He opened a folding chair next to the lounge. "Sit, Mother. Want some tea?"

"No," Grace replied. "I was about to leave, let Charles rest. For these first few days at least, I think short visits are best."

"She's right, Roger," Charles said, and Grace kissed his forehead, hugged her son, and departed.

Heavy-hearted, Grace walked back to Bob's apartment unable to erase from her mind the memory of her husband as he wasted away from cancer, and she knew the anguish, the sleepless nights, the physical and emotional exhaustion that lay ahead for her Roger.

39

OPENING DAY

Hannah turned over in Bella's bed and snuggled into the soft down pillows. Not until she heard a truck door slam and a motor start did she look at her clock.

"My goodness, it's after eight." Hannah threw back her covers, slipped her feet over the side of the bed, and moved with alacrity to the bathroom, where she splashed cold water on her face. In the mirror she saw that her left cheek bore a red blotch where her hand must have pressed while she slept. A cold compress might help. Water from the tap flowed cold and clear from a deep well, and Hannah wet a washcloth and held it to her cheek. Now the entire cheek assumed a rosy hue. Hannah shrugged. The redness would fade. She hurried to dress. Downstairs in the kitchen, Hannah grabbed a glass of juice and brushed aside Anna's protestations that she not leave without breakfast.

"You have big day, *Señora* Hannah. I make eggs *pronto,*" Anna said, but Hannah shook her head.

"I overslept. Got to get to the park."

The lobby of the office at Bella's Park was empty. The entire building was much too quiet, but it was not until she raised the shade of her office window and saw Max walking rapidly toward the office trailed by workmen, and Hank and Laura, that Hannah understood that something was seriously amiss.

Minutes later voices rose, feet scurried, and as if on cue, the phones began to ring. Max stepped into Hannah's office. Tousled by wind, Max's hair stood out beside his ears. His agitation showed in his reddened face. "Some damned fool left a faucet on outside, and we've got a hell of a flood at the Indian Settlement." He pointed down at his shoes, which were muddy, and sat to remove them. "The place is a mud field, as if it poured all night." He flung his cap on a table. "If it's not one thing, it's another."

"What will you do?"

"Make a quick trip home and change these shoes," he said. "What can I do? We can't open that area to the public."

"They'll have lots to see at the homesteads." She meant to be consoling, but it wasn't coming out right, she could tell by the way he looked at her.

"I know that. It's just that the Indian Settlement's probably the most important part of this park to me," Max replied.

"I'm sorry about the flood."

He grinned, suddenly. "Heck, what am I fussing at you for? What do they say, nothing in this world's perfect? My mother used to say they always put a flaw into a Persian rug, a reminder that man cannot be perfect or create perfection." He laughed. "You're right, of course, there's plenty for visitors to see and do. With the rides over in the north pasture, and your clowns and jugglers, and one hiking trail cleared and blazoned, the gardens, and the Covington Homestead, there'll be a lot for folks to do."

"And they can see the overall plan by looking at the model in the reception area," Hannah said. The model sat on a large sheet of plywood covered by a plastic dome.

"They'll see that next year we'll have a lake with canoes and rowboats."

"There is no end, is there, Hannah, to what we can do here?"

She smiled. "No end, Max. For the rest of our lives, I imagine, we'll be busy on this land."

He stood there, muddy shoes in his hands. "So, will you marry me, woman?"

She understood his gruffness. She thought of the new baby. "Yes, I think I will."

"Think?"

She flushed. "I will."

Max's face changed. His eyes danced, and his craggy face softened. "Now, that's the best news I've had in years."

For a moment doubt assailed Hannah. "Same deal?" she asked. "I live in the farmhouse with Grace and Amelia, right?"

He nodded. "Same deal. Grace not staying with Bob?"

"She says not. I'm not so sure. I kid her, tell her Bob should move in with you, and Anna could cook for us all." She was half serious.

His eyes grew speculative. "Bob doesn't really like apartment living or Loring Valley. Not a bad idea. Let's work on that. I'm rambling around in that big old house. Anna's pining for someone other than myself to take care of, and mumbling in Spanish, waving her arms as if she were on stage playing to an audience. She's been all sunshine since you've been there." He placed his shoes carefully on a mat inside her door, then walked toward Hannah and placed his hands on her shoulders. "When?"

"When what?"

"When can we get married?"

"There's much to do these days. After we're settled in our farmhouse."

" 'Mrs. Maxwell'—how does that sound?"

Hannah lifted her chin. "I intend to keep my name."

He kissed her cheek and smiled. "Can't win 'em all, I guess."

Opening day at Bella's Park went gloriously. People arrived smiling and departed smiling. A dignitary from Mars Hill College cut the ribbon stretched across the front of the office, a county high school marching band, in full regalia, played a Sousa march. Karla Margolin from the conservation organization RiverLink delivered a short speech commending Hannah for her efforts to obtain the land, and Max for his foresight and generosity in purchasing it. The small crowd clustered on the lawn clapped. Then the doors were thrown open, and the day began.

On the patio outside Hannah's office window, children squealed with delight as their faces were painted, and they clapped for clowns and jugglers on the rear lawn.

Amelia and Mike photographed the events of the day, and Amelia brought a Polaroid for individual shots, which she distributed: children with painted faces, families, a couple sitting on the log bench on the porch at the Homestead, a boy turning cartwheels, a girl, her face lit like sunshine, staring down at the Pizza Garden. Hannah's students were wonderful guides, and the Children's Garden delighted parents who, along with their children, found the beanpole tepee, gourds, birdhouse tree, and especially the Pizza Garden with its different color vegetables enchanting.

The men, women, and children of Cove Road arrived with all their kin. Herrill cousins ranged from a toddler in arms to an elderly uncle with a cane. Brenda Tate handed out maps of the grounds. Molly, in period costume at the Homestead, explained the uses of herbs as medicines back when the first Covingtons arrived in the area. Pastor Johnson delighted in his role welcoming arrivals at the front door and directing them to the model on the table. MaryAnn made certain that he stayed seated on the high bar chair Max provided and brought the old pastor juice or coffee.

Throughout the day, Hannah caught glimpses of Hank and Laura. Once she saw them stop, as they rushed past each other, to snatch a quick kiss. She was satisfied that all was well in that arena.

But it was Max whom Hannah watched in awe. A seventy-five-year-old dynamo, his presence was everywhere: comforting a child who could not locate his mother, giving directions, hastening after a workman toward the Indian Settlement, taking phone calls. When the soda machine accepted money and did not produce drinks, Max opened the back, fiddled, and fixed it. When the pump in the Canal Garden ceased working, Max hastened to repair a break in the water line. When two boys scrabbled, slamming and kicking each other on the front lawn, Max intervened and took them to his office. Whatever he said to them, they came out smiling.

Wayne Reynolds excelled at overseeing the rides, and Lurina and Old Man wandered the gardens, sitting often to rest. Grace found them there and brought them cakes and iced tea.

"Hannah's done a right fine job in this here garden," Old Man said.

"The roses smell good as them Ma used to grow in our garden, back before the freeze of 'sixty-two killed 'em," Lurina said.

"They're old-fashioned roses," Grace said. "Hannah chose them because of their fragrance."

"Hannah done good. People gonna sit here just to smell the roses," Lurina said.

On the far lawn Bob and Martin Hammer set up a putting green and gave putting lessons. It surprised Hannah how many people lined up to swing those clubs.

During most of the day, Grace stayed close to the food concession stands, to make sure, she said, that vendors used gloves before touching the food they served.

The press came and interviewed staff and visitors, and the WLOS-TV crew from Asheville arrived with their cameras.

From the opinion cards that were filled out, people declared the Covington Homestead true to its time, and some said that it reminded them of stories their grandparents had told them. The gardens, others said, were absolutely beautiful, the hiking trail well marked and safe, the guides friendly and helpful.

One person who signed herself "Amanda Crow" wrote in a fine calligraphy that she adored the gardens and especially enjoyed being escorted by a most charming young lady, who simply could not have been more courteous. Amanda Crow remained a mystery woman, but Hannah framed her note and took it to school to show her class. "Anyone remember this lady?" she asked

"I do." A girl, Amy, at the rear of the room, raised her hand. "She wore gloves and a hat with a net to screen her face from the sun. She spoke with a funny accent and kept asking me how old I was."

"Well," Hannah complimented Amy, "you did a fine job. Mrs. Crow was very impressed with you."

Alma Craine wrote that she had no idea that Anson's land could be turned into such a lovely place, and many of the opinion cards simply congratulated Mr. Maxwell and Mrs. Parrish. The fireworks, others said, were spectacular, a real treat.

Buddy thanked Hannah for her efforts to preserve the

land from development. "I wouldda helped you," he wrote, "but I couldn't go against the others."

When the day ended, after the cleanup crews arrived and left, when the offices were closed and locked, and Bob, Grace, and Amelia and all the staff had departed, Max and Hannah stood on the front lawn. Overhead stars salted the sky. "A grand success," Hannah said.

"Thanks to you, and everyone else," Max replied.

They went, then, to their separate cars and drove to Max's farmhouse.

A pot of decaf, compliments of Anna, had been left on the stove, and a coffee cake plastered with almonds sat under a plastic cake cover. "Hungry?" Max asked.

"Not hungry as much as keyed up."

"Let's sit outside a bit. I'll just get a mug of coffee."

"Well, if you're getting coffee," Hannah said.

Max poured two mugs full, while Hannah cut the coffee cake and placed several pieces on a plate. "Might as well take this, too, just in case."

At that moment life seemed nothing but comfortable.

40

OF MEN AND WOMEN

Several days after the opening of the park, the ladies sat at their new kitchen table in the breakfast area overlooking the front lawn and Cove Road enjoying a cup of tea. Plowed under, raked, and seeded, the front yard sprouted grass through straw spread to protect it from birds and heat. From Max's driveway a truck carting cows to market rumbled onto Cove Road.

Amelia's bedroom furniture had been delivered yesterday. And Hannah's and Grace's furnishings were in place upstairs. Bathroom toilet paper was stacked and towels hung. In closets hangers waited for clothes. In their bedrooms through open windows, curtains fluttered in the breeze.

Max had offered, and they had accepted, a distressed-looking dining room table stored in a barn, and eight chairs. In time they would restore the pieces. Their new porch rocking chairs were padded and comfortable enough to bring indoors in winter and be used in the living room until they were able to furnish it. The extra bedroom downstairs could also wait.

Hannah toyed with the spoon with which she stirred her tea, turning it over and over in her hand. "The problem is men have come into our lives and raised the old dilemma."

"What dilemma?" Amelia asked.

"Well," Hannah went on, "when we three met, our lives were definitely on a downward spiral. We'd given up on dreams and settled for doldrums. As for men in our lives, that seemed highly unlikely."

"Then out of the blue came Amelia's Cousin Arthur, whom she didn't even know she had, and this place," Grace said. "And we decided to commit to one another, to move here, share a home, take care of one another."

"Then Grace met Bob, and we waited to see if she'd marry him and move away," Hannah said.

"Well, I didn't, did I?" Grace said.

"And I met Lance," Amelia said. She stared beyond them into the distance. "I might have married him, if he'd been a decent human being."

"And now there's Max proposing to Hannah," Grace said.

"What's pretty amazing is that each of us has even met a man," Hannah said. "I assumed that part of my life was over, and was glad of it. Men are distracting and time-consuming."

"They certainly are." Amelia ran both hands over the rough surface of the table.

"Do you think," Grace asked, "that God is testing us, testing our commitment to one another?"

"Why would He do that?" Amelia asked.

"Why do you always have to have some wider, meta-physical meaning for things, Grace?" Hannah asked. "Life happens. It's random. Through our activities we happened to meet some men, simple as that."

"I never met anyone after Ted died, and my life was busy volunteering at church, and at the school," Grace said. "No, Hannah, I think it's more than that."

"I'm not going to argue with you," Hannah said. "You know my feelings. Why complicate things seeking esoteric meanings?"

"What of our commitment to one another? Here you are planning to marry Max," Amelia said. "You, of all people."

"And why not me?" Hannah bridled for a moment. Then laughed. "Look. Let's face it, none of us really wants to change the way we've been living. We like things as they are, and will be again, the ease of it, the sense of owning our own lives and time. Men impose, or we let them impose, a sense of ownership. No one says it out loud, but we feel it, through guilt. . . ."

"You're right," Grace said. "Like if we're late getting home, or if we don't have meals for them, or don't go someplace they want us to go with them."

"When I'm in love, as you both know, I want to do everything with him," Amelia said.

"We know," Grace and Hannah said at the same moment.

"So what are you saying, Hannah?" Grace asked.

'I just hope that we can keep it the way it's been. I've made it very clear to George Maxwell that I will never move out of this farmhouse." Hannah's chin tilted. "Ours is strictly a business arrangement, with economic long-term considerations on both our parts."

Amelia asked, "If Max were to die, God forbid, would you put that property in all our names like I did this place?"

Grace felt slightly sick. It had crossed her mind, also, but she found it well nigh impossible to bring it up. Now Amelia was bringing it into the open. They had made it a point to be open and honest with one another. How far could you carry honesty?

Hannah did not hesitate. "Certainly I'd do that, and

add Miranda and Laura. Listen, for years I've worried that Grace would leave us to live with Bob. I could have killed Lance, what he was doing to you, Amelia. I am not moving into Max's house, not going to be Mrs. George Maxwell. I'm Hannah Parrish, and that's who I'll be when they lay me in my grave, and if I live long enough to inherit Max's property, I will put it into our names and my girls'."

"I almost wish we had never met a Bob, or a Lance, or a Max," Grace said.

"There have been good times, too. Don't discount them," Amelia said.

Hannah studied Grace, who was bending over the table, over her teacup. "What are you looking for, Grace, answers in tea leaves?"

Grace jerked up and sat straight.

Hannah went on. "It's a matter of being clear in our own minds exactly what we want, and making that clear to Bob, or Max, or whomever."

"I thought I'd done that," Grace said. "Bob never gives up."

"Then he'll be disappointed again and again, won't he? That's his choice, his problem," Hannah replied.

"But it's my fault, too," Grace muttered. "Isn't it?"

Hannah raised her eyebrows. "If you give him mixed messages, it is. Everyone is responsible for his or her feelings and behavior. I've been telling you for months, now, tell Bob the truth, and say it clear and firm. If he chooses not to believe you, that's his problem, not yours. You vacillate."

"I do not." Grace lowered her eyes. "I do, I know, I do. I feel so guilty. There's his heart, you know."

"His heart's in better shape now than before the angioplasties. Maybe you're not clear what you want." Hannah stared at Grace.

Grace looked away. She wasn't clear, and she ought to be.

"Maybe he's accustomed to getting what he wants," Amelia said. "Like Lance was."

"God, Bob's not like Lance," Grace said.

Silence filled the kitchen as each retreated into her private thoughts. After a time Amelia said, "Bob's not like Lance in most things, but maybe this one thing." Lance had been such a no-good person. She had been devastated. Yet it troubled her when the others made disparaging remarks about her affair with him, perhaps because it still shamed her to think of how long she had been a willing participant in the whole sordid mess.

Hannah said, "Well, I will not live with Max."

Grace cleared her throat. "And I will not stay with Bob."

"And I never want a man near me again," Amelia said. But in her heart she was not so certain.

Later that evening the women sat down at Max's kitchen table to draft a letter to the women who had written to them regarding housemates. They had thought a great deal about it, discussed it, but no matter how optimistic they tried to be, it seemed to grow clearer all the time that choosing housemates was a serious matter.

"You can't just pluck people out of thin air," Hannah said.

"Maybe an ad in the local paper?" Amelia asked.

Grace laughed. "Like the ads for dating?"

"How do people who put those ads in handle it? A stranger calls . . ." Amelia said.

"Could be a fine person or a bum," Hannah said.

"Don't they usually meet for coffee first, something like that?" Amelia asked.

"Okay, a woman wants to find someone to share a

house with her. What would an ad say?" Grace asked.

"Let's not go there," Hannah replied. "Leave the wording up to them. I think there's some kind of legal responsibility here, the possibility that we could be sued if things went wrong."

"We could ask Emily," Grace said.

Emily, when they called her, argued that they should not touch this matter, that it was assuming enormous responsibility and leaving themselves open for a lawsuit should, for example, one woman rob or injure another in some way. "People being what they are," Emily said, "you never know what someone will do. I suggest you share your own experience and leave it at that."

"Emily's right, you know," Grace said. "All we know about this is our own experience."

"Right you are, Grace. Just think of my reaction when Ellie Lerner asked if she could move in. Relationships are complicated. Take time to develop."

"As does trust," Amelia said. And the others nodded in agreement.

The letter they finally drafted read:

Dear
We have given careful consideration to your request for our help in finding a housemate or housemates. We would like to share our experience with you.

We met one another in a boardinghouse and lived in that environment, sharing meals, and our mutual states of depression at the turn our lives had taken. Yet, unhappy as we were with the dullness of our lives or the negativity of our landlady, it was not until Amelia came into an inheritance of a farmhouse in rural North Carolina that it occurred to us to take matters into our own hands, pool our resources, and find a place of our own.

Because we lived under the same roof for more than a year, we had a sense of one another and had built a certain level of respect and trust for each other. This, as you can imagine, takes time.

Perhaps you know someone in similar circumstances with similar goals. You might discuss your hopes and dreams with that person. Perhaps you might tell others of your desire and word might spread, attracting someone of like mind and interests. Should several of you decide to share a home, we suggest that a trial period would be useful.

We regret that we cannot advise on how to screen others with whom you might share space and time and that we cannot be of more specific help. One thing we would urge. Do not rush into this. Take your time.

We wish you the best of luck.

Sincerely,

And they signed their names.

Emily approved the letter, and had it typed for them, and they spent several evenings addressing the fifty-odd envelopes.

"I wish we could have been more concrete," Grace said.

"Who are we, gods to lay out a plan for others?" Hannah replied.

"Someone should open a matchmaking service for finding housemates," Amelia said.

"That's a job I wouldn't like," Hannah said.

"Maybe someday someone will," Grace said.

41

THE MEN IN THEIR LIVES

Max gave Hannah's remark about Bob moving in with Max serious consideration, and arranged to meet Bob at a restaurant in Asheville.

Bob arrived directly from his golf game. "Seen Sunday's paper?" Bob asked as he sat down. "They gave the opening at Bella's Park rave reviews. A whole page of pictures."

"We're delighted with the reporting and the story on the evening news," Max said.

The waitress arrived, pad in hand, and they gave their orders. Max leaned forward. His fingers drummed the table. "Bob, you know about Hannah and me?"

"Grace told me. Congratulations. What are they going to do with their farmhouse? I can't see Amelia living there alone."

"Didn't Grace tell you, this is a business arrangement between Hannah and myself. I want her to inherit my estate without a tax burden. We never planned to live together." He drank deeply from a beer the waitress set before him. Bob sugared his iced tea. This was one of the rare restaurants that did not presweeten its tea.

"That's okay with you?" Bob asked.

"Sure it is. We live together, now, like siblings, you could say. It works for us."

"That wouldn't suit me," Bob said. "Grace will be staying on with me."

"Really?" Max had heard differently from Hannah. "Then no need to suggest what I had in mind."

"What did you have in mind?" Bob asked. He motioned the waitress for a refill of tea. "I use that powdered stuff at home to show cooperation with Grace and her diet." He added more sugar and his spoon clinked against the sides of his glass as he stirred. "After playing eighteen holes, I can't get enough liquid. Shoot, Max, what's on your mind?"

"I thought Grace was moving back home, so I figured . . . well, I've heard you say you're not nuts about Loring Valley. What the heck, Bob, I live alone in that big, old place—four bedrooms, and Anna muttering about how empty the house is and eager to cook for company. I thought, maybe, you'd move in with me. The women would be right across the street. Some nights Anna could fix dinner for all of us, like a big old family, you know."

"Well, I'll be damned. I don't much like Loring Valley, and I certainly don't like being trapped by weather at the top of that mountain. But, as I said, Grace is staying. Maybe she and I will buy a place on the flat somewhere between Covington and Mars Hill."

"Just an idea," Max said.

"Not a bad one if circumstances were different," Bob said.

They spoke no more of the matter, but went on to discuss a ball game, and the flood at the Indian Settlement.

Bob looked at his watch. "Got to go, Max. I'm meeting Grace at the doctor. Her toes have been bothering her."

* * *

Grace and Bob waited for her doctor in an examining room with its wall mural of a waterfall plunging over rocks into a deep pool. "I think these murals are meant to relax patients. I like them better than looking at a blank wall, but they don't relax me one bit," Grace said.

Grace sat in the single chair, Bob on the doctor's round stool. The moment the door opened, Bob jumped off the stool.

"Morning, Grace." Her doctor flipped pages on the chart in his hand.

My chart's getting fatter, Grace thought.

"Well, I see you've taken off nineteen pounds, Grace. I congratulate you. And remember, the more active you are, the better your body can use whatever insulin it produces."

Grace explained about her toes. She had taken off her Adidas walking shoes and now pulled off her socks. He examined Grace's feet.

"Good. Good. No ulcers, no changes in the shape of your feet. Now, tell me . . ." He pricked her toes with a pointed instrument. "Feel this?"

"Ouch. Of course I feel it," Grace replied.

"That's good. If you'd lost feeling, I'd be more concerned. People can lose feeling and not even know if they have a cut, can't even feel a pebble inside their shoe."

"That's horrible. I don't want to lose feeling. What can I do? How can I stop the progression of this neuropathy thing?" she asked.

"I'd suggest a podiatrist, let him check your feet regularly," the doctor said. "Also, you can check your feet daily for sores or red areas, or infected toenails. Wash your feet in warm, not hot, water. Dry them well. Use talcum powder between your toes to keep your feet dry after a bath. Rub your feet morning and evening with a good lotion or even just petroleum jelly. If you get corns or cal-luses, which you don't have now, I'd suggest using a pumice stone, or let your podiatrist take care of it."

"I've never been good at cutting my toenails," Grace said.

"Then let a podiatrist do it," he said.

"Wait a second." Grace dug in her bag for pad and pencil. "I have to write down all of this. I'll never re-member."

The doctor opened the door and called, "Miss Baynes." The nurse appeared in the doorway. "We have a care sheet for neuropathy. Get one for Mrs. Singleton, will you please?"

"Thanks," Grace said.

"Oh, another thing," the doctor said. "Wear shoes and socks at all times. Don't go around barefoot. It's easy to step on something that could injure your feet. Socks made from wool help keep those toes dry. Well"—he leaned back—"I think that's everything. Here's a prescription."

"What is it?" Grace asked.

"It's for the lowest dose of Elavil. It'll stop that tin-gling, burning sensation. Help you sleep at night."

"Hold on now," Bob said. "Isn't Elavil an anti-depressant?"

"An old one, been on the market for years. Very inex-pensive. They found out that the lowest dose helps neu-ropathy. Interesting."

Grace took the papers from the nurse, and the pre-scription. Bob shook the doctor's hand, and they departed. "Sorry, honey," Bob said in the elevator. "Who the hell knew a little diabetes could cause so much trouble."

Grace was reading the information the nurse had handed to her. "Listen to this, Bob. It says that I should wiggle my toes for five minutes twice a day and rotate my ankles to improve blood circulation. And I'm going to have to remember not to cross my legs. If you see me doing it, tell me."

Grace's nose was buried in the information sheet as Bob led her across the street to the car.

"I'm going to have to buy new shoes, too, ones that have what they call big toe boxes, so my toes don't get squashed."

"Better safe than sorry," he said.

"Yes, indeed," Grace replied. Tell him now that you are moving back to the farmhouse, she urged herself. You have a half hour's drive home. This is the time.

Bob slipped a cassette into the machine and the rolling thunder of the opening chords of Beethoven's Fifth Symphony filled the car. Grace listened, moved as she always was by the music.

After a time Bob turned the sound down. "Max came to me with the oddest proposal. He suggested I move in with him. Said Anna liked to cook for more than one. I thanked him, of course, but I told him you were staying with me. By the way, when's Amelia moving out? That'll be a relief."

"You told him I'm staying?"

"Of course you are, my love," Bob said. "I thought we'd agreed on that." Without waiting for her reply, he continued. "You've no idea how happy you've made me."

When had they agreed that she was staying? Why couldn't she remember that conversation? "I don't want to get married, Bob," Grace managed. "You know that."

"Sure, honey, I know that. But we're going to have a great life together."

You gutless ninny, Grace told herself. Tell him. How can I tell him? He's as happy as a little boy with his first bike. Damn it. She looked over at Bob, his firm strong chin, those great big hands with the hair sticking up from his knuckles. She did love him, and he did need her.

42

HANNAH'S
REACTION

Laura and Hannah put in a long day at work. Getting back to normal took as much or more work than preparing for the opening of Bella's Park. This morning, finally, truckers had arrived to haul away the disassembled carousel and other rides. Even with trash bins scattered strategically about the lawns, gardens, patios, and the area around the Covington Homestead, candy wrappers, bottle tops, and cups must be picked up from the grass where they had been tossed. The lack of courtesy this implied infuriated Hannah.

"We have people to do this job, Hannah, take the rest of the day off," Max urged.

"I most certainly will not," she replied. "Not until this place is spick-and-span."

Tonight mother and daughter planned on having dinner alone together. Hannah was pleased when Laura invited her. Undoubtedly, her daughter wanted to talk about her upcoming wedding and the anticipated baby. They had come upstairs to Bella's room while Hannah changed from her work clothes, and Laura settled on Bella's luxurious lounge. She ran her hand along the smooth chenille upholstery. Everything in the room was soft and feminine. Laura knew her mother liked the room, which puzzled her, for she had never considered her mother either soft or feminine. But then, there was so much about Hannah she was discovering.

Hannah changed into dark brown slacks and tucked in a tan dress shirt, then pinned a round pearl pin about the size of a fifty-cent piece just below the collar on her right. She brushed her hair back from her face and dabbed on a pale shade of lipstick.

"You look nice, Mother, and I see you've made yourself very much at home here, haven't you?" Laura said.

"Why not? Bella and I were friends. I feel that she welcomes me."

Another surprise. Her mother admitting to feeling welcomed by a dead woman.

"Max is easy to be around," Hannah said. "He's made me welcome, as has Anna."

"And, still, you're moving back to your farmhouse?" Laura asked.

"Yes, next week," Hannah said.

"And you're going to marry Max?" Laura shook her head. "An odd arrangement." She looked at her mother quizzically.

"That's what it is, Laura. An odd arrangement. Max is leaving me this property, and he doesn't want me to pay taxes. If I'm his wife, I won't have to. It's that simple."

"It's the kind of thing, if kids did it, parents would have plenty to say," Laura said.

"If you have something to say, go ahead," her mother said.

"I don't, Mother." She laughed.

Hannah laughed. "I had quite a time explaining it to your sister. She thinks I'm nuts, can't figure why I wouldn't want to live with Max."

"What did you tell Miranda? Why don't you want to

live here permanently, Mother? I can't imagine an arrangement like that between Hank and me."

"Our needs and goals are different, my dear. You're so much younger, and you're going to have a baby." A wide smile spread across Hannah's face. "I'm so happy about that. Marvin's right, you're going to have a boy, and I'm going to love and spoil him."

"You really believe that I actually heard Marvin?" Laura asked. "I've been telling myself that's crazy."

"What I believe, Laura, is that those are the things Marvin would have said to you."

"He always did want a little boy," Laura said. "But it's ridiculous to think that I actually heard his voice."

"Trust your intuition," her mother replied. "I believe it's a boy, and the name Andrew feels right."

"I'm going to tell Hank it's your father's name. I can't tell him it's Marvin's dad's."

"Hank knows you loved Marvin. He saw you through the worst of it, after the hurricane, when you were so ill and depressed, remember? I doubt he'd have the slightest objection if you told him the truth."

"Well, I'd rather say Andrew is the name of your father, okay?"

"Whatever you want, Laura, is fine with me."

They slipped into a moment of quiet reflection. The day had been delightful, not hot, not cool, the kind of day that fills your senses with pleasure. Now a soft breeze stirred the curtains, sending them rippling into the room like waves on the seashore.

After a time Laura spoke. "So, you're moving back with Amelia?"

"And Grace."

"Not Grace. Grace is staying with Bob. Grace told Amelia last night. They both cried. You'd think, if she decided to live with Bob, Grace would be happy about it."

Hannah stopped rocking. The room grew still. The curtains lay flat against the wall as if they, too, were sobered by this news. A mix of sounds—cows, a truck's wheels crunching on gravel, José singing softly in Spanish. Grace staying with Bob? After all she'd said? After buying furniture? Anger poured over Hannah, pricking her skin, sending her blood racing, her stomach knotting. Hannah took a deep breath.

"So, when is the wedding for you and Max?" Laura asked. "Want to make it a double wedding?"

"No. Max and I will duck into a courthouse and do it one day when we happen to be in town. We have the license." It took every ounce of control for Hannah to sit there quietly when she wanted to rush out to find Grace, give her a good shaking, and demand to know what she was doing. Chicken-livered Grace. A wuss, unable to speak her mind. How could she cave in after all their discussions about why she did not want to live with Bob? Damn Bob. Damn Grace.

Piqued, Hannah considered staying here with Max. And what of Amelia? If Amelia had a man who wanted to marry her, would she turn that down to live with two women? Hannah thought not. But Grace was different. And what hurt the most was that she had not told Hannah, that Hannah had learned about it secondhand.

"Mother, what's the matter?" Laura asked. "You're all flushed and your hands are so tight your knuckles have gone white."

Hannah bolted from the chair. "Darn right, I'm flushed. Listen, Laura, you and Hank plan whatever kind of wedding you want."

Laura scrambled to her feet. "Simple, Mother, we want a simple—"

"Fine. Look, I have to see Grace." Hannah strode from the room, their dinner date forgotten.

Laura heard her stomp down the stairs, heard the front door slam. Good Lord, she thought, Mother did not know about Grace staying with Bob.

Grace was alone at the apartment, huddled on the couch crying, when Hannah burst through the door. "What the hell is going on?" Hannah demanded.

Grace held a pillow to her chest as if to ward off a blow. Her eyes were puffy, her nose flaming red. "Please, Hannah, please understand. I have to stay. I'm torn in two about this. He needs me."

"I need you," Hannah blurted, then covered her mouth with her hand for a second. "And Amelia needs you." How in the name of heaven had she allowed herself to care so much? Hannah collected her thoughts. Consequences. That's what life was about. Comings and goings, loving and losing. Being knocked down, picking yourself back up, recovering, and going on. Grace must do what she had to do, and Hannah would proceed with what she had to do. Which was what? Move in with Amelia, of course, as planned.

Grace was crying now. She held out her hands to Hannah. "Forgive me, please."

Without a word, and without accepting Grace's outstretched hands, Hannah turned on her heel and strode from the apartment.

It was not until she was down the hill and turning not right toward Cove Road, but left toward Mars Hill, that Hannah realized that she was speeding. She slowed and cruised along the country road at thirty-five miles an hour. Her mind flashed back to that day in the kitchen in Branston when Grace had agreed, finally, to do the driving to Covington, if she didn't have to drive faster than forty miles an hour.

In spite of herself, Hannah smiled. So many good

things had happened to them since coming to live in Covington: new loves, new work, new friends, rapprochement with their children. Amelia had unearthed a hidden talent and was involved in a career beyond her wildest dreams. Grace had become a person in her own right in the last four years. She had learned to say no—until now. Through her kindness and interest in people she had expanded their circle of friends into an extended family. She, Hannah, had found meaningful work, and there was Max. How grand that at their ages they could still plan, dream, and implement their dreams. This was living, really living, not merely existing as they had done at Olive Pruitt's boardinghouse. So why treat Grace this way? It was the very nature of Grace to care deeply, to feel responsible. Didn't she treasure Grace for the very qualities that drove her to stay with Bob: loyalty, commitment, responsibility?

Hannah pulled into a dirt road and turned her van around. Within fifteen minutes she stood at Bob's apartment. Unable to locate her key, Hannah rang the bell. There was no answer. She rang again, knocked, then pounded on the door with her fist, calling Grace's name. Where was that key? Had she dropped it somewhere in her fury? She couldn't remember. Was that gas she smelled? Oh, God, what had Grace done? Her heart racing, Hannah banged both fists against the door. Grace must have been torn in two to begin with, and her words, her coldness had driven Grace over the edge.

At that moment, as if in answer to a prayer, Amelia's car pulled into the driveway. "Thank God you're here, Amelia. I think Grace is in trouble. Open the door, quickly!"

Amelia scrambled from the car and raced to the door. Inside they were greeted by a frightening silence.

"No one's here, Hannah," Amelia said after a quick

tour of the apartment. "Why did you think Grace was in trouble? What kind of trouble?"

"I was horrid to her, Amelia." Hannah sank into a chair at the kitchen table and dropped her head onto her out-stretched arms. In her fear, she had only imagined the gas smell. "I yelled at her, and when she reached out to me, I walked out."

"Because she decided to stay here?"

Hannah raised her head and nodded.

"I never imagined Grace would actually let Bob talk her into this," Amelia said. She sighed. "I'm going to miss her."

Hannah nodded again.

"Well, she's not here," Amelia said.

And not dead either, Hannah thought. Thank God.

Without fanfare, Hannah and Amelia moved home. Roger helped Bob and Amelia transport Amelia's boxes and cam-era equipment. Max and Anna carried Hannah's several boxes from Max's house to hers. Anna's eyes brimmed with tears, and she sniffled constantly.

"For God's sake, Anna," Max said. "She's only going across the street."

"But so soon I miss her, *Señor* Max," Anna said.

"Tell you what, one night a week you make one of your delicious dinners, and we'll invite Hannah, and maybe the others, and you can set the table festive the way you used to do."

They stood at the edge of the grass, holding boxes, waiting for Brenda Tate's car to go by. Brenda slowed and stopped. "Moving day? I'm glad our ladies are finally getting back into their home." She rolled up her window and rolled it down again. "Oh, and Max, congratulations to you and Hannah."

"The whole darn place knows, I imagine," he said as Brenda drove on.

"They happy for you and *Señora* Hannah," Anna said. "I no understand. Why she no stay here, *Señor* Max?"

"Too complicated to explain, Anna."

They stepped onto the road and walked across to the ladies' farmhouse. Four white rocking chairs sat on the porch along with wicker end tables and a swing. Lurina occupied the swing. Her white hair hung in a long braid across one shoulder and down the front of her white smock. Her toes barely touched the floor. She waved to them as they approached.

"I came along with Wayne," she said. "Excitin' movin' into their own place again, don't you reckon?"

"Sure is." Max started up the steps trailed by Anna.

"How you doin', Anna? You get them boxes laid inside, Max, and come on back out here and set a spell with me. Hannah's makin' flowerbeds, she and Wayne."

Max noted the curved green hoses laid on the ground to form flowerbeds that would soon be dug and mulched in preparation for planting next spring. Wayne and Hannah were intent on a bed across from the stream, close to the south side of the house. A package of cigarettes rolled in Wayne's sleeve was as standard as was his baseball cap, though he never smoked around Hannah and the ladies.

"I'll be back," Max said to Lurina. Max and Anna headed for the door. Moments later, Anna started back across the road, while Max pulled a rocker close to the swing. "Swings are mighty relaxing," he said, fanning himself with his broad-brimmed hat.

"Mighty relaxin'," said Lurina. "You and Hannah gettin' hitched?" she asked.

Max nodded, then explained the situation to Lurina,

who listened intently, her head cocked to one side like a bird's. Around the corner, they heard Hannah laugh and Wayne join in.

"Well, Max," Lurina said, "you and Hannah are good people, you got good sense, so I think you know what you're about." That said, her toes touched the floor and the swing moved back and forth.

"I thought you'd understand," Max said.

Lurina laughed her delightful young girl laugh, and Max joined in, and Hannah appeared with Wayne, whose hands dripped dirt. Twists of Hannah's hair clung in wet clumps just above her ears. Wayne wiped his forehead and then his hands with one of the bandannas Grace had given him last Christmas. They flopped down on the steps.

"What's so funny?" Hannah asked.

"Life's funny," Lurina said.

"Maybe it is," Hannah replied. She accepted Max's handkerchief and wiped her face. "Hot in the sun."

"Miss Hannah's sure gonna have a terrific yard when we done plantin'," Wayne said.

No one spoke of Grace. Better that way, Hannah thought.

43

IN THE NEW
FARMHOUSE

On August 23, Hannah and Amelia sat in the living room.
They had moved that very day. Amelia removed her
shoes, stretched her feet, and wiggled her toes. "It's going
to be wonderful, this new house, isn't it, Hannah?"

"I suppose so," Hannah said.

"I know you're upset with Grace, but it'll be all right.
Maybe she'll change her mind, and if not, maybe we can
invite in a housemate to take her place."

Hannah stiffened. "Definitely not."

"Okay, so we won't."

The silence that followed spoke of unease and sadness.
Amelia refused to fume and fuss about Grace. Grace
hadn't moved out of town, not even as far as Mars Hill.
She was just around the corner. Amelia believed that she
understood why Grace stayed with Bob and felt that Hannah was overreacting. As far as Amelia was concerned,
their home was rebuilt and life was good. Hannah should
focus less on Grace and more on Max, Laura, and her
work. As for the finances, well, Hannah had a steady income from her work at Bella's Park, and her own photographs were producing an income. They really did not

need Grace to share the expenses. They'd be fine, and maybe, in time, she and Hannah would grow closer.

That week, folks along Cove Road stopped in with pies, cakes, and other foods. Alma Craine proudly presented Hannah and Amelia with a smoked ham. "Frank smoked it in our new smokehouse out back," she said. "He always wanted a smokehouse, and now he's got one, and we got ham for everyone this Christmas. Shame Grace ain't here to share it with y'all."

Hannah looked away.

Brenda and her daughter, Molly, who was now Max's full-time assistant and happy to be working close to home, brought jars of homemade fig preserves. Amelia opened a jar immediately.

"I adore figs," she said.

"We have a big old tree back behind the barn," Brenda said. "Help yourself anytime."

They became oddly quiet. After a time Brenda said, "We sure miss Grace."

"Hannah more than any of us," Amelia whispered, for at that moment Hannah came into the kitchen where they sat. "Figs, Hannah?" Amelia held the jar toward her.

"Hi, Brenda, Molly," Hannah said, ignoring Amelia.

They chatted awhile about shorter days, and blanket weather these nights, and then—Amelia was certain Brenda could sense the strain between herself and Hannah—Brenda and Molly took their leave.

"Would you like me to make dinner tonight?" Amelia asked.

"Another tuna salad?" Hannah turned up her nose and walked from the room.

Days passed. Rather than growing closer, Amelia found herself and Hannah living increasingly as if they were strangers. There were evenings when they did not bid one another good night, days when they hardly spoke. How could this be? Left alone in the kitchen one day, Amelia dug her spoon into a jar of fig preserves, and not until the jar was nearly empty did she realize what she was doing. She looked about her. This efficient new kitchen had been designed for Grace. Grace would have loved cooking in it. Amelia's heart sank whenever she walked by Grace's room, furnished and empty at the same time. Their lovely new house, with its shiny wood floors and pretty rugs and its nice new bathrooms, was filled with tension, and she couldn't, it seemed, do or say anything right.

Didn't Hannah like her? Had she ever liked her? Many a night Amelia cried herself to sleep, or she lay awake worrying about how to please Hannah. Nothing pleased Hannah. Nothing but Grace coming back. Didn't Hannah realize that she missed Grace, too? Amelia reminded herself that she didn't have to stay here. She could sell her third of the property and buy a place near Mike, in town. Much more convenient to the theaters, and art galleries, and shopping.

Now, as she sat in the kitchen alone, tears spilled down Amelia's cheeks. Damn Grace. Why did she abandon them? She'd been by twice, only twice, and stayed a very short time. And Grace looked miserable, eyes puffy, unsmiling, hardly speaking. Amelia thought she'd burst into tears any minute. What was happening to them all? Where were the jokes—silly jokes—but fun, that they told one another? Where were the happy faces they had brought to the table each day? Hannah rarely smiled. She scowled. Max couldn't lift her spirits, and lord knows he tried. Hannah brushed him off and suggested he go back home, and she kept putting off a wedding date.

Amelia screwed the top onto the fig jar, licked the stickiness from her fingers, and picked up the phone in the kitchen. "Roger?" she said. "Can I come over? I'd like to talk to you about your mother."

But before Amelia talked with Roger and Charles, she determined to talk with Hannah.

If there was anything Hannah would have chosen not to do, it was sit across the kitchen table and face Amelia. Hannah had no answers. She hated herself for her cruel treatment of Grace and now of Amelia. Amelia tried so hard to be thoughtful, even to the point of staying out of Hannah's way. Today Amelia had literally pulled Hannah's arm until Hannah walked with her to the kitchen. She had set a chair for Hannah and exerted soft pressure on her shoulders until, with a grunt, Hannah sat.

"Well," Hannah asked. "What is it?"

Amelia placed both elbows on the table and leaned forward. "It's about us. If you'd prefer, I'll sell my third of this place and move into Asheville."

This was the last thing Hannah expected. She had braced for whining, for complaints, tears, but not this studied calm Amelia presented, nor her short, definitive alternative. It was falling apart, her dream, their dream of sharing a home and caring for one another. A sob caught in Hannah's throat.

"No," she said.

"No? Why not? Tell me. We hardly talk to each other. It's as if we were strangers. And you snap at me no matter what I do. I can't live like this," Amelia said, and then her voice changed and tears formed in the corners of her eyes. "Hannah, I feel that you hate me."

"No, no, I don't hate you, Amelia," Hannah replied. She pressed the palms of her hands against her cheeks. Regret and sadness filled her eyes. "I hate myself for being mean to Grace, and for being nasty to you. I lie awake at night and promise myself that tomorrow I'll smile and invite you to lunch and apologize. And then it's daylight, and I rush to work and snap at everyone. Max says I'm turning into a bear, and he's going to turn me loose in the woods. I feel so out of control."

"It's the end of a dream, isn't it, Hannah?" Amelia asked. "I hadn't realized. Of us all, yours is actually the deepest commitment."

"A dream. Yes. It is a dream, isn't it? And I won't let go of it." Hannah's hands fell to her lap. "Time to let it go, isn't it?"

A flush suffused Amelia's face. "There's still you and I," she ventured in a soft, tentative voice.

"Yes, there's you and I," Hannah said. She reached for Amelia's hands. "Can you forgive me, Amelia, for being so damned stupid and so cruel?"

"There's nothing to forgive. I had my awful time with Lance and then after the fire, and you and Grace tolerated me. You're having a hard time now. It will pass. And, Hannah, Grace is just around the corner. Please go to her, talk to her."

Hannah stiffened. Drew away, crossed her arms. "I can't. Not yet, anyway." She was silent for a time. Amelia's eyes never left Hannah's face. Finally Hannah said, "I wish I didn't feel so betrayed and abandoned. Grace's leaving us seems to have unearthed in me every feeling of abandonment or betrayal that I've ever had in my whole life."

"Grace is torn by this too. I'm sure of it."

"She told you that?" Hannah asked.

"No, but I feel it. I don't think she really wants to be with Bob," Amelia said.

44

LISTEN TO YOUR HEART

Two weeks after Roger and Charles came to Loring Valley, Roger called Miranda. "We're not coming home for a while. Being in Covington has done Charles a world of good. His color's better, he sleeps better, and his spirits have certainly improved. The view from our terrace relaxes him, and Grace spends time with Charles almost every day. Just seeing her buoys his spirits. They play gin rummy." He laughed. "Charles wants her to win every game."

In his mind Roger could hear Grace saying, "Come on, Charles. Let me lose one, okay?"

"I don't want you to get bored and stop coming," Charles had replied.

"As if I'd ever do that. I enjoy your company, and I never get tired of hearing about the time you rode an elephant in Kenya, or about the markets in Morocco. I haven't traveled out of this country, and probably never will. I travel in my mind through you," his mother had replied, laughing.

"So," Roger continued. "Go ahead and hire help, and pray Charles gets better, will you, Miranda?"

"Don't you worry about anything. We'll be fine here. Philip thinks he'd like to go into the business. I haven't a clue where his theater plans went, but he's switched to a business major at college. I was going to discuss this with you when you returned. . . ."

"Let him go ahead and start now. Good a time as any."

"I'll pray for Charles," she said. "He's going to be fine."

"Thanks, Miranda."

When Grace arrived the following day, the top of the dinette table looked like a map of the world with all the flyers and books about Alaska, Majorca, Spain, Italy, Canada, South America that Roger had gotten.

Grace and Charles attacked the pile.

"The Amazon, now that would be fun, don't you think, Grace?" Charles asked, holding up a flyer showing a boat cruising down a long river.

"Too adventurous for me," Grace replied, showing him another flyer. "How about Banff in Canada. We'll stay at a lodge way up in the mountains and go heliporting to an alpine meadow. See, it shows a helicopter discharging passengers in a flower-filled meadow."

Charles smiled up at Roger. "You think I'll ever be strong enough for a trip like this?"

"Of course you will. Why, since we're here, you've made great strides in regaining your health and energy."

So Grace and Roger planned trips: a cruise to Alaska, Spain for the bullfights, and Majorca, or was it the island of Madeira where, Grace had heard, the roads were lined with oleander and bougainvillea? "It sounds so beautiful," she said. "Glorious blue sea and stunningly vivid flowers against a heavenly sky. Who could ask for more?"

"I could," Charles said. His mood changed. "I could ask to be completely well."

"Yes, you could," Grace acknowledged. "And you will be."

Charles's eyes filled with tears. "You've been more than a mother to me."

Amelia picked a day when Grace, Roger said, had errands in Weaverville. She arrived at their door with an apple pie from the grocery.

"That's kind of you." Roger took the pie from her hands. "We'll have it smothered under ice cream. We eat sugar-free everything when Grace is here."

"She's sticking to her diet?" Amelia asked.

"No," Charles replied. "Not a diet, a new way of eating. She has to, you know, diabetes is no joke. She's been trying out recipes on us. Some I don't like at all, too bland, others are delicious. It's quite an adjustment for Grace. She's dumped potatoes, and white flour, and pasta from her pantry. Rice, she says she must have with meatballs and prunes, and she says she won't give up her special rice with cinnamon, raisins, and almonds, or her avocado pineapple dip, which is terrific. Her doctor says a little bit of it won't hurt her, that it's actually a matter of portion control, and sugar control, of course."

"It sounds like she's getting it under control," Amelia said. "She's certainly lost weight."

"Twenty-one pounds last count," Charles said.

"Mother goes to the mall in Asheville three mornings a week now and walks," Roger said.

After a few minutes Charles excused himself. "I'm bushed, going to lie down."

Amelia and Roger were alone in the living room. Amelia noted that a couch had joined the two recliners. "Nice couch," she said.

"Charles needed a place, other than bed, to rest during the day."

"It's nice. I like the leather and the dark green is attractive."

They sat at opposite ends of the couch and faced each other across the empty center section. "What's on your mind, Amelia?"

"Your mother. Do you think she's happy with her decision to stay with Bob?"

He did not reply for what seemed like forever. Amelia felt the stillness in the room like a cloak about her shoulders, heard the hum of the refrigerator from the kitchen as if it were the roar of a tractor's motor.

Roger cleared his throat. "Why do you ask?"

"Grace has always been cheerful and optimistic. I haven't seen her smile since we moved back to the farmhouse. Have you?"

"Well." Roger scratched his head. "She does with Charles, but maybe that's for his sake. Mother could always hide her feelings if she thought they would make someone unhappy."

"We hardly see her. I get the sense that it pains her to come to the house, and when she does, she struggles not to cry, and leaves as quickly as she can. Pretty soon we're not going to see her except by appointment, and then it'll be at some restaurant, some neutral place. Would she act like that if she were happy?"

"We need to ask Charles about this. She's here almost every day, plays gin rummy with him, or they plan trips to exotic places they'll never go to. That seems to lift both their spirits." He jumped from the couch, went to Charles's door, and tapped. "Charles. If you're not sleeping, come on out here, Amelia wants to talk to you."

A moment later Charles opened the door and joined them in the living room, where he settled into one of the recliners and pushed back so that his feet were elevated. "What is it, Amelia?" he asked.

"Hannah and I are worried about Grace." Amelia leaned forward and looked intently at Charles. "How is she, do you think?"

Charles did not respond immediately. He pulled the lobe of his ear, and his teeth grazed the corner of his lower lip. "She doesn't say much. If I bring up Bob, Grace changes the subject. I don't know how she is, actually. It's selfish of me, but I don't want her to stop visiting with me, so I don't bring up anything I think makes her unhappy." He stopped talking and began to bite a fingernail. Then he said, "I never felt it was right, somehow, her not moving home with you and Hannah. When she lived with you ladies, she was happier than I've ever seen her, right, Roger?"

"Mother's a mature woman," Roger said. "I don't feel we have the right to question her decision."

"Even if we can see that she's unhappy?" Amelia asked.

Roger turned away.

"Trouble with Grace is she's too kindhearted," Charles said.

Amelia twisted the emerald ring on her finger. She had bought the ring in New York and hardly worn it until after the fire. It was one of the items she had saved that night, and it had come to symbolize survival and a return to normalcy. "I thought you'd have some ideas. Should I plain out ask her, do you think?"

"She may be my mother, but you're closer to her, Charles," Roger said. "How about asking her how things are, or something like that?

Charles's brow scrunched. "Lord, I hope Grace is all right. You two have me worried about her now."

Had she chosen to say so, Grace could have told them how trapped she felt and how buried in a private despair of her own making. She had already hurt, maybe permanently alienated Hannah, and, now, if she left Bob, he might hate her. Feeling like a foot soldier defeated in battle, Grace struggled with depression, while Bob, oblivious, laughed and joked and could not contain the sense of having won a long-sought prize.

Although he acquiesced when she insisted on having her own room, and smiled as he helped her move her clothing and books into the guest room, on other occasions he pouted, teased, and urged until she finally agreed to begin the night in his bed.

"I love falling asleep alongside you, and we don't have to make an appointment for sex," he said. "When I'm asleep, you can always go to your own room."

I'm not your child, she wanted to yell at him, but did not. I don't want sex as often as you do. I feel used, can't you see that?

But he didn't see that. Bob showered her with kindness. He brought her flowers, set the table, washed the dishes, bought a television set for her room. He was a good man, and he loved her. She loved him. But, thank God, he was absorbed in golf, and she had most of the weekdays to herself. Only she spent those days looking at the clock, waiting for it to be five o' clock, waiting to begin dinner. She recalled a time when Roger was little and started school. She spent all day waiting to pick up her son. Her baking for the entire neighborhood had evolved from worrying and waiting. But now, with this confounded diabetes, cookies without sugar tasted as flat as they sounded. She hadn't baked cookies in months, and was beginning not to enjoy cooking. Easy to diet without an appetite.

Although Grace planned to return to volunteering at Caster Elementary School in September after school was under way, with Tyler at school in Mars Hill and Lucy starting middle school, it seemed somehow meaningless. These changes in her attitude and mood frightened Grace.

As the days grew shorter, Grace had grown increasingly morose. Unable to bear visiting Hannah and Amelia at the house, she spent hours walking aimlessly about the mall, angry at herself for not being assertive, for not telling Bob she was unhappy with this arrangement. How could she tell him that his whistling in the morning grated on her nerves? It seemed so petty. Or that she hated his enthusiasm for everything when she felt so low, or that it cheapened her, leaving his bed to return to her room at night.

How could she say that she hated sitting on the couch with him after dinner and discussing, politely, which program to watch. It irked her when he poked fun at *Wheel of Fortune,* which she found relaxing. And she hated the TV dramas with shootouts, car chases, or surgical procedures that he preferred. But when she rose from the couch, he would reach for her hand, kiss it, and say, "Oh, stay a bit longer. I love us sitting here together."

Sometimes, as Grace walked the hard tile causeways of the mall, she talked to herself about being weak-willed, and she remembered all those times she had enumerated to Hannah and Amelia the reasons living with Bob would be untenable. *You can't go home again,* Thomas Wolfe had written, and Grace wondered, if she returned to the farmhouse, would things ever be the same? Then Grace would check her watch yet again and hasten home to welcome Bob, to hand him a beer, or a scotch and soda, to make dinner. Why did she feel she must do all of that? He didn't ask her to do so.

One day, while sitting on a bench in the mall observing passersby, it struck Grace that Bob understood what his needs were and he took care of them. He wanted them to live together. He persisted, and succeeded. From what she could tell, he assumed that she was as pleased with the new arrangement as he was. She, on the other hand, had sacrificed her needs to please him. Had she been true to herself, she would be back in the farmhouse with Hannah and Amelia.

But then, one evening a few days later, a straw broke the camel's back. After a day of golfing with Martin Hammer, he arrived home flushed and cheerful.

"Grace," he said after they finished dinner, and he had loaded the dishwasher and set it whirring. "I've been thinking. What say you come on out to the club with me? There's a golf class for ladies starting Friday. Several wives of the guys we play with are taking lessons." He strode over to where he had propped his golf bag in the foyer and extracted a club. "Hold this, see, it's smaller, see if it feels right for you." He walked toward her and, still holding the club, kissed her cheek. "It would be great fun, you and I playing golf together."

Grace reacted with a violence that startled her. "Damn it, Bob! Leave me alone! I hate golf. I don't want to follow a ball around a golf course." She pushed him away.

He set down the club and raised his hands defensively. "Okay. Okay, just an idea. Just thought it might be nice, you and I . . ."

Grace's hands flew to her head. "I can't stand all this togetherness. I need space, privacy."

"I'm gone all day most days. Isn't that enough space and privacy?"

Grace sank to the couch. She worked the end of her bandanna into a long twist and wound it through her fingers. "It's not you, Bob. It's me. It's my fault, really it is, but I want to go home." She heard herself and was appalled. This was a child, not an adult speaking. But she did want to go home. Grace rocked back and forth. Tears streamed down her face. When she could, she stammered, "I'm sorry."

He kneeled beside her. "Grace, darling, why didn't you say something? What have I done?"

"Nothing. You haven't done anything but love me and want me near you. And what I feel is stifled." She looked at him, saw the pain in his eyes, and nearly reneged. "I'm not blaming you, my love. I'm grateful for all your love and kindness, but I miss my stream, and my room, and my rocking chair, and not feeling responsible to anyone for when we eat, or anything." She took his face in her hands and kissed his cheeks. "I do love you, Bob. I loved our arrangement these last few years, before I moved in. It felt so right. Can't you accept that? Can't we go back to how it was?"

Bob sat back on his heels. His eyes reflected hurt and concern. "The last thing in the world I want is for you to be unhappy," he said. "Why did you stay?"

"I thought you needed me, that you were afraid you'd have another heart attack and be alone."

"That's always a possibility," he said, "and yes, I was afraid at first, but less so now. I'm more philosophical about it. A guy toppled over on the golf course a few days ago. The ambulance took him to the hospital. They had a hell of a time finding his wife. I gained a new perspective. It's not how you get to the hospital, it's knowing that when you open your eyes, someone you love is standing there, like you were."

"Then, you don't need me here?"

"I don't *need* you, Grace. I *wanted* you here, for my own selfish reasons. I hadn't a clue you were unhappy." He lifted her chin, and her eyes found his. "You think I want you unhappy? Hell, no. One day I'd come home and you'd be gone, and maybe by then you'd be so pissed off you'd never want to see me again." He drew her into his arms. "I love you too much for that. Pack up, my girl, I'm taking you home."

His words shocked Grace. "You mean that?" A weight lifted from her heart. It had been so simple. Fool, not to have said her mind right from the start. But how would Hannah react if she just appeared? "Right now? Tonight?" she asked.

"Yes. Tonight. For years we've been happy living in separate houses. Get going now. Start packing." He delivered a gentle pat to her behind and followed as she started for her room. "Hell, Grace, maybe I'll even rent or sell this place and take Max up on his offer."

She had drawers open in the dresser, and had started to set pajamas, underwear, her robe, and slippers in the open suitcase on the bed. "What offer?" she asked.

"He suggested if you weren't going to stay here that I share his home, like you ladies share yours. Says Anna wants more folks to cook for." He handed her shoes from the floor of her closet. "That way, I can spy on you with binoculars from across the street." He laughed.

She chuckled. "You can't see into my room from Max's house, thank heaven. It's Hannah you'd be spying on. Her room faces his place."

"Don't want to spy on Hannah. Well, then, we'll have a signal. I'll run up a flag when I want to visit you, and you can wave a red flag 'No' or a green flag 'Yes' before I come over."

She snuggled against his chest. "You stayed over when you wanted to before. You'll be welcome anytime." She stood on tiptoes and kissed him. "Thanks, Bob, for understanding. It'll be better, you'll see."

He held her from him and looked lovingly into her eyes. "What the hell. Life goes on." Then he said, "Hey, sexy lady, how about we have some fun one last time before I take you home?"

Grace looked at her dresses in the closet. She'd take them on hangers. She wanted to be with him, now, to lie in his arms, to make love. From habit, they walked arm in arm from her room to his.

45

HOMECOMING

It was eight-thirty when Grace phoned Charles. "Wonderful news. I'm going home."

"Oh, Grace. You weren't happy, were you? And I was so wrapped up in myself, I didn't see."

"I wouldn't have inflicted my troubles on you, Charles. It was something I had to work out myself."

"Well, love, I'm delighted you've worked it out. When do you go home?"

"Tonight."

"Tonight?"

"I'm nearly packed. I just wanted to tell you that this doesn't end our gin rummy games. Roger will drive you over to our house, and I'll come to you when you want me to."

"I'll be delighted being in your home with all you ladies. I always loved the atmosphere."

His words sobered Grace. "I don't know how great the atmosphere will be, at least initially."

"Well," he said. "Hannah and Amelia miss you terribly."

"They do?"

"Yes. I know, because Amelia was here talking about it."

"Was she? What did she say?"

"Concerned if you were happy, saying how much they missed you," Charles replied. "They'll welcome you with open arms."

And so it was!

Grace simply arrived, and to her surprise and disappointment, no one was home. Luckily, she had a key. Amelia had given it to her, saying, "It's still your home, too, and you never know when you might want to come over."

Bob helped her carry her things from the car and up to her room. He kissed her hard, told her how much he loved her, looked wistfully about, and left. Grace studied her two suitcases, several boxes, a clothing bag. Was Hannah at the park? Her car wasn't at Max's. Should she drive down to the park and surprise Hannah? Should she try to reach Amelia through Mike's cell phone? No. She would unpack first.

Her hangers, with their blouses, skirts, and shirtwaist dresses, filled less than half of the twelve-foot rod. Her underwear, pajamas, and socks did not fill two small drawers of her new dresser. Within minutes her books jammed the several shelves of the new bookcase. Too small. Well, there was room for more shelves. Grace ensconced her toiletries on a shelf in the bathroom cabinet, below the shelf where Hannah's lipsticks, aspirin, Ben-Gay rub, and other over-the-counter items sat in neat array. She considered a bath, then decided to relax by the window. She closed her eyes. Immediately the gurgle of the stream drifted up to her. Peace. If anyone asked Grace to recount her exact feelings of that moment, Grace would say that relief permeated every cell of her mind and body.

After a time she rose and walked slowly about the room and the bed several times. Then she studied her face in the mirror over her new dressing table, and was pleased to note that her forehead looked smoother, that her eyes sparkled, and even her hair seemed shinier.

Grace trotted downstairs. She explored all the rooms as if seeing them for the first time. While she'd been gone, they had purchased not two, but three chairs for the living room. Two of them were pulled close to and facing the fireplace. She added the third to form a semicircle. The guest room was unfurnished, but there were towels in the downstairs bathroom, and soap, and a vase of plastic daisies that looked so real, Grace bent to smell them. The kitchen was perfect, the kind of galley kitchen she had always wanted.

When she had opened and closed cabinets and pantry doors, Grace decided that she must shop. Within minutes she was at the market at Elk Road Plaza, hoping to run into people she knew, even though it was now after nine P.M.. She wanted to hug friends and neighbors and tell them that she was home again, but she pushed her cart up one aisle and down another, filling it with vegetables, fruit, grains, chicken, fish, ground round for meatballs, and prunes without seeing a familiar face.

Back at the house Grace unpacked and put away the groceries, and still no Amelia or Hannah. Would they be excited seeing her car? Would they run up the steps? Would they welcome her when she threw her arms about them?

Suddenly tired, Grace went upstairs to rest a little, she thought, as she threw herself, fully clothed, upon her bed. The bed, with its pillow-top mattress, felt wonderful. She stretched. It was so good to be home.

Grace started awake. Someone had slammed the front door. Someone was racing upstairs, and flinging wide her door. Amelia threw herself at Grace, hugging her, thumping her arm, crying. "You're home, oh, thank God, you're home," she said when she was able to catch her breath.

"I'm so happy to be here," Grace said as she returned Amelia's hug. "Where is Hannah?"

"Hannah never comes home anymore until late. Let's phone her. She'll dash home if she knows you're here. Why didn't you call one of us?"

They were standing now. Grace smoothed back her hair.

"You look marvelous, Grace. You're half your size. I hardly recognize you. Gosh, we've missed you so much." Amelia threw her arms about Grace again and hugged her tight.

Feeling like the prodigal daughter, Grace returned Amelia's affection. "God knows, I've missed you, too."

"What say we run down to the park and surprise Hannah, drag her home?"

"Good idea," Grace said.

Moments later they were on their way. At Bella's Park lights lit the reception area, but the front door was locked. They rang the bell, once, twice, three times before Hannah's firm footsteps moved toward them on the other side of the closed door.

"Who is it?" she asked, her voice crisp.

Amelia looked at Grace and put her finger to her lips. "It's Amelia."

The lock turned, and the door swung open. Amelia stepped back. "Look who's came home."

"Oh, my God, Grace," Hannah said. "You've come home? Is it true? Come in, come in, don't just stand out there."

Inside, they stood for a moment appraising one another, and then Grace put her arms on Hannah's shoulders. "I've come home," she whispered.

Hannah's chin quivered as she struggled to hold back emotion. "Thank God," she said, and welcomed Grace with a powerful hug.

It was very late when they finished the tuna salad and hard-boiled eggs that Amelia had left in the fridge. Still, it was a fairly warm night, and they decided to sit on their porch. Across the road a dim light issued from Max's den. He's watching the eleven o'clock news, Hannah thought, and she did not feel the least bit like joining him.

After an impeccably clear day, a day in which the mountains were visible at great distances, the sky was clear and luminous with stars. Quiet filled the night, filled their hearts. It seemed to them that they had never been apart, that there had never been a fire, or months spent dealing with loss and change. Sitting on their porch, it seemed as if nothing had changed in their lives. Yet so much had changed. There was much to say, and no need to say it. A chapter had ended. A new chapter was about to begin.

"I'm tutoring twin girls this year," Grace said.

"I'm going to start working on that second book. You were right, Grace, I won't use Olivia's photo on the cover, but it'll be the very first photo when you open the book."

"Do you have a cover picture?" Grace asked.

"Daylilies. A field of daylilies, and if she's willing, I plan to ask Marion Mundy to be in the picture, perhaps at work in the field, or picking daylilies. I've been meaning to take Hannah; now I'll take you both over to meet her."

"What ever happened with Ellie Lerner? I haven't seen or heard from her in weeks," Grace asked.

"Brenda says the space she's living in is too small. They're talking about sharing Molly's place that Ellie rented," Amelia said.

"That sounds perfect," Grace replied.

They rocked for a time in silence. Stars stepped aside, bowing to the crescent moon as it rose above Snowman's Cap. "Beautiful. So many stars tonight," Amelia said.

After a time Grace asked, "What are you planting at the park now, Hannah?"

"Japanese garden," Hannah said. "And I'm planning a woodland garden with mosses, ferns, hostas, things like that."

"God, life is good," Grace said.

"I brought the time capsule back from Max's last night," Hannah said.

"Great. Now that we're together, we can add to and rebury it in the backyard," Amelia said.

"I remember that night when we buried it the first time," Grace said. "The moon was full, and we worried the people across the road, whom we did not know then, might see us and think we were crazy."

"If Max sees us, it would hardly matter now." The runners of Hannah's rocker squeaked.

"Should a new rocking chair squeak?" Grace asked.

Hannah threw back her head. "Who cares?"

"You're right. Who cares?" Grace said.

"Let's get our stuff together and rebury the time capsule when the moon gets full," Amelia said.

"Let's do that," Grace said.

Hannah reached over on either side and placed her hands lightly, one on each of an arm, of Grace and Amelia's rockers. "It'll be special. Celebration of return, the three of us home together again after what seems like such a long time."

"Yes," Grace whispered, "together, and home at last."

GRACE'S RECIPES,
BOTH OLD AND NEW

AVOCADO AND PINEAPPLE DIP

(Grace has made this for so many years, she can't re-call if she made it up herself or someone passed along the recipe.)

You will need:
  One ripe avocado
  1 large can crushed pineapple with its juice or syrup

Peel and mash the ripe avocado.
Add one can of crushed pineapple, using some but not all
    of the liquid.
Season to taste and serve cold with crackers.

COLD REDUCED-CALORIE
ZUCCHINI SOUP

  3 small zucchini cut into pieces
  2 cups of homemade or fat-free chicken broth
  1 8-ounce pkg of reduced or low-fat cream cheese
softened
  ½ bunch green onions chopped well
  Salt and pepper to taste
  ¾ teaspoon of dill—fresh is best
  4 ounces of plain fat-free yogurt

Garnish with fresh chopped chives

Place first five ingredients in a saucepan.

Cook over medium-high heat, stirring occasionally for
  fifteen–twenty minutes or until the zucchini is medium
  to soft but not mushy.

Place, a cup at a time, in your blender and mix until
  smooth.

Cover and chill for 6 hours. Stir in the yogurt. Garnish.
  Makes about 5 servings and keeps well in the refrigerator for several days.

CHICKEN/TOMATO/CELERY
TORTILLA WRAP

1 6-inch low-fat flour tortilla—try to find whole wheat
  flour tortillas

2 tsp reduced fat mayonnaise

2 slices of cooked chicken

2 tbsp fresh tomato chopped well

1 tsbp finely chopped celery

1 tbsp finely chopped fresh basil leaves

Lay the tortilla flat. Spread with mayonnaise.

Lay the chicken slices on the tortilla.

Spread the tomato and finely chopped celery and basil on
  top of chicken slices.

Roll the tortilla to make a rolled sandwich.

**Don't miss the next heart-warming
novel in nationally bestselling author
Joan Medlicott's *Covington* series...**

AT HOME IN COVINGTON

Grace is grieving over the death of her son's partner from
an AIDS-related illness, and Hannah finds her present
disrupted—and her beliefs about the past shattered—when
she receives a mysterious old diary in the mail. Amelia
suggests a Caribbean cruise to lift all their spirits, but not
even an exotic vacation can ease her brewing conflict
with Hannah. Amelia has other welcome distractions,
like her photography workshop in Maine, but will she
want to live with Hannah upon her return? Grace must
also face up to her diabetes—and she has yet more cause
for concern when her young protégé, Lucy, becomes
involved with an Internet predator.

Now available in paperback from Pocket Books

POCKET BOOKS
A Division of Simon & Schuster
A VIACOM COMPANY

10449